# EVER AFTER

*novel*

# Anita Sullivan

Burning Daylight
Colorado

I acknowledge Robert Moss, author, for both the idea and the term "House of Time."

To my brothers Paul, Eric, and Peter

*Cover Design:* Anne Kilgore

Burning Daylight is an imprint of
Pearn and Associates, Inc.
1315 Kirkwood Drive # 905
Fort Collins, Colorado 80525
Email victorpearn@ymail.com

*Library of Congress Control Number 2015937435*

Sullivan, Anita
*Ever After,* by Anita Sullivan.
ISBN 978-0-9897242-4-1

Printed in the United States of America

1st edition.

# Contents

# Part I

## The Arbiter

Lions eat a lot, but when Mick came, he brought two female lions with him and that's flat. They aren't his, they're mine, the ones I dreamed about for so many years before I became thirty years old forever.

The lions stay when Mick goes, but they don't eat until he comes back, and meanwhile they fade into a kind of lumpy haze. I can still see them, but can see objects through them as well. It took me awhile to even notice this, because it seemed so normal. It is normal; I only mention it because of the food part. I had no idea what to feed lions, and just sent out an intention (or more truthfully, a panic call) for "whatever will please them." I didn't bother to explain that they had arrived with a person attached.

Eugenia is here too, a couple of times a week. We measure time in the old Maya way now, with the double calendar, except that we completely changed the day names since we're in charge of setting up our own mythology in this place. Today, for example, is Yellow Sing Second Leaf. We spent about a week, the three of us, sitting at the table in the garden and making a huge chart with double wheels. Now each morning I come down into the cafeteria, spin the wheels, and whatever Day name comes up, I consult the chart to learn what character the upcoming day is likely to present, and plan accordingly. If it's bad enough, I go back to bed with a book and a cup of hibiscus tea – sometimes I think I ought to wear a hard hat on such days, in case of an earthquake or some sort of random spirit-knot passing through our space like a collapsed star. It could happen.

1

I am living in a villa with many rooms, along a rocky hillside above the Mediterranean sea. The general design is my own, yet I specifically requested the inclusion of secret apartments for later discovery, with trunks of exotic fabrics, glass cases filled with delicate carvings of birds, centuries-old manuscripts in the languages I already know – English, Spanish, Greek and my father's native Portuguese – all to keep my overdeveloped sense of romantic notions continually stimulated for the decades (maybe centuries) I expect to live here. I opted for floor-to-ceiling windows set deeply into thick walls, skylights, arched doorways without doors, spacious rooms with high ceilings, but some as low and simple as monks' cells. The hodge-podge architecture is meant to offer an organic beauty, but also to prevent the deadly claustrophobia of boredom and loneliness from defeating me in my new life. Air! Give me air! And sea light coming in through windows that open onto terraces and into walled gardens. I must tend the gardens myself, so says the Arbiter, but I will be given the youthfulness to do so (and the wheelbarrows and shovels and pruning shears too, no doubt).

I can have anything I want for breakfast. On this, my third day, I ask for croissants, mangos and strong, dark coffee. Breakfast, oddly enough, appears more or less out of thin air, but for other meals I have to do my own cooking, my own dishes. Will I finally opt for death simply because I am sick and tired of doing the dishes? Scrubbing out the bathroom is worse. But I will not sink into sloth, I will not!

I don't anticipate that getting up in the morning will be a problem. Even during my final years on Earth (good heavens! I am still on Earth, but how else to say it)? When I was in my eighties and no longer had reason to rise at a certain fixed hour, I found that the initial bleakness of waking up alone would slowly leak out of me, like honey dripping through a hole in the bottom of a cup, until finally, when it was gone, I would abruptly sit up and throw the covers off, totally <u>unable</u> to remain still any longer. I trust the same will happen here. As for keeping track of time, I have a grandfather clock down in the music room. I brought it along for the excellent quality of its chimes, not because it's a clock, or because it was my grandfather's. I can hear it when I am sitting at the piano or the harpsichord. I included French doors for that room because I love the way the glass squares break the view into little frames. This never fails to jerk me into a different kind of attention when I look through them. Pale pink bougainvillea brushes across these doors, somewhat obscuring the glass on the left side. I am like the Lady of Shallot, a prisoner in her tower, caught in an odd spell.

I know that I have died, but am still alive. *I can live! I can live as long as I wish!*

This is a huge responsibility; I believe it's a chance to bring about a real change in how human life works. I must keep my wits fully about me. For sure, a Faustian bargain has been struck, but one that it may be possible to supersede, by a kind of metamorphosis, by the deliberate and gradual loss of the *capacity* to die. This is a very advanced thought to have on only my third day of immortality, and it worries me. I giggle as I run up and down stairs and open doors and sniff the air and feel my new young limbs free of creaks and pains. I am doing six impossible things before breakfast, sure, but what about after?

Anita Sullivan

## Eugenia Arrives

Eugenia came first, actually. She came towards the end of that early dark period when my joy did, after all, leave me, when I stopped writing things down, when I was sleeping twenty hours at a time, or staying "awake" for days in a state of thickened consciousness, forgetting who I was and walking into walls thinking I could walk through them. Slipping into that kind of insanity was so easy then, with no other humans to balance myself against. I kept holding onto the ends of the days, because I recognized the difference between dark and light, and at each end I would cry loudly and repeatedly "Eugenia, Mick, come!" No matter what else was happening, when the light changed I would sit cross-legged on a bed or floor, wherever I was, and deliberately call up their faces, and feel their personalities. It was like praying. We were all old when we died, three friends who had known each other for forty years.

Eugenia came at night, holding a candle, and wearing a long nightgown. Her thick curly hair was blooming out around her face and she seemed breathless. She looked even younger than my earliest memory of her. I stepped out through the kitchen door at the upper terrace, breathing wisteria fragrance, and when I saw her it was as if a bucket of spring water had dumped onto my head. I was clear. I blinked and could see everything. There was nothing left to be known by me. I walked barefoot onto the bricks and stood in front of her, thinking too many small things all at once, such as breakfast and canaries and sex and the crusades and the house I lived in when I was eight years old with the flame vine on the tiled roof, not sequentially but all at once, making a huge warm fabric like a robe around me.

"Are you really here?" I whispered. She nodded, her eyes shining. We both jerked slightly, as if we wanted to hug each other, but we didn't, not from uncertainty or shyness but rather out of a general courtesy, because it would have seemed that we needed to verify the vibrant and immediate fullness of one another's presence. And we did not.

"It's too dark. Let me make some coffee," I said, and went back in.

As I turned, I realized, yes, there <u>was</u> just a little rim of light around the outline of her, giving some indication that she had broken through some piece of cloth or sky to get from There to Here. I nodded in appreciation and wondered if it would stay with her, like a halo, for as long as she was here. But I didn't wonder how long, because "how long" has no meaning now for me.

"Where are we?" she asked when I brought the coffee, and some really nice pastry with almonds and pistachios and dates on a red lacquer tray. "Is that water down there?"

"The Mediterranean, of course," I grinned. "I suppose you're in England in a wee rose-covered cottage?"

"Something like that."

We sat for awhile in silence, sipping and trembling in eagerness to know how to continue. I think we even cried a little, but still didn't touch. *No human contact.* Would she vanish if I reached across the table?

"How did you know – ?" I began to ask.

She put up her hand to stop me, shook her head, and closed her eyes the way she often did when speaking. Eugenia figures things out by silence, I by speaking. I bit my lip to keep from saying too much too

Anita Sullivan

soon. I realized that all along, during this entire year of being alone, there had always been a right way of doing, and lesser right ways, and I had always moved towards the appropriate as if it were a holy flame. Why is this? Were we making a universe more quickly this way than we would if we operated strictly on whim?

"How many of us, you think?" I said quietly. She tilted her head.

"Mick will soon come, I'm sure. Beyond that, who knows? I have no clear sense of it all yet, do you?"

"No." I resisted the urge to start making a list of all the people we both longed to have join us. This isn't a fairy tale we are living, with three wishes per person.

"I do have the feeling this arrangement doesn't go back to the Neolithic" I said, a bit dryly. "Which is some relief! I mean, I don't think there are millions of us hidden away in little pockets of space-time all over the planet, leftover from the time of Plato or Gilgamesh or some such. That could get really weird!"

She laughed. Then after she had fully absorbed what I said she nodded. "A recent experiment. Yes, I agree."

"And obviously, full of loopholes!" I added, waving my hand loosely around to take in the present situation.

"Yes!" she said, widening her eyes in a quick mock terror that disappeared almost immediately. She still refrained from jumping right into an explanation of how she made the trip. Maybe it happened too quickly for memory.

"Were you surprised to, to—find yourself here?" I asked. She frowned a little, not at my question but with the difficulty of a clear answer. "No," she shook her head vigorously so that her hair almost spun. But she was unable to say more.

"We could wait twelve years for Mick to show up," I said. The kind of dumb statement one makes hoping it will trigger something else.

"Maybe time is different now," she said slowly.

"Do you have an idea of how we can bring Mick here? I mean, knowing him, he must be dreaming his head off, trying to find us. How can we help -- ?"

"Let's wait. I still don't have a clear sense of how --- " She raised one shoulder as if fending off something. I felt the dark stirring, and I realized (again) how words serve only to shift the defining silence already inside us, from one position to another. I breathed out slowly, feeling completely content.


[Journal Entry]


The Arbiter reminded me that each person who goes into this voluntary post-life Exile makes her own rules. "We don't micro-manage," said the Arbiter, "Not in this enterprise any more than the earlier one" (by which he meant, of course, Life). I refer to the Arbiter as "he" even though he is more like an angel than a human, and angels are without gender. But somehow I think a female would have set things up differently.

At any rate, I asked lots of questions before agreeing to try this plan. Such as, "Is this same opportunity offered to every single person in the world, young and old, at the exact moment of their deaths?" and he would not answer that, by which I assumed the answer was No. I

Anita Sullivan

wanted to say, "How come we aren't told about it in advance? It's not even mentioned in any eschatology, so far as I know. Plenty of stuff about paradise *after* death, of course, but not *before*. You've kept it a dark secret." Then he admitted that I am part of a relatively new Experiment, and that the details of its operation remain fundamentally arbitrary, mysterious, and even potentially dangerous. He let that one slip, and it haunts me, even as it gives me an adrenaline rush. "Dangerous" meaning what?

"What about insanity?" I asked him, "What happens if I go insane and thus can't choose death any more? Do I just lie there, dribbling, for all eternity?" The answer came ringing inside my head, the way all his answers do. "No, you would die of starvation. You are, after all, still alive. Except," he added, as if thinking of it for the first time, "We probably would assume insanity to be a Request to Die." Dying, in this Experiment, is thus an option at any time, but a choice to be taken with care and a waiting period (i.e. second chance), after which it happens cleanly and painlessly in sleep. "What about anti-depressants?" I asked next. "I mean, living alone isn't normal for humans, it will take some getting used to. "Sure," he said. "Give us your symptoms and we'll send something down. We're not shamans or psychiatrists, but our role is to *help keep you alive and healthy as long as you wish.*"

Basically the only Rule is "No direct contact with the world you left behind." I can watch films, old TV programs, play computer games, even get onto the Internet—so long as it's all stuff done before my time of death. Eat my heart out.

If this is an Experiment, how do we know if it succeeds or fails? I asked that question too. But there he cut me off, as if I had already exceeded my Three Wishes in the fairy tale. "You can't treat me as if I were a person," he reminded me gently. "I'm only a Voice, the voice of the Rule, which might come from inside you, which might come from the collective intelligence of the entire universe. But it's not a personal voice. You must not think you can call it up whenever you want companionship. The Rule is not set up in advance by careful deliberation of some committee; it's simply the result of the situation." Circular reasoning if I ever heard it.

Because I am a goal-oriented person, I will go into this new life with some set plans, even if I grow weary of them later. The first one will be about dreaming. I will keep track of my dreams as well as events in my waking life. More than ever now, the two are likely to be the same. My friend Mick used to insist that all life was an aspect of dreaming, and that the distinction between waking and sleeping dreams was really an illusion. I used to disagree by insisting he was wrong to overlook the deprivation of the senses in sleep. Now I think the whole pattern of those arguments may shift, and I will be able to bring a new perspective to dreaming.

I may find that the distinction between sanity and insanity is also more difficult to recognize. In fact, this is a chief drawback of the whole Experiment, and why I must assume the Arbiter and his minions know something they are not telling us.

## The Next Morning

The next morning came along, as they tend to do. Eugenia and I were still awake, so it was the same day for us. We went down to the sea. No sooner had we started to meander along the beach than we

Anita Sullivan

found something washed up on the shore that we didn't recognize. It was blue, roughly cylindrical, about twice the diameter of my middle finger. Could have been a lumpy kaleidoscope, since it was stopped at one end by glass, but hollow otherwise. It seemed to be made of plastic, not the cracking kind but the rubbery kind. I giggled.

"What's so funny?" Eugenia was turning it around to catch the sun patterns the glass made on the sand.

"A futuristic prophylactic!" I said, "except it's not really the future yet, we haven't been here that long."

She frowned, looking at it carefully, then shrugged. "Shall we keep it?"

I grimaced, then I suddenly got excited. "Hey!" I said, "Hey, wow! I just thought of something!"

"Tell me!" she urged, setting the object carefully back on the sand. And we climbed some crumbling steps of island stone and sat among the weeds, hugging our knees in the early morning chill, waiting for the sun to gain strength.

"Well, you know, we're not supposed to have any contact with the world. But what does that mean? I mean, I guess we're in some kind of suspension, out of the space-time continuum, if you'll pardon me sounding like an old *Star Trek* film. But this – " I gestured grandly at the ocean innocently lapping at the beach below us, "This is the MEDITERRANEAN SEA. It's the same water that's touching the real world out there. I mean, I don't think we're living on a movie set, with some artificial pool in front of us. So, if something gets washed up on the shore . . . ." I ducked my head and brought my front teeth together meaningfully, unable to continue for a minute. But she got the point.

"Oh yes! I live on the sea too, or at least a block away from it. The Atlantic Ocean. Things wash up on shore there too. Maybe a bottle with a message in it?"

"All kinds of possibilities. Robinson Crusoe here we come! I guess they – " I waved at the sky, "I guess They would make sure no humans came here, no ships or swimmers – very likely it's not even physically possible. We're in a parallel time zone. But what I'm thinking is that we actually *share* some things. And quite possibly, a few teensy items could squeak through the time barrier now and then, eh what?"

Eugenia looked with new interest over at the blue plastic cylinder. "You mean this actually could be something from the outside world, the real world!" she said softly.

"I suppose it's been drifting around in the ocean since before we both died," I shrugged, "but maybe not. And if we happen to be still here 100 years from now, maybe something will come washing up on the beach that's brand new—that was manufactured after we died! And THEN we would actually have some notion of what is going on in the world we left behind!"

She tipped her head sideways. "Do we really want to know?"

I sighed. "Yeah, you've got a point there. I find that I really don't care much what's happening 'down below'!" I laughed, thinking of Dante's hell, where the coffee is always cold. Sometimes I get tired of my tendency to flit back and forth from serious to silly. It seems to indicate a basically trivial soul. I turned to Eugenia.

"The old reasons for curiosity are gone now," I said, totally serious.

Anita Sullivan

"And enthusiasm," she added, paddling her hand around in the sun on the stone beside the step as if she were stirring water.

"But still," she tilted her head and looked directly at me, "I still find myself wanting to do new things, don't you?" Then we both grinned, as we remembered once again her sudden and recent arrival. And she had not vanished into thin air, nor seemed likely to any time soon.

We wandered the beach all morning, had lunch, then decided to sleep for awhile. Sleeping had at once become more important, especially with two of us. We were both practiced dreamers – our joint dreaming, after all, had allowed Eugenia to travel from England to Italy in full physical form. Should we immediately try to include Mick in our world? Would this be too much like an act of hubris on our part? Did we need to wait an appropriate time so that some sort of gap would be filled, or balance restored? We talked about these concerns, but neither of us felt a strong instinct prohibiting us from making an immediate attempt to "dream him in" as Eugenia quipped. We both believed he was also still alive, that he would have chosen to be part of this experiment too. In fact, he had died seven years before me and six years before Eugenia. I was the oldest of the three, but I had lived well into my eighties.

"I'm a bit torn between doing something right away, and holding off for a few days. How about you?"

"I'm not torn." Eugenia was often clear when I was wishy-washy, and sometimes this annoyed me (sheer envy and self doubt), since hers was never a confidence driven by false pride, but rather by uncanny insight and intuition. I never could discover in myself an equal wisdom. She continued slowly, her eyes closed. "I would like to set an intention, not a really fully conscious one, but at a deeper level. I think setting an intention together could be really powerful, don't you think?"

"Oh yes!"

"Something really simple," said Eugenia. "We would like Mick to know where we are, and to join us here if he is able and if he so wishes."

"A little awkward, but good enough," I murmured, and we said it aloud several times until we had each internalized it. Then we went off to our naps. I went to a room on the middle level of the house, an open mezzanine furnished with a charming little love seat with a high back and sides made of beautiful polished teak, upholstered in pale orange velvet with aqua and white flowers. I have no idea where it came from, I never would have chosen it myself, but the little sofa turned out to be much more comfortable than it looks When I lie down on it I feel hidden, as if I have gone clear off the screens of the Arbiters, so far out of their observation zone that I feel—in this one place in my house—empowered to become dead in the usual sense, and I would then simply disappear; I would not show up on any chart or in any book of statistics past or future (my serial number lost forever). Since in my present life I am already once removed from reality, this second removal is doubly precious to me. It is a silence within silence, yet it has a limit, so that I don't feel the lurking terror of falling into an infinite series of interlocking silences. At any rate, it's a terrific place for a nap, because I know I'm always the same when I wake up as I was when I went to sleep, even if I don't feel that way.

Eugenia said she wanted to sleep outside, under a tree up on the hillside behind the house. She took a pillow and a silk comforter and went off, in her nightgown still, looking like a Victorian painting of a

Anita Sullivan

child. When I woke up I lay quietly and thought, "Is Eugenia still here?" After all, I had dreamed her here in a previous sleep. Maybe this little nap, instead of bringing Mick here, had sent her back to England.

I went into the kitchen and began making pasta, a simple dish which requires sautéing garlic and hot pepper in olive oil, then discarding them and stirring the pasta into the oil. A bit of lemon juice, some fresh parsley. I had made bread the previous day. I kept thinking of things to say to Eugenia. Being alone tilts you far inside yourself, and it can be like treading on velvet, so quiet you know you have metamorphosed into a being that lives without breathing. Speaking to another human being becomes a raw, primitive action, yet so necessary. How could the Arbiters dare to offer humans such an option as paradise alone? Even Adam did not have to wait long.

I had just dreamed of being inside a large apartment with a semi-circle of windows across one side. I was looking out over trees and meadows going quickly by, as if I were on a train. The whole building was traveling, and I was enjoying not living in a fixed location. And yet, I knew that if I went out the front door I would be in a small town in Alabama, every time.

"Why Alabama?" I smiled, shaking my head as I went out to the terrace. It was mid-afternoon, a little hushed bee-drone and bird-murmur did not quite drown out the heavy sense of the sea in the distance. Not quite a sound.

Eugenia came down into the kitchen with an inquiring look and I made a face indicating my failure. "Did you find anybody?" I asked, the most comprehensive question I could think of to slake my confusion and curiosity all at once.

"I saw Mick," she said indifferently, and began to help me set the table as if she had lived here all her life. "I saw him, but he didn't see me. He was crossing a parking lot. He walked right through me."

"How did he seem?"

"Fine. I didn't get the sense he was out looking for us."

"Ungrateful wretch!"

I felt a surge of the old misery and annoyance and ignored it as I always had. When Eugenia sets an intention, she always dreams about the thing she sets an intention for. Naturally, she *saw Mick in her dream*. But not me, of course. I dreamed of something else entirely, unless I could rationalize by telling myself "I was looking for Mick with an entire building."

We ate in silence. Suddenly I set down my fork with a clang and folded my arms, leaning my chair back somewhat recklessly.

"What's wrong?" She spoke a little sharply.

"Why the hell are we doing this? The universe is totally fickle. Why do we kid ourselves that our stupid little dreams have anything to do with what actually *happens*?" My voice became shrill, and I shut my mouth firmly as well as my eyes, as if to close down all further conversation. The wolves' shadows lurched forward from the edge of the garden again. My ears buzzed and pinwheels circled the insides of my eyelids. When I finally felt able to open my eyes again, Eugenia was gone.

[Journal Entry]

Today when I was playing the harpsichord in the library I suddenly heard it in a totally new way, as if I were acting out one of

15                    Anita Sullivan

Zeno's paradoxes. I was able to distinguish each harpsichord string being plucked—precisely and with some delicacy—while simultaneously receiving the overall impression of something much larger, as if the harpsichord were the pool of a waterfall with a single column of mist rising from its middle. I only mention this because I recognized one of those rare *superimposed* thoughts that simply pop up now and then from nowhere rather than emerging through slow evolution. I would expect to have more of those in this place. It's as if we learn all that we know twice over, the first time from the inside out (by virtue of who we are), and the second time from the outside in (by virtue of what we do). Now I have more time to do the second part. *But nobody to tell.* It makes me weep. So I must write.

I wish you were here, David. We could have a long discussion about music and sound, and compare the piano to the harpsichord as we were accustomed to do, you being a pianist, and I a keyboard technician and tuner. You've been dead for 20 years, and I for only a month, but now I may learn to miss you in more refined ways as my memories of the past blend with those of my new life.

I do believe, though—and this is a very wicked and subversive thought—*that communication is possible among the humans caught in this voluntary exile.* I would not have chosen this after-death option if I didn't believe that. We are prevented from physically leaving the grounds of our chosen place of solitude, that's the cardinal Rule. But what's to prevent us from traveling to one another in our dreams? I don't mean just dreaming about other people, I mean actually moving from one place to another through dreaming. Mick and Eugenia and I and a few other friends spent quite a number of years working on this, and we came dizzyingly close a few times. People thought we were crazy, but fortunately nobody had any idea how serious we were (even David didn't know, bless his heart). In some ways we were like the people who jumped off cliffs flapping their feather-coated arms, convinced that humans should be able to fly, except that we didn't die in the process. Certainly there is nothing to prevent me from renewing the practice now. I believe the Arbiter and his group do not know of this possibility.

## Mick Arrives, But

I sat in my chair for a long time obsessively composing an imaginary summing-up to Eugenia to calm my fears that she would not come back. It went something like this: Consider: Yes, we really can travel by dreaming, we just proved it by Eugenia's arrival. Now we want to bring Mick here too. But is that all? Don't we eventually want to branch out and seek other human company as well? *What sort of human company?* How much control do we have, especially since we have no idea how many others like us there are "out there." How can we call people up when we know nothing about them? We might not have the skill to keep out a host of really weird people. Or we might end up being irresistibly drawn to their houses, or castles or yurts or wigwams . . . (here I began to giggle, and had to start pacing the floor to calm myself).

But I knew what was really happening. I had fallen into one of my pessimistic spells, and Eugenia had disappeared to avoid listening to me. Living alone for something over a year had taken its toll on me, mind and spirit, and now I seemed unable to keep from stumbling regularly into sinkholes of total irrationality. A cloud would come over

Anita Sullivan

my mind, like an evil spell, blotting out the ability to think. I began to talk to myself aloud. "Actually, irrationality is the very thing I need to develop—but a <u>positive</u> version of it. Everything we're doing here is already impossible, so why not just keep jumping off cliffs? Mick and Eugenia are good at that, but me? I'm always the voice of—no, it's not caution, it's not reason, it's just plain old pessimism."

As I continued to pace the floor I knew I had hit upon what was making me feel so guilty and depressed. Will I never change? What the hell does it take, anyway?

Over the next few days I plunged into my library of dream books, and found some legitimate cause for caution, in terms of trying to dream our way into Mick's world. I read again about "planes" of reality which the dreaming soul often travels through, some of them pretty shady regions, like the red-light district of a huge city, peopled with mangled and underdeveloped spirits. I don't want to risk opening some kind of conduit through which these souls can begin to stream. I can just see them, draped over the benches and tables of my garden, the sofa in my sitting room, setting up their sleeping bags in my little cafeteria like a bunch of hippies. Telling us their life stories. Arghh!

But, on the other hand, I do want the company of a select group of wise and witty and kind and loving people (somewhat like myself, eh what?) I kept looking up from my books to smile and frown at the inherent difficulty of the situation. Here we are, supposedly set up in an ideal, stress-free paradise. But no, that's actually the key point of this whole Experiment, isn't it? To help us get to the core of what con-stitutes full human happiness. And here I am manufacturing new conditions for unease.

So, true to form, I spent about a week trying to devise a dream filter. I practiced protection rituals, casting tents of light around my living space. I knew from years of experience that dreams are of many kinds, and one of those kinds is "'Other' coming in." Not all dreams, as some psychologists still insist, emerge from your own psyche. The engineering problem I was up against was to isolate the right kind of dreaming technique and to turn it into a method.

In the middle of all this, Mick did show up. I didn't dream him here, as happened with Eugenia – that is, he didn't come while I was asleep and dreaming about him. He simply stepped in through the gate in the wall, closing it carefully behind him and looking devilishly pleased with himself.

"I'm your next door neighbor," he said. "Wondered if I might borrow a cup of sugar?"

For once I was at a loss for words. I just sighed and shook my head and looked at him. I had no idea how to react, I couldn't even manage to say "Good Lord!" or to laugh or render shock. Finally I just closed my eyes and said weakly, "How the hell did you do that?"

Meanwhile he was blundering around the place, and so didn't even hear me. "Hey! This is cool!" I heard his voice from the balcony off the bedroom, which has a marvelous curved railing made of slender filigreed stones carved into the shapes of vines and flowers. "I'm in Italy too!" he shouted down from the smaller balcony off the upper gallery, the one which faces the mountains. "We may actually be neighbors!"

"Why am I not surprised?" I muttered, putting down my trowel and dusting off my knees. "I am not in Italy!" I shouted back. "It's just general Eastern Mediterranean!" Mick was born in Mexico, his father was Mexican and his mother a green-eyed Irish lass with a Ph.D. in Hispanic literature. He grew up speaking Spanish first, and had only ever lived in Oregon or Mexico all his life. Yet for some reason he was fixed on Italy, even though he never managed to travel there during his lifetime – he never could save enough money or take time away from his practice as a counselor, and his wife and three children were always falling ill with one thing or another. But he dreamed of Italy all the time. He had a regular place there he always visited, people he had gotten to know. He was even learning Italian through his dreams, and would tell incredibly complicated stories about the village life there. "I don't need to go, I've already been there!" he would say, and he meant it. Almost.

"You staying for dinner?" I shouted, figuring he'd hear me somewhere.

"Sure!" he yelled back. So I got out my basket and began to clip parsley and fennel and artichokes, at a leisurely pace. A few new potatoes coming along down by the spring. I'd need mushrooms, a bit of asiego . . . maybe a dry Cretan white wine.

"You didn't bring company did you?" I shouted again.

This time he came bouncing down the hall stairs and out into the garden in a hurry. "Oh, god no!" he said, "I fought them off like mosquitoes!" And he burst into a cackle of laughter, his greenish eyes alight with mischief but also with a memory. He shook his head as his laughing died away. "You wouldn't want to know what I've been through to get here. I'll come another way next time, if I can even get back." He looked at me with a strange expression. "You may not be able to get rid of me. I may not be able to get rid of me, I don't know!" And shaking his head, he walked over to the edge of the garden and stood there looking out. "Funny, isn't it, how we can't just walk away, you know what I mean? We're like dogs with electric collars." He turned around. "Do you ever feel like Adam and Eve in the Garden? Paradise which is actually hell, because you're trapped inside its rules?"

I said nothing, thinking of days when I had lain half awake in bed for hours staving off a ceiling that looked like boiling concrete coming down on my head.

"We're slaves," he said with a long and elegant shrug. "They're experimenting with us. I get the sense that almost anything we do is welcome, you know what I mean? All this bullshit about the Rule – the Rule is whatever we can't do. Even if we kill ourselves trying. They don't really give a flying fuck, they just want to see what we can *do!*" He paused a moment, squinting to organize his thoughts. I always love it when Mick goes on a rant. He doesn't lecture like so many men do, he just speculates wildly aloud. There's always an undercurrent of uncertainty, of mobility in his philosophy.

"I don't mean to sound paranoid," he said. "It's hard to talk about 'Them' without sounding that way. But I mean, what is this all about anyway? You know what I think? I think they're trying to actually *prove* that immortality is fundamentally impossible for regular humans, and so justify tossing us all into some ash pit somewhere and starting over."

"What?"

"I mean, the gods, or whatever, screwed up right from the start. Immortality doesn't work because it means no children, no variety, no change. But then you go and create a bunch of mortal beings who know they're going to die, *and they don't want to.* We're damned if we do

Anita Sullivan

and damned if we don't, so it never really works, you know what I mean? And they've just never figured a way out of this stupid paradox."

I shook my head. "I don't believe they're still dealing with *that*," I said. "Give them credit for knowing something we don't. I mean, they did manage to do this—" I waved my hand around. "So they do have some power." I gave him a quick grin and grabbed him by the elbow.

"Hey, Mick, let's talk about this over some food. I'll show you my cafeteria. Just come carry some things, will you?"

I had made some scordalia, sautéed some artichokes with parsley and mushrooms, and finished with a little corn and pimento salad, and a raspberry sorbet. It was the usual hodge-podge from the great refrigerator in the sky, supplemented by my own *jardin*. The parsley and artichokes I had grown myself.

The cafeteria is at the lowest level of the house, hidden from the sea by masses of small hedges and trees at the edge of a low stone wall. It is a room with a counter on the side and six small square wooden tables with simple wood and wicker chairs. Semi-circular in shape, with windows going down from the ceiling but stopping about two feet from the floor, so when you're sitting at a table, you feel a little sheltered. This is where I eat on special occasions, waiting on myself from the kitchen, and then sitting at now one table, then another. My cafeteria, I must say, was a stroke of genius.

"Wow!" said Mick when we came in.

"Choose a table," I commanded him, and when he did, I went behind the counter and came out with a tablecloth with lovely earth colors, dark yellow, brown, deep orange. He grabbed it from me and shook it over the table with a flourish. We were both grinning. I handed him the silver.

"Here, set the table, light the candle, and then sit down and I'll wait on you!"

"No, you should let me wait on you!" he said, "You've been waiting on yourself all this time."

"Tomorrow is soon enough. When Eugenia comes back we can take turns. And whoever else shows up!" I knew I was opening a conversational can of worms here, but I wickedly skipped off into the kitchen, which is up a short flight of stone stairs from the cafeteria, so that it looks in two directions, the private and the public.

"What's this about Eugenia, did she beat me here?" He threw back his head and gave a long cackling laugh before I could even nod. I poured the wine – a dry pinot grigio – and we both sat down.

I told him about her visit, how suddenly it had ended, and how we had tried to dream him here to join us.

He breathed out suddenly and his eyes widened. "You did!" he said. "You did dream me here. I was out wandering around. I had started traveling but didn't know where to go. I had just started doing that. I was a little nuts the first couple of years, I think – it's hard to keep track." He was speaking rapidly, his sentences choppy. "But last night I was running down a grassy pathway in the woods somewhere near here – I'm sure it was near here – and suddenly began to fly a little. I flew over this place about three times, and it looked, well, it's hard to explain. I suddenly knew that it was a place in my own reality, you know what I mean? I mean, our reality, not the old one."

I nodded.

Anita Sullivan

"So, I decided to come on over. I thought right away of you and Eugenia. I had dreamed of you both, of course, a bazillion times, but of course I didn't know if you were dead yet, and if you had decided to do this immortality stint too!" Again he laughed. "Sounds so stupid to talk about it that way. 'I'm not dead yet!'" He made a silly face and relaxed his limbs suddenly into a rag-doll pose, practically falling off his chair. He was quoting an old Monty Python film. "That's our motto, isn't it? 'We're not dead yet!'" He gave it the phony British accent, and I raised my eyebrows and grimaced, leaning back in my chair with my glass of wine. I wished Eugenia were here, and Patrick and Tim and Donna and Jess and you, David, and I went off into a happy haze of listing old friends I would invite to our imaginary party. I felt positively immoral to have such a sudden lust for other people again; I had trained myself out of it so rigorously during the past year.

"What about this café?" he said, standing up suddenly. "What a great place! What made you think of it?"

"Public and private," I said.

"Ah!"

"I had an image of myself coming down the stairs every morning to my little café. If I could see all these tables here, it would give the impression of a public space."

"But without any people here, wouldn't it be worse?"

"No, not really. It's still a public space. That gives it magic, and possibility. It's not that I actually expect people to come in the door, it's not a matter of fooling myself, it's just that the space itself feels somehow—different because of what it stands for."

"As if it were a little church," Mick said softly, sitting down again.

We ate in silence for awhile, and I felt suddenly giddy at the prospect of conversation on a regular basis. As if I were looking at a painting held up in front of me, entitled "Conversation," and I knew it could be put back down again and replaced with something else. Being human suddenly seemed too enormous a task.

"What are your plans?" Mick asked when he was finished eating. He seemed restless, about to leave his chair again but not quite ready.

I gave a snort and shrugged. "Bring in some friends. Hang out. Learn how to keep from asking 'why bother?'" I shrugged again.

Mick got up and started walking around, idly picking up vases and candlesticks and putting them down again. We were both silent a long time.

"Funny," he said finally, "the 'why bother?' voice never occurred to me much during my lifetime, and it hasn't really bothered me here either."

I narrowed my eyes at him. "Mick," I said, "you just finished saying that the first couple of years you were a little nuts. Don't tell me you didn't freak out when you found yourself back inside a thirty-year-old body again with no females around. Just for starters."

"Yeah." He sighed and tried to smile a little. Mick has a great gift for kidding himself. He stops just short of lying, and we always know he's doing it, and he always knows we know. But it's part of his way of moving through the world.

"Yeah. I admit I was depressed, even though I thought I could beat it—I thought just being here would be enough. And that I could figure out stuff to do that I'd never been able to try before, you know what I mean? So basically I just started traveling through dreaming."

Anita Sullivan

"Keeping busy," I said.

"Yeah, but dreaming is definitely not busy-work. I was getting somewhere with it, actually traveling, different levels of reality, I mean, new stuff. When Eugenia comes back, we could go off on some adventures. We could do some more of that shared dreaming work we used to do, you know, when we all slept together in the same room." He looked mischievously over at me, and once again I was reminded how much he resembled a faun. Not that I had ever met one. But I always thought of him as a forest creature, especially in the sense that his personality is unusually narrow but very deep.

Suddenly I felt wary. Mick had married quite young a sickly and jealous woman with whom he had much in common; she was a gifted psychic and herbal physician. But his own rather Pan-like personality had given him an eclectic attitude about sex, and he had persisted in finding it wherever and whenever he could. Eugenia and I had fought off his advances relentlessly and still managed to hold onto him as a good friend. In his 50's he had finally agreed to his wife's demands that he be true to her, even though such behavior was not yet strictly part of either his temperament or his philosophy. Then she had died suddenly, leaving him with three teenage children, and he had resumed his amorous relationships, but much less like a faun or satyr; more out of mutual respect and delight.

Still, how would we deal with this matter now with all eternity ahead of us and probably few prospects of other humans able to join our company? I realized I wanted time to develop a clear policy about sex, at least, which had not been an issue before. No sooner do you get people than you get bones of contention. We might eventually have enough dream travelers to form a little community, and need our own set of rules about many things. I shivered and tried to think what to say next.

As I was muddling, two lions appeared outside the café windows.

They were gazing meaningfully in at us with tawny eyes. Two females, very large and healthy looking. My thoughts were as frozen as my posture, except that I was very glad they were outside, and that the door was closed.

Mick gave a little squawk and then an exasperated snort.

"I thought I had left those guys behind!" he said, coming over to stand next to me. "That's what I meant when I was talking about the troubles of getting here."

"Are they real, you think?" I whispered.

"They sure look real to me!" he chortled. Mick has an almost annoying way of reversing emotions, so that when everybody else is angry or terrified, he is laughing. I was prepared to settle into out-and-out terror, and he was diverting me right at the beginning. This was not comforting, only confusing.

"It's just like the dreams I used to have of lions," I said. "They were always outside trying to get into my house, and I was always going around closing doors to keep them out. Can we get rid of them, you think?"

He shrugged. "I suppose they might come with me if I went away again."

"We've got to try that!" I gasped, as they began to move along the building, as if looking for a weak spot. One of them rose up very slowly on its hind legs and leaned against the window. But they didn't seem desperate or angry.

Anita Sullivan

"It's one thing to dream about them," I said. And racing through my head was a paradoxical scenario: *I go outside; the lions kill me; at the moment of my death the Arbiter appears and offers me the chance to remain alive for an indefinite period under certain circumstances. I accept those circumstances and set myself up in a second Italian villa. Mick arrives with two lions . . . .*

Once again I had the feeling we had arrived at the soft underbelly of the whole post-life, pre-death experiment. I closed my eyes and shivered.

"I gotta go!" said Mick. "Show me another door. I'll just go out the gate the way I came in. I know what to do after that."

[Journal Entry]

For many people, this life would seem like paradise. Yet after a few days of sleeping in the sun and eating anything you wanted, and watching movies, masturbating six times a day – or whatever – you might look around and say, "O.K., what now?" If all you are capable of is seeking comfort, you'd be doomed. The whole point of this experiment is to get past that initial stage. Let human ingenuity finally show its true mettle. Therefore, I don't believe this is a good place for someone who died before about age 60. Which I did not.

In a recent dream, David, you and I were hurrying across the enormous central room of Pennsylvania Station in New York, passing through that secular-cathedral light which is golden and blurry and filthy and mysterious all at the same time. I could hear our shoes clicking on the hard floor; I could sense brown and gray people streaming out from around us as if we were a magnetic field in the shape of a circle. I could see how your face was lifting towards where I was hurrying away from you, and towards you at the same time. And the main purpose for this event was to convey a set of impressions about a specific kind of beauty. There are at least a million specific, unique kinds of beauty. We harbor them inside our spirits like chemical elements or compounds, which only wait to be activated. A kiss will do it. A light sleep, a fragrance, a music. One for each of the million.

You and I had never been in Penn Station together, and I have no idea if you were ever there without me during your whole life. Yet the picture and the sounds and the feelings were as precise as if we actually had gone through these few moments and I was only remembering them extremely well. Something in my spirit was making this up from my body cells as if they had been paints. This is how dreaming and being awake are actually the same, except that the waking dreams usually elude you because you cannot turn quickly enough.

I believe that if I can practice turning quickly enough, then I might have discovered a way to have human company in this place. How long will it take? Aye, there's the rub.

Meanwhile, the details of this Experiment can be somewhat amusing.

Case in point: I'm supposed to fix my own lunch and dinner. "We are not a restaurant," (as the Arbiter told me in his opening lecture). Yet, aside from the breakfast exception, which makes no sense, I have ordered pie, dolmades and pasta salad from the grocery deli department (the imaginary one in the sky) and it comes through just fine. I mean, I don't have to grow my own wheat and thresh it and grind it to make the pasta noodles like the Little Red Hen. So, how do

Anita Sullivan

they know where to draw the line? I'll put that in italics, *How do they know where to draw the line*? I have learned that this is an intelligently-run universe at base, just as I had hoped, which means they really don't micro-manage. And that means they operate on a somewhat ad-hoc basis. Ask – and sometimes you shall receive and sometimes not, depending on who's at the Desk that evening. I may try pizza again in another week or month or year, and maybe if I word the request just a little bit differently . . . .

So, I'm going to dream myself up another person, who is going to visit me, and whom I am going to visit.

This Experiment, after all, constitutes a kind of solitary confinement. And humans are not supposed to be able to tolerate that. That means either "They" are innately cruel, or else *there is a way through.*

But more precisely, I don't want to take pot luck; I want my visitors to be people I know. Mick and Eugenia would be the most likely choices, since I can't call upon David. Oh, that seems so strangely final ("full fathoms deep my true love lies . . . ." He will not return, he is done, and here I am with a future, a future . . . .)

So, I will find a way to invite Mick and Eugenia to come here, through dreaming. Maybe others too, eventually, even strangers.


I saw a hoopoe in the garden this morning. But it wasn't just a bird. That hoopoe was a sign. Either Mick or Eugenia sent him out, testing the lay of the land, I'm sure of it. The hoopoe is a pretty bird, about the size of a kingfisher, with a long slender black beak like a needle, lovely pale orange neck and head, black and white feathers, a white tummy. A ruff of orange feathers sticks up on top of his head, making him look royal and tough at the same time. The little chap hung around most of the day, doing mildly bizarre things such as perching on the edge of the table on the patio and pretending to fall off, then catching itself with a big flap of wings and loud scratchy cackles. I know hoopoes look a bit like jays, with that tuft on their heads, and I suppose maybe they have the same adolescent sense of humor that jays have. I don't know; they are European birds, and I never lived in Europe before. I suppose because I'm in a Mediterranean villa, I have to have hoopoes instead of jays. I fed it chunks of bread from my hand, it was all too easy. It looked me right in the face, cocking its head sideways the way birds do. As if to say, "We've got something going, you and I, don't we?"

Now a rufous hummingbird has come. The hoopoe may have been random, but this is more serious. We share the hummingbird, Eugenia and Mick and I. They don't exist in Italy, yet here it comes, like a little helicopter, hovering in the dusk above the heliotrope and while I fixed my eyes onto it, suddenly it falls away as if I were weeping marbles; I can feel the weight leaving. I know it's no use to look any more for it today.


WHAT DO I DO WHEN A LIGHT BULB BURNS OUT? It's depressing. One of the big gorgeous chandeliers over my kitchen table popped a bulb this afternoon, setting off another serial set of doomsday thoughts in my one small brain: one by one all the electrical and mechanical devices in this house will break down, or clog up, and I will be the only moving item in the landscape, huddled before my little pile of ashes, waiting for my own bulb to burn out. Item: Do I have to fix my computer when it crashes? I do tune and repair my own piano and harpsichord; the wash I do by hand in a big sink with a washboard. What about the toilets (there are 4 bathrooms in this place)? One by one by one by one. . . . I HATE plumbing! I will neither plumb nor sew.

Maybe I should take to singing instead of talking, or reciting poetry. Those were the first uses of language anyway, so I believe. I will revert to poetry and song.

David sang tenor in choirs before we met and yet I never once heard him sing. Not a peep out of him, not even in the shower. "You haven't missed anything," he would smile when I mentioned this to him. I kept trying to trick him into singing, starting a song in the car or in the kitchen when I was cooking, but no use. He didn't sing when he was doing dishes either. But he always had a song going on somewhere deep inside him, just as I did. We probably moved all day to those songs, without thinking about it, different melodies. Even if it were the same song it wouldn't be the same. We talked about that too.

I am in the grip of the sea. Every day since the start of my time here I have walked on the seashore. I have my own beach, which I get to by going down a long flight of stone and concrete stairs, along the side of an enormous rock.

The house does not sit directly on the shore, I specified that it not do so; rather it is back and around a slight curve, so that from the top story I can see water, but I do not hear it. The sea is too noisy for my taste, even this middle-earth sea, this enormous inland lake which mostly paws gently at the shore, like someone absently caressing an animal from an armchair.

To reach the sea I go down the rock stairs and across an ancient set of garden walls, some of stone, some of dirt. Inside still grow remnants of old vegetables among the long reeds and grasses. They used to tether cows here, or goats, to keep down the weeds in the fallow plots. This was a community garden, and I can still smell the people here with my inward palate, so sharpened now by silence and solitude.

Every day I am coming to understand more and know less. I can feel my entire shape changing with the seeping-in of understanding, the seeping-out of knowledge. Eventually I will lose my words, but I will not know it when it happens.

I sit on the lip of an old terrace, in front of an abandoned villa at one side of this little cove, and the sea breeze blows my hair. The yard is littered with old broken chairs, clay jars, plastic lids, nails, amphorae. The detritus of generations, maybe even centuries if I dug down between the cracks in the concrete. There is a small rectangular pool on the side of the house away from the sea, inlaid with decorated tile, even a bit of mosaic, although it is not ancient. I dreamed of an enormous white plastic angel standing in this pool, its bottom half beneath the water. At first it was erect, about twice as tall as an average human, but gradually it filled with water and began to bend gracefully at the waist, touching the water with its fingers and its wings. I was part of it in some way, like a lesser appendage, a little dark figure on an inner tube bouncing around its navel. Soon we were floating on the surface of the water together, quietly in the sun.

I believe now I have always belonged to a minority which floats in the plasma body of human imagination like an antibody made of other, or might-have-been: an alternate aesthetic which would have grown into a different architecture, a different expression of the connection to the universe's largesse. This exile is not new, I have always been here.

Anita Sullivan

Every day as I come up the stairs to the path over to my house, I pass a small lane leading out in the direction I am not able to go, marked by a painted wooden sign on a post, which says "Via Buona." That means "Good Street." The sign is not old and faded, but could have been painted yesterday. David's last name was Good. Is this a small finger of previous reality into my world? Is it a joke? Are they the same thing? *If you come to a fork in the road, take it.*

[Here the Journal Ends]


## More About Lions


We ran upstairs through the kitchen and the library and out onto the upper terrace. "What if you bring them with you every time?" I said, knowing I sounded like a Greek mother again, always expecting the worse in every situation.

Mick shrugged and rolled his eyes. "I'll try to come a different way next time," he said. "I can come any time, you know. Don't worry, they might even be O.K. They could be guides, you know."

"I know, I thought of that. But I'm just not brave enough to face up to them yet!"

He nodded and moved off cautiously towards the double wooden gate in the wall that faced the sea road. I watched him until the gate closed, then I scuttled back inside, shutting the door firmly behind me. It took me about half an hour to work up the courage to go down into the café again. What if they were still there?

I didn't go downstairs again until I had cleared up my attitude somewhat. In my dreams I had always both loved and feared lions, as I was doing now, but they had never done me any harm. "They've come back to taunt me into making up my mind" I thought, and carried this silly thought like a feather down the stairs.

They were still there, lying like two statues on either side of the stone bench, shoulder-high in flowers. But there was an insubstantiality to their bodies now; they looked gray rather than tawny, and I could almost see through them. I began to wonder if they were in the process of fading away entirely. Should I go out and try to communicate with them in this intermediate state?

Yes, I should. Otherwise I would be crouching inside my house for days, weeks. What did I have to lose except my life, ho ho?

I stepped out the café door and moved towards the bench as if I simply intended to sit down and look over the flowers towards the high wall beyond. Bees, I remember, were droning in the wisteria along the wall, in the climbing roses. I was suddenly overcome with a complex of intersecting images that pricked in me an attitude I had never felt before. This one was geometric and rich with pale colors edged in pale gold-dust luster, and gave me a thin and wicked kind of energy, as if I had become a flung disc.

"Hello," I said silently. The lionesses turned their heads and looked over at me, but didn't move. I felt a surge of companionship in a courtly sort of way. We were like three circles touching at the edges but not interlocking.

And I relaxed, and we lived happily ever after. It took about six or seven hours, I think, looking back now with other people here and the lionesses pacing through the garden day and night like a couple of house cats. I just sat there until something happened. After all, I didn't have anything else to do. The bench was hard, so I went to the upper terrace and brought down a lawn chair. But one of those little uncon-

Anita Sullivan

scious personality nodes inside me made a decision that must have gone something like this: "I'm not moving from this spot until somebody tells me what's going on." And so I just sat. Either my attitude changed, or they sent me a subliminal message, I don't know. We never talked. They never made a sound, and I didn't receive any communication from them the way I would have expected. Just a big, gorgeous silence. Nevertheless, I think, like the fox in *The Little Prince*, we must have tamed each other. And after that I was free to move around when-ever Mick would show up and the beasts would slip fully back into this reality again (instead of being "one world behind," as I now like to call it).

Djan, when he came, did talk with them, and I was a little envious. It was a kind of mind-speech, the advanced communication you read about that certain desert or jungle peoples developed, and all humans likely carry the latent ability for. Mick could do it too. Eden had a natural love for animals that transcended any notion of fear, so he would pet the lionesses, make faces with them, even roll around with them in the grass and they seemed to love it. And Eugenia had a kind of empathy with them that she never talked about, but made it so they were never far from her when she was outdoors (they didn't come into the house, I don't think they were able to). I was the only one who did not communicate. Or, at least, not in an intellectual or emotional way, and what else is there? I think there is something else, actually, and even now I hesitate to try putting words to it. I wouldn't even call it *communication*, but more a kind of identity. I don't need to talk to them because in a sense the lionesses are part of me. Not of my body or spirit, but of my soul: the "soul" which is particular to me as long as I'm alive. They are a manifestation of the "part-ness" aspect of all life, so that we—the lionesses and I—do not need to do more than tremble and revel in the constant joy of our *capacity* to know one another as separate beings, even as we are one.

That evening I went up to the balcony off the bedroom, sat down on a bench all propped up with pillows, and wrote in the journal I've been sporadically keeping since my first day here. You would have thought there would be little to say in such a life, yet recently (with the lions and all), a kind of plot seems to be forming. Will there be a shape to our lives – not simply one day after another?

A silk tree was blooming below me off to the left, and soon a fiery red and green hummingbird came along and began to feed there in the wispy, slender pink blossoms. Between feedings it would come and perch on the balcony, inches from my moving hand. I felt an ecstasy almost like a breeze moving through our mutual space, and I knew there was a bird in my throat at the same time one sat on the railing, and that the ecstasy was outside me, not of my own doing, but that it was a good thing for random ecstasies to be roaming the world alone. I began to sketch the bird.

That evening I flew out for the first time myself. I know this for sure because although I had stopped keeping track of dates for awhile (until a bunch of us devised our new system), I do remember it was a week after the lions and I came to terms.

Before I talk about that adventure, though, I must go backwards first to balance my narrative in the matter of attitude. Mick remarked that he had been "a little nuts" the first year (or did he say "year or two"? I don't remember.) This whole business of living alone forever in one place in a body that never grows old is most definitely insanity-making. Humans need other humans, and they need to travel.

Anita Sullivan

The Arbiter and her/his/its gang—or Necessity, or Evolution, or what-ever has managed to make such an arrangement, must be something *other than human*. This I have come firmly to believe. It's the same way women used to joke that a man must have designed the kitchens in their houses. No proper human god would subject human beings to a life so impossible, so unnatural as this save for a sort of savage curiosity, and I do not believe such an attitude is behind our post-life exile, not in the least. I think we are being tested to see how far we have already come, and if we can make the next big jump – the one which allows us to tolerate immortality. Granted, the last jump might well be to learn how to tolerate immortality living alone in one place. Is that more impossible and unnatural than living forever with others? Something inside me shouts "Yes!"

But, to balance my narrative. For the first several months I dutifully followed the Rule as it was given, as if I continued to have no choice in the matter. I strove mightily to live alone in one place indefinitely and remain sane. Not only sane, but productive. Not only productive but happy. I trusted that on the days when my whole mind split apart like a continent turning into a collection of islands, that it wouldn't be a permanent split. When I completely lost control, I somehow knew that Arbiter-And-Group would lean down and put me back together again as a female humpty-dumpty, and even my cracks would seal up again, so I would emerge a stronger and finer egg than before! What else could I assume? On days, nights that I would sink into oblivion, feeling myself going down, the world swirling around me as if I were suddenly moved into a different portion of the electro-magnetic spectrum, thus losing the name of "matter" – on those days I trusted that my inability to hold onto my mind would not ultimately lead to the end of my life here. There seemed to be no reason for this trust. Why ever should I not lie in my bed, or on the floor, or in the flower bed, or wherever I happened to fall, and stay there until I starved to death? Nobody had given me any guarantees against that kind of irresponsible dying. But I assumed because *I didn't want to die yet* that I would not. And, I didn't.

This is all I will say. I didn't record anything during those periods, of course, because I could not. I don't know how many there were, or how long each lasted, but there were many. I do not know if they would have continued, like a chronic illness, for years. In my previous life I had taken medicine for clinical depression, and I was not taking it here. I told the Arbiter I wanted to go clearly into this new life, and I expected an interim of hell before my philosophy swung round (although it was surely in arrears to my physiology, as I should have known it would be). I believe I became someone else during that first year, even if I was unable to morph into a being who could withstand eternal solitude. I was stronger in a way I believed would serve well going into this new phase, this phase of travel through dreaming. "Toujours gay, Archie!" David used to quote sometimes, from *Archie and Mehitabel,* and bless his heart he was not saying this when I was in a black mood, to try to cheer me up. He knew what it meant. I don't invoke that line very often either, because it is, for me, so powerful I hate to risk overusing it. Fortunately, it still surprises me every time. If I ever do decide to die, I might even ask to have it put onto my gravestone. Always depending on what I discover between now and then, of course.

Anita Sullivan

## I Venture Forth

When I finally flew out on a dream journey it was much easier than I imagined. It's one thing to dream of other places, and quite another to go there in the flesh by way of dreaming. Not an "out of body," but a "whole self" experience, I guess. Certain places are open, others not. To this day I have never visited Djan or Mick because they have chosen to keep the portals closed that lead to their dwelling places. Eden tends to prefer that we come one at a time to his odd little cabin in the Maine woods, and Eugenia did, finally permit us to make the rare visit to her extended cottage on the South Coast of England.

I started on my trip by climbing stairs in sunlight to the top of a wall, or what seemed to be a wall. As my head rose over the top, I found that the wall became the floor of a room with glass walls, so that I felt myself in a bubble of outside-within-outside, if that makes any sense. There I waited until others arrived—the "other people" you often encounter in dreams, who look vaguely familiar, but who never resolve themselves clearly into anyone you can identify. We climbed onto a rug that lifted off the floor and flew out one of the windows, over a city, down a wide river busy with ships and barges. Then came a humming sound, as if hundreds of small birds were trilling at the same frequency. My vision became clouded as we (I believe) accelerated and began to move off into higher regions.

The carpet came down in an empty parking lot in front of an adobe wall. A sign inlaid in the wall in blue tile said "Henningsen Gallery." Two bicycles were chained to a metal post beside a flagstone pathway.

"I was hoping for, maybe Paris . . . ." said a deep voice behind me. I turned so quickly I almost fell over.

A tall black man with a wonderful head of grizzled curly hair was leaning his chin on his hands, which were nested on top of a knobbed walking stick. He was sweeping his glance around the place with a squint of concentration, possibly amusement. I don't know if he meant me to hear him, but his comment was like a tiny grain of salt landing on the enormous cloud of doubt and confusion whirling around my head, making it vanish—Poof! I blinked.

"We can't go to Paris," I thought, and my brain started following that train of thought, idly, as I turned back around and saw a sign with an arrow, "Gardens" pointing away from the adobe wall. "At least, we can't go to Paris as it is now, with lights and food and cars and other people . . . ."

"The undead," he said even more quietly. He spoke like one who is always in communication at various levels in various ways with the people around him, so that what he actually says is like an underground river making one of its sporadic appearances above ground.

"Where are we?"

I could feel him step forward to stand beside me, and we looked at one another. He smiled and nodded courteously, his face breaking into wrinkles that showed how smiling had likely been his normal mode for quite some time. His eyes were dark brown, but sparkled with bits of silver that came and went on the surface as if to deflect any attempt to focus too closely.

"Judging by the adobe wall, the American Southwest, perhaps?" he said, waving one hand at the scene. We both paused to look around more carefully, still without moving from the spot. Behind

Anita Sullivan

the wall we could see the top portion of a house with a series of stacked towers, each one dominated by an unframed window glass set deeply into the adobe, and the whole edifice leaning at a slight angle, as if to catch the sun at a precise time of day. We moved forward at the same time to peer around an opening in the wall, and saw that the flagstone path led to a recessed porch, supported by hand-hewn, dark brown wooden pillars. A sign on the tall wooden doorway said "Open: Ring Bell."

"Tempting, wouldn't you say?" he remarked with a slight grimace.

I glanced behind us, and realized I was looking for the carpet that had brought us here, the other people. But there was nothing but a small circular driveway with a few parking spaces. I wondered if the cars were actually there, and we were unable to see them. This thought made me slightly dizzy, and I swayed. He reached out and caught my elbow.

"It appears we have been left to pursue our own adventure."

I remained silent, since he seemed in some way to be taking care of any preliminary conversation we might need, and I felt a little curl of comfort that he would talk to me this way.

"Have we been exiled here?" I asked, my voice coming out in a little croak.

He nodded thoughtfully, as if thinking over my question, not as if answering it, and then chewed on his lower lip awhile.

"We both know how to return, whenever we wish."

"This your first trip out?" he asked. I nodded again. "I don't think this is a portal, any rate," he continued. "This is a real place. It's usually best to explore slowly. Each place is a gift – can teach you how to move through more quickly, teach you to learn what you're looking for."

"I was hoping for some other people."

He folded his arms across his chest, incorporating his walking stick inside so that it stuck rather comically up beside his left ear. Leaning back a bit, in a cowboy-like stance (and he was wearing jeans, a belt with a silver buckle, soft brown leather boots up to the middle of his calves, and a bright aqua shirt that hung like a serape a foot or so below his waist.) he drawled at me in a kind way. "Well, Ma'am, I choose not to take offense at that remark!"

And of course I laughed. Then we introduced ourselves: I'm Carley. I'm Djan. I'm from Oregon but I live in a Mediterranean villa; I'm from Australia, Northern Territory. Out exploring? Yes. First time out? Yes (Carley); No (Djan). Met any other people? Yes (Carley). Some old friends (cautiously); No. Not until now (Djan). Long time? About a year (Carley). More like about three. You lose track (Djan).

And that's how I met Djan, who turned out to be a splendid addition to our company.

Our first adventure together involved little more than strolling around the grounds of Henningsen Gallery, resting ourselves 'neath the local Tum-Tum tree (I asked Djan if it might be a Baobab and he came close to snorting in derision. It was merely a large, highly-contorted cedar). We spoke of many things, but not of the past—neither the immediate, nor more distant (each of us now has two distinct "past lives"). Djan exuded a certain Old World courtesy which precluded many questions I might have asked other strangers, yet we immediately enjoyed a meeting of minds of a kind that allowed our joint narrative to

Anita Sullivan

run along half with, half without words. Most of all I wanted to ask him about Australia, and about his own, likely Aboriginal, heritage, but I felt that those questions would be answered in their own good time.

After awhile we both drifted back to the parking lot, and looked again at the bicycles. They were both locked, but Djan figured out immediately that the rather simple toothed combination locks could easily be manipulated, and soon we were bouncing off down narrow dusty streets past a variety of adobe-styled houses. It was spring, and besides abundant flowering trees, and lilacs and other colorful flowers tumbling over the walls, dandelions were furiously blooming beside the dry ditches, making their own outsiders' garden.

We found a prairie-dog town, filled with the cheerful little creatures, and stood happily watching them for awhile. I wondered how come we were able to pass so many houses, where living humans probably were carrying on their lives, and yet we saw none of them, nor signs of their recent activities. At one point I laughed as the thought occurred to me that we should search through their trash cans. Would they be empty also? Or would they be full of trash from two or three years ago? I stopped my bike and put the question to Djan.

"Oh, one paradox at a time, please," he said, and squinted somewhat fiercely in concentration.

"It raises the additional question," he said slowly, pausing at odd intervals, "whether the trash I would be able to see would differ from that trash you would be able to see, being as how we died at different times, you know." He shook his head, his eyes gleaming with amusement and maybe something deeper than that.

"Reminds me of Schrödinger's Cat!" I said cheerfully. And when he asked me to explain, I couldn't remember exactly how it went.

"Something about there's no way of knowing ahead of time whether the cat inside the box is actually dead before you open the box . . . ."

He nodded. "Yes, it would have to work that way, wouldn't it? The trash is not *either* present or not present as a single entity, it's only temporarily there depending on who is looking at it. Hmm . . . I would surely not like to be one of the Old Ones in charge of this particular enterprise. Too many mutually exclusive possibilities exist, many of which might be on a collision course with one another." He stuck out his bottom lip and frowned while he imagined some of these possibilities.

So we didn't look into the trash cans, but we parked our bikes (no need to lock them) and climbed over a barbed wire fence with a huge sign proclaiming Indian Land belonging to the Taos Pueblo. The sun was warm without being too hot, and the sky was a pulsing, vivid blue. We wandered through dry arroyos and up and down hills until we were hungry, thirsty, and weary.

"Nice place to live," said Djan lazily, as we walked back to our bikes. I knew he was thinking that one of the dreamers in our group might well have chosen this as a lovely spot to set up an ideal house. Briefly I wished that we could do serial immortality, moving every ten years or so to another landscape. Well, maybe even that could be arranged in time.

Although later we would discover that Djan had amazing scrounging abilities within the limits of our Experiment, and very likely would have been able to locate food and water for the two of us, he chose on this particular day of our first meeting to pretend ignorance, and we returned to the parking lot. After re-locking the bikes to their posts, we simply propped ourselves against a couple of shady tree trunks, dozed off, and dreamed ourselves home. Not before I had described to him in great detail the location of my villa, and invited him firmly to come for dinner the very next day.

"The very next day I can manage it," he replied gently. By which I knew he did not mean months or years. We parted in contentment.

## The Island

The very next day Eugenia and I decided to go out together. We called it our "walkabout," and planned to bring packs with food and water. I told her about Djan but she thought, reasonably enough, that we need not wait around for him, since he could probably find us somewhere else if he wanted company. Nonetheless, I left a note on the front gate, right under the bell pull, inviting him to make himself at home.

"Do you think we can choose where we want to go?" Eugenia asked.

I shook my head.

"Why not?"

"Think about dreams," I said, feeling like an old curmudgeon. Was I telling the truth or was I just acting out some internal need to quash the hopes of this fine young woman standing there with the morning mist clinging to her curls? "How often do you dream about the exact thing you expect? Dreams are symbolic. Besides," I flitted quickly to a different aspect of the subject, "Where do we want to go?"

She shrugged. "I don't really care. I think we should ask for guidance and assume we'll be going somewhere we ought to be going."

"What about your house in England, I've never seen it?" I suggested. It seemed logical.

She wrinkled her nose and shook her head. "Not this time!"

"Well, pot luck, then!" And we both closed our eyes, relaxed, and waited. We had decided in advance that even though there was no assurance that we would end up in the same place, we would start out together with a focused vision of the glassed-in room on top of the wall, assuming that if we managed to find our way to this launching spot we could then be more in control of where we actually traveled. I was able to describe the room to her pretty exactly. As I was drifting off, my imagination flashed me a bunch of superimposed images, some of them with words attached. I saw a small Greek village with a path going down beside a stone wall. "Unicorn," was a word that came drifting in, and then a couple of words I couldn't understand, along with the flash of white teeth in a grin, and yellow eyes. After that I was plunging in a dizzying slow tumble with my eyes half open, seeing alternating flashes of silver and dark.

Thump! I sat up, damp and chilled, at the bottom of a shallow well. Above me, about shoulder level, sunlight illuminated a couple of bright yellow poppies.

I stood and found that my elbows easily rested on the grass at the edge of the well. I took a deep breath and looked around. To my right was the stone wall of a house, with an opening left for a window. It looked brand new, as if the house were still under construction, and in fact as I looked up I could see that it had no roof. In front of me was a low stone wall, probably the boundary of the property. Near the wall on the left was an old apple tree, crouched and gnarled. Between the abandoned well where I stood and the apple tree were the remains of a

Anita Sullivan

garden. Nobody was in sight, and I heard nothing, not even distant voices, not even a breeze. But I could hear myself breathe. Carefully I hoisted myself out of the well, throwing my pack and walking stick out ahead of me, taking no pains to be quiet.

I sat down next to the yellow poppies.

I probably should write that sentence in huge capital letters, because I have no idea how long I sat there. I am probably still there. I could feel sun on my shoulders, but also on my face and chest, which came from the poppies. I knew the yellow smile at the center of the universe and I was at once vulnerable and clear. I sat and sat and sat.

A man came along to disturb me. He was driving a unicorn in front of him, hitting its shining rump with a thick gray stick.

When he saw me he took the white cord around the unicorn's neck and tied it to the apple tree. The beast began to graze.

"Apo poo eesay?" he said gruffly. I shrugged. Suddenly, although I could understand his Greek, I was so unwilling to speak as to be unable.

He disappeared around the corner of the stone house and came back shortly with a bowl of apricots and two glasses of water. He sat on a little three-legged stool on the grass and we shared this frugal lunch. Now and then he asked me another question and I smiled and shook my head. He assumed I didn't understand Greek.

Somewhere through the meal I glanced at the apple tree and saw the eyes of the unicorn, and that they were yellow and gleaming, not the way unicorn eyes should be, and I knew then that the beast was an illusion. Maybe, like Persephone, I had eaten of the pomegranate and now would be trapped here forever. Then it occurred to me *I am already trapped somewhere else forever, you can't have me*. This was such a ludicrous thought that I laughed. This startled the unicorn, who turned into a white goat. The man jumped up and roared. He started to chase me, but I didn't run because I was too lethargic with inner peace. Instead, the scene changed and I found myself rather roughly flung down onto a bed of pine needles in a small forest of island mountain pines. I knew immediately that I was still in the same area, but safely out of harm's way for at least awhile. My walking stick and pack, however, did not accompany me.

Slowly I stood up, stretched and looked around. The pine forest covered the side of a hill, sloping down to a dirt road. Across the road and on either side of the forest were fields of furiously-blooming heather. Dimly I could hear the heavy hum of bees out there, although in among the trees it was very quiet. I also noticed that the landscape was very rocky between the carpets of dried pine needles, and as I began to walk around, I saw heaps of these gray rocks arranged into small vertical rectangles, each enclosing a round clay pot. All I could see was the rim of each pot, because its opening was loosely covered by a slab of stone with a little notch at the side. These seemed to be some kind of storage jars, half buried into the hillside. "Cairns!" I said aloud, not remembering exactly what the word meant, but feeling it to be appropriate.

For the present I didn't explore the odd stone formations any further, although they were scattered loosely around the landscape in all directions. Instead, I wandered up the hill into the sunlight, where I could see boulders that looked large enough to sit on. I was beginning to feel impetuous again, wanting food, wanting actions, wanting explanations.

Anita Sullivan

When I came up to the boulders there was Eugenia sitting cross-legged on top of one, talking to a slender woman in a long dark blue skirt, white blouse and a red cotton scarf which she had partly around her head, partly around her shoulders. I squinted at her, wondering if she, like the unicorn, were an illusion and would soon turn back into her real self. Could she be a dragon, with fangs? Come to think of it, why are we meeting other people here? What place is this?

I was squinting and thinking so hard I stubbed my toe on a stone and said "Ouch!"

"Hi, Carley!" said Eugenia. The young woman looked over at me with quick interest, hardly surprised by my sudden clumsy entry into their conversation.

"This is Ifigenia," she said. "She's one of us – you know," she shrugged and gave a little impish smirk. *One of the Undead* I understood her to mean. And then I wondered about the man and the unicorn. What were they?

"I am from Athens," said Ifigenia in perfect English, with a sweet accent. "I died of cancer at age 51, and left behind my husband and three children. I wanted to come here, back to Ikaria, my island where I was born."

I pursed my lips and said nothing. My old fear was returning. *How many people are we going to let in*? I wondered, and felt uncouth for having such a thought.

"I've lost my pack and my stick," I said, gesturing in the general direction I might have come from. "Before we go back, I think I'd better go get them. There was a man and a unicorn . . . ."

"A what?" said Eugenia, widening her eyes.

"The unicorn turned back into a goat," I added helpfully, and started back down the hill. I was conscious that my behavior was rude, and this bothered me a little. Will we all gradually become totally uncouth as we continue in this eternity business? Why should I pretend interest in this new friend of Eugenia's when right now I don't feel like meeting anyone? The small conflict began to intensify in my mind, causing me to pause, switch direction again, and almost weep. Maybe I am a unicorn turning into an old goat.

"Sorry," I said a bit breathlessly, arriving back at the boulder. Eugenia and Ifigenia had stood up, probably to follow me and be helpful.

"What?" said Eugenia again.

"I was rude. I apologize. I didn't even say hello to you." I nodded to Ifigenia.

"It's all right, you don't have to be nice to me," she said, her face completely serious. "I will stay here on the island, and if you want to visit sometimes, that will be good. We could be slow friends." She put out her hand and I shook it.

"What's this about a unicorn and a goat?" Eugenia persisted.

I told my little tale and Ifigenia gave a deep sigh. "That is Petros," she said. "He is, oh, what do you call it, a *magus*. Not a good one, but harmless. He goes around turning things into other things, but with little reason."

"Oh! Does that mean he could change us into something else?" I asked.

She smiled and shook her head. "No, I don't think he has the strong magic like that. He tries to make stones into ships, and houses

51    Anita Sullivan

into castles. They change, but not completely, and not for very long. Just a sneeze or a laugh will make them go backwards again!"

"Prospero's island," I murmured, but Ifigenia heard me. Her dark eyes lit with the personal kind of enthusiasm which transgresses the boundaries of early friendship.

"Sometime like apes, that mow and chatter at me . . . then like hedgehogs, which lie tumbling in my barefoot way," she said. "Yay, verily, our isle is somewhat enchanted, filled with the wayward spirits of ancient dreamers come back to claim their old arts."

I swallowed. "You mean that truly?"

"It's very complicated, this island," she continued, as if giving a lecture to an educated group of tourists. "There are levels of realness, of reality, very difficult to navigate. You can be in danger from an old necromancer trying to suck your soul, and not even know until it's too late, and yet the place is full of flying beasts and running beasts and sometimes very noisy with all the roaring and chasing, but it is all happening on a reality two or three times out, so you have nothing to do but walk through it with your hands over your ears. If you stay here for long, or if you come again, I would advise you not to pass very far along any road without a guide. Even I, who was born here, do not know the place as a repository of spirits that it has become. I believe Ikaria, this island, is very full, it is unusually full." She nodded as if to emphasize what she was saying, and waved her hands for emphasis.

I glanced around, as if to confirm that the air was probably filled with spirits I could not see. The same way that you can't see the thick swirl of dust you are always breathing, without the sun hitting it at a certain angle, so you always assume the air is "clear" when in fact it is usually quite full of particles. I looked over at Eugenia.

"What do you think?"

She had her head tilted to one side, listening intently. "I don't know about you," she said to me, "but it seems to me that this is an ideal place to learn — what the possibilities are. That's what I most want to know. What is *out there.*"

"What to avoid and what to glom onto?" I added. Inside my head I was madly vacillating between abject caution and wild abandon.

She nodded.

I turned to Ifigenia. "Are there protections we can do?" Ifigenia said she could teach us a few basic, local protections, but could not be our guide. She explained that we must each locate our own personal guide as a primary protector, sort of like traveling inside a glowing helmet. Then, for each plane of "island reality" we would need a corresponding guide. I had a vision of the two of us loping along one of the island's narrow footpaths with a little retinue of talismatic creatures on all sides of us, maybe even beneath our feet. Angels, wolves, beetles – who knows what? I looked at Eugenia.

We made the decision for wild abandon, bid Ifigenia a warm goodbye, and stumped off down the hill.


We Go After Humbaba


I was shivering and giggling, a delayed reaction.

"This is bizarre," I kept saying, "We're going on an adventure, la! la! la!"

Eugenia was too sweet natured to tell me to shut up. She with her walking stick, and I without, were following directions from Ifigenia to one of the island's many footpaths. First we were supposed to walk along a road past a monastery, downhill into a small village, past a church – and so on.

"I wonder if we are going after Humbaba?" I said. I was actually talking to myself, and had forgotten Eugenia.

"Humbaba" she repeated, patiently, knowing I would realize soon that she didn't know who I was talking about, and that I would explain.

"He was a monster," I said slowly. I didn't know where to begin. It's such an enormous story.

"The Epic of Gilgamesh. Ancient Sumerian story. Instead of one hero there are two. One of them's a king and the other one is a, well, a kind of wolf-child."

"Oh, you mean he – or she – was brought up by animals in the wilderness?"

I nodded. We were walking side by side, since we hadn't yet come to the footpath. I told her the story of Gilgamesh and Enkidu, how they got together and decided they needed an adventure. We came to the footpath and started uphill. A mist was rolling down from the mountains.

"So, what happened when they went after Humbaba?"

I shivered and stopped. "Nobody had ever seen Humbaba. Nobody knew what he was even, not a god, not a human. He wasn't just a simple 'Evil Monster' like the fairy tales. In the story – well, he could have been a 'she,' I suppose, or maybe even a sexless being. Anyhow, they just knew he was big, and strong, and had certain powers. Humbaba was leftover from an earlier time. He or she was in charge of the sacred cedar forest."

About this point I think we lost track of the directions. First we came to a road sign, announcing the entry to a village called Ξανθί (ksanthi). Ifigenia had said something about going through a village, but then her directions had been brief.

We left the path and started down the dirt road between the houses. Before we had properly gotten into our new stride, we found our way blocked by a white gull and a black crow pecking for food side by side. The air felt charged around them, and I knew they were actually important, not just symbolically important. I reached out and pulled at the back of Eugenia's sweater.

"Wait!"

She stopped. We stood completely still, as if willing ourselves to turn into part of the landscape, and believing we could. The two birds, like a couple of old ladies, doddered past on either side of us. Did they leave a little smear of enchantment on the outer rim of our mutual space?

"How do you tell the good guys from the bad guys?" I whispered, as we turned to look at them. We both laughed nervously.

"We probably shouldn't be thinking that way," said Eugenia, wrinkling her nose and making a half serious, half comical face.

When we turned around again, along came a child on a lopsided bicycle. The front tire was bent so severely that the bicycle moved along like a ship in heavy seas, so that on each downward swell the child had to step off and begin over.

"Ya sas!" it said cheerfully, and stopped to regard us with interest. We realized then that the two houses we could see, somewhat buried in vines and trees, gave evidence of being lived in. We could hear people inside, talking, calling out, and the clanking and clattering sounds of daily activities. Eugenia and I looked at each other. This is not supposed to happen. Has somebody forgotten the rules? We are not allowed into the world as it is now. Therefore, *what world is this*?

Eugenia had a brief conversation with the child, speaking in English and being answered in Greek. I felt uneasy.

"I think we should keep going," I said. "This is some kind of illusion. We could get caught here."

We walked quickly through the village, not meeting anyone else. We both tried to remember the directions – some monastery or church was supposed to turn up next, after we crossed a little bridge over a rocky stream. Then I remembered something else.

"Ifigenia told us we needed local guides, remember? 'One for each plane of island reality,' I think she said. But then we went charging off without finding out how to get these guides."

"We really are naïve, aren't we?" said Eugenia, and we didn't know what to do next. Should we call off our whole adventure just because we didn't finish our preparations?

"I thought she was getting a bit carried away. I mean, we'd never get anywhere if we had to keep calling in a new guide every five seconds . . . ." I was just warming to my subject when Eugenia interrupted me.

"The birds," she said.

We turned around, but they had disappeared. Were we meant to follow them?

At that point in the road we had come to the end of the village, in front of us was the little sign which showed Ξανθί with a red line through it, so that you knew you were leaving. Just outside the village was a bench, half hidden in the bushes, and our eyes were drawn first to the bench and then to the other side of the road to what the bench was facing. As if we had been sitting on the bench, we saw a narrow, rocky driveway leading so directly up the hillside that only a vehicle with a powerful engine would be able to negotiate such a slope, no matter if the driveway had been asphalt.

We stopped and, figuratively speaking, leaned on our walking sticks.

"Finish telling me about Humbaba," said Eugenia. She has a genius for sticking to a point.

"They go after him. Two macho guys on a hero quest. Enkidu knew right away it was the wrong thing to do. He kept having bad dreams about it. When they came to the sacred forest you could just feel the whole thing was wrong. I love the story, because it's not a cut and dried case of Good versus Evil. There is a deep old power to Humbaba, and the story is tragic in more ways than one. But, anyhow, they kill Humbaba after a big fight. They cut off its head, and cut down some of the sacred cedars too, just like a couple of vandals."

"Maybe cutting down the cedars was the same as killing Humbaba," said Eugenia slowly.

"Yeah!" I nodded vigorously. "I think this epic is truly unusual. At least the Humbaba part of it is unusual. It seems to be about nature, and about how we first became alienated from it. It's about the separation of man from nature, and the consequences."

"What were the consequences?"

"Well, in 'Gilgamesh' it was mainly that Enkidu died from a wound he got in the fight with Humbaba. Some kind of poison, it sounds like, that slowly paralyzed him. The rest of the story is all about Gilgamesh trying to win Enkidu's life back by going across the river of death and meeting up with some immortals. I don't remember that part too well. He fails, of course."

I was looking up the driveway, feeling the call of adventure.

"So, why are we going after Humbaba?" Eugenia persisted. "Shouldn't we be on his side?"

I shrugged. Why am I always shooting off my mouth before I have time to think? "I think what I meant was—" I chewed on my upper lip in an exaggerated grimace of mental concentration. "Going after Humbaba means we might be charging off into an adventure without knowing how much damage we can do. I mean, we aren't heroes, and we don't have magical powers, but we aren't normal human beings, exactly, either. We might ought to think about our responsibility." I shrugged again, not willing to pursue this line of thinking any further, since it would conflict with my immediate wish to continue exploring. Eugenia seemed quite happy to drop the subject of Humbaba too.

"Let's just have a look up there!" I said, gesturing with my head. I have no idea why – after all this talk about Humbaba and about needing guides – we didn't conclude that the only safe, logical, and morally-responsible course of action was to turn around and either leave Ikaria altogether, or at least find Ifigenia and ask some more questions. Maybe it was the birds. Actually, yes, I believe we had both seen them as signs that it was O.K. to continue on our way. They could be guardians of some gate, and their behavior gave us permission to blunder on through. At any rate, against all logic, we turned together and began moving up the driveway like a couple of All Terrain Vehicles.

# We Find Humbaba

I had never returned to my initial landing place to search for my pack and walking stick, so I had to rely on Eugenia for water and food, and I slipped several times  as we climbed the steep and bumpy driveway towards the sky.

Soon the drive made a graceful bend to the left, and we could see a whitewashed stone wall running along the bottom of what seemed to be a garden. It was a beautiful wall, not the usual peasant-cottage pile of rocks roughly filled in with lime slurry to keep it together, but flat along the front and with little space between the stones, as if some skilled masons had spent quite a bit of time shaping the edifice. But we still couldn't see a house because of the steep angle and the tangle of vines and bushes fringing the top of the hill. As we continued to stomp and clump our way up the drive, a white tower, a low sprawling white house, and a gate simultaneously sprang into view.

"Towers and spires," I muttered, quoting a fragment from a poem that David used to recite about a magical city. I never could remember much more than this. Something about "the thronging dark" came later, I believe.

So firmly did we have ingrained in our minds not to expect to meet other humans, that we felt no hesitation in undoing the latch on the gate. We had to lift the whole gate up in order for it to clear the ground and swing out, and then once we were inside, had to grab it and lug it back into position. The stone masons were perhaps not also gate masons.

Up a flight of stone steps onto a flagstone terrace. Round clay pots full of soil and dead plants. No flowers blooming, but signs that

Anita Sullivan

they had bloomed in the recent past. Then we were suddenly standing at the end of a whitewashed stone house stretching away to the left, with small windows whose wooden shutters were latched open. The shutters and window frames were painted either blue or red. Although we heard nothing from inside, we both froze. Something about the feel of the place indicated that it was occupied. I remembered the sounds we had heard in the village below, and I think Eugenia was thinking the same thing. We had stumbled upon some level of reality with people in it.

Soaring up behind the house, but apparently not attached to it, was a tall, square white tower. The house roof itself went up into a peak and ended in a squat square of its own, as if hiding perhaps a roof garden. Out of the walls of this mini rooftop fortress popped a row of animal figures made of wrought iron, very simply and elegantly formed. I saw a bear, a wolf, something like a goat. Although the figures were life-sized, so far as I could tell, they would not show from a distance; you would have to be exactly as close as we were now in order to know they were there.

We stood still for several minutes, listening, hesitating to do anything else. By mutual consent, we seemed to have decided not to talk. Eventually I found myself edging to the left, around the place where the house made a curve instead of a corner, and discovered an inward squiggle in the surface of the dwelling into which the house builder had poked an elegant ceramic sink. A copper pipe led down from the roof, through the mouth of a gargoyle, and out into a basin large enough to do laundry or even to take a bath if you stood up. I ran over to peek in, to see how deep it went, and saw a faucet cleverly disguised as the gargoyle's left ear. I was about to reach out and turn it to see if water would start running, when I heard singing.

At once I whirled around, saw Eugenia coming quickly towards me from the front of the house, and from around the other side a man dressed in jeans and a white shirt. We made a little dance, the three of us, in the way we moved together, and then suddenly stopped.

The man recovered himself first. "Welcome!" he said, and stuck out his hand. There was a brief battle between old habit, which would have bidden us to extend our own hands quickly in response, and a new habit of caution built up during the time that had elapsed since we were last part of a normal human society. New habit won out, and both of us stood quietly as if we were only watching a film and any minute would come the credits snaking their way across the screen.

"Welcome to my castle," he continued, letting his hand drop, but not seeming bothered by our behavior. "We don't have visitors often – hmmm, some to be sure from time to time, as one would expect. But you must come inside and have a coffee with us. My girlfriend Georgia is around someplace – *Georgia!*" he hollered. Then he went over to the sink and turned the gargoyle's left ear. Immediately a lovely stream of clear, musical water came pouring down into the basin. He rolled up his sleeves and washed his hands, drying them on a towel that had been lying folded on a stool beside the basin.

"The best in medieval technology," he smiled as he turned around in the act of folding the towel. "We'll give you the full tour after you have dined with us." And he motioned us with both hands back in the direction we had come, towards the front door, somewhat as if he were herding sheep.

Anita Sullivan

I had already determined that he was not Petros, and this gave me some relief. This man was shorter, although he also had dark curly hair and dark eyes. There was silver along his temples, and he looked to be about sixty. "Are you alive or dead?" I wanted to ask him. Maybe there was a better way to phrase that question.

We decided to take him up on the coffee. After all, we had come up his driveway in search of something, and we had found something, so we might as well suffer the consequences. I was scurrying through my store of knowledge about alternate realities, and remembered that in some belief systems you are still alive after you die, except that you are no longer in your "gross material" body. Instead, you advance to the next level, the name of which was presently escaping me. Here you stayed until you had worked out some more karma. Then you advanced to a level where you no longer even had the illusion of a body. I longed to talk about this with Eugenia, but we continued to be silent as we walked through the low front door.

I was surprised at how small and dark it was inside, even with the shutters open, and with the roof giving the impression of a much higher ceiling. In the corner of the roughly oval-shaped room was a fireplace. Along the back wall a built-in bench covered with kilims, the colorful woolen rugs common in Greece and Turkey. The rest of the room was taken up with a low table, a couple of stools, and a bookcase full of books. On the table before the bench were some ashtrays, a scattering of papers and books, and a tray of crumbs. A curtain beside the fireplace separated this room from the next one. I was musing over the use of cigarettes after death when the curtain was pushed aside and Georgia came into the room.

"Ya sas!"

"Ya sas!" I said back to her, hearing my voice come out in a strange rasp. She proceeded to ask us in Greek if we would like coffee or something else to drink. She was chubby, with glasses and long black hair, a young woman who would have been quite beautiful if she lost 50 pounds. This in itself, along with the seeming late middle age of the man, let me know for sure that these people were not like us, "Pre-dead," or whatever other grossly inadequate term one chooses to use. "Whatever!" I said to myself, and mentally rolled my eyes.

We sat and had coffee and talked.

"I am Kalypsos," said the man, and I felt a chill across my shoulder blades. *Did you have a sister about 3000 years ago?* I seriously wanted to warn Eugenia, but I kept taking sidelong glances at her and could see that look on her face that showed she was being careful. He told us about how he built the house.

"I taught philosophy at the University of the Aegean for forty years," he said. "All those years I was building this house, stone by stone. I work with my head and my hands." He smiled and turned his palms up in front of his face, looking down at them.

They seemed to assume we would stay for dinner. What would we tell them? We hadn't decided on a story ahead of time, and I was rapidly losing my ability to do the math, in terms of what the possibilities might be, not to mention the consequences of saying too much. I excused myself to go to the bathroom and was directed through the curtain into the next room, which turned out to be a combination kitchen and bathroom, the bathroom walled off from the kitchen with a kind of bamboo curtain. In the kitchen were bowls of ripe peppers, tomatoes, potatoes – all looking quite solid and real. I became more

Anita Sullivan

puzzled. If you can't tell one reality from another, then why have different ones? What questions should I be asking? Are we in danger?

Georgia asked me how I had learned Greek. We talked a little Greek and I told her about my visits to Athens. Eugenia said we were exploring Ikaria on the walking paths. This made us seem like innocent tourists. At one point in the conversation I saw a certain light come into Kalypsos' eyes and leave again. As if it came from somewhere else and was shining through him. As if he had unwittingly lined himself up between a narrow line of reflecting panels, a position he had been skillfully avoiding. I stood up.

"I believe we must continue on our way, we are expected somewhere this evening," I said.

Kalypsos stood with me, making a slight bow. "Would you ladies do me the honor of first a little tour around the garden, my small estate? It will take maybe ten minutes at the most." His voice was deep and musical, and at that moment seemed to have added on a couple of extra overtones. I could feel a heaviness beginning at the two pressure nodes behind my ears, and I took that to mean the onset of an enchantment.

Eugenia picked up the pack, I the walking stick, and we followed Kalypsos outside into the damp autumn sunshine. At least, looking back on it now, I believe it must have been autumn, since the heather blooms most furiously at that time. He led us through the intricate pathways of his garden. Proudly he told us he was intent on preserving native species, especially of herbs and of the plants peculiar to that part of the Aegean. My head swirled with the botanical talk. All the while we were moving towards the tower, a separate building down at the lowest point in the garden.

As we came up to the tower, Eugenia and I went in first, and we heard the heavy door close firmly behind us. It was as if we were two pool balls slipping into their pockets.

"We are imprisoned in a tower." It wasn't even a thought, more like the title of our predicament.

Inside, the sun through the narrow windows made nice little rectangles on the dirt floor. Outside, we could hear Kalypsos singing again as he walked away. His song was not in Greek; it wandered in the way of Arabic chant, wild and beautiful. We both stood quietly for a few minutes, listening and looking without moving.

Eugenia walked over to the nearest window and looked out.

"We're on top of a cliff," she said.

"Why am I not surprised."

"Yeah." She stayed there, looking out.

*We can dream our way out of this*, we were both thinking. But neither of us spoke those words yet, out of some superstition, or reverence, or fear.

Into my head came a silly verse, and though I couldn't remember which tense it was supposed to be in, or whether the sun was masculine or neuter, I said it aloud:

"The sun is shining on the sea
shining with all its might
and this is odd because it is
the middle of the night!"

Eugenia turned around. "What's that?" she asked.

Anita Sullivan

"I think it's from 'The Walrus and the Carpenter' by Lewis Carroll," I said. "Seems relevant somehow."

She sighed and returned to her fretted contemplation of the sunlit. I closed my eyes, trying to think rationally instead of giving in to one of various urges: to scream, to laugh, to move around and explore the architecture of the tower (maybe there was a better view from an upstairs window), etc. etc.

"It's humiliating" I muttered. "I guess Ifigenia was right. So much for our bird guides." I was getting it all out of my system at once, clearing the channels.

"We found Humbaba after all," she said, not turning, but with a smile in her voice.

This knocked me back a bit. I've always been one of those people who think that life is a story. The other half of people seem to believe that life is just one damned thing after another, with no form to it all. But for absolutely no reason I happen to believe, secretly, that the universe has clumps of something like Significances or Stories floating around in it. This has nothing to do with religion, it is just a natural phenomenon, part of the quirky way our particular universe happens to be constructed. This means, in practical terms, that we all basically make our way from one Significance to another, like jumping from stone to stone across a creek. Sometimes there is a gap, and we have to wade a little, get our feet wet and risk slipping or cutting our feet. But mostly we can count on there being a new plot every few feet for us to land on. It's like the "portals" Djan was talking about, I guess. Maybe Eugenia and I had just stepped through a portal into another plot. Make yourselves comfortable, folks . . . .

The idea that was occurring to me now was this: *Maybe in some sense we are presently caught inside a story similar to "Gilgamesh" and things will turn out better if we operate on that assumption.* As if Eugenia and I, having dreamed our way to a Greek island, somehow got caught up in a little "Gilgamesh plot" that happened to be—but wait a minute! The guy's name was Kalypsos, like the male version of Calypso, from *The Odyssey*. And since we're definitely not Odysseus, we must be more like members of the crew. Are we going to be turned into swine? No, better that we stick to the Humbaba plot for the time being. This is a much-abbreviated version of what went tearing through my head, resulting in a resolution of action. Meanwhile, Eugenia was doing some of her own thinking, bless her.

"If it were Humbaba, though," she said, "We wouldn't be here, would we? I mean, we wouldn't have gotten caught. Unless – !" She turned with a big smile, her eyes reflecting the little patch of blue sky I could see outside through the top of the rectangle beside her head. "Unless maybe we can do it differently this time!"

"Oh, you mean we get killed by Humbaba, yay rah!" I said.

"Not necessarily," she continued, ignoring me completely. "I mean, we don't know how it *would* have turned out if they hadn't fought him and cut off his head."

"But going after him in the first place – him or her – was the main mistake," I said, squinting in concentration.

"We didn't go after him, we just stumbled onto him," she pointed out.

"Well, if there are so many differences in the plot, it must be another plot!" I grumped.

Anita Sullivan

"No, you see, Carley, wait a minute – " she was trying not to run ahead of her thoughts. "We did go after Humbaba, because that's what we were *doing* today, almost as if that were our assignment. We're going back into that place, that particular mystery. It's obviously a big mystery, one that it's O.K. to explore.

"Yeah! The mystery of Humbaba!" Her idea was making sense now. "We're just dwelling on a certain aspect of the story, and exploring it more deeply."

"And you know," she almost interrupted me in her excitement, "Kalypsos does have this garden where he collects all sorts of rare and unusual species of plants and trees. Not a cedar forest exactly, but a garden. He is a kind of keeper, a sacred keeper maybe."

"So what do we do now?" I asked, after we talked a little more along these lines. "I mean, it's really hard not to think of him as a bad guy, isn't it?" I shrugged and glanced around the room.

Helpless Maidens

*Pick the lock!* I thought. It had been my intention earlier, but we were distracted.

Eugenia and I explored the tower, went up the very sloppily constructed stairs to the second and third floors, from which we gained even better views of the abyss into which we would fall if we tried to leave by the windows.

"This seems to be a pretty new building," said Eugenia. "You would almost think he built it on purpose to keep prisoners in."

"Bluebeard!" I said absently. Then I made a face. "Oh, let's not get ourselves into <u>that</u> story."

"It's all your fault that you know so many stories," she smiled.

By mutual consent we ate something from her pack, since I believe we were both expecting to break out. We never felt the least doubt that we could leave whenever we wanted, the only question was exactly how. In this we may have been wrong, but our confidence at least kept our spirits up. I kept having a picture in my mind of a pile of brand new tools lying on a clean stone floor. A screwdriver with a red handle, and some other long pieces of metal, gleaming with purpose. This vision led me to the idea of picking the lock. However – minor detail – we did not in fact have these tools.

"Do you have a screw driver?" Eugenia asked, as if reading my mind.

I shook my head, then contradicted myself by rummaging in my pockets.

"I've got a paper clip!" she said.

"Oh! and here are two more!" I cried. "Those big ones that will evolve into bicycles!"

We stood up and raced down to the front door. I tried the handle (something that we hadn't done yet, by the way) and sure enough we were locked in.

"Go get the pack and stick," I said, "just in case this works!"

We took turns, and it was Eugenia who finally made the final crucial adjustment with the chain of paper clips. The right combination of jiggling and fiddling, and the fact that the lock didn't seem to be as up to date as the rest of the material in the tower. At any rate, about the time dusk was gathering around the exotic herbs in Kalypsos' garden, we lifted the old brass latch on the tower door and walked out onto his labyrinth of stone paths.

Anita Sullivan

"Do we sneak off, or do we go find him?" I whispered. We had neglected to settle this detail before our escape.

Eugenia glanced up at the sky, all soft and dimpled with new stars. "At least we don't need a roof over our heads," she whispered back.

"I must admit I'm curious why he locked us in," I said.

"Do you think he's dangerous?"

"Well, even if he is, I can't see just *leaving*," I said, my voice squeaking a bit as I carelessly let it rise above a whisper.

"Ah, ladies!" came a familiar voice, followed by a lantern and the white shirtsleeves of Kalypsos coming down the path from the house. "My hospitality did not sit well with you, then?"

"We'd like to leave, and we want to know why you don't want us to," I said firmly.

He stood before us now, and looked down at us through his dark eyes, which glittered in the moonlight.

"You are still alive," he said softly, almost a hiss. "I would keep you here and observe you awhile."

"We're not the only ones on Ikaria who are still alive," I said quickly, before any of the other things I had thought of had a chance to crowd in and get spoken.

This surprised him and caused him to toss his head slightly. I think he was afraid I had guessed some secret. But I didn't want to play games, I just wanted information.

"I take it you're not alive, then?" I continued, somewhat rudely.

He placed his free hand on the front of his stomach and smiled lightly. "I no longer have the silver cord," he said, as if this explained everything. "Here on the island we exist in many planes – psychic, noetic, theophanic. I am, shall we say, a traveler through, and a connoisseur of these planes."

"You don't need to lock us up," said Eugenia. Her voice sounded mild, but I could hear that little steely edge that showed me she was not to be trifled with.

"Perhaps not," he said. His tone was too smooth, and I couldn't help jumping to conclusions such as *no, you can shoot us up with narcotics and make us do anything you like*. But greed for information kept taking precedence over common sense.

"When were you alive?"

He laughed for quite awhile. If he had had a gun, it would have been the ideal time to jump him, since he was bending over and slapping his knee. Eugenia and I looked at each other, narrowing our eyes.

"I am between incarnations," he said slowly, when he had recovered. "I have certain unusual knowledge and abilities with plants. It seems that I will be permitted to remain here and continue my beloved work for an indefinite time."

"What do you do with your herbs, are they for healing?" Eugenia asked, trying to sound naïve.

"Some, yes, some . . . ." He seemed preoccupied, and I could sense that he was formulating a plan to keep us here. I also calculated that he didn't have any powers of his own, only those which his plants could give him. But he might well be ruthless in what he was seeking to learn from these plants. And then, if he had live subjects to experiment on . . . . The traditional failure of wizards is their greed for knowledge for its own sake.

Anita Sullivan

"What are you wanting to find out?" I asked him. "Just random information, or are you working on a particular experiment?"

His eyes flashed, and part of the flash was a grudging admiration for the question. It occurred to me that he would be a neat person to have on your side. I wondered if that were possible.

"That I cannot tell you," he said. It was a lame answer and he knew it.

*What if we leave you with a pint of blood and skedaddle?* I wanted to say, and actually stifled a giggle. Instead I shook my head.

"We simply cannot agree to help you with experiments when we don't know what they are about," I said. "It's possible we could help you quite a lot if we could trust you. But that might take time. I don't know about you, but we have quite a lot of time." It was an olive branch, and I swear he was tempted. But old habits prevailed.

"Let's talk," he said, and turned towards the house, expecting us to follow. I sensed he would have no power over us until he could make us swallow something, or sniff something, and thus he badly wanted us to come inside. It was time to leave.

"Out of here!" I hissed to Eugenia, and we burst into a run, heading in the other direction, downhill, knowing the paths were set up in a labyrinth that we could easily become caught in, but that at the bottom of the hill was indeed a small cedar forest. If we could reach it and have a few moments of quiet, we could dream ourselves back home.

Behind us Kalypsos began to sing again, in a lovely counter tenor voice, the same wild, plaintive lyric chant he had sung twice before, only this time with more volume, more rhythmic vigor. Soon the space around us was pulsing, as if the whole garden were strung with thick bands of air, and his voice were playing them into a fierce resonance. We were being directed by clumps of sound, unable to enter certain spaces because the noise was unbearable. Soon we found ourselves moving away from the house, around the back, towards a shadowy clump of vines. These vines, as we came closer, seemed to be writhing. As we zig-zagged wildly, our hands over our ears, the first strands began to catch our ankles, and soon we would have tripped, tipped over, and probably been trussed up neatly like a couple of chickens. Instead, we collapsed more slowly, deliberately, retaining a bit of our dignity and self-control by falling slowly to our knees. Scarcely five minutes after we started running, Eugenia and I had become two helpless maidens kneeling on the dirt behind the wizard's house, panting as he came up to us and stood, holding up his lamp bless his nasty little heart, and gazing down at us. We looked up and found him laughing.

A Beauty Comes In

Although for some reason I was not as frightened as I ought to have been, I was very worried. Kalypsos was "Wizard" just as surely as Athena was "Pallas" or Zeus was "Thunderer." He behaved like one, he had a tower for locking up people, he was able to extend his normal human physical powers, and he was proprietor of a magnificent garden of native and exotic plants, which I began to suspect might be much more extensive than what we had so far been shown. Maybe he had gardens and fields tucked away in other dimensions.

Wizards, I grimly reminded myself, are like scientists or portrait painters, they always want subjects to experiment on (or to paint, as the case may be). Into my mind kept flitting a shadowy sketch of Eugenia and me in a laboratory, surrounded by burbling beakers; our eyes are closed and our heads tipped back, and Kalypsos is ladling some lovely dark green liquid into our mouths. Soon we will turn into a couple of swine, or go into convulsions, or who knows what. I kept veering away from this vision and coming right back to it. The only color in it was the green liquid, everything else had a silver and charcoal hue.

I opened my eyes and looked directly up at our wizard as he continued to contemplate his prey. His eyes were black as paraffin candle soot on the ceiling of a whitewashed church, and very bright. But around their edges I detected a bit of that opaqueness that you sometimes see in people with cataracts or glaucoma. It struck me suddenly that this was a sign of age. And with this thought there swept into my whole body a realization of where we were. Not "where" by way of specific place, but more like tradition. We were inside a kind of archetypal "enchantment" bubble, hardened into reality by thousands of years of tradition, in song and story, and in action as well. Two thousand years of alchemy reinforced by some tens of thousands of years of the shamanistic practices of our hunter-gathering forebears. Well, maybe leave out the shamans, they might be different. Nevertheless, *we were starting down a very old path. And unless we inserted, very quickly, a completely anomalous action of our own, we might become, like Odysseus' young man Elpenor who fell asleep on a witch's roof and was granted a couple of lines in the song.*

I looked over at Eugenia.

She had her lips pressed firmly together, and I could see by the way her eyes were glowing that she was trying to decide whether to speak or to remain quiet. Both of us were being quite rational there on the flagstones.

The figure of Kalypsos seemed to flap over us like a large, shabby owl. Time was stretched. He could have been dancing around a fire, with us in the center peeking out of our cauldron. Even if he didn't know quite what to do next, the Story would soon nudge him into the correct action. Modern veterinarians use stun guns to put their large animals to sleep. Would he poke a needle into our arms or sing us to sleep? I looked up at him again and he was still laughing.

*He seats himself in Frederick's chair*
*And laughs to see the good things there*

This little verse came into my mind, from who knows where in my childhood, and I spoke it aloud. In your face, Wizard!

Kalypsos became completely still, like a doll. A puzzled look came over his face. I stood up and repeated the words, making my voice shrill and heavily accenting the second and sixth syllables of each line. Then I turned it into a song. On about the fourth repetition, Eugenia joined me.

And the vines uncurled from our feet. They seemed content with the counter spell, if that's what it was. I had hoped to break a pattern, but instead it seemed the tradition was large enough so that almost anything you did either resonated with a part of it, or it did not.

We stood up as quickly as our knees would allow and edged away around the back of the house, the opposite way from how we had come in, some hours earlier, and found the gate. After we had unlatched it, hauled it out, gone through, and hauled it back into place, we

Anita Sullivan

didn't stop to look or listen, but skittered clumsily back down the drive in the dark.

Through some combined effort of walking, dreaming, and perhaps the hidden assistance of our bird guides, we came back to the pine forest we had left in the afternoon. A late, waning moon was just rising, and its light came down through the tall trees to a point about four feet from the bottom, so that the forest floor was without light. We could reach our hands up into the moonlight and see our fingers appear. I suddenly felt like weeping. We were a couple of butterflies gone to rest in the dumb integrity of the dark.

"It's holy, isn't it?" whispered Eugenia. Tears began to stream down my face. Something had come in, something or someone very old, beyond old. The quality of the silence became like a fine dust, sifting through all the gaping holes in our cells, coming out at our feet, again and again. Soon we would rise up on little mounds of silt.

"Come, Carley, we're going back!" I heard Eugenia's voice, firm but urgent. She took my hand. Soon I felt the familiar spinning sensation, the heaviness in the temples and at the top of the spine. And then I was in my bed with real sunlight flooding in through the long windows.

## Part II

Heloise

A person who has spent a year in solitude can easily be overwhelmed by one day with a friend. After returning from Ikaria I wanted nothing more than to keep my mouth closed for an indefinite period. Listening to others is far less demanding, I have found (remembering back to being the mother of five year olds, who ask a question approximately every ten seconds), than being required to "mount" the huge panoply of mental and emotional attention required for ANSWERING. Eugenia, I figured would likely have the same response, so I didn't even need to warn her that my villa would be "closed" for a time. Mick was irrepressible as well as persistent and highly skilled in the intricacies of dream travel, so I could only hope he would read the note I put on the gate, and take my lack of response for what it was.

I had heard nothing from Djan, but I felt a lingering warmth and strong sense of his spirit. This allowed me to forget about him, at least to the extent that I assumed he would "just know" when was the right time to show up. This kind of thinking was unusual for me, and probably represented at least the beginning of an important shift in character. But I didn't think about that either.

I became a hermit again, for days, maybe weeks. Cooking, pulling weeds in the garden, sitting with my knees up on the bottom steps of the ruined villa by the sea, or on the sand, staring sightlessly at the water. In a bemused fashion, I gave some thought to dying. It seemed a reasonable action to take now, not out of boredom or despair, but as if I had achieved the peak of wisdom my brain and soul were capable of, so why continue? Paradoxically, my so-called wisdom was soporific, and I dwelt in it like an opium eater, without the benefit of full, active intoxication, but more like a *suspension*.

One small event broke into this rather opaque state of consciousness. I kept hearing the sound of a bell, at random intervals during the sunlit period of the day. Each time, I rocked backwards as if I had been physically struck. Each time, I did not anticipate the sound, having forgotten it totally. I only call it a "bell" because that was the closest translation I could find to something hitherto outside my experience. Obviously, I remember it now because I am speaking of it. This is odd.

Later, it turned out that both Mick and Djan had, during this period, been traveling extensively. Both of them were keen for plain adventure in the episodic way that I found so abhorrent, and they were developing pathways and skills to become, as Djan put it, "frequent flyers."

Also during this period, Djan discovered The House. Most basically it was an imaginary meeting place, a launching spot— somewhat like the glass room where Djan and I had originally started our own journey, only more complex and solidly established. Wisely, Djan figured that if we designed the floor plan of an imaginary house together, the normal differences in our vision of this place would be insignificant because the complexity of our common understanding would fill in the gaps. This was extremely important, as it turned out, in allowing us to travel together safely to locations of choice, rather than one person ending up in New Mexico and somebody else in India or Patagonia, simply through a simple mistaken picture in the mind.

The House shimmered in the center of a lush valley, between exotic trees, at the edge of a meadow on the edge of the River of Time. On the outside it could look like a palace, a temple, or whatever your fancy chose. But inside, a labyrinth of gleaming hallways was lined with earth treasures from the beginning of the world, large and small, simple and ornate, artistic and practical: as much museum as house (this was Djan's idea). You could lose yourself for years wandering these passages with their lighted display cases, and each time you touched one of the objects you were invited to visit the time and place from which it came.

If you chose to bypass this labyrinth at the entrance (which I probably will always do, since museums make me claustrophobic), you would go under a lovely archway made from samplings of all the trees in the world, and come to the foot of a wide but shallow stairway leading up to an airy lobby, the "navel" of the house. This space is cathedral-like, topped by a domed ceiling circled by windows of colored glass. Lining the dome is a painting of something glorious, whose colors bleed and folded into one another like lucent clouds, so that when you are gazing up at it you are totally clear what you see, but when you look again, and see something else, you know it was not the same but can't remember the previous scene. At least that's how it happens for me.

The floor of this lobby is made of tiles in soft earth colors, and laid out so that the surface is even but not flat. Walking across the room your feet tingle in a way that is slightly erotic. Although pillars support the edges of the domed lobby, it is impossible to know precisely the final shape or dimension of the space. A fountain with a clear pool is located just off center, where light from the high windows takes turn

Anita Sullivan

playing in the water. Comfortable benches are scattered throughout this area, and this has become our formal place of rendezvous, especially when we are going away together on a journey.

Doorways, cloisters, and hallways are visible randomly between the pillars, but they are not always in the same place twice. However, the library door always shows up straight ahead from the top middle of the wide stairway, and dimly through the open doorway can be seen the Librarian, whose head is in the shape of the stylized Ibis on Egyptian tomb paintings. The head seems to float, tantalizingly, always in profile, always at the same distance from the floor.

It occurred to me more than once that there was something both amazing and deeply reassuring about this place. The fact that an imaginary house could exist in the minds of all four of us, based only on a brief description from Djan, and that we could meet there time after time, seemed to be a miraculous certainty in the midst of what could become an ever-broadening and terrifying chaos for us all. For me it finally and beautifully affirmed all my secret beliefs of childhood, that the fairy-tale realms really did exist outside my own mind, or the mind of the person who "made them up." Djan explained, eventually (when we were ready to hear it), about the "imaginal realm" of the ancient Sufi mystics, the "Eighth Climate" as they sometimes called it. During my own lifetime, like most people I knew, I was taught to regard "the imagination" as insubstantial and fundamentally a *secondary* reality, a spin-off from the primary one. We believe all of our dreams and visions to be unreal, as an insurance against the insanity of delusions, and thus never learn to make fine distinctions between what we make up, and what the universe makes up. The mystics—by which are included a huge variety of ancient, mostly tribal traditions—see certain of these visions differently: like a set of equal realities, each with its own quality, or integrity. For those of us trained in the "duality" perspective, making the change is simply a matter of stretching (or perhaps skewing) our understanding of what is *real*; so that we can step through the picture frame (the rabbit hole, the back of the closet, or whatever) and know *I didn't imagine this place, it was already here.* Once we make that big jump in understanding, we become comfortable with the realization that in the imaginal realm it's the essence that counts, not the details. Thus, once we all were of one mind about the essence of The House, we were free to "imagine" or to "make up" its architecture, its furnishings—to our own specifications.

One morning a dog came into my garden and I knew she had been sent to bring me to the Library.

She was a Basset Hound with the soul of a wolf. She was long, wide and low, with a large head, all classic Basset characteristics. But her mug was somewhat narrow (bordering on aristocratic, shall we say?), and she was all one color, a lovely silvery gray. When my arm hung straight down by my side the tops of my fingers would just touch the short hairs on her back, a thing which turned out to be comforting on more than one occasion later, when we were wandering in the dark. If she faced me and lifted her generous black nose, she could poke it straight into my navel. Gazing at her, you could swear she had a poker-faced sense of humor, so that you always felt convulsed by the laughter she must surely have been suppressing behind those bland brown eyes.

"Heloise!" I said when she scratched at the gate and I pulled the rope to open it. She lifted a languid paw, which I shook briefly, and then stood out of the way to let her waddle in. I was delighted to see

Anita Sullivan

her. We spent the rest of the morning getting acquainted, straightening out certain matters regarding digging holes in the garden and what foods she might prefer, and how getting up onto my bed was strictly forbidden but sleeping in the same room was encouraged. It was immediately clear that she had come to stay, even though she was a messenger dog, and thus had certain regular duties that would call her away from home, maybe for extended periods.

"After lunch," I assured her, when I understood her message was to invite me to the Library for a conference with its Ibis-headed master. I was honored. "After lunch, Heloise, I'll take a nap and we can go."

She gave me to understand that I must prepare for this visit. "Bring food?" I asked. She curled her lip. "Make up a list of questions?" She inclined her head in assent. "What kind of questions?" She turned away, climbed the steps to the upper garden and lay down under the table, head resting gravely on her front paws. I was to figure this out myself.

So I took out a legal pad and pencil, made a cup of peppermint tea and sat by the kitchen table where I could just see the dog as a mound under the garden table outside. I decided to treat this as a chance to gather really important information, but not necessarily of the kind you could find in books. The Librarian, I sensed, had inside its head (not a he or a she) a pattern of Changes rather than actual facts, and this pattern would line itself up as an Answer opposite whatever Question you presented. Only one question. Oh, what a responsibility!

"What do I most want to know right now?" I thought.

*Should I stay alive?*

But that seems so inane. Maybe if I ask a really small, silly, specific question, such as *What should I have for dinner tonight?* I will get a better answer. How about *Where shall I travel to next?* No, not essential enough. Something larger, grander. How about *What is the true nature of life?* But of course that's not the kind of question that has an answer. Or maybe (I felt a wave of greed) I could find out who or what is in charge of our Experiment.

The Librarian is our own discovery, therefore not part of the Experiment. The Librarian is not one of Them. Briefly I allowed this little narrative to run through my mind, but dismissed it immediately with a frown. "Moving right along . . . !" I said to myself, and continued to chew my pencil.

Outside, Heloise slid sideways heavily and fell into a deep sleep. She was hinting that my time was almost up. I closed my eyes, seeking clarity. Then I thought of my question:

*What do I need to know?* Never mind whether the Librarian can answer this or not, it's what I will ask. With this thought, I went up to my Victorian sofa in the sitting room and prepared myself for dreaming.

Almost instantly I felt Heloise standing beside me, quickly taking the position of the dutiful dog lending support to its mistress. I could feel that we both curled up on the sofa, and the sofa was whirling through the air with the two of us peering over the high arms with large round eyes of wonder and innocence, like characters in the *Wizard of Oz* series. When we finally stopped it was a surprise to find the sun coming down through a skylight onto my tee shirt, spilling over onto Heloise's back and onto the gleaming black and white floor.

# The Library

Gorgeous, thick square tiles, black and white and gray, glowing with a satiny polish and denseness of material the likes of which I had never known. Everything here was in outstandingly good taste, and the floors were simply one example of it. A set of patterns was spread across the tops of the tiles, gently etched with a slight indenture into the surface, geometric patterns, repeating themselves every six or seven tiles in a larger grouping that I thought might work something like the change ringing of English church bells. But the patterns also went *down* into the thickness of the squares, and even *up* into the air above them. I found myself sniffing and making slight dance-like movements, overwhelmed by a mere floor. I suppose in a fairy tale I would be said to be enchanted, and if evil were afoot, I might be at the mercy of it, but this was not so.

I lifted my head and found myself directly across from the nether end of the Librarian's beak. Its eyes were small and gray, *matching the tiles* (I couldn't help but think). But round, like marbles. Because of how they were arranged in the odd face, they gave it an expression of fixed astonishment.

"Hello, here we are," I said.

A little musical phrase came out of the air around the Ibis. It was its version of speaking. I smiled, for the whole scene reminded me of a cartoon. The word-cloud seemed to hover above us, with musical notes substituting for words. I knew what it meant, even if I didn't know what it was saying. We started walking down the middle of space.

*What do I need to know?* I said, maybe aloud, maybe not.

The Ibis wanted me to see a collection. We walked, or floated, through a sunlit room over the tiles, past rows and rows and rows of books on silver shelves going up as far as the eye could see, and no ceiling in sight, but sun way up there definitely coming in *through* something. Heaven must be like this. Maybe if I die they would let me work here in the library! I had a smile on my face so broad it began to hurt.

"One by one," I heard. This meant it was my turn to be in the library. Infinite time for an infinite number of people, one by one, to see what each person most needed to see.

*What it means to be alive.* This was the answer to my question. But of course, it was only another question. How many questions must I ask before I arrive at the first answerable question? I felt a chill in the pit of my stomach.

*This is a Library.*

The Librarian had spoken again. Its words were like the tiles beneath our feet: simple and deep, small and complex, mysterious and comprehensible.

*A Library is a place of turning, between knowledge and belief.*

As I translated "place of turning" we turned abruptly to the right, heading slightly downwards, and found ourselves in the Ancient Greek poetry section.

A number of unasked questions were suddenly answered. Yes, the library holds music, speech, noise, smells – all the paraphernalia of the human senses. I could spend an eternity in this library alone and never go out. This library is a duplication of the entire world, a map as big as the thing being mapped. But although this thought made me a little dizzy, it did not occupy me for long. I have never been much intrigued by acquiring knowledge in the serial, rational way that happens when you read an encyclopedia. Surely this Library must have more to offer than that?

*Poets have access to First Knowing.*

The librarian was speaking again.

The smile on my face evaporated, no longer needed. I felt settling onto me a large, flat happiness; no subtlety, no ecstasy or terror lurking at its edges, as if I were a bench in a garden in the sun. "May I?" I asked, stretching my hand out for a book.

Soon I was, in fact, on a bench in the sun – the sun coming from the sky but filtering through all those *shelves* – of Word-Catchers. Books. Knowledge. Information. Mind Patterns. A held universe. Whatever.

Beside me on a low, lacquered table was a small pot of tea and one tiny cup. Heloise lay dozing on the floor where my feet would have been if I had been sitting in normal upright position. But I was not, I was leaning against one rounded arm of the bench with my feet up.

Is this a place where one can stop?

Will I live for another thousand years, only to learn, very slowly and thoroughly, how to stop? But because I still don't understand, I am here in this library reading in the sun. Already I know it is not information I seek. But information is not what this library offers. Not exactly.

I opened the book on my lap and read:

*In happy fate all die a death*
*that frees from care,*
*and yet there still will linger behind*

*a living image of life,*

*for this alone has come from the gods.*

*It sleeps while the members are active;*

*but to those who sleep themselves*

*it reveals in myriad visions*

*the fateful approach*

*of adversities and delights.*

This was Pindar. A fragment from some of his lost poetry. I was slightly annoyed. This was exactly what I had come to the Library to find, and now I had found it, I couldn't read anything else on this day. How could I?

Heloise moaned in her sleep, and looking down I saw her large, ungainly front paws jerking, as if she were out chasing a rabbit. Maybe she was remembering how it was to be a wolf. *To those who sleep themselves* I smiled down at her. Now that she was sleeping, did she see, wholly and completely, the second life that the gods held back in secret for her? Was there an Abelard somewhere in her past or future?

I frowned.

Does this mean that I must die in order to realize fully the "myriad visions" of my own life, of Life itself? What in the world does he mean "to those who sleep themselves"?

I began to have an inkling of something. I remembered what Kalypsos had said, or the gist of it anyway. He had said "I am between incarnations." Here was a person who was dead in the clinical sense, yet he seemed quite alive. Was he "sleeping"? Is this what Pindar meant, the great long dream of the dead? Are we—here in post-life exile—being excluded from that? *Or are we doing essentially the same*

Anita Sullivan

*thing?* There is perhaps less difference than I am able to imagine between being dead and being alive.

This was my conclusion for the afternoon. I wondered if frivolous reading were allowed in this Library, and I rose from my bench, somewhat stiffly.

"Where is the sofa, Heloise?" I smiled down at the dog, who, like me, was stretching the stiffness out of her muscles. "We must find a way to fold it up and carry it with us after we arrive places. You'd think a Library could have more comfortable seating arrangements."

We went off to find the Librarian, and of course got lost, since the Library is a labyrinth. We wandered up and down dappled pathways, soft upon our feet, and never got tired, although I am sure we were walking on tile the whole time. Eventually we came to the entrance, where the Librarian's profile showed vivid and clear against the darkness of the large domed vestibule outside. We said goodbye, and it gave us to understand that we were allowed to return at any time.

*The Library is infinite, but it is not the only infinity.*

These were the parting words I got from the Ibis. They affected me like an elixir. Suddenly I felt a kind of readiness for "the fateful approach of adversities and delights" that Pindar had mentioned.

I felt a need to be in touch with Mick and Djan and Eugenia again. I hoped they were feeling the same need.

Ladle Rat Rotten Hut

"We can't seem to raise her," said Djan. He sounded like the captain of a ship.

"She could have decided to die, couldn't she? And how would we ever know?" This was Mick, looking strained but sounding almost annoyed.

I sighed. "I'm sure she wouldn't, without letting us know. We've never made any promises about that, but I don't think any of us would do that, not any more!" I looked at each of them hopefully. We were sitting in the café on a hazy afternoon, wind blowing at almost gale strength outside.

"We probably should formalize that promise, as soon as we all manage to reassemble," said Djan. "Perhaps also address the matter of traveling alone."

"Eugenia and I did agree that we wouldn't go traveling alone, right after our trip to Ikaria. I haven't been anywhere since—except the Library." I was making a full confession.

Minutes before, I had finished telling Mick and Djan about our experience with Kalypsos and the magic-seeming Greek island, now weeks ago. None of us had seen Eugenia since. Already I felt stirrings of a longing to return to the island, and was hoping at this gathering to find someone to go with me. But Eugenia had ignored our usual call.

"Do you think you were put under a spell while you were there?" asked Mick. "I mean like swallowing a pill that gives you a secret irresistible desire to go back?"

I swallowed. Inside me I felt the curling away of this thought, like smoke. *No! Not possible!* the smoke-thought was saying. We had drunk coffee there at Kalypsos' house, but eaten no pomegranates. I think his magic would depend upon our presence. Yet he did work with plants . . . .

"I suppose it's possible," I said in a small voice. "Maybe we should go there to look for her."

"What about her house?" said Djan. "Do we know she is not at home?"

"No, we really don't," I said, starting to feel desperate.

"We can't go there," said Mick. "I've tried. She has to be at home, and invite you in."

I nodded at Mick. I, too, had tried to imagine and dream my way across to a cottage in Cornwall, and totally failed. It was as if she had blocked out any access to that place.

"So, she could be there," Mick persisted. Djan squinted and slowly shook his head. *Massive*, I thought irrelevantly.

"I don't think so."

"Why?"

He raised his shoulders up to his ears and half closed his eyes. Then abruptly, he relaxed and smiled over at us. "Just native intuition," he drawled. Then he stuck out his lower lip and got a bit more serious. "I don't invite people to my house either. And that's a normal part of the Rule; nobody can come in unless your portals are open. Deliberately and gladly open. But I believe that her present occlusion is not of her own choosing. That is not to say I feel she is in danger, only that she has somehow gone— "he paused for a minute and looked up at the ceiling, then smiled and looked back at us again. "Out of our radar range I guess is the only way to put it." He reached for more coffee and we all sat back and watched the wind blowing blossoms by the windows. The lions lay facing each other at the end of the garden bench.

*Why can't they be of some use?* I thought. And then I heard Heloise making her slovenly way down the kitchen stairs, belly slithering whispers across the stones, loud enough to be heard between gusts of wind. It was eerie. Life is a story, after all, but you must give certain details their full due in the plot.

"I think!" said I, making that short sentence into an announcement. "I think Eugenia set off into the forest alone and has gotten waylaid by the Big Bad Wolf."

They looked at me in silence. Djan leaned back dangerously in his chair, pressing the tips of his fingers together and looking merry and enigmatic at the same time.

"Is this the voice of non-native intuition speaking?" he inquired mildly. I nodded. "Would you care to elaborate?" I shook my head. "Not yet," I said, and looked out towards the lions again.

Mick, usually glib, continued to say nothing. He stood up and walked between tables to the little counter near the side door. He went around behind the counter and leaned his elbows on it, so he was looking over our heads. I could just see him by turning my head slightly to the side.

"Don't you wish there were more of us?" he said suddenly. I knew what he meant. I thought about David. I thought about my two sons, my two granddaughters, who had been in their late teens when I left. I had felt lucky to see them grow up even that far, but it's never enough. My eyes filled with tears and I brushed them away fiercely, clumsily. If I had a pet wolf I'd name it Nostalgia. This thought made me almost smile. I looked around for Heloise, and spotted her over by the middle window, gazing out very alertly. If her ears had been capable of going up, I'm sure they would have been up.

"Tell us the story of Little Red Riding Hood," said Djan's voice out of the shadow. He wasn't really speaking to either of us.

Anita Sullivan

I said nothing, not ready to be distracted from my private musings.

"A little girl." Mick took up the challenge. "With a basket. Because her grandmother is sick. Her mother gives her a basket to take through the woods to grandmother's house. A *red* girl." He began to laugh, then to cough. "Wow! It's such a simple story, and I can't even remember it right. How does it start?"

"Little Red Riding Hood," I chimed in. "She's been such a *good* girl that her mother makes her a red cloak, which she wears all the time."

"Yeah, that's right! And one morning her mother bakes cookies or was it some cheese, strawberries . . . ? whatever . . . into the basket. And for the first time, she is allowed to go out by herself, through the Deep Dark Florist – I mean, Forest!" Mick was being shaken by one of his unaccountable laughing fits, and was struggling to overcome it. For once it was annoying him, maybe even frightening him.

"Go on, don't stop! Her mother said to her – "

"Don't take any rides with strangers."

"And so she starts out on a bright and sunny morning."

"But lurking in the undergrowth"

"With slobbering lips and gleaming eyes"

"The Wicked Wolf."

"Who hasn't eaten for seven days and seven nights."

We were tossing the story back and forth, call and response. Into my head suddenly came a fragment of the version David and I sometimes read to each other; it used real English words that sounded similar to the story words, but were not quite right:

*Wail, wail, wail, set disc wicket woof, evanescent ladle rat rotten hut! Wares or putty ladle gull goring wizard ladle basking?*

Not quite right. Real words, set down in the wrong place, trying to figure out what to do. Like us. We were all ladle gulls inner lodge dock florist.

Breathless, we stopped and looked at one another.

"Eugenia has gone somewhere, I feel sure!" I said softly. "I know Ikaria really appealed to her. She made a friend there. It's the kind of place you need to go back to. What have we got to lose, to try there first?"

We began to talk all at once: "We'll take the lions!" said Mick. "Heloise is a wolf!" I said. "We need to set an intention, let's form a circle!" Djan said, calmly. "We're going to grandmother's house!" Mick shouted, his green eyes blazing.

"We'll ride on their backs." Djan spoke again, and finally we heard him and were quiet and even obedient. We went out into the garden, where the wind was still blowing steadily, making the air into an indefinite space. Mick climbed onto one lioness, Djan onto the other, and I sat on Heloise, although not actually placing all my weight on her. We linked hands, closed our eyes, and didn't stop to think how absurd we looked, or how absurd we might actually *be*. We thought "Ikaria" and "Eugenia" and "Grandmother's House," together, and were off.


Grandmother's House


We were sitting in a row with our feet sticking out, looking through black iron bars.

Anita Sullivan

It was a wrought iron balcony, about waist high we discovered as soon as we stood up. It faced the sea, where a huge orange sun was just sinking into pale blue water the same color as the sky.

"When is the sun really DOWN?" said Mick.

"When it gets dark," said Djan, his voice twice as dark. "I wish we had managed to arrive in the morning, but ah well."

Behind us was a small white church, Greek Orthodox style with a dome in the middle behind the short square bell tower in the front. Beside the church a narrow flagstone pathway ran between two outbuildings, then veered off. The whole compound was perched on a hillside high above the sea. A sign in front of the church told us this was a Monastery of St. Theoktistis. We tried the door of the church, but it was locked.

"Where's grandmother's house?" asked Mick.

Cautiously we explored around the outside of the church, the buildings, listening at all times for sounds. Heloise came along with me everywhere I went. I wondered about the lions, but quickly realized that they were the large white rectangular blocks on either side of the church door. It made perfect sense at the time, the way dreams do. Everything can turn into something else, but not just *anything* else.

By this principle, "grandmother's house" could be something other than a house.

Gradually we separated, extending our exploration in different directions. Djan went downhill on a path that led up from (as it turned out) an overgrown parking lot. Mick went inside one of the buildings and opened cabinets, poked around between chairs and tables. I went past the buildings to where the flagstones turned a corner and started uphill, before petering out and essentially turning into a miscellaneous scattering of "wild" stones. As I picked my way over the irregular ground into an area of oak and olive trees, I looked up, and gasped.

There perched on top of a huge boulder was a tiny house with a roof that looked like an enormous mushroom. The house was white-washed like other island houses, but the roof overshadowed it as if it were wearing a hat as big as itself, perched at a slightly rakish angle. As I looked longer I realized the "mushroom hat" flaring out over the top was actually a single slab of stone, and the house was tucked between this slab and another one underneath it, as if held gently in the huge jaws of a whale. Beside the door was a small dark window, and leading up to the door was a stairway carved into the boulder, steep as a ladder.

I rose up on my toes, poised to go up those stairs. Heliose growled.

"Mick! Djan!" I called out, and turned to run back down the path.

Soon we were all standing at the bottom of the stairs, our necks back, looking up. The house's walls were stones that had been smoothed and painted over with a layer of thick whitewash to fill in the cracks, but now were mottled from years of exposure to weather. I should say "was mottled" because truly we could only see one side of the house, and it could have been a false front for all we knew.

"The front door is red!" I cried.

"I believe you have before you Grandmother's House," said Djan to Mick, his voice rich with delight. I gripped Heloise's back at the chill I felt after he spoke.

"What should we do?"

Anita Sullivan

Djan shrugged. Mick said nothing, and we all stood there as the light faded.

"I don't think we should wait till morning," I said in a small voice. It seemed for a minute as if they had turned into stone themselves, and I was feeling their great, heavy stone souls beside me, cold, but able to become molten at the snap of a finger. This odd sensation stayed with me long enough that I turned my head to look at them.

Shadows were seeping in from under the trees, from beneath the boulder holding up the house, from the hills all around. They were blue shadows and seemed to flap.

"Do you think Eugenia is up there?" asked Mick. His voice sounded like dry stones rattling on a windowpane, not like a voice at all.

We sank down onto the ground. Quite suddenly we had run out of energy, but more than that. We had collectively come to the end of a whole rope of ideas about who we were and what to do next. We sat in the dusk, what the Greeks call "lykofos," or "wolf light," another name for twilight.

Djan's brown eyes, Mick's greenish-blue eyes, became bruises against their faces. We stared at one other. Suddenly we were three people alone together in a world we did not understand. We needed to know each other, and we did not. How do people get to know each other? We had forgotten that mysterious process. I felt tears running down my cheeks. Mick doubled over, as if in pain. Djan's face was pinched and his eyes seemed enormous.

We kept looking at one another until the light bled away under the sea. The hollow around us began to fill with mist. We reached for each other's hands, moved closer together until our hips and knees were touching. I have no idea how time passed, if it was normal time or some other kind, but out of weariness we tumbled into a heap on the hard earth and fell asleep in a tangle of limbs.

*If this is Grandmother's House, have we arrived before or after the Wolf? Maybe the Wolf has already eaten Grandmother and we are here before Little Red Riding Hood. Maybe we are Little Red Riding Hood. Maybe we are the Wolf. In the story, there are only three characters. We are three.*

In the morning we went up the ladder-stairs to try the red door. Mick was first.

The door opened easily. He ducked his head and went cautiously into the dark room. Djan and I were right behind him, and soon the three of us were standing in the middle of a little chapel, not a house at all, with space for maybe seven full-sized adults on a Sunday morning. We looked at faded icons on the walls, crumbling bits of scarlet tapestry, tarnished brass candle stands full of sand to hold up the tiny beeswax candles.

Djan took two steps forward to peek behind the carved and gilded wooden screen at the front of the room, behind which the priest would have carried on the private part of the ceremony. Maybe the priest was there, even now. I shook my head to clear it, and reminded myself to stop thinking of such things.

Mick had moved back towards the door, and found beside it a hollow chamber opening back into the rock. Pushed back into this natural storage chamber was an old steamer trunk. We could hear him pulling it out.

Anita Sullivan

"I think we're starting our search at the end," I said to Djan. "The dream brought us here, almost as a joke, or maybe out of bad timing. But Eugenia isn't here yet. At least, that's how it — "

I was interrupted by a cry from Mick, a mixture of horror and glee.

"Wow, come here!"

The trunk was full of skulls, yellow and polished, as if many careful hands had taken them out and put them back, over and over again for centuries.

"The monks who used to live here, you think?" asked Djan, gently cradling a skull in his big hands.

We took them out, half a dozen in all, and passed them back and forth, feeling them as intensely as we saw them. The light was dim, coming through from the window in the chapel, lending our movements an indefiniteness that seemed to soften the nature of the trunk's contents. We looked at each face, noting the individual qualities of the bones, the shape of the eye sockets, length and spacing of teeth.

"They could be nuns," I said.

"It seems like we're either too soon or too late, y' know what I mean?" said Mick. He wasn't speaking about the skulls, but he might have been.

We put them back, one by one, and shoved the trunk back into its hollow.

"I think we have to go somewhere else," I said again, and felt my face lengthen.

"A quest – we have to go on a quest to find the princess," said Mick. He stood up and promptly banged his head on the stone ceiling. "Damn!"

"You O.K.?" asked Djan, and Mick nodded dumbly, his eyes watering.

I peered out the front door. At the bottom of the stairs Heloise was whining. There was no way she could climb up. I looked down into her brown eyes, not dark and not light, but the color of some essential forest substance that probably doesn't exist in fact, but only in aggregate. This did not come to me as a thought, but as an understanding, and it gave me huge comfort.

As part of our plans, we agreed to leave the lions here, in case Eugenia came when we were gone; also "for general guarding purposes, and to reinforce the sacred space," as Djan put it, somewhat wryly.

We decided to walk in one direction until we came to what seemed to be the end of the island. Then we would go back the other way. If the island turned out to be as wide as it was long, our task would be more complicated.

"You'd think we could figure out whether Eugenia is here, without actually having to cover the ground," muttered Djan. He shook his head and continued muttering, but we couldn't hear him.

"What about food," I said, not even making it a question. "If this were a real fairy tale, we'd have a cornucopia or something. Do we have to keep dreaming ourselves back home for supplies?"

This is how we first learned of Djan's scavenging talents. He lifted a hand to silence us both, and a peculiar expression came over his face. One eye almost closed, his mouth twisted sideways, his head bent forward. Then his head began to nod, or rather to bob, like that of someone with a tremor. In a few seconds he grinned and gave us a thumbs-up sign.

Anita Sullivan

"Got it covered," he said. "Wait here till I get back.

"But what if Eugenia is just hiding out somewhere?" said Mick. We were walking along a dirt road munching on cucumbers, bread, and a dry, salty Greek cheese. The sun was high. "How do we know she's been abducted?" He said the last word slowly, as if he were sticking pins into it.

"We're acting on intuition," I said.

"Whose intuition?" Mick shot back. "I don't really feel anything at all about where Eugenia is. I want her to be here again, and not to die, but that's her business, not ours. Why can't we mind our own business? Do we have to keep track of each other all the time?"

I opened my eyes wide. This was the first time we had so actively disagreed. I felt horrified, rather like a maiden-lady schoolteacher who has overheard one of her pupils swearing.

"This is true." I could feel Djan struggling not to seem too fatherly. He shook his head, his dark eyes genuinely troubled. "But we are such a small company of friends in such an enormous territory. No hurt to look out for each other, if we sense the possibility of harm or danger."

"Yeah, like Djan said earlier," I felt myself starting to babble, but went on anyway, "we probably ought to get together and draw up some sort of guidelines about all this – when Eugenia gets back. I mean, we all want to be independent, and feel like we can have privacy and all that, but we all *care* about each other, Mick. I think that's the main thing."

Mick was looking away from both of us, and now he turned back. "Sorry," he said. "I'm just so sick of being reasonable, I don't even know what that means any more. Today I just hate everything, y' know what I mean?"

"We ought to have the flexibility of changing our plans," said Djan, sounding very reasonable. I smiled. "Our present plan is to be on the island of Ikaria and to look for Eugenia, because Carley has a strong intuition that she's here. And because I have an intuition that she is—er, somewhere—that we can't yet know. Carley and Eugenia came here together and found the place to be – what would you say, Carley, – sort of like Prospero's island? A place of magic and powerful mystery?"

I nodded. "The island feels to me like a miniature version of the whole universe. A cauldron! As if every weird possibility that has ever existed has come over here to stay alive, even if it's died out everywhere else. All the gods nobody believes in any more, the half-baked magical spells, they can all come here and do quaint deeds and fully flaunt their pride."

"It's a big circus full of layers and levels of air. I think if we spend some time here, we'll go through whatever stages we need to go through, much faster. But that's the 'reasonable' way of saying it, sorry, Mick!"

I had intrigued him. The way to disarm Mick is always to engage his imagination.

"Well, of course I'm *worried* about Eugenia!" he said, as if contradicting my thoughts by showing some feeling. His oddly handsome, puckish face was flushed. "I think I'm really mostly pissed off because I don't get any messages from her. I guess I'm vain. I thought I would be the one she'd send messages to. But she hasn't, and so I'm just shooting off my mouth here." His ruefulness was charming and genuine, if fleeting as sunlight across a leaf. Djan and I laughed, and the tension was broken.

"Any idea where she *is* on the island?" Djan asked, looking at me. I shook my head.

"Maybe she's been caught by, oh, what's-his-name, the necromancer guy?" said Mick, "the one you both escaped from?"

"Kalypsos," I said. "Yes, we talked about that before, but we got distracted by the Little Red Riding Hood thing. I have a strong feeling of not wanting to go back to see him, and yet the opposite feeling too. So, I don't trust anything I feel about him."

"Seems like we ought to figure out something more specific, instead of just wandering around," said Mick. "I mean, at least decide if we go back to Kalypsos's place or not." He gave a little shrug. "I'm all for leaving him alone for now. I mean, even if it makes some sense that she might have gone there." He turned to me. "Why else would you think she had come back here, anyway?"

By this time we had seated ourselves on a stone wall under the shade of a huge plane tree. And we made plans all over again, each of us realizing that these plans would have to be renewed on a daily basis. Ad hoc government for our little tribe. What we hoped was not our *diminishing* tribe.


Dante


We gave ourselves three days to tramp around the island, to explore on foot. The weather was warm, and it was easy to find shelter at night, to wash our faces in streams. We decided to stay together, keeping constantly alert for any helpful signs. During that time we saw no unicorns, but plenty of bees, goats, a few chickens, and we were haunted sporadically by the sound of children's voices, without ever seeing the children. Djan seemed to think the people we heard, but never saw, were the newly-dead living out their lives in the next plane. I shrugged this off, although it sounded logical enough.

"Are they any danger to us, or us to them for that matter?" asked Mick.

"I think it would be impossible for us to interact with them," said Djan. When I asked him about Kalypsos and Georgia, whom we had most definitely interacted with, he had an answer for that as well.

"In between incarnations," he said, as if this explained it.

At one point we saw a group of people clad in long white robes and carrying candles coming down the path towards us, singing. We stood still, not knowing what to do, and they passed through us, leaving a cool, moist sensation.

Each time we came to a deserted building we explored it. This included many isolated houses, churches (some were locked, and we contented ourselves with peering into the windows), olive-pressing sheds, small barns, shepherd's huts.

"Is there a chance Eugenia has gone into another level of reality, where she is invisible to us?" I asked. "I mean, 'in between incarnations' sounds like it could be an enormous place." I was a trifle irritated. Why do we have to have all these categories? Can't we just chalk it up to whim? We've fallen between the cracks, we're in the place where "They" don't micromanage, where rules have petered out.

Djan looked at me a bit oddly, as if to say *I already explained all that.* But we were doing very well together, sweaty and weary and discouraged. What kept us going was a deep seated unease about

Anita Sullivan

Eugenia. As the hours wore on, we began to come to the conclusion that she was not here on the island at all. In fact, that became a conviction rather than just a rationalization for going back to the comforts of home.

On an afternoon we were walking along a path high in the mountains, with rocky hillsides falling gradually but steeply away to our left, down to a distant village, where we could see the usual white church dome and cluster of stone houses, walled gardens. The sun was making a loud lemonish swatch around us, keeping us silent. We came into a wild and lonely area with no more village, and no houses, only low scrub and scattered stones, a few oak trees. I turned again to look downhill, and what I saw made me stop.

I was looking down a wide valley at a couple of distant hills framing what was probably the sea, but it was too hazy to identify. At the bottom of our immediate hillside was a flat, rocky meadow, covered in its center by a large black square, probably cloth or plastic, but resembling tarmac. And on this black square some creatures were moving slowly around in a random fashion, like prisoners taking their daily walk. At the edges of the black square stood soldiers with guns over their shoulders, dressed in camouflage. All of the figures were smaller than I would have thought they should be, given the distance, and I kept blinking to make my sense of perspective come clear. Were these toy figures, or real? It seemed as if we had stumbled upon a dead zone.

I turned back to Djan and Mick, who had noticed me looking, and were gazing downhill. By the expression on their faces I knew they were seeing the same thing I saw.

We stood and looked and looked. The creatures in the middle of the tarmac (I am now calling it) were people dressed in loose gray shirts and trousers, bent over with their heads almost to their knees. They were walking around in circles, very slowly, as if trying to follow some orders but too weary to obey them. Every now and then one would fall down and began to crawl slowly to the corner, as if trying to get out of the blazing sun. At the corners of the tarmac were piles of bodies. The number of people moving slowly and aimlessly around the tarmac did not diminish. Yet we never saw any new people coming in. Sometimes one of the soldiers would shout and point, and all of them had whips. We could not hear anything, it all seemed very far away, as if we were looking at an image projected upon the countryside, not a real event.

"I see Eugenia!" cried Mick suddenly, and he went charging down the hill before we could stop him. I started to run after him and Djan put a hand on my arm.

"Better we stay here," he said, his voice strained and almost hoarse.

We watched, each of us on our toes ready and wanting to run after him, but restraining ourselves. It would be a plunge into bottomless despair, into oblivion. Mick kept running, making lots of noise and causing stones to roll down the hill. He disappeared into a clump of trees, and we waited to see him come out at the edge of the tarmac, to confront a soldier, but it didn't happen. I squinted at the figures crawling around, and they seemed to be beyond help, like something out of Dante's hell. *Yet I knew they were being punished for nothing.* I tried to see if Eugenia was there, and once it seemed as if a person in the middle stood upright, and it might be she.

Anita Sullivan

"We must try to dream this place to a close," said Djan. "May these forces of tyranny lose their powers, now and forevermore," he murmured. We clasped hands and closed our eyes. Then I realized Heloise was not with us any more. I opened my eyes.

There, at the edge of the tarmac, a soldier was confronting a gray dog with long floppy ears, who barked at him. The soldier tried to point a gun at her but she bit him in the leg. He tried to kick her and his foot might as well have been striking a stone wall. In spite of myself, I began to laugh. Beside me, Djan was laughing too. Our laughter rang down through the ravine, and up the hillside. The lemon sun allied itself with the laughter and began dislodging stones. Soon a small avalanche of stones and boulders came rumbling past us, down through the trees.

"Mick!" I shouted. And again, "Mick, look out!" My voice seemed to echo mightily against any halfway vertical surface in the vicinity and to reverberate with the noise of the stones, to resonate with the strange yellow light, which in itself had taken on a resonance and was pulsing like a huge bell. The entire scene seemed to rise up into a conflagration, so that we were looking down at a fiery cloud that roared and rang.

Then we were engulfed by it, and we could not help but put our hands over our ears and to bend over, closing our eyes. We did not fall down, but stood there for what seemed like a time past our endurance, time enough for an entire day to have gone by. When we were at last able to look and listen again, the tarmac had completely vanished, and a clear sweet dusk was filling the landscape. Heloise and Mick were climbing the hill towards us, side by side.

"Wow! I'm starved!" said Mick when he came to us, and he collapsed onto the ground, tears running down his face.

Djan, being Australian, knew how to make a small fire out of twigs, and we boiled water for tea. We found a grassy place under some oak trees and decided to stay here for the night.

*Of their own devising* . . . this phrase kept drifting into my mind as we sat quietly around the fire, not talking yet. I never know where they came from, these random phrases from stories that drifted into my head. Did they fit into what was actually going on around me, in any kind of relevant fashion, or did they represent frivolous mental energy on my part? *Of their own devising* . . . *of her own devising* . . . how did Mick's recent encounter with the dark cadre of soldiers, how did it fit with whatever was happening to Eugenia? Is there such a thing as a waste of time?

"I was wrong. She wasn't there. It was a trap, and I fell for it hook, line and sinker," Mick was saying. A shadow seemed to have settled inside the bones of his face and was looking out. He might be some time getting it to leave. I thought of all the fairy tales where people take on pain for someone they love, and hold it for years. The sister who sat in a tree weaving little jackets for her twelve brothers, out of stinging nettles.

"Who were they?"

He shrugged. "People working out some terrible karma, is all I know," he said. And we left it at that. Heloise, on the other hand, seemed to have sustained no damage. In fact, her wolf soul had grown a smidgen larger, and was making her fur look shiny. For a long time I

Anita Sullivan

smiled vacantly into space and let my fingers wander around between her ears as she leaned up against me.

We were unable to sleep, and decided to tell one another the story of our past.

"Like Scheherazade and the 1001 nights," I said. "We can take turns and tell as much as we want. But eventually I want to hear *everything*!"

Mick said he didn't want to start, so Djan volunteered.

"I was born in Australia, the Northern Territory, near Darwin. My father was an aborigine who had been orphaned and brought up by missionaries, hence my somewhat classic education. My mother was originally from Niger in North Africa, another long story in itself. Pop earned his way mostly as an itinerant newspaper editor and missionary rolled into one. There were six of us, and we were never in the same school for one entire school year, so we ended up being essentially home schooled, though they would not have used that term at the time. My father kept getting into trouble with his editorials – he was very much opposed to government policies regarding the aborigines, the "black fellas" as we were called. So, we kept having to move, and we never had any money. Sometimes Pop would get himself a church for awhile – though there weren't many available for black Christians (nobody believed we were smart enough to be converted, though they kept trying to convert us). We would move into a different drafty house every few months. I was the youngest, and a sickly kid, so even when my brothers and sisters were going to school, I was often at home with a fever. I remember essentially living my youth in a waking dream. I think that's why I spent much of my adult life wandering from one job to another. Why I never married . . . ."

He told us of how one of the tribal elders came to the house to ask his father's permission to start teaching young Djan some of the aborigine traditions. "I don't know why my parents agreed. After all, they were Christian, and these were the very pagans they had dedicated their lives to converting. It makes no logical sense, even if they did have race in common. My mother was born in Djanet, a little town in Niger near the Ténéré Desert, a place whose name means Nothingness. She was small when she left there, but something about the place got into her soul. She used to tell me tales about the fabled walled city of Djaba." He sighed and looked up at the darkening sky. "I sometimes see the shapes of that city of the perpetual purple dusk of noontime . . ." he paused, and said no more about it. *We are all haunted* I thought, and wondered if we could somehow pool all our hauntings how it would extend the cave wall. Pooling our hauntings, yes, that's one way of talking about the way we dream together. My attention was wandering, but I noticed that Djan had stopped talking.

"Where was Eugenia born?" he asked abruptly. Mick's eyes widened and he took a quick breath.

"South Dakota," I said. "I don't know the name of the town, or at least I've forgotten. She left there when she was about six, but used to go back for the summers. To her grandparents' farm."

Djan and Mick looked at each other and nodded. They knew something they weren't telling.

"She's gone there," they both said, or one of them said, or maybe nobody said.

Anita Sullivan

I frowned. "How do we dream ourselves to South Dakota? It's just a name for me, I've never been there, I don't know what to imagine."

"The shapes that Djan was just talking about!" Mick said excitedly. "You know, Indians with feathers in their bonnets holding spears, riding on horses. The windswept plains. The Presidents carved on the rock!"

"That's in North Dakota, you dweeb!" I said.

"O.K., the Badlands then, whatever!"

"Do you think she even needs us?"

"Yes, she's stuck. If she doesn't need outright rescuing, she needs reminding. "

We had a long, stupid generic conversation trying to figure out what to do, in which we all said things any of us could have said, and it all melded into a nice warm lump of intention that we proceeded to pat into shape.

"What about my intuition that she was in Ikaria?" I whined.

"You were mixing up the past and the future with the present," Mick said somewhat loftily. "Easy enough to do."

"I'd like a shower before we go," I said in a small voice. It was very quiet. The fire had died down and the pre-dawn wind was starting to flow over us in a thicket of gray.

"With eternity in the palm of our hands, it's hard to know when to hurry, when not," murmured Djan. He was squatting and poking idly at the dying coals. His eyes gleamed. I was overwhelmed by the sense of history coming out of his shape, the ancient, noble peoples he represented on both his mother's and father's side. It was as if he were a funnel for this history, and it poured freshly up into the air, lending strength to us, simply because we had acknowledged it. I threw my shoulders back, wiggled them around, crossed my hands behind my back and stretched my arms.

"Let's just go," I said, and then added, "After all, this is as much for us as it is for her. Why wait?"

We lay down in a semicircle with our feet pointed in towards the dying fire and dreamed ourselves into the country of the Lakota. In point of fact we ended up on the outskirts of Vermillion, South Dakota, a small college town with sidewalks and gardens and huge frame houses. This could have been Kansas, or Iowa, or Ohio, there was little of "the West" or "the Plains" about it, except for the flatness and the dust in the wide streets. We squinted at this dust, which seemed to be swirling slowly as if it had just been disturbed by something that had vanished moments before we arrived.

"How the hell did we get *here*?" Djan drawled, hands in his pockets, swaggering in his boots down an empty sidewalk.

"A gunfight!" said Mick, and we looked at him thinking he was joking, but he was not.

"She's been shot at," he went on, tilting his head to one side as if sniffing. I looked down at Heloise, who was the designated creature to be sniffing things out. Behind us was a motel and gas station. We were on the corner where a stop light hung, of course unlit. If we crossed the street cars might go right through us, our atoms completely skirting one another in the vast spaces between them. I thought of dust motes. Of bees.

"She's gone to a safe house," I said.

Mick rolled his eyes. "Whatever," he said. "Show us the way, then."

111                    Anita Sullivan

"We need an alley. There was an alley. Some gun shots." I started marching down the street towards the campus of University of South Dakota, away from the center of town, although we were still several blocks from it.

Djan had taken a quick breath when Mick said "gunfight" and I knew he was thinking of those irresponsible adolescent spirits who roam between the worlds and gain their substance from the obsessive fantasies of people living and dead.

We strode along in the dawn on the uneven sidewalk, crossed the empty street, skirted the Student Union, walked past the music museum, and in another couple of blocks started up a sort of hill. On our side were public buildings, across the street white picket fences seemed to bristle at us, putting up their petty row of defenses. Why was there an air of battle? I kept shaking my head, raising my shoulders to shrug it off.

Then a crack split the air. Although I may never have heard gunfire in my life, I knew it now, and felt my insides threaten to melt. Like a squadron of small tanks we turned immediately away from the sound, into a narrow passageway between two brick buildings. The alley I had been seeking. It grew narrower. The shot rang out again, but we heard no footsteps other than our own, nor could we sense that a bullet had struck anywhere; there was no ricochet, no sound of any-thing breaking apart. We just kept running, with our heads hunched forward. Heloise was behind us, our rear guard, and I remember dimly wishing we could stop long enough to stuff her in amongst us so her wide body would not be such a ready target.

The alley did not end as soon as it should have. It went on unnaturally, and began to grow narrower and steeper, until we all realized we were no longer in Vermillion, but in a larger city, cut off almost from the sky by towering walls, basement stairs going down into apartments with black wrought iron grills on the windows and garbage cans and bicycles sitting outside. Although the gunshots came no more, we felt pursued nonetheless, by something that hissed and flapped, though we did not turn to look. All of us were breathless, almost staggering, when we came to the end of the alley, ducking under an overhang to find our way completely blocked by a massive door studded and braced with iron. We fell upon it, pounding with our fists, but none of us uttering a word.

## The House of Bees

The door opened quickly and we were taken in. It closed behind us with a satisfying Boom! And then we were *enveloped*. I couldn't say "by silence" because it was not: we heard the low hum of insects, a hint of water, an even more quiet hint of music – was it the noise of jasmine and roses filling our heads, was it the blur of white butterflies in the corner of our eyes?

"Come in," a low female voice said. The outline of a figure in pale orange beckoned us down a short flight of steps through open glass doors and down into a room full of furniture made of honey-colored wood, including a grand piano in the corner, more double glass doors leading into a greenhouse garden. From there, louder now, came the hum of bees. Thousands of them. As we stood there uncertainly looking around, we saw Eugenia in the garden with a working apron on, doing something with jars and spoons. She seemed oblivious of our presence.

Anita Sullivan

I was unaccountably overwhelmed with the thought of my two sons. *They will die and I will never know.* This thought had come to me before, of course. But here, in a place of extreme quiet and contentment, it took on a different meaning. The nostalgia was almost logical, if you can imagine such a thing. As if the inchoate emotion driven by the small thought, "My sons will die and I will never know,"— as if this emotion suddenly took a real shape like a small ceramic bowl I could hold in one hand and turn slowly, puzzled by its changing pattern in the air before my face. I stood quietly, letting the thought totally engulf me like one of those tidal waves in dreams that comes crashing down on the house you are crouching inside of, and the roof of the house holds firm. And you wait for the next one, willing yourself to be dumb. Now I didn't have to be dumb any more. *It's all right for them to die. They are tied to you forever in love.*

I blinked as the thought released me. Hummingbirds were plying the blossoms of various red and orange flowers. Beside me, Djan and Mick seemed as equally in thrall as I was.

"This is a real House of Bees!" said Mick, with a nervous snort of laughter.

Eugenia turned at that sound and saw us. Her face lighted up and she came hurrying over. Nothing stood in the way of her embracing us, and so she did. An urge to leave rose up in me and was countered by an equally strong urge to sit down with glasses of wine and listen to the humming forever. Forever. We would have that option, would we not?

"Circe will bring us wine," said Eugenia.

*Circe?* I turned to look for the creature in orange, whose face I had not been able to see clearly. Circe, indeed! My eyes narrowed.

Surely this is a totally different situation than the one in Kalypsos' garden. I glanced quickly at Djan, and his dark eyes were puzzled. His large, lithe frame looked tense, poised for action.

"So, what if we are turned into swine, but allowed to remain here forever, dumbly swilling pleasure? Isn't this the classic idea of heaven?" I thought as we were guided into a solarium, with high windows bleeding into a glass roof, but the walls opaque, made of some material like lapis lazuli, or maybe Egyptian faience, deep in the richness and subtlety of its colors. We sat down in chairs woven of some tawny grass, our feet on a thick warm rug. Heloise immediately flopped down at my feet with her chin (if I may use the term loosely) resting in crossed front paws. She seemed alert but not alarmed.

"So, tell us your tale, my dear," said Djan.

"These are the Bees of Sorrow," said Eugenia, gesturing with one hand towards the adjacent greenhouse. The bees seemed to be confined there, for none had followed us into this room, although a double door was open between the two spaces. "I was drawn here to care for them."

I saw Djan's eyebrows draw together at the expression *drawn here*.

We were brought wine, by gauzy creatures who were definitely not human: naiads gazelles, or dryads. Creatures of the air. This was a House of Air, even though the sound of water was not absent. It was a water of air. My head began to play word games off in a corner to itself, even as I listened to the conversation I felt no urge to take part in.

"Tell more," said Djan, as she stopped. She seemed to assume we knew all she knew.

Anita Sullivan

"The Bees of Sorrow are sent out into the world so that despair will turn into sorrow more easily. It's like a chemical process, where you put drops into water to make it coagulate. Sorrow is a thing people can manage; despair is not. This is the place where the bees are born, and return to."

"Are these real bees?" asked Mick. "I mean, the bees we see every day in the flowers, are these the ones?"

She shook herself a little, as if fending off the question. As if fending off questions in general, and closed her eyes for a few seconds.

"I don't really know," she said slowly. "I think these are more like the souls of bees, and they go out and enter the bodies of the bees already there."

"So, do they have to sting people, the people in despair, so their despair will break up into parts, and become sorrow?" I asked suddenly. Then made a face at how ridiculous this question sounded.

Again, she shook herself, took a deep breath. "These are real bees," she smiled. "Something in the nature of Bee-ness allows them— only bees—to do this task. I don't think the stinging figures in at all, it's not what they're all about. But all I know is, only Bees can do this thing, and this is the House of Bees, the Bees of Sorrow."

"Are there Bees of something else?" This was me again. Somebody had to ask these questions.

A peal of laughter came from behind us, followed by a ripple of merriment that went around the room like a breeze blowing through curtains. I turned to look, and saw something that did, indeed, look like curtains. Probably our host of attendants listening in on our conversation.

"I don't think so," she said. "I believe this is the task of bees in the world. They crystallize sorrow."

"Is it like making honey?" Mick burst out suddenly. "Do they turn Sorrow into honey, something sweet?"

Again, the peal of laughter. Eugenia shook her head. I had the feeling this conversation could go on for a long time, as it had gone on for a long time on Earth among philosophers. Writ large, it was the problem of evil, the nature of happiness, the purpose of existence.

"I care for them," she said simply. "They are messengers. They go out, and sometimes they are injured, or tired, or ill, and they return. There is no queen bee, only those of us who care for them."

No queen bee? These words rang in my ears. Suddenly I had an understanding of what went on in this house. It was the hive. People and other creatures recruited from many realities would come here and do a tour of duty, looking after the bees, helping them be born, nurturing them, sending them out into the world. This was a linking place between the abstract and the real, between the metaphorical and the actual. It was a middle-level actualizing place in the cosmos, "below" that of Origin. This was as far as my mind would let me go. But a sense of the honor we had been accorded by being invited here, stole over me. I felt warm and drowsy. My urge to leave began to drain away, without activating any alarm systems.

"Are you going to stay here, then?" Djan's voice was harsh, unnaturally loud. Heloise raised her head. My eyes opened wide. I felt annoyed. Why bring that up now?

"Outside this house is a city," she said. "It is the city of the world. The bees must go through this city on their way to their tasks. Many of them die, about half of them die on the way through. There is

Anita Sullivan

poison, there is sickness, pollution, violence. We are in the center of that city. It is the city of repository of all the world's despair. To leave this place, we must travel through the city as the bees do, as the birds do in their migrations, risking the muck and the slime, the thick mists to confuse us and weigh us down. That is the only way out that I know."

We were struck silent by that. The next normal question would have been, "Well, then, how did you get here? How did we get here?" but it didn't seem a necessary question, since we obviously had not come here by slogging our way through a difficult city. Or had we? I remembered the Arbiter telling me, in essence, "This is not a test," and my realization that the Arbiter was wrong. We had all survived a year or more of living alone, in exile from the world of our fellow humans. Such a task might be the equivalent of slogging our way through hell, mightn't it? I kept this thought to myself.

"What do you mean the only way out?" Mick said suddenly. "We dreamed ourselves here. We dreamed ourselves together. Why can't we dream ourselves back out again?" His voice took on an anxious note, as if he expected some Evil Power to come in and say, "Heh! Heh! Little do you know, the Rules have changed . . . ."

"We could dream ourselves out," Eugenia said very slowly. Her eyes were clear, and she was speaking as one who had come to an understanding on her own, not as one who had been indoctrinated. I sat up, revived, and took another sip of the lovely, limpid, smooth red wine. "But in a sense we would never be really out. This place ties us in a way – it's hard to explain. In our own houses, I mean in the new lives we have been living, you know – we are disconnected from the "real" world of living human beings. But since we are not truly dead, we are also disconnected from the spirit world, or at least not able to move as freely there as we would if our souls had gone out of our mouths. But here, in this House of Bees, we are in a kind of neutral place. All realities are actual here. And that means we can't just dream ourselves out of here, because parts of ourselves – some levels of ourselves – would stay behind."

After we had sat thinking about that for a little bit, Djan said, "I guess you mean that we would in effect *lose substance* if we left here by dreaming." He was not asking a question, but trying to figure it out. "It would be a sort of dying by degrees. That is, we would arrive home and find that we were weaker, or more transparent, and might even, then, actually die."

We all nodded, getting this point, and feeling angered, frightened, intrigued by it, round and round. We could sit here for years feeling that way, and wondering "Why leave, if it's that much trouble?"

"We've come to that place in the Story," I said, partly to stimulate us away from this circle of thinking, "where the heroes have to be held captive in the Enchanted Tower for centuries waiting for some magic to happen. But I suppose," I added brightly, "We can't be in despair, can we? I mean, not in this place."

But we can feel sorrow, because I do right now. And anger, and terror, and suspicion, and confusion. But wait a minute – sorrow? Do the bees work on people inside their own House? The thought was paradoxical enough to make me relax.

"You've been here for awhile," said Mick, who had not touched his wine but sat stiffly in his comfortable chair taking deep breaths, his eyes large. "What do you want to do? I mean, we came here because we felt you were asking us to come. And that means maybe you wanted some help. Is that true?"

I felt a little shattering in the air, as if Parzival had remembered to ask the question in the Grail Castle, first time around, instead of making the entire world slog through another century of anguish. I could swear the windows let in more light, but somehow this was what was making the room seem darker, fuller. We were made aware that changes could take place here, unbalances, deteriorations; whereas we had quickly come to believe the situation was eternal, fixed in this House of Bees.

Eugenia didn't answer. She was obviously struggling. She didn't want to say yes or no and have it mean something she did not fully intend. Or was she unable to answer? Was her mouth sewn shut? I looked over at her mouth to see if I saw any threads there, feeling not the least silly for this. I could not see any.

As I was leaning across, squinting in my far-sightedness to trace the lines of Eugenia's mouth, Heloise stood up and waddled across the room. I have to say "waddled," even though she moved as quickly as if she were a small bird hopping across a garden. She gave Eugenia a little nip on the knee and then sat down on her haunches and looked at her, waiting. *Come on, honey, there must be another way* she could have been saying. Or, at least, I wanted her to be saying.

Mick relaxed suddenly in his chair. He seemed either not to have noticed Heloise, or else he interpreted her act as merely playful. Merely playful, indeed!

"Let's just hang out here for awhile," he said. And then shrugged. "Maybe we could actually be of help, volunteer work, you know what I mean? Why be in such a hurry to go somewhere. Now that we're all together again, we might as well be here as anywhere. I mean, unless you're ready to go right away?" He opened his greenish eyes wide and looked across at Eugenia. He was taking the risk that he would know, no matter what she said, what she really meant.

She looked directly back at him. "I will show you the work," she said calmly. I closed my eyes and found myself sticking my lower lip out, biting down on my upper lip, a thing I see others doing but never do myself. Will we drink of the waters of Lethe? Will we forget who we are? Will we even know if we've been turned into swine? But maybe I'm worrying for no reason. Creatures obviously come and go in this place, and so we can, eventually, leave. This is a world of new stories, not just the old ones. I've never heard about this particular story, the Bees of Sorrow. Might as well settle into it and see what kind of a turn it takes.

All this and more went whizzing through my mind as we stood up and went out into the greenhouse with Eugenia, into the vast array of greenhouses that stretched as far in all directions as we were able to see, all of them hazy with the perfume of a myriad of flowers, blurry with bees.

Anita Sullivan

## Part III

### Vorweile Doch

And so we stayed for a year and a day. Might as well have been. We didn't keep track by putting notches on anything, and we hadn't devised our own day sign system yet. But looking back, it feels like about a year worth of sleepings and wakings went by in this strange and wondrous House of Bees.

There was furniture. That seemed odd to me until I realized this place *had come into existence because someone dreamed it, and then died.* It seemed eternal and generic in the way that such places always are in the middle of stories: perfection is usually generic. Yet it seems perfection is a species, not a genus, so there are many different kinds.

I slept in a tower room, just as I had always fantasized as a child. The room was larger than I would have thought, with space for a small single bed, a lovely wrought-iron rocking chair with its own matching footstool so you could put your feet up and push yourself back and forth as you gazed out the lancet window into the bee gardens. No windows in the house looked "out," they only looked "in" to the garden. As if it had become the entire world.

Eugenia, Mick, Djan and I hardly saw one another during the period we were at the House of Bees. Or rather, we saw each other every day but could devise no urgent reason to speak. Nobody spoke much in this house. We each had our daily tasks to do, and they were so absorbing that we had no mind left for any other absorption. Yet at the end of the day we were not exhausted, just sweetly tired, and we went into the brass and marble bathroom for a misty and steamy shower, where we were scrubbed by invisible hands, and then off to instant sleep.

I am remembering some of this because I wrote it down. My memory itself tells me almost nothing. As if I had been a piece of cloth torn in two and sewn back together; there is a seam now in my middle, but I have no idea how it got there or why, or how much cloth I may have lost. We were prisoners, yes, but also willing and simple servants – drones in the hive you might say.

We learned to heal wounded bees, and to revive ill and exhausted ones. We learned to sew on gauzy wings with the thread of spider webs, the strongest material in the universe. Day after day we stood barefoot on a ground strewn with fragrant grasses before small glass tables with our tiny instruments, our tweezers and needles, our files, spatulas, our pin vises, brushes, and we re-created the Bees of Sorrow so they could continue to fly out into the poison of the world and keep the level of madness from growing into a tidal wave to destroy all life. It is a holding pattern, not a way of change, but without it, change would spiral into unmitigated hell. At least that is what I was led to believe, and I still believe it.

We worked alongside creatures from many realities, many parts of the universe. Maybe this was a kind of Peace Corps for some of them, a tour of duty on Planet Earth. We had little contact with our fellow workers, and in fact could not see most of them, only had hints by the motions around us, an odd sound here and there above the bass level humming, as if the whole constituted a huge passacaglia. I think I spent my time there half drunk with music, my soul tilted to one side, listening, listening. It was a relief not to speak, yet alone in my tower room I dimly thought of the silence of not speaking as a kind of yin to

Anita Sullivan

the yang of another kind of silence, and could feel the two spinning together, around me, and through me.

Probably the furniture – remember I was speaking of furniture – allowed us to leave. Not that we ought to have left. I don't believe we were in danger there, except of forgetting who we were, and I suppose under the circumstances of this whole experiment that may be only a matter of preference. *Vorweile doch, du bist so schön* as Faust was driven to whisper in Goethe's tale, discovering that he had finally reached a small reprieve from his natural state of restless anguish, but he was talking about a moment, gnat-sized amid the wash of hours in his life. We, however, were growing to feel that way about an eternity. And I suppose for us that constituted a kind of dying. So, it came to an end.

One morning I descended from my tower and, passing through the living room with its odd collection of sofas and chairs and the grand piano, I saw Heloise asleep on a sofa.

"Who's that?" was my first thought.

"She's sleeping on my sofa," was my second thought.

And then memory came rushing back, like the tidal wave I mentioned a little while ago. All at once I remembered who I was – my entire life before I died, and everything since then. All very clearly, item by item, as if eternity broke itself down into so many discrete grains of sand in my mind, each full but small enough not to take up too much space. There was space for it all.

"Heloise!" I roared finally, when that grain of sand caught my attention, and I ran over to wake her up. Where had she been all this while? She was with us when we stumbled into this house, down the alley, the four of us. Why had I not missed her? She had not slept in my tower room, nor had she been at my feet every day while I ministered to the bees. *Where had she been hiding?* Full of joy and reproach and confusion, I fell upon my faithful wolf-dog to embrace her.

And she snarled at me. The look in her normally mild brown eyes, light brown eyes the color of delicious root beer, was wild and vicious. I was frightened at this reappearance of the ancient wolf, and I backed off. She kept coming at me, as if herding a single sheep, until I bumped up against Mick working at his table. Then there were two sheep. Eventually she had the four of us back at the sofa, the same flowered Victorian sofa I had vowed not to leave behind in our travels. Had this resourceful dog traveled back to my Italian villa and smuggled it into the House of Bees? Past Circe and the other nymphs who moved constantly at the edge of our peripheral vision? I don't know. Heloise had turned into a mad wolf, a thing with fangs, ancient and severe, and we obeyed her. We had stepped suddenly from our story into hers. Up onto the sofa the four – no, the five – of us went, and were gone from that place. I suppose there was a bevy of orange-gowned creatures looking up at us from below, their garments winking and gleaming in the filtered sunlight, but nobody tried to stop us. We came, and in due time we went. Soplice.

However, the powers of our wolf dog did not run to navigating a sofa back out of the City again. Somehow, we took a wrong turn, thus heading into the center of the foulness rather than out to its edge. Our wee sofa came to rest with its tidy four polished teakwood feet sunk into a bog of mud, and our choices became immediately to sink further while seated on the sofa, or to try wading out in the direction of what looked like solid concrete at the edge. All the while a green stinking mist was rising around us, threatening to knock us unconscious as well as to keep us from seeing each other.

We all jumped off about the same time. Our habit of not speaking had taken hold of us so strongly we were acting almost as if we didn't know each other, or as if we were each existing in a totally separate world. But as soon as our feet touched the ground, we realized we were going to be wading through a thick, sticky, horrid glue-like poisonous mud and might not be up to the task.

"Help! Ugh!" We all cried out, and found ourselves looking at each other and reaching our hands out, both to aid and be aided. As a result, we started walking four abreast across what was some kind of an industrial holding pond full of chemical sludge, our eyes and nostrils burning. An instinct told us that together we might have more of a chance than separately. And so we lurched and slogged our way across, in a race to keep from sinking so far that we could no longer move at all.

Heloise had veritably skimmed across the top of the mud, or maybe slid in some platypus-like fashion, so that she reached solid ground very quickly and was able to bark and growl encouragement from the sidelines. As we came closer, as our "organism" oozed closer to her, she reached out with her teeth and held onto sleeves for awhile, then ran and found a stout stick that she put into Djan's hand so she could pull. Gradually, coughing and retching, we managed to get across the stinking marsh and pull ourselves up onto a kind of concrete wall, where we sat, dumbly grateful.

Above us, around us, was a din of clanking and grinding, and the ground shook slightly with the deep hum of industrial motion.

"We are in hell," said Djan. His voice was flat with despair, unusual for him.

"We can't stay here, we'll die," I said. But nobody moved. We raised our eyes and looked around. As far as we could see on any side, rectangular ponds of mud or pitch or slime reeked and gave off gasses. Every now and then something would make an ear-splitting screech, as of metal on metal, and we had no guarantee that a huge sharp wheel would not come rolling down the middle of some hidden causeway to split us in half. The murky light was occasionally lit briefly by an orange or green glow, or by some color I have never seen before.

"Which way do we go?" said Eugenia. She was showing the only spark of energy in the whole bunch. She sat next to Heloise and had one hand on the dog's back. None of us even thought of trying to dream our way out of this, it was not any more in our philosophy. I could feel my head beginning to loll crazily under the influence of the acrid fumes. We all blinked constantly.

Heloise also seemed confused, but being the doughty creature she was, she stood on the wall and barked hoarsely, trying to arouse us. Maybe we should try to walk to the end of this rectangle of concrete and hop over to the next one. And so on, ad infinitum, until we keeled over. This thought winked on and off in my dulled brain.

Just about that time we heard, between the rumbles and hisses and screeches, a faint metallic noise that was definitely not from machines. It came and went, came and went, yet gradually grew stronger and more constant.

"Geese!" I gasped. It was an ancient sound, unmistakable, and stirred the blood of all four of us, despite ourselves. Our heads turned in

Anita Sullivan

the direction of their coming as if we were watching a sports event in a stadium.

And through the dim light, under concrete spans, weaving and wending their way through a hell of intersecting pipes and girders, tanks and bridges, flew a small flock of bright green and yellow geese, with wide frightened eyes, necks stretched straight, wings flapping steadily. They looked like lost children. We watched them go just over our heads, and they looked briefly down at us with that blank transparent gaze of wild creatures which is totally inexplicable in its power, since it says nothing at all, nothing at all.

We stood up and followed them, as if we too were migrating birds, caught napping by the well. Although we could not fly, I believe we did manage to run for awhile, so anxious were we not to lose sight of these folk who were so valiantly making it through the City, the place of poison. Like the bees, they too were on their way out to do their work in the world, and nothing was going to stop them.

Of course, we did lose them, but by that time we had come out from under the heavy buildings into a lighter gray sky, so that we had a better sense of what was ahead of us. The miasma of stinking chemicals grew less too, so that breathing was at least possible without gagging. And we settled into a pace of leave taking, with our spirits bolstered enough so that we were ready to continue on until we came to the end of this place, or died, whichever came first. The birds did this for us.

Later, in the dark (for we traveled all night) we found the body of a goose lying on its side, feathers completely clogged with oil and mud. We stopped, and all of us wept over its small form for quite a-while. This was wrong. Nothing later would change that.

# Monkeys on Typewriters

We probably would have walked home – "home" being our separate dwellings in our own private level of reality – if it hadn't been for Djan. Maybe it was the shock of the poison City, after such a long period of tranquility. At any rate, we forgot that we normally traveled by dreaming. We forgot that we were not in the real world any more, that our weariness and stink and hunger and fear and disgust was temporary in a different way than it would have been if we had been still alive in the usual sense. So, through every alteration in this strange symbolic city, this repository of all that is very worst in human cleverness and greed since the beginning of the world, we just kept on walking.

"It's not squishy any more," said Mick matter-of-factly. The mud had dried on our shoes, on our skin, in our hair. We all looked ridiculous, like robot figures in an amateur theatrical production.

The geese were gone. The sky was colorless, we were trudging along an empty highway with steel and concrete walls separating us from heaps and piles of metal, containers, garbage, the refuse of construction projects never completed or never begun.

Djan stopped suddenly. "Why are we doing this?" he said a-loud. He wasn't speaking to us, or to himself, it was as if inside him a little voice machine had clicked on.

Nobody said anything. We stopped too, and leaned our elbows on whatever level of the endless rows of concrete and steel we could reach, peering through cracks at the contorted mass of forms piled before us. I squinted slightly, imagining that I could see a line of monks on a ridge in black cloaks, their heads all leveled off at the top like

Anita Sullivan

small mesas. The image amused me slightly, and made me wish, also slightly, for a drawing pad.

"It's like monkeys on typewriters writing the Shakespeare plays," continued Djan. "If you give them time enough, they will eventually – *eventually* – come up with at least one entire play, with all the letters in the right order, all the spaces between the letters. Except, you know it's not going to happen. You just don't remember why. And I just remembered. I just remembered!" He turned, his eyes glowing with a light that seemed suddenly the only beautiful and real thing we had seen for quite some time.

"Warga-warga, that's why!" he cried, pushing his fist out in front of him, as if into an imaginary soldier's belly. He pursed his lips and squinted, and pushed his fist out again. It didn't occur to any of us that he had gone nuts, because he was so obviously filled with a healthy flood of real feeling. We each held our own spare supply of ecstasy, I'm sure we did, like honey. Not for nothing had we spent an entire year inside a bee hive.

"You see," he explained, dropping to his haunches and squatting comfortably on the pavement. "In order for the monkeys, or the computers, or whatever they are – in order for them to come up with even one Shakespeare play, they must be prepared to go through all the possible permutations and combinations involving letters and spaces and punctuation, every single one, whether or not they result in words. Even in one language, since we're assuming only one language here, right? But that's the trouble. *All the possibilities haven't been done yet.* Far into the future, people will speak, and writers will write, and they will keep coming up with different combinations of letters, words, and punctuation. That in itself, I believe, would be enough to scotch the experiment. But there is more." He held up an index finger and looked at us closely. "What if these inimitable monkeys took the notion one morning to write 'Warga-Warga'? And then 'Warga-Warga-Warga'? And they kept doing that, and nothing else, forever? What's to stop them? It's not outside the realm of possibility? You see, nothing is outside the realm of possibility. Possibility is infinite. Thus, you would never, *for sure*, get your Shakespeare play."

He paused dramatically, as if we were supposed to be as excited as he was by this discovery. I thought it was pretty neat, actually, and was turning it over in my mind. Eugenia had her head to one side, looking thoughtful and a little bemused. But Mick said, "What does that have to do with anything here?" Not peevishly, just rather innocently. We had all the peevish leached out of us, I think, maybe for good. But I didn't think of that until later, and when I did it was much more exciting than the monkeys on typewriters.

"We're doing Warga-Warga here, and we need to stop," Djan said, and stood up with a shrug. "It's like we're trying to prove something we don't need to prove. Are we doing penance? Lord knows the world needs it, but our misery is not going to dissipate a single stinking breath, or bring a single beauty in. Not here. Our work is elsewhere, out with the bees in the fields. This place is an archetype, a fullness of the Ugly. We need to be reminded of it from time to time— *and then move on.* " He shook his head after this speech, as if clearing his mind and his eyes on behalf of all of us, then looked each of us in the eyes with a slow, beautiful smile. At that moment, I truly loved him. We all sighed, probably a collective sigh.

Anita Sullivan

"We should be dreaming our way out of here!" said Mick, anticipating Djan's next remark. His voice sounded rich, full, with all its usual overtones.

But Eugenia shook her head slowly. "I don't think that would have been possible, Mick, up until now. It might be possible now." She looked up at the sky, as if checking some kind of weather.

"Why do you say that?" Mick asked.

She sighed and shook her head. "I don't know. It's like the air came out of the balloon, at least temporarily." She smiled and opened her eyes wide, and just being confronted with that sudden bit of blue made me hanker after color painfully. I started to imagine red peppers, and yellow squash, then bread and coffee . . . I was only half listening to the conversation, but it was lingering at the edge of my consciousness in a strange way, like the calling of geese, or the calling of some old voice in memory. I was having one of those ideas that happens without words, a pile of tiny fragments starting to form in a secret place, where you can feel their weight, their hot breath almost, but you can't go there yet. If ever.

Heloise, who had been walking a little ahead, now came back to see what was delaying us. She stood wagging her tail, long tongue lolling out the side of her mouth, her oddly proportioned head seeming suddenly large and out of control. I felt as if I were looking at the Dog in the Moon. I wondered if we were supposed to jump over her.

"But we can!" said Mick. "This city goes forever—I mean, really, we've gotta make up our minds and just get the hell out of here!" The old imp had crept back into his eyes and his voice. We had stopped walking when Djan started talking about the monkeys and typewriters, and now we all sagged slightly, like scarecrows having been lifted down off our poles. We laughed, and stretched, snorted, sneezed, coughed, wiggled.

"I think we can jump out," I said cheerfully.

"Amen!" said Djan in a deep voice. I felt his strong hand take hold of mine, and I reached out to take Eugenia's hand. We stood in a circle in the middle of the street, in this wasteland, seeking the power to make it fade away behind us, to dissolve into a different reality before the vividness of our own beings. Eugenia had her hand on Heloise's back, and Mick's hand was on top of hers.

But this time we went nowhere. We opened our eyes and found that we were still a tired, hungry, filthy group of potential immortals rapidly losing calories. Around us an ugly gray city stank and rang.

"I don't mind walking," said Mick after a few minutes, his voice cracking. "But I really think we need help. I mean, there's no place to get food – here."

I had my eyes closed, trying to plan. Silk Purses out of Sow's Ears, I thought, and Pearls before Swine. Why was I thinking about pigs? Stone Soup, I said to myself, and then realized what my mind was doing was like a starter engine trying to start a car whose battery was dead. I was trying to remember a story for us to latch onto. A story with food in it, banquet halls, cornucopias, cafeteria lines, pantries. But all I had the energy for was odd fragments of proverbs. Pathetic, it was, simply pathetic.

"To die, to sleep, perchance to dream – aye, there's the rub!" muttered Djan, looking off into space and rubbing his chin. He, too, was trying to latch onto something larger, something that didn't involve walking and going nowhere forever.

Anita Sullivan

"We *are* the monkeys on typewriters," said Eugenia, in a small voice. She is always surprising me, that girl.

"Is there a high place from which we could reconnoitre the landscape?" mused Djan, half talking to himself as he often did. We were on a bridge, with huge girders. We looked up. Djan shrugged and began to climb. Better you than me, I thought, since I have terrible dizziness at anything higher than a small tree.

He came down again a short time later, grinning.

"There's a shopping center about, oh I don't know, a day's walk," waving his hand to the left center. I could not say without a compass, which direction was which, since the sun didn't even show up as a dim circle behind the gray crust plastered over the known world.

"Is a shopping center an improvement?" asked Mick. He was not trying to be funny.

But Djan was convinced, so we headed that way, hoping we would get there before our tongues started to swell and grow black. I wondered briefly about Heloise, if she could find water in this industrial desert. This was not the natural world by hardly anyone's definition.

We walked through another night, stopping more frequently than the night before, breathing deeply to keep our energy up. Halfway through the night we fended off an attack from a flock of bats, if "flock" is the proper noun of venery. They never actually touched us, but wheeled around our heads making prickly sounds that sometimes we could hear. They were small, ugly, black, with thick noses and bristles sticking out of their foreheads, as if a passel of crones had been shrunk and given wings. They were trying to steer us in a different direction, or so it seemed, but we resisted any change. The flapping and the breezes and the mild unpleasant smell they left behind, like the whiff from moldy basements when the door is held open too long, left us with our skin crawling, and undermined our weak resolve much more than it should have.

"Surely this is not an omen!" said Djan, trying to be light-hearted.

"Who cares if it is?" said Mick, and he burst into one of his cackles. "We're already in Hades!"

"Maybe we should honor them," said Eugenia thoughtfully, looking at the shadowy figures as they dipped around us. She stood for a long time, her eyes closed, then opened them again and shook her head. "No!" she said, not smiling. "They don't have anything to do with us."

We trudged on, and by dawn we had indeed come into a shopping center, complete with grocery store and cafes. Here we were able to find food. Djan the Scrounger, as I dubbed him, made the rounds with Heloise while the rest of us sat wearily on a circular concrete bench that was built around a collection of plastic plants. We were expecting at best, canned food, but he came back with steaming tortillas, beans and rice, juice and hot cups of yerba mate tea.

"Don't ask!" he said, raising an index finger, his brown eyes full of laughter. After we ate, we all stretched out like a row of homeless people on the concrete benches and slept.

I woke up in the dark, cold and stiff. I felt like a figure in an old Farside cartoon. A low-browed, hairy figure who had been trapped inside an iceberg for 10,000 years, Thag was sitting at a desk in a bookstore signing copies of his memoir, the title of which was *It Was*

*Very Cold And I Couldn't Move.* I managed to wiggle up onto an elbow, and looked down to see Heloise sleeping calmly below me.

*How can you sleep at a time like this?* I thought. This dog had come to me in a magical and mysterious way, and I had assumed she possessed powers beyond those of a mortal canine. I had been led to believe – or at least I had come to believe – or rather, I had known right from the first moment I saw her – that she was a spirit guide in disguise. So why wasn't she doing her job? She had instigated our escape from the House of Bees, but what for? So we could starve? So we could endure the usual miseries of our previous existence all over and over again? But here in this poison City she seemed to have lost her power. Why?

I flopped over onto my back, ignoring the dull pain of my lower back muscles, and tried to make my intuition and imagination work. What do you do when you are cold and you cannot move? How can you send out positive elemental energy any more when you have turned into a small dynamo of ill will? A cluster of little despairs came fluttering at me like icy rain against a window, *Why stay alive if this kind of thing can happen? What good are you doing anybody? What have you learned that's so different from what you knew before? The ratio of misery to happiness doesn't seem to have improved. The stupid experiment is just stupid. How long is this going to last?*

But mostly, *Why can't we dream our way out of here?* Eugenia seemed to understand the answer to this question, but I didn't. Here we are, all four of us practiced dream travelers, and we are sleeping the dreamless sleep of the dead, of stones, of poison gases, of turbines, of smokestacks, vats, mill wheels, cauldrons – all things that crush and spew and make the world worse.

What's more, I had lost my Victorian sofa. I sat up, gripped by a quick sadness. Closing my eyes, I tried to see the sofa, to force myself to remember exactly its color, shape, the pattern on its four pillows, the way its high arms had polished teak fronts with a little knob on top, peeking out from the upholstery material, the four feet – not legs – trim and neat as a dancer's ankles. Yes, the color was pale, pale orange, with a pattern of . . . oh, what was it? Fronds . . . yes, small sweeping gestures in dark orange and aqua, splashed with delicacy in a decent hue across the bottom pillows, up the side pillows. The whole sofa was a study in tension between grandeur and kitsch, a perfect balance. I smiled and opened my eyes again.

But this time I couldn't see anything at all. Not only was it cold and I couldn't move, I also couldn't see, even my hand in front of my face (I quickly tried). There was no fog, no swirling, no breeze, no sound. I knew the others were beside me, just as I could feel the concrete bench digging uncomfortably into my backside. Still, something had changed, and I could only suppose that was good sign.

"Story-less, they wandered through the land . . . ." Another fragment flitted through my mind. And I realized that everything of importance that we had been doing, separately and together, had happened because we had latched onto a story—*on a bat's back I do fly, merrily.* Now we were without one, and it was like being heartless. I shivered and sat up. Eugenia was always giving me credit for having a story ready for every occasion, but it was not that way at all. Stories just showed up.

But not here, not in this place. We were going to have to go after one, like hunters. Jump starting, leaping from one half-baked story fragment to another, was not working. If stories were linked, and one

Anita Sullivan

led to another in some kind of huge pattern – as I was now beginning to believe – how do you get from nothing to something? "Vy is zer somesink instead of nossink?" David used to go around asking, in a phony German accent, mimicking the philosopher Tillich. Now I could ask it the other way around. So, I did. I leaned over and brought my face down to the place where Heloise would have been if I could have seen her, and I hissed: *Vy is zer nossink instead of somesink?*

But I already knew the answer, because I remembered *The Thirteen Clocks*.

## Light Enough to See It By

"Something that would have been purple if there had been light enough to see it by, scuttled across the floor."

(James Thurber, *The Thirteen Clocks*)

We stood in a row peering through the bottom third of several tall interior windows. We stood on a stone floor, the stone window ledges just below my shoulders. A ragged sort of light was moping around the place, as if it weren't sure whether it was leftover from the evening, or was hinting at the early part of a new day. We seemed to be inside the back hallway of a castle, looking through to a grander section, as if we were in the servants' quarters.

We were still cold and stiff, but at least standing up, and the feel of the air alone indicated that we had left the poisoned City behind at last. We were in a row, close enough so that our shoulders almost touched, and wedged into a rather small dark viewing area as if we had been plunked down in this particular spot for a purpose. Strangely, we also seemed to be relieved of our grainy coating of hardened mud. I felt clean, not rested, not free of hunger or cold, but clean. One of the Seven Deadly Virtues, as David used to say.

Nobody said a word, and I realized we had arrived in the middle of James Thurber's *Thirteen Clocks*, inside the castle of the Cold Duke, at a certain critical moment covered by a single sentence in the tale, waiting for a person, or object, to cross the floor of the room we were seeing through the open windows.

"How are we going to look for something that would have been purple, in the dark?" I thought in a sudden panic. Surely it must be almost dawn, and the place would only grow brighter by the minute. The story would continue with or without us, but we had a hostage to pluck out of thin air, as soon as there was light enough to see it by.

"Royalty," said Djan, nodding somewhat vigorously. I looked over at him and realized that in his previous life he had developed a tremor in his old age, one that caused him to nod all the time. But here, in this reality, he would never have to do that. I swallowed and then remembered what he had just said.

"We're looking for a child," I told the others. "She is about ten, has ash blonde braids down to her waist; and she's a princess."

*But in the story, the thing "that would have been purple" was round and small, and scuttled across the floor. It couldn't have been a princess, princesses don't scuttle. Besides, there was already a princess in the story. No story would ever have TWO princesses. You must be wrong. You are making this up.*

"No, I'm not making it up," I thought. "Every story has interlopers who keep trying to take over, or wander in by mistake, and have to be quickly quashed. Thurber noticed her and realized she was out of

Anita Sullivan

place, so he gave her a disguise and a quick exit. Our timing has to be exactly right . . . ." I grabbed the far side of the window ledge and fiercely wiggled myself up until I was able to slip over the sill and drop lightly onto the ballroom floor. In the story she was in a dungeon, but we were catching her before she got that far.

"What are we doing, Carley?" whispered Eugenia, as if she hadn't heard me just explain. Mick looked alert but quiet.

"Kidnapping a small princess," I whispered back. "Anybody have anything interesting in their pockets?" I could see her now, coming down the long room. We might have very little time before the Cold Duke showed up and was unable to see her as clearly as we could.

"A balloon," said Mick with a little smile. "I like to decorate my house with them."

He handed it to me through a window.

The balloon was purple. I blew into it until it swelled into a small ellipse; then like the witch calling at the door of Snow White's house, I held it out and waggled it back and forth directly in the pathway of the princess. She stopped and came over to look. Having never been instructed not to talk with strangers, she took my hand gladly when I whispered that she was going to my Mediterranean villa with me. She had no idea where that was, but if it was a place that had purple balloons, she was all in favor. We climbed back through the window together and dropped on the floor into the hall, just as the Cold Duke's boots could be heard clicking on the uncarpeted stairs.

## Pandora's Box

Fortunately we were too tired and hungry for the enormity of my rash, illogical act to sink in immediately. We all managed to arrive safely back at my villa and everyone elected to stay for the afternoon, since there was so much to talk about. Our quick elision from the poisonous City to our regular seats around the glass-topped table on my upper verandah seemed no less than miraculous. But why did we stop off on the way to pluck a minor character—actually an imaginary, or barely-existent character—out of a story, as if we had been running an errand for someone on the way home? Were we to keep her here until someone came to fetch her? She surely didn't belong to our company.

The princess was content for the time being to explore the house, garden, the path to the sea and all its weedy terrain between. I didn't worry about her as I would have had she been my own child, or even had she been alive in the normal sense. I had no idea whether or not she could drown in the sea, fall off a cliff or a balcony, or run away. I only knew I had been the instrument to bring her here, the material cause I suppose Aristotle would have said, or was it the formal cause? I never can get them straight.

In the afternoon we gathered out on the upper verandah with tea, wine, and a variety of *merendas*.

"Where's she gone?" asked Mick, spearing himself a stuffed artichoke.

I shrugged. There was a silence, and the others looked uncomfortable.

Eugenia shook her head. "What, Carley – what is this all – about?"

Anita Sullivan

I realized they held me responsible. They thought I did it on purpose. I brought my front teeth together in a kind of wince. "I was trying to get us connected to some kind of story, so we could get out of that place. And what came into my head was *The Thirteen Clocks*. But beyond that, I have no idea." I shook my head and shrugged. "It's like something took over."

"We now have a child in the house. That's really weird!" said Mick, after a pause in which nobody thanked me for getting them home.

"Achh!" said Djan, closing his eyes and resting his forehead onto the tips of his fingers. He muttered something guttural in a language I had never heard, then looked up at me. "You don't have any idea, do you?"

I felt my throat tighten and tears sting my eyes. I looked down to my hands clasped in my lap and began quietly to cry. Because I did know, suddenly, what he meant.

"Oh, my god!" said Eugenia, as she too caught on that we now had a child in the house. Mick stood up and let his hands fall to his sides, making fists. He looked up at the flawless blue sky. "Is this part of the experiment?" He turned, his green eyes flashing. "This is turning into a big nightmare," he continued, almost desperately.

"We've made some choices," said Djan. He looked up into the sky and closed his eyes for a few seconds, then shrugged. "Our choices have set in motion certain consequences, for which we now bear responsibility."

"What do you mean *we*?" Mick said, trying to keep his voice even. "I don't remember being consulted. We were all there together in the city trying to figure out how to get back home. But then, bang!

Suddenly here is this *child* we seem to have kidnapped. She's about ten years old. Where did she come from? What right did we have to take her? Are we going to keep her here and watch her never get any older, year after year?"

"Is this what we're really afraid of?" asked Eugenia. "I feel it too. Have we made a wrong thing happen?"

"But we did rescue her from something," I said. "The Cold Duke, who is definitely totally a bad guy. She was in the wrong place, and we came there at just the right time."

"But you were the only one who even knew where we were," said Mick. "It was like you were dictating. You just leaped out in front of her and lured her away. How do you know she didn't belong in that story? You seem to think you've got the right to change stories around any old way that suits you. Like you're on a mission or something!"

I began to cry again, soundlessly.

"But it seemed the only way to get us home," said Djan quietly. "There seemed to be only a small number of choices open to us, of back roads we could locate to bring us from that place to this one, so different from one another. I don't believe we acted out of greed, or ignorance or rashness, we were latching onto something *available*."

I nodded, shuddering with sobs. I was angry with myself, but also puzzled and frightened.

"We should go find her," said Mick.

"We don't even know her name," Eugenia observed quietly.

"Porphyra," I said. And then she came to the door of the kitchen, as if she had been inside the house waiting to be called. She smiled shyly, showing a gap in her front teeth. She was wearing blue

Anita Sullivan

jeans and a pink blouse, and held a stuffed rabbit in her hand. It was pale purple.

The rest of that afternoon went by like small cumulus clouds passing over one by one: the scent of flowers, the five of us chatting, the drone of bees, Heloise snoring. But most of all we had the yellow buttery soul and lavender/silver spirit of Princess Porphyra poured into the pitchers of our ears, filling us with prickles of joy and wildness.

She had no curiosity about where she was or how she had come to be here. She did not talk about parents, or country, nor did she show fear or anxiety about being somewhere other than home. Either she assumed we knew all that, or she did not know herself. She had no name for the place we had found her, the Castle of the Cold Duke and his ward Saralinda who was about to wed Zorn of Zorna; she only remembered waking up cold and bored in a small room, and coming downstairs to seek company. So I suppose I was right in assuming she had been a basically redundant character created to cover a potential gap in a story.

Was she still alive, in the same sense we were? This seemed unlikely, but we were neither fit nor willing to pursue such a question at the time. Our afternoon was like a purple balloon, under whose spell we allowed ourselves to remain while we followed the age-old ritual of getting acquainted. That she was a child in a place where children could not be, we put behind us in the simple joy of her company.

"I went down to the ocean, I haven't been on the beach for a long time," Porphyra said. "Heloise came with me, to keep me company. I didn't see any other children, but I imagine there are some nearby. We will go exploring tomorrow. My bunny is named Lambris!"

she giggled and held her rabbit up for our inspection. "He is my best friend."

This was how the afternoon went. She talked and we nodded and smiled and answered questions when they came.

Djan wandered off to the kitchen to prepare some dinner. Porphyra went along and turned out to be quite capable at washing vegetables, especially scrubbing carrots with a brush.

"I have a feeling we will learn her life story grain by grain," Djan remarked with a smile when the two of them came back bearing trays and lanterns. In the interval, I had managed a short nap, while Eugenia and Mick had wandered down to the tangle of old terraces at the bottom of the cafeteria.

"The lions are back!" Eugenia mentioned in the middle of dinner. Porphyra tilted her head to one side, her eyes wide.

"You have *lions*?"

"Yup!" said Mick, looking down at her like a fellow conspirator. "I brought them here. They're really special lions. Everybody figures out a way to talk to them. I'm sure you'll get along just fine."

"What are their names?"

Mick shrugged and widened his eyes at us, opening the field for answers. Nobody said anything. It was a question that simply had not come up before.

"We don't know their names," Eugenia said finally. "But they are female lions. They – they help us out sometimes when we travel to other places."

Porphyra jumped up and down in her chair. "Oh, I love traveling!" she said. "I believe you are my parents now, and so I can live with all of you, can't I?" she added. Was she an orphan? I tried to

Anita Sullivan

comfort myself with this idea, which meant that we had not kidnapped her. But what if the story itself were her home? But which story?

"Actually, that was a matter I wanted to discuss with you, Porphyra," said Djan, leaning back in his chair and regarding her from under his thick eyebrows. "I think it would be good at the beginning, if you would come back with me to my house in Tasmania. Quite a few interesting animals and birds live in my back garden, and there is a really fine path up the mountain with magic caves and pools, and a whole bunch of terrific trees to climb . . . ."

And that, basically, was how the matter of Porphyra was settled. We took her in, not knowing who she was, or whether she would grow up, or die, or whether her stay with us would be only marginally longer than her stay inside the story where we had found her. For one brief moment, in that long afternoon of cumulous-cloud thoughts, events, sensations – for one moment I had a horrible notion that the secret role assigned to us (without our knowledge) by the Arbiter was to wander through eternity from one Story to another, fixing leaks in the plots. We would know no rest until we had worked our way slowly through every novel, every short story, every folk tale, every myth in existence since the beginning of time, perhaps mercifully being spared the necessity to take care of all the close variants. Nevertheless, with time off in between for rest and recuperation, that alone would take us hundreds, if not thousands of years. A kind of Arabian Nights run amok. But I quickly dismissed the notion as unlikely in the light of what had actually happened to us thus far. We were definitely carving out new ground. Still, the notion had passed across my brain like a bat flying over the moon, and it stuck in my memory like a small photograph.

# Part IV

## The Vatch Hook

I have decided to play one Bach piece every single day for the rest of my life. I think it will change me, but I can't think of an analogy that would explain how. I believe it will work on a structural level, with cells maybe, allowing small tendencies to develop that would not have been there otherwise. With Bach, the tendencies would have to be good ones, so I'll take my chances. Only the choice of *which piece* might occupy my attention for a few hours.

Just think, if I played Scarlatti instead, how different my world might become. But I don't want to think that way. I have chosen a path.

I generally tune my harpsichord in quarter-comma meantone temperament, at A-415. This is the tuning system used for centuries on keyboards, nobody knows how long. Immersing myself in these subtle tone relationships is equivalent to a kind of *geography*. I go into a country whose contour, colors, shadows, and meanings rise and engulf me, tickling me into a certain frame of mind. For me the music is the portal into this place, and all the rest need not really exist, I can infer it. Subtlety is what makes life worth living, and suddenly I am craving it in all the aspects of my life. The same *number* of events occur each day, but the distance between them is much, much smaller. Any day now I will be able to float through walls.

I've been playing the harpsichord for a couple of hours each morning, very early, sometimes even before I make my coffee, which seems subversive, overindulgent. Am I just an old drunk, substituting beauty for alcohol, and still taking the same risks of growing blurry around the edges? Moderation has always been a thing that puzzles me.

Why does it not come naturally, as our preferred choice in all cases, since it gives the best results? You'd think natural selection would have selected out excess long ago. Yet even birds will get drunk on fermented berries given half a chance, and humans are notorious for doing things that are not in their best interest, individually or in groups. Why is this not impossible, after several million years of being hominids?

Porphyra seems to have settled down quite comfortably living with Djan, and he seems as reluctant to give her up as she is to go elsewhere. In his previous life, so it turns out, he had not married, but he had a niece who was about this age when she died. So now he can be "Uncle Djan" again.

The question of playmates does continue to be an issue. We have explained to her as clearly as we are able, the situation. She understands that we can't just invite kids in for her to meet, nor can we go out into the world to look for them. Fortunately, she doesn't seem to blame us for the condition, and yet she wishes for friends her own age, and she believes that surely the universe must be willing to take care of this need. We are not the universe, but we continue to feel some responsibility for her situation, and wonder where she really belongs.

She has made friends with the Librarian, of a sort (I should add), since it is not clear whether the Librarian is a "who" or more of a "what." At any rate, we travel there together to the House of Time about once a week. I go and find myself a sunny alcove where I will spend a long morning sipping mint tea while reclining on a sofa and basking in the shining peace of the place with a stack of books beside me, while Porphyra will be up front at the desk sitting on the floor with her hands clasped around her knees, chattering away with the Ibex. She speaks; he does not. But they communicate. Sometimes they stroll among the rows and rows of shelves, as if it were a forest. I don't believe she looks at many books, although I don't really know. On the expressionless face of the Librarian is a patina of serene satisfaction, and I have a sense that by making this creature happy she is doing more than just that, but I don't know exactly what.

It was Eugenia who suggested we return to Ikaria to find children to play with Porphyra.

"You remember, there were kids there? That little boy on the bicycle? And we heard voices from inside the houses. It's the only place that's ever happened."

Mick and Djan agreed that they had never found people anywhere in their travels, all the villages or cities they visited had been quite deserted, in accordance with what we had been led to expect from the "Rules".

"Ikaria is different. Somehow the rules are out the window there. It's Prospero's island!" Eugenia pointed out. I agreed, somewhat reluctantly. We decided not to go all of us together, but to leave one person behind, at least, in the House of Time, in case a rescue operation is needed.

On the first trip out, I elected to stay behind. The story, then, is a summary of their individual accounts.


They went back to Ksanthi, the village where we saw the boy on the bicycle. It was noisy; chickens and pigs were ambling around in the streets, "Big pink pigs!" Porphyra told me, her eyes round with delight. "BIG pink pigs." I knew what she was talking about, I have seen their rosy bulks snuffling in the soft dirt of the olive groves as if they were the primary creatures on earth, and everyone else had conveniently been turned into something very gray and small.

Did they find children? Oh, yes, and but –

Well, what do you mean?

"They kept disappearing!" said Porphyra, her mouth pursed into a puzzled expression. "We were doing a somersault contest over on the grass by the little church. And the boys were doing it first, because they thought they were so important. And then the girls started, and suddenly the wind blew and nobody was there any more." She shrugged, holding her elbows.

"Did they come back?"

She nodded. Djan, Eugenia and Mick watched her, letting her tell the story.

"It was weird, but it was O.K. too. After awhile I got used to it. They blinked out, and then they came back. I was nervous, sort of, at first. I even asked them where they went, but they didn't know what I was talking about."

"Did you have fun?"

She nodded. "Yeah, I guess so. I talked to Stavros a lot, and he told me about the wizard up on the hill who keeps the plants. It's kind of a secret, and he was probably not supposed to tell me. He said that a couple of them have sneaked in over the fence at night and watched him talk to his trees. There are fires . . . ."

We were silent, waiting for more. She must be talking about Kalypsos. A quick little plot began to hatch in my brain: send a child in, protected by innocence, to gather information.

"Do you want to go back?"

She shrugged again and picked at a thread on her sweater sleeve. She looked directly at me, then, with her best impish gaze, this little nereid-in-the-making, and she said, "I could be a spy for you Carley, your secret agent!"

I opened my eyes very wide, as if to feign innocence, but also to signify my reaction, "Two minds with but a single thought!" But Eugenia broke in immediately.

"I don't think that's a good idea, Porph. That wizard on the hill has power, and he might capture you and turn you into a frog." She was not joking.

"True," I said, swallowing. Why do I feel such an illicit desire to continue this matter? Speaking of moderation, as I was earlier, all my life I was blessed with never really wanting anything that was bad for me, at least never in excess. But now I felt a kind of evil desire curling around my heart like a serpent. And I don't even believe in evil any more than I believe in the need for power.

The rest of the story was simple: they waited for Porphyra, sitting on a grassy hillside looking out over trees and rooftops to the distant sea. The sun shone, bees buzzed, nothing much happened. Porphyra was not always in view, so they didn't see the children disappear and reappear, as she did. We decided that was not anything to worry about, unless it upset the little girl too much.

"I trust it's not a trick she is likely to learn herself," mused Djan, half joking. I believe we all tucked that thought away to brood over in private.

Towards sundown, Porphyra went off with Djan to Tasmania and the three of us sat over tea in the cafeteria.

Anita Sullivan

"I have to confess," I said right away, "I feel a strong wish to go back to Ikaria and try to get back into Kalypsos' garden. I don't really know why. It's not that I'm bored, it's more like a need to finish something, but I'm not sure it's a healthy need. I just wanted to confess it, because I am a little afraid."

"Afraid of what?" asked Mick after a long pause.

"Afraid of what I might do. I might wake up one night and go off by myself. After the way I went after Porphyra I don't really trust myself any more, my instincts I mean."

Eugenia held up her hand. "Do you remember a science fiction story once, I think you may have recommended it to me, Carley—but there was something in it called a "vatch hook," remember?" She smiled at me, her eyes dancing because for the first time she had come up with a story.

I shook my head.

"I feel sure you loaned me the book, Carley, but never mind. I only remember that people — creatures and people — could have power over each other's minds in a way that was a little different than the usual science fiction formula. They had something called a "hook." You would cast it out, and if you got it into the mind of the other creature, that creature was attached to you without knowing it, until you let them go. The hook could be something like a virus. I wonder if Kalypsos has a hook in you? If so, there may be a way to find it."

"Sort of like getting rid of worms in a dog!" muttered Mick, and then he cackled a little to cover his nervousness. But it was an apt analogy. I took a deep breath and felt better already.

"Yeah," I said, "I don't think Kalypsos is some huge powerful figure carrying out some great plan to take over the universe, so that we don't have some obligation to go back and risk our lives foiling his plan. That's my instinct, anyhow," I nodded to Mick, getting back to his earlier comment. "So, it does feel like a kind of *itch*, this urge to go back and find out what he's doing. It's not normal curiosity, though. I don't trust it. How can we get rid of this hook, this worm – this hookworm?" I grinned.

Eugenia had her eyes closed again, and was getting ready to speak as she did when she seemed to be listening to a voice from far inside her. Just then I had a really great idea, but I kept my mouth shut in order to let her finish thinking.

"All I can think of is that you have to promise, you have to *really promise* that you will not go back there by yourself, no matter how strongly you feel the urge. And you need to keep track. Write down everything you think or feel about Kalypsos, about that place, if you have dreams about it." Her eyes sprung open. We all thought the same thing at once.

What if the wizard could draw me back there through dreaming?

"No," said Mick. "Not if you don't give full permission. And especially – !" he was just remembering something, and he made a wry face as if to chide himself for not thinking of it sooner. "The five-pointed star! I forgot all about that. Do you know how to construct one? It's a good protection against practically any outside mind inter-ference."

We both shook our heads. So, Mick stood facing us with his legs slightly apart, right hand sticking straight up, and told us how to visualize the construction of a five-pointed star, beginning above the center of the head, going out to the tip of each finger when the hands

Anita Sullivan

are extended to each side, and the two bottom points at the feet. The whole thing would be three-dimensional, so when you were "constructing" it in your mind, you would think of it as thick enough to enclose your whole body.

"Do that every day, first thing."

"I wonder how long it lasts?" I couldn't help saying. Am I really that scientific?

Eugenia giggled. "It's not like aspirin," she said. "Take one every four hours."

"And call me in the morning," added Mick, letting his tongue hang out of the corner of his mouth and rolling his eyes.

"So, you have to promise, Carley." It was Eugenia again, after we stopped laughing. She has an amazing way of sticking to a subject.

"But I've gotta swear on something," I said, running into the house. "A book of poems!" I shouted as I leaped up the stairs to the upper level room where the sofa used to be. And my favorite little furniture piece was back, muddy but intact.

So, of course I ran back downstairs to tell them the news, and they had to come up and see for themselves, and of course I forgot all about getting the book, and the promise was not made, and I never told them about my great idea. But above all, we forgot to take into consideration the logical possibility that protecting yourself with a five-pointed star only works to *keep things out*, not to eject things that might already be in there.

# Eden in the Garden

A honey-colored sun was coming through the lancet tops of my upper-living-room windows as I lay morosely on my sofa all afternoon sorting through possibilities. It wasn't information I hankered for, it was adventure. In the dichotomy between nomads and sedentary peoples, I am definitely a nomad. Or maybe, like the landscape painter Edward Lear, I am driven to keep moving by my own temperament, which inclines towards depression (or as they would have said in his time, "melancholy)." People who are inflicted with a natural melancholy often dispel it by regular changes of scenery, and by piquant challenges to their normal state of comfort and safety.

I tried to remember my great idea of a few hours earlier, but it had vanished. Instead, I was caught in a shabby little mood of deciding "what to do next." Eugenia's light-hearted talk about a "vatch hook" had me worried. How do you tell the difference between healthy curiosity, and someone messing with your mind? Just because Kalypsos had obviously tried to capture Eugenia and me didn't mean it was truly dangerous and foolhardy to go back there, did it? *Do I just want the challenge of confronting him? Do I want to show off my power? I thought I was immune to that kind of thinking. Do I want to sit at his feet and learn his craft?* I couldn't really trust my answers to those questions. And that brought me back to the vatch hook. Was Kalypsos "calling" to me, like an enchanter? Like a *fellow* enchanter. Ah, yes, that began to ring a little more true. My vanity was involved, a place of weakness for everyone. Then it was my duty to resist! But all these arguments and thoughts failed to break a conviction that I needed to return to that garden. I went round and round with arguments for a

Anita Sullivan

couple of hours and was starting to get hungry. "Why do I want to go back to Kalypsos' garden when there are so many other places I could go?"

*I want to get to the bottom of something. I don't want to just keep dream traveling all over the world, like a tourist, seeing one sight after another. It's not worth staying alive for that. I want structure, plot, meaning in my universe! Kalypsos' garden felt like one of those central places where maybe you can actually figure something out.* I was feeling whiney and irritable by this time. So I got up to fix a cup of tea and finished up some leftover hummus, a handful of olives, some figs. Then I climbed the stairs again to the sofa, now basking in the perfect in-between light, what the Greeks call "lykofos" or "wolf light" just after the sun has gone down but before darkness.

I had made no decision to do anything, but I inadvertently began to concentrate my thoughts on Kalypso's house, how it had looked especially after Eugenia and I had opened the gate and gone up to the terrace with the potted plants all dried out. I was still trying to figure out exactly what I wanted to know about him, about the work he was doing. Did I need to go inside again? I thought of his odd dark little living room, and wondered where the stairs would be to the upper floor . . . . I had obviously overwrought myself with obsessive fretting, and as the sun went down, I dozed off in this state. Concentrating my thoughts and lying on that 'magic' sofa . . . . Foolish girl! Oh, foolish girl!

I woke up on top of a sunny hill in a patch of wild fennel. Fennel can grow pretty tall, and since I was sitting on the ground, I was effectively concealed in a little forest of these plants with their bright green feathery leaves. Since it happens to be, next to parsley, one of my favorite grazing foods, I reached out, broke off a handful, and began munching the licorice-flavored herb. I heard nothing but a mild breeze, saw nothing but perfect blue sky over my head. I could have been at home in my own garden, except for the abundance of this one plant, but I knew I had dream-traveled again: the sofa was gone, I was outside, it was the middle of the day, and Heloise was nowhere in sight.

Cautiously, I got up onto my knees and poked my head up through the fronds. A few yards away from me, also on his knees, was someone in a white tee shirt, straw hat, and dark blue jeans. He – I was fairly sure – seemed to be cutting fennel stems and piling the leaves onto a piece of cloth on the ground beside him. A fennel harvester. His arms looked young, well developed, and he seemed to be humming slightly to himself as he worked. This was not Kalypsos, nor was it anyone else I had yet seen on Ikaria, if indeed that's where I was. I turned quickly to look around me in all directions, and saw that yes, I was indeed in Kalypsos' garden, a good distance to the rear of his house. I could see the square tower in the distance rising above the low sprawl of the villa itself. Should I clear my throat? Should I just lie down and dream myself back home before I started getting into trouble?

"Hey!" I said.

He turned around, not terribly quickly as one startled, but as if he might have heard a bird going past and wanted to check on it.

We looked at each other. He was a young man, more likely in his 20's than my age, with large blue eyes and long reddish-blonde sideburns sticking down beside his straw hat, which was firmly lodged over the tops of his ears. A puzzled look came over his face, then he shrugged a little and grinned. I grinned back.

"You never know," he said, shaking his head.

I made a face to indicate I didn't understand.

"I mean," he shrugged again, more elaborately, "in a place like this, you never know who will turn up. Are you alive between incarnations, an elemental, magic, or one of those, those – people who live on after they die?"

Suddenly, for no reason, I got the hiccups. I opened my mouth to answer him and instead made a noise like a frog singing in the reeds. Then we both laughed, which caused me to hiccup more.

"Here," he handed me a plastic jug, having courteously unscrewed the lid, and I took a couple of slow swigs of water, breathing carefully after each one. In a little bit I was back to normal.

"Thanks," I said. "What are you doing?"

"Oh, I'm picking some fennel for the guy who owns this place," he waved his hand back at the house. "He's a wizard, I guess you'd say. He's doing elixirs, going through the alphabet. Right now he's on 'm', I think." He grimaced a little. "I know fennel doesn't begin with an 'm', but then he's Greek!"

I decided to sit back down again, but then I couldn't see him very well, so I stood up and walked over closer, slowly so he wouldn't think I was jumping out of the bushes at him.

"That's Kalypsos," I said, squinting a bit to see what his reaction would be. He had stopped picking fennel and was sitting on the balls of his feet as if ready to chat for a bit. He nodded at the name, and looked at me more closely now that I was easier to see.

"You look familiar," he said, then flushed a little in embarrassment.

"I've been dead for several years," I said laconically, "and when I died I was about 87. Aside from that, who knows, we might have met sometime."

"Yeah," he said, and his face grew serious. "I keep forgetting. It's the same for me, except I died the age I am now, 24. So, I decided to stay this way."

"You must be from the U.S." We might have been two tourists meeting at a bar in Rome.

"Washington, D.C. I was a pilot. I died of the flu. It was my first job. Kind of pissed me off, if you know what I mean. Still, I thought I'd take a crack at this immortality thing, even though the rules were kind of hard, you know – " he stopped, looked at me a little sideways, knowing we were both starting in the middle, but what is the beginning in a situation like this?

"How did you get here?" I waved my hand around.

He shook his head and rolled his eyes. "Long story. Need heap big campfire, many marshmallows – except I hate marshmallows." He half closed his eyes in a kind of conspiratorial look, closed his front teeth together and made a little hissing sigh, as if deciding to confide in me. "I started dreaming my way around. It was a thing I learned from my brother and sister."

I felt a twang of nostalgia, thinking of my own son and daughter, but I nodded so he would continue.

"I think I got caught on my first trip out, I'm not exactly sure. All I know is that I seem to have some kind of bondage deal to work out with Kalypsos. He can't hurt me, in terms of, you know, putting me under a nasty spell and then cutting off bits of skin for samples. But I have to come over here to the island and be his servant once a week. Mostly he sets me out here in the garden doing stuff with plants. I'm learning a lot, actually. Might come in handy later."

"What happens if you try to leave, or if you just don't come?"

"Oh, it doesn't work that way," he shook his head. "As soon as I go to sleep, bam! I'm here. It's like a broken record. I can't go anywhere else any more, the way I used to. Not that I ever got really good at the dream travel, I was just starting into it. I guess that's why I got caught, I was an amateur. Anyhow, regular as clockwork, I report to work." He sighed and fell forward onto his knees, just for a change in position, then stretched his arms behind him and yawned. "I just hope this won't last forever. I know we're supposed to live alone, and maybe this is my punishment, but I really don't think so. It's too weird, it's too – oh, I don't know – random!"

"Do you have any idea what he's doing with these plants?" As soon as I spoke, I felt a surge of greed inside that surprised me. I felt my soul turn to look at that greed, the way a mouse would look down at a spider on the floor in front of it, two different small creatures not knowing what to make of one another. Should I close my ears to the answer? But this wasn't a normal question and answer conversation anyhow; it was totally unpredictable. I was enjoying myself immensely.

"Yeah, actually, I do, although he hasn't told me." He squinted up at towards the house, as if looking at his watch. How much time could he take from his task? "It's hard to explain. I mean, I don't think he's working alone, doing his own thing. I think he's been chosen to do some—well, it's not even an experiment." He wrinkled his forehead, trying to find the words. "Do you read Plato?"

"Well, I have read some, yes."

"He's doing some Platonic thing. You know, with the Forms. He's working somehow with the Absolute Plants. Like here, with this fennel," he picked up a stem and held it up to the light. "What is the absolute fennel supposed to look like, and taste like, and what is it supposed to *do*?" He stopped again, as if he had started down another dead end path, and tried to think of a different way to explain. He turned and waved his hand around the garden.

"This place is in between everything. Whatever happens here is not physical, exactly, and it's also not theoretical. It's in-between, like a basket hanging from a balloon. This garden, for example, is infinite." He stopped, tilting his head slightly, and quickly bent over the plants. "He's coming!" he whispered.

Quickly I flattened down on my stomach and slithered as far away from him as I could, back into the fennel where I had landed.

In a little while I heard light footsteps, coming not from the direction of the house, but the opposite way, up the slope from what I had always assumed must be the "end" of the garden, a stone wall perhaps, or a fence or someone else's orchard. Apparently not if the garden was infinite.

I thought I would be able to hear them talk, but I could not. Their voices were too low, and there was no wind to carry them. After awhile I found myself relaxing in the sun, the quiet, noticing a series of delightful smells. Maybe the rest of my life would consist of moving slowly from one garden to another, learning the bees by name, working my way through the alphabet of plants, that particular infinity . . . .

"Ah, you have returned!" I heard a lazy voice drawl over me. I was in such an odd frame of mind I almost failed to recognize it as a

Anita Sullivan

voice, the words as language. But I managed to sit up and put my arms around my knees. I looked up into those black eyes. What could I say?

"May I assume your willingness, then, to give aid to us in our enterprise?" He stood with his legs slightly apart, arms folded.

"I don't know," I said truthfully. I was struggling to make judgments. In some ways he seemed like a typical Greek small farmer in his 50's, with his taut, compact body, curly hair, sun-browned skin, and the air of male authority such men usually reek of that makes them so difficult to communicate with in any meaningful way. Yet there was a depth to his eyes, a grace to the way he held himself, that signaled the possibility of wisdom, even of uncertainty. Could such a mien be dissembled? Did he know how much of a sucker I am for diffidence? Next to intelligence, love of beauty, humor, and grace, that is. I shrugged and stood up, so we would at least be negotiating from a position of physical equality.

"Yes, I came back because I am curious about what you are doing. If you are doing anything that harms people, I don't want to help you. If you even know what 'harms people' means."

I figured I'd just say what I wanted to say, and if he understood me, all the better. If not, I didn't really care.

"Harm doesn't come into it," he said, and his tone was dismissive. I wrote him off again, at least in terms of honest, direct communication. I glanced quickly around behind him and as far to each side as I dared without obviously turning my head. I couldn't see the young man anywhere. But I was tempted to take a chance. After all, if Kalypsos had people like this young man working for him, even if not exactly willingly, he was probably just carrying on a scientific experiment, not doing the work of a powerful necromancer trying to subvert natural laws. Nor was it the possibility of death or even torture that made me hesitate. There on my knees among the fragrant herbs I was amazed to recognize that I had developed a stance about my life. This stance included a strong reluctance to take an active role in any large project that might have a huge moral outcome, even if I were convinced that the project was meant to change Universe for the better. My path here is a different path.

"I can't explain what we are doing here," he continued. "Not that I would not wish it, but it is impossible. Plants are the physical plane connection, and although there is far more involved than merely plants, that is how you will perceive it, and how you will begin to work. The work is continuous, vital, difficult, and occasionally dangerous. I can only say this: our work does not lead to making any reality better or worse. We only work with the manifesting, so that it may continue . . . ." His voice grew soft, almost hoarse. His eyes held mine in a way that would have been hypnotic, because they were steady, penetrating, deep, and totally impersonal in that way of animals, caves, stars. Yet I didn't feel enchanted, in fact I felt invigorated and clear.

"What would you like me to do?" I asked.


A Centaur


*"Then he laughed for the seventh time, drawing breath, and while he was laughing he cried, and thus the soul came into being."*
(Marie-Louise von Franz)


He wanted me to keep the centaurs out of his garden.

Anita Sullivan

Shrugging eloquently, the palms of his hands turned up, his dark eyes looking skyward, Kalypsos was the picture of the put-upon necromancer, or necromancer-in-crisis I might have said. The subtext of his request could have read something like this: *Normally I would not waste your talents upon such a shabby task as this, Kyria, but the creatures will not listen to reason, and force is impossible . . . .*

He spoke as if this was the role he had planned for me all along, even back when Eugenia and I were tangled up in the vines behind his house and I had been convinced he wanted to throw us into a vat to extract our vital essences. He hinted that two of us would, indeed, have been preferable, but made no direct suggestion that I should go back and bring Eugenia here as well. A bird in the hand, he probably figured, sensibly enough.

We walked around the periphery, its low, irregular stone wall that wouldn't keep a goat out, much less a full grown centaur. Probably not even a cat or dog, certainly not rabbits, unicorns, or just about any other creature I could think of, not to mention most vines and weeds. But during this stroll, which lasted about an hour (so much for the garden being "infinite)," I came to understand something important about Kalypsos: *He could not leave.* He was confined to this garden for eternity. His life depended upon its continuing to flourish. But not only that, he was passionate about the plants under his care. The nature of this passion I didn't quite understand, since there were a number of possibilities. He could be raising plants in a nursery, to send out some-where into the cosmos on a regular basis for restoring others which had died or gone extinct. He could be experimenting with new species, crossing samples from a whole myriad of eons and realities, and in some sense aiding someone's attempt to introduce new powers into the world. He could be simply trying to keep himself alive by tending a normal but especially large and vigorous garden of herbs, vegetables and flowers. But for whom? He could be a pantheist who worshipped plants and had some sort of mystical connection with their souls, like the people at the Findhorn Garden in Scotland. He could be a wicked, or semi-wicked, or barely wicked alchemist who was experimenting with extracts from plants for his own maniacal and power-hungry ends. This had been my first assumption, and I now laid it to rest for good. Kalypsos was not in this place to do his own thing, and he was not the tool of some large evil power trying to get its foot in the door.

But centaurs?

"I'm not very big," I pointed out. "I can't wrestle them to the ground. They have hooves, anyhow, and I've always been afraid of horses. Can't you just set me to work pulling weeds or something?"

I found that talking to him this way he missed about half of what I said, but it gave him the impression that I was paying attention. He picked up the stem of some nearby plant to chew on, and waved his hand out over the countryside beyond the stone wall. There I could see the dark points of cypress trees amid shorter trees, shrubs, all tumbling down slopes with here and there another stone wall peeking through the vines, and all of it ending up in a ravine, at the bottom of which would be a dry stream bed lined with boulders. Did the centaurs live here? I had never seen one, but I knew they were half man, half horse. Ikaria was the kind of place you would find them still showing up.

"Among the Old Creatures of earth, they hold the highest position," said Kalypsos, as if reading my thoughts. "Because they are half human they can speak both the language of humans and the Old Tongue with equal fluency. They are immensely powerful, and very

Anita Sullivan

strange. Some say they were the first here, before gods and heroes broke in two, before humans took to the plow and lost their facility with the Old Tongue, long before that for certain. Unlike the gods, however, and unlike the ancient stones in your own ancestral land of Britain, they do not require belief to keep them alive. In this, they are truly unique and powerful."

"What kind of trouble do they bring you?"

"They break things," he said shortly. "Their weakness is wine. They are always after wine. Anything stored in an urn or a jar is fair game to their hooves. Though they kick with fair skill, amazing dexterity for creatures so large, nevertheless they do immense damage over time. I bury my urns, or I keep them high in the towers. But this only angers them, and they leap the walls and thrash around in the garden like large dogs, destroying months of work, delicate cross-breedings that have taken centuries to perfect. It is . . . it is simply outrageous!" He puffed out his cheeks and expelled his breath in a huge sigh. Even someone who presumably had all eternity in which to work, could be excused for loathing vandalism.

"Why do you think I can help? What do you expect me to do — to actually do?"

He looked directly at me, squinting slightly so that his black eyes were shadowed by his eyelashes and seemed darker than normal. For some reason I suddenly felt as if I were back inside a familiar church with a vaulted roof, sitting in one of the wooden pews in the quiet. It was a Lutheran church where I used to take piano lessons when I was a teenager, and later where I used to tune the piano every month, even though I was never a member and never went to any of the Sunday services. I would sit there in the pew waiting for my lesson, and

I never felt so secure in all my life. Something about the high back of the pew, and the quiet, and how the light came in through lavender and gray and pale green slits of glass spread at random up and down the side walls of the church. Everything whimsical, everything in balance, just the way life ought to be. Sometimes after my lesson I would sit there and talk with one of the other students, or with several of them and the teacher, and it was like a little cul-de-sac in space and time. We felt this was exactly what we should be doing. I smiled now as I remembered that, and realized the memory of it gave me a new strength.

"You will be able to listen to their laughing and not go mad," Kalypsos said with a wry little grin. "Maybe laugh back. I don't know what will keep them out, but it is not physical strength or I would not have asked you."

Now it was my turn to squint. "Asked me" indeed! Like that young man I had met, was I now going to be trapped into coming here every time I fell asleep? But clearly I was volunteering for this task. I was intrigued by this assignment (being ignorant of its full danger). In fact, I thought the first thing I would do—if Kalypsos was ever going to go away and leave me alone—was to find that young man and see if he knew anything about the centaurs, and maybe if he would help me, at least with ideas. We could sit in a church pew together for a couple of years and make plans.

Kalypsos did leave, and I was able to wander around until I found the lad again, still on his knees in the sun.

"Tell me your name!" I blurted out, as soon as he saw me.

"Eden," he said, sticking out his hand.

"Carley," I replied. We shook hands, then I quizzed him about the centaurs.

"Never heard of 'em," he said, removing his cap to scratch his head in genuine distressed puzzlement. "I mean, I know the word, and it's not surprising to find things like that around here. But beyond them being half horse and half man – which half, by the way?" He stopped himself and grinned, as his imagination tried to put together the halves in a variety of ways. I explained that it was the back half that was horse, so they had four horse legs, but the torso, head and brains of humans. Well, brains maybe, but I don't know about minds.

"Can they whinny?"

"Good question! I know Kalypsos said something about their laughter driving people crazy. So very likely they make some kind of non-human noises."

We were both quiet, thinking about these creatures. I was seeing them jumping over the stone wall in the dusk, herds of them, graceful and wily.

"Go away! Shoo! Shoo!" Eden was chuckling and making sweeping motions with his hands. He looked over at me. "Just practicing," he grimaced. I smiled and shook my head. Then I stood up, dusting my jeans.

"It's really not your responsibility," I said. "And I don't know how much time and energy I feel compelled to put into it myself." Then I paused and frowned. "What do you think, is this garden important? Is it worth defending from the centaurs?"

Eden stood up too, and looked back towards the house along the tangle and mass of greenery, dark and light. "I just can't believe it's a real problem," he said slowly, a bit puzzled. "I guess I expect different rules here, not the usual problems we had back – back in the real world. I mean, wouldn't he have automatic protection here, if he's doing some big universal project?"

"You think he's making them up?"

"'Life is an illusion,'" said Eden softly. Then he turned around and flashed a grin. "I don't believe that, whatever it means anyway. And yet I do believe it at the same time. Why do things we aren't used to always have to seem like an illusion?"

"I thought it was the other way around," I murmured, only half listening. "The stuff we take for granted is the illusion, and the reality is stranger than we can imagine, so we don't even notice it when it happens."

And I was noticing a centaur in broad daylight.

Eden, seeing my shocked glance, turned towards the back of the garden and saw it too. Far enough away to be only a shape still, without much detail, it seemed to be nibbling at the tip ends of some feathery plant.

"Yeah, how do they eat, come to think of it?" said Eden, a very direct and practical young man I was beginning to see. "No hands to pick up stuff, and yet they can't exactly graze, can they?"

"Yes, they have hands," I informed him. But my breath was coming quickly. Illusion or not, it suddenly seemed very difficult to me to think I could take part in banishing such a creature from this garden, or any garden.

"Should I go talk to him?" I asked. But Eden had already started in that direction, walking casually as if he meant to go there anyway, garden gloves in his fist and straw hat jammed firmly back on his head. I hurried to catch up.

Anita Sullivan

The centaur stood its ground as we approached, watching us through its odd goat eyes, while continuing to chew. It was the size of a huge horse, so that the man's head rose still a few inches above Eden, who must have been six foot two or so. Curly dark hair, beard, huge bronzed shoulders, and a stillness that came from its presence like a reverse magnetism, fending us off. We approached the creature like human figures in one of those Renaissance paintings who are holding up their arms to shield themselves from the glory of God.

Such an animal could do much damage in a garden, for sure, and this one seemed none too careful about where he placed his hooves. Leaves and stems lay crushed in little heaps around him. Anger flared in me, suddenly and unexpectedly, out of proportion to what the situation seemed to call for. After all, this centaur was simply a large and exotic pest, was he not? I mean, here we are in a potential paradise, and we are spending our time sorting out petty quarrels between neighbors just as if we were back home in Peoria? How many levels of reality to we have to slog through to get past this essential *pettiness*? This creature is too glorious to be taking on the role of a mere nuisance. Can't somebody deal with this? Are the Arbiters up there now doubled over in laughter, and if so, they are jolly well part of the problem.

A host of such thoughts were surging through me, raising my blood pressure even as I was raising my head to regard the centaur as a work of art. Amazement, admiration, fear, and yes, a kind of heart-shattering adoration—in that order. I felt myself being *taken over*.

"This garden," I stammered. The beginning of trying to do my job. Did centaurs speak? I looked over at Eden, who was staring. The centaur looked at both of us, and we saw that his huge eyes had that slit yellow pupil down the middle, and this gave the impression – the *illusion?* That he was thinking thoughts we could not understand. Eden and I started talking then, and found ourselves carrying on a conversation while still fixing our gazes on the centaur.

"Did you know that Kalypsos cannot leave this garden?" I asked.

"No!" He gave an emphatic sigh. "Hmm, that explains some things," he said.

"It might be a punishment," I went on.

"Maybe – not a punishment any more," said Eden.

"What do you mean?" I shook my head.

He shrugged. "Well, the prisoner getting used to his cell kind of thing. I mean, if you were stuck in this place" – he paused. "Stuck? That's impossible. It goes on forever."

"No, it doesn't, I walked around the entire garden wall with Kalypsos earlier today, and it took about an hour."

"Another illusion."

"Besides, it <u>can't</u> be infinite, look out there beyond the wall, there's other stuff out there, what's that?"

"Another infinity."

"Oh," I said. "Well, wouldn't Kalypsos want that infinity too? Or at least, if he saw *someplace else* wouldn't he want the freedom to go there? Don't we all long for freedom above everything else?" But even as I said these words I was thinking *infinity in a grain of sand, eternity in an hour.* What if Kalypsos was satisfied, totally at peace, in his confinement? Why were we talking about the satisfaction of Kalypsos, anyway?

"He mainly wants to keep his garden healthy," said Eden.

Anita Sullivan

"Do you think there are many centaurs?" I asked, lifting my chin a little higher towards the creature who stood in perfect stillness before us, like an enormous gate.

"Ikaria is a small island," said Eden, his voice light. "Here we need only one unicorn, one wizard, one witch, one teller of bees . . . ." I could feel the words coming out of him as if from a different spirit. Surely he would not have known all this of his own accord.

"Then perhaps," I went on after a long silence. "Perhaps this centaur is meant to be a Guardian of the walls. If the walls are truly infinite, as you say, he would be able to patrol them with little damage to the plants, since he would never come back again to the same spot."

The centaur began to laugh.

I doubled over as if struck in the stomach. The sound bubbled out, mirthful, silly, old, and infinitely sad. Oil and water, the way you can believe and not believe something at the same time. *But you cannot be alive and dead at once, they're not the same!* I wanted to cry out but my ears were too full. The sound turned itself into a physical presence that came at my face, forcing me to abruptly reverse directions, to bend over backwards until, like a gymnast, I fell into the position of a backbend, but on my elbows, not the palms of my hands. I was like a crow on an interstate, contorting itself into an unnatural position in order to avoid being run over by a car. Yet the weight of the beast as it passed over me like a shadow, without touching, was close to unbearable. I choked, I felt a white heat split my body in half from neck to groin; a stench rose from the earth beneath me, steam. And more laughter, as if knives were prying bones quickly from the sides of dogs as they howled, cutting them off sharp, one-two-three, then off into a garbled sighing wail of utter resignation, a galloping and galloping that lurched my head from side to side as if someone were striking it like a gong. Then I was violently sick inside a pinwheel of colors, before I lost consciousness.

## The Fisher Queen

Eden picked me up, slung me onto his shoulder, and climbed over the stone wall. Not an easy matter for a guy whose foot has just been shattered by the hooves of a centaur as he was trying to keep it from destroying someone – namely, me. He tried to stab it in the haunches with his garden shears, for lack of any other readily available weapon, and for lack of any foresight as to the likelihood of doing more good than harm to either me or himself. In the confusion that ensued, the creature released me in order to kick Eden, and then something else happened that he explained much later, when we were both sitting on the terrace of my villa, nursing our injuries.

"A look came over the centaur's face," Eden said, and a look came over *his* face too, a mixture of revulsion and awe. "As if it had suddenly realized something. Changed its mind. Sort of like demonic possession, when the demon goes away. I could swear it *was sorry* for what it just did, really deeply sorry. I mean *deeply*." He stopped, looking for words that wouldn't sound moronic and repetitive. "It was like he had committed all the crimes of the whole world, over again. Like he had done this before, and couldn't stop, and kept waking up. I could feel that, and see it in his face. Like this was a punishment for him, and when he woke up he was totally wise. I saw all this just after he kicked me, when he had stopped rearing up and was standing there on all fours looking down at you on the ground, and me on the ground

Anita Sullivan

too." Eden shook his head, his voice choking, almost in tears. I could see him re-living the incident, looking at it again, pacing around the edge of the scene. He smiled, as he found a way back in. "Like office hours," he said softly. "We could come to him during these break times, when he wasn't crazy, and he would be as tame as a bunny rabbit, and he could teach us amazing things about the world that nobody else knows. *Nobody else.*"

Eventually, Eden pulled himself over to where I was lying, and saw that I was unconscious and bleeding a little from the mouth. He checked me over but my clothes were not ripped, only wildly disheveled.

"Obviously you were injured," he said, "but I couldn't see any evidence that – er, any part of the – er, animal had actually touched you anywhere."

"You mean, I was neither stomped upon nor raped," I said matter-of-factly, with a deep shuddering sigh. This was days later. He nodded, frowning.

"What happened to the centaur?" I asked.

"I have no idea," said Eden, wrinkling his forehead. "I truly did not stop to see. I think I felt pretty sure he wouldn't bother us any more, but I was still in panic mode, and all I could do was just get us the hell out of there."

"You know," he said, somewhat later, "I bet he hasn't reformed at all. I bet he's still as dangerous as ever." A painful, puzzled look shadowed his eyes. "Maybe he's been this way for a bazillion years. Back and forth, back and forth."

When he got us over the wall, he felt we had entered a safe zone, and so he collapsed.

"Infinity hopping," he said with a little smile. We were sitting on the upper terrace of my villa, dosed with medicine, neither of us able to walk. Eden would be up and around again soon enough, but not without a limp that has yet to go away. Me, I'm still waiting to get back to normal walking without pain. Is this what they call the *turning point* in ancient Greek drama? I am alive, but I am not the same as before. What will the Arbiter do now? Have I fulfilled my role by taking a totally new path, by proving some new possibility? Deep inside I could feel melancholy seeping and seeping.

The others arrived soon after Eden climbed over the wall. Maybe they were already there. At any rate, he looked up through a mist of half consciousness to see a group of people coming up the slope: Eugenia, Mick, Djan and Porphyra, looking like enormous heroic silhouettes backlit by the sunset. Bringing me back was some-what tricky, since I wasn't able to do conscious dreaming quite yet, but they didn't want to leave me there on the rocky hillside with darkness coming on.

"We circled our wagons," was Djan's laconic explanation of what they had done. "We stopped over in the House of Time, partly to familiarize Eden with it for future reference. Finding your place was a little harder."

"Mick brought me here," said Eden. "We just went flying around together. It was that simple. I followed him, and we flew over this place, and he said 'There it is!' and we came down."

"The same way I found you the first time, remember?" said Mick.

Despite a chronic pain that radiated from the center of my chest down through pelvis and legs, and up into my lungs, and a complex

Anita Sullivan

memory I was still too terrified to explore, I was warmed immensely by the group of friends around me. These were people with whom, yes, I wanted to spend eternity. Maybe we would become an archetype, an ideal. But no! I no longer believed in such things. Rest in the eternal moment. Rest, rest.

Eugenia, Mick, Djan and Porphyra took turns staying with us while we recovered. Eden said he was living in "a little cabin in the woods in Maine," but he seemed quite content to convalesce in my villa, which had many spare rooms. I had deliberately designed it that way, knowing I would need the sense of an endless house if I were to spend many years alone in one. I had the romantic notion of wandering through unopened rooms like Bluebeard's wife, rooms with the furniture draped in white and the heavy drapes closed; rooms with secret passages behind bookshelves and fireplaces; rooms with odd-shaped windows of colored glass. The need for solitude, though, when it asserts itself fiercely (as it will), does not allow another person in the house, no matter how large the house, and how unlikely it is that second individual will actually show up at any given moment. Besides, hunter-gatherer societies depended for their stability upon the last resort of escape: if people didn't get along with each other, somebody left. So, inasmuch as we resemble that ancient human culture, we continue to need our own houses.

Porphyra and Eden immediately struck up a friendship. Oddly enough, it was based at first on cooking. Eden had dropped out of high school at age 17 and gone to work at a variety of fast-food places, gradually working his way up through vegetarian restaurants to a couple of long-term jobs in high-end gourmet restaurants in large cities. Only when he was faced with the prospect of spending the rest of his life with an apron on did he finally pull himself together and go to school to become a pilot. "The chef's cap just wouldn't stay on my head," he grinned, indicating his high forehead, which at age 24 was already indicating future baldness. Still, he remembered much about cooking, and soon was spending long afternoons sitting on a kitchen stool with his lame leg propped up on a chair, directing Porphyra in the culinary arts.

She, having no background that any of us could pry out of her, had no aversion to nutrition. She didn't say "Eeeeew, tofu!" or beg for pizza, ice cream and soft drinks, having apparently never known such things. And being a very independent and lively person, it wasn't long before she was thinking up variations of her own, some of them without the full sanction of her teacher. Fortunately for all of us there was a certain limitation inherent in the way we received our raw materials, from the "pipeline in the sky," as Djan called it. That is, you had to request something specifically before you got it: "Like sending your husband out to the grocery store," Eugenia pointed out once in frustration, "instead of just browsing the shelves to see what comes to mind." Nevertheless we did experience some very strange breads, puddings, pies and stir-fries during that period; some of them we actually buried quietly in the garden, since we hesitated to feed them to the lions, or to leave them out for the birds.

I was basically an invalid for a year. I no longer traveled in my dreams, except to the House of Time to visit the library, and then I always insisted upon going alone, with Heloise. I was able to walk only for short periods each day, no more than fifteen minutes at a time, and even then with the aid of a cane. My legs were slightly numb, subject to cramps and spasms if I moved them too quickly or in an awkward

Anita Sullivan

direction. I could only sit with my feet together flat on the floor, could not crouch or sit cross-legged, and turning over in bed at night was often painful. I was experiencing the full import of the Rule: that we remain mortal and thus can do damage to ourselves. The Arbiter was not going to put out a wand and go Bing and cure me! I had a regimen of creams and tonics, some reasonably hefty pain killer for the bad times, but beyond that the healing had to proceed at its own pace. And its pace was not what I would call normal; I seemed to stay exactly the same, growing neither better nor worse from week to week.

"I feel like the Fisher King," I said one day, "Or rather, the Fisher Queen."

"Who's that?" asked Porphyra.

So I told her the story of Percival, out of the Grail legend, who was riding through an immense forest for days on end, seeking the Holy Grail, and one day came upon a castle whose King had to be carried in to the Royal Feast on a litter because something was wrong with his legs. Percival noted that the King was ill and lame, but out of politeness he didn't ask, "O Sire, I see you are in great pain, what grievous wound have you endured?" Instead, because his mother had taught him to be polite around older people, he chose to remain silent. And because of his silence, the spell on the King was not broken, and the world suffered another year of drought. At least that's roughly how I remembered the story, with some extras regarding enchanting maidens who filed in during the banquet carrying the Grail. Later, when Percival tried to find the castle again, he couldn't, because it only appeared to people when the necessity arose. You couldn't find it on purpose, because it had no real location. I always loved that story.

"But we know why you are wounded, don't we?" Porphyra asked. Then she turned red and her eyes got huge, and suddenly she burst into tears and ran off up the stairs. And I got cold chills when I realized she didn't know, because it finally hit me that I didn't either. My brief encounter with the centaur was not a classic case of mortal woman gets raped by god disguised as bull or horse. The centaur was obviously not disguised as anything. And if physical rape had been its desire and intention, I most likely would be truly and finally dead by now. Yet the centaur, magnificent and ancient as he might be, had lost control and reenacted a ritual of greed and madness. The animal did me grave harm.

"I've been poisoned!" I realized suddenly. "And since nobody knows how, nobody knows how to bring about a cure. I could stay like this for eternity."

## Memory

Since my dreaming has gone dark, I practice remembering. I try to reconstruct a segment of my childhood. Poets and dreamers have said it is good to do this; certain mystics used to recommend the daily exercise of lying in bed at night trying to remember in detail everything you did from the moment you wakened in the morning. I tried this exercise a few times, back in my 40's I think, but it always made me feel slightly nauseated, and I never got past that, so I gave up. But now, during the long days of convalescence, I pass my time asking myself sudden quiz questions out of my past: what color was the kitchen floor in the house you lived in when you were going to college? What did you do on the day of your 12th birthday? The list keeps growing of questions I can't answer. Today, cautiously, I am approaching the house I lived in when I was a teenager.

I can see the outside of the house quite clearly, the narrow yellow boards, the identical windows facing the sloping front yard. I enter the back door, through the dark kitchen with the double enamel sink, past the pantry with its red and white boxes of oatmeal, blue tins of Maxwell House coffee, cans of peaches, corned beef hash and beans, the pantry where my mother sometimes saw a mouse. After that was the small bright room where my mother had done her sewing. Always this room was overflowing with soft piles of folded cloth, loosened from being mere bolts, carelessly re-wound into their rectangular shapes. Patterns, lace collars, zippers, spools and spools of thread. I can feel myself smiling and pushing them out of the way as I had always done, in order to enter the dining room. But after that, nothing. In my imagination I stand at the far edge of the dining room and peer searchingly forward like a soul about to cross the river into Hades. But all the many other rooms of the house remained shrouded in a mysterious and impenetrable fog.

"Dining room! Bedrooms!" I say to myself severely, closing my eyes. But I have lived in so many houses. Does this matter? Will I remain ill until I remember if we had a formal dining room table, or a rug on the floor, or if there were windows in this room where I lived – when? I don't even remember. Have I drunk, already, the waters of the Lake of Forgetfulness under the white cypress tree, across the meadow of asphodels? But there is a choice – for if memory serves me, the other lake, the twin on the opposite side of the throne of Hades, is called the Lake of Memory.

*"Let the healing begin!" cries the bell-wearer, from the end of the hall. A path opens for her down the length of the room so that she can be fleet, as she is wont to be. She wears the motley of a Fool, but the colors are silver and green, healing colors. Not a woman in the Kingdom who does not wish to be a bell-wearer when she grows up, though it is a position one person only keeps for a year. We all feel the strength of her message — Harmony, 'fitting together' of all that would otherwise fly apart if not so firmly bound: like logs on a raft. A daily tempering of unruliness. "Be at peace with one another, let quiet fill your hearts." It is a message lost on this assembly. It is lost on me. I don't need wine to make me reckless, my life is going from round to flat in one small set of hours at the end of this day, like a river when it meets the sea. The bell-wearer jingles past me, I can smell the oil of her anointing, hear the sputter and hiss from her torch. She will leap out through the long window at the other end of the hall, out into the garden. Her feet are bare. I long to loosen my own sandals. I long to loosen something.*

I can't remember my own life, but my head is stuffed with stories of people who never existed. The others have gone home. Porphyra too, for all I know, since she never came back down the stairs after leaving me some hours ago. I feel weighted down, and useless, deeply useless.

My villa was not built for a wheelchair, there is hardly a smooth patch of flooring anywhere in the place. Also, practically everything is on its own level: cafeteria, kitchen, music room, then the upper floors. They left my wheel chair in the music room so that I could play piano and harpsichord and go down the four steps to the kitchen, two essential daily activities. For going to bed I use my cane and am able to make it up the sets of shallow stairs to the top floor. This much I can accomplish now, and thus my willing set of nurse-maids has been shooed off to their own houses. Later they will tell me of their travels, if any, or regale me with details of the birds and butter-flies that came into their gardens, or a new idea they had for a calendar, a recipe, a game, a riddle. Meanwhile I continue to find myself op-pressed by a sense of obligation. Something I am supposed to remem-ber. Like Sherlock Holmes, must I take out my magnifying glass and look for clues? I think about this for awhile; imagine myself peering at three (why three) whitish-gray hairs set on a dark green background (velvet)? They are not human hairs. But this makes me feel slightly nauseous, the way you do when you're right-handed and trying to write with your left hand.

By way of breaking out of such musings, I wheel myself into the kitchen to scramble some eggs with green onions, mushrooms and grated parmesan. Coffee, fresh brown bread and butter, marmalade, a bowl of apricots. Painfully I drag it and myself down to the cafeteria, into which buttery sunlight is flooding. Heloise, who has been outside lying by the benches near the lions, comes up to the door and asks to be let in. I'm sure if she could have reached the latch she would have come in by herself. I smile as I imagine her raising one of her long ears to press upon the latch. I must build her a door of her own – when I am next able.

# Part V

## Bloduedd

Hello, Eden here. The whole part about the centaur might not have happened if I hadn't been on the scene, so I'm going to jump in here and keep things going while Carley is ill. Carley told me she's been writing things down. Not like that guy in Tacoma, or wherever it was who kept a diary of *everything* he did every day. Like, "I got up at 7:03 and put on my black socks and blue slacks and I looked out the window and it was raining and the temperature was 43 degrees. Then I went to pee. "His study was lined with spiral notebooks. I can just imagine one of his exciting, action-packed days: *I am sitting here at my table writing about sitting at my table writing* . . . . Shudder.

So, no, I'm sure Carley's not doing that.

Me either. In fact, I'm more likely to noodle around about ideas and lose track of anything actually going on. This whole pre-dead thing is pretty mind-blowing. I still haven't gotten used to it like the others have. I keep thinking about my earlier life, before I, you know, "died." Carley and Eugenia and the rest, they don't seem to remember any more. Or at least they never talk about it. I don't really understand that. After all, it could be like a huge long childhood, and people do talk about their childhoods.

Maybe after you die your soul can't get used to the idea that you're dead, so it hangs around for awhile before it finally says, "Oh, what the hell, I get the picture, O.K.? I'm outta here!" Maybe I'm like that, because I died so suddenly and so recently, I still have connections to my earlier life. I wasn't really done yet, and I still feel sad about that. I hope it goes away, the sad part at least.

183

But I won't write down my earlier life. It might sneak in from time to time, but I really don't want to do a biography, it's too painful. "Eden Robinson was born in Richmond, Virginia on February 17, 1976. He was the second of four children, his older sister Natalie and the twins Dan and Donna . . . ." Gosh, I wonder how the twins are doing? I really miss them, they were just finishing high school when I died. We were planning to do a back packing trip together in the Rockies that summer. And Natalie, whew! We all did our best with her "personality disorder" thing, but there didn't seem to be much hope. I mean, if my folks were going to lose a kid . . . but no, it's just a broken record to think that way. She was screwed up, but we loved her as she was. I wonder if I'll ever stop being sad about missing them all? It seems so nuts this way, they're supposed to be mourning *me*, not vice versa. I don't know if it's better to let myself think about it or to try not to. But I do feel sorry for them, and especially for Mom and Dad, because I died so suddenly and sort of uselessly. I really feel guilty about that, I know it's stupid, but I do, and I don't know if staying alive here a million years will ever make any difference. I know it happens all the time, all over the world, kids dying. But it still hurts like hell. Now I'm crying, which is stupid, I guess. I wanna be still alive. But I am still alive. It's crazy, but then life is crazy. Which is another thing. Shouldn't life be the most ordinary, comprehensible, normal thing? Why do we keep saying stuff like "Life is strange!" We shouldn't have to.

But I've gotta stop thinking that way, or at least stop writing it down. Get back to the story.

Carley is just plain out of it now. For awhile she seemed to be getting better, although it was very slow. But she was walking around some with her cane and not moaning so much. Then Porphyra and I came cruising back from a kind of stupid trip we took, where we ended up out in space, and everybody kind of freaked out. Sure, it was a real adolescent stunt, and we had no business taking such a risk. But when Carley found out, for some reason it pushed her over the edge. After that, she really did shut down. Now she mostly sits around, like an old person, and hardly talks. Eugenia and I are pretty much taking turns living at her house. It's like she just stopped getting better. Like she's waiting for something to happen. And we all wonder what we're supposed to do to break the spell. We keep trying to figure it out.

We've been having weekly conferences in the cafeteria, the five of us. We report what we've been doing during the week, and plan what to do next. It makes us feel better, anyhow. Djan has been wandering all over Australia looking at rock art sites. He thinks there will be some clue there in the drawings. "We are witness to the re-enactment of an old ritual," he says, or something like that. It doesn't make any sense to me, I mean, there aren't any centaurs in Australia, so I can't help but wonder why he's concentrating his time there. I guess it's because it is familiar to him, since he was born there and all.

Eugenia wanted to go back to Kalypsos and confront him with the fact that he had been pretty much the cause of Carley's trouble. She asked Mick to go with her.

"We thought he would have an antidote," said Mick. "To me it seems obvious that Carley's wound is a slow poison, and maybe not just physical, you know what I mean?"

They had arrived in the little alcove outside the house, where the cistern stood with its gargoyle spigots. I told them I knew all about that, having washed reams of plants there. Georgia and Kalypsos were

Anita Sullivan

standing in their bare feet, pants rolled up, sluicing and washing, laying leaves out as tenderly as babies along the wide stone walls to dry.

"We came right to the point," said Eugenia. "We told him our friend had been attacked by a centaur and was badly hurt. We asked him if he could suggest a cure." She sighed then, and closed her eyes.

Mick shook his head. "He basically told us he didn't 'do' healing, can you believe that?" I didn't believe it. I got a little angry, actually. But he insisted that his work is, oh, how did he put it, Eugenia? His work is 'in the plants themselves.' It's not that he doesn't *know* which plants have medicinal powers . . . . It's like he's under a contract, and it prohibits him from being a shaman, or a wizard."

I thought "how convenient," but that was as far as it went. Then Djan said, kind of harshly, "Was he lying?"

"I don't know," said Mick, looking at Eugenia. She shook her head slowly, her mouth scrunched into a wavy little line.

"He more or less told us," Mick said slowly, looking over at Eugenia again, "that we'd have to get the information from the centaur himself. 'The witch who makes the spell must unmake it,' he said, something like that, right?"

"Well, it's kind of true, I guess," I said. "I mean, I don't think Kalypsos' job is figuring out new uses for plants. He's not like doing pharmaceutical research. He probably hasn't got a clue how to cure the, er, what happened to Carley."

Djan nodded and half opened his mouth, but Mick interrupted.

"You'd think by now that every cure for every illness on the planet would have been discovered. Humans have been closely working with plants for, migosh, millions of years. Why do we need more research for crying out loud? Somebody knows what to do for Carley! Somebody already knows!" His voice squeaked a little.

"A cure may very well lie with the centaur himself," Djan said after awhile. "This is deep magic, old magic. It has to do with transgression, and balance." He stopped, and brought his fingers together as he always did when he was retreating into non-verbal thinking.

But Eugenia hadn't quite finished with her initial frustration.

"He managed to figure out a way to make his vines move, and to trip me and Carley up, so he does have some powers with the plants!" Her eyes were flashing, as if she wanted to go back and continue the argument with him.

"He's probably afraid of the centaur, after all he did ask Carley to protect him from it, or from *them*." I said. I had suddenly remembered Kalypsos talking about the centaurs like a group, or a herd, even though it seemed like one was enough for an island. One centaur per 20 square miles . . . . How could they ever have run in herds, what country would be large enough for that? Africa? My brain started going off on a tangent.

"Yes, and also it's the nature of herbal remedies that they tend to be general rather than specific," Djan was saying. "I mean general such as: cramps, heart irregularity, loss of hair, rheumatism, and the like. But the poison from, uh—certain attention by a centaur would be very ancient as well as very specific, and no human would likely know the cure. It wouldn't exactly be alive in the folklore . . . ."

*It might not exist* we were probably all thinking. But then I remembered the look on the centaur's face. Remorse was the only word for it. If centaurs were fundamentally bi-polar—oh, god, like my sister Natalie—they spent half their lives trying to compensate for what they did in the other half. Surely, then, they would have an Old Magic cure for their own poisons? I decided to let that thought rest, and wait till the right opportunity to bring it up to the group. Not much point in raising false hopes when we were so worried.

Which brings me to Porphyra. I hate to say this, but she's a real fly in the ointment. I mean, she's great, she's fun, a neat kid, and we all love her . . . . But besides being a *kid,* I know she's not exactly like us, because they told me the story of how they found her. So she doesn't really fit in here in our group. It's all well and good in other places, we run into all kinds of spirits and creatures who aren't exactly human. But here at Carley's it's kind of like a safe house for us. We all need to be the same. And because Porph doesn't exactly fit, nothing has been going right. Yeah, that's it. I don't know where she is from, she doesn't talk about it, and when I ask her, her eyes get big and she doesn't seem to know what I mean. There's something missing with her. Or else there's something extra. Because now she seems to be growing.

First of all she got lost trying to get back to Tasmania without Djan to take her there. Or, at least that's what we think now. We had sort of forgotten about her when Carley and I came back, not right away, but after my leg was getting better, and everybody was going home more often again. Somehow in the back and forth, Porph got left behind. And something spooked her, something Carley said, I don't know. So she just disappeared. She went upstairs before dinner and didn't come down. So, I went after her by dreaming, since there was nobody else around but me.

I half expected to find myself back on my knees with a trowel and a bucket, slaving away in Kalypsos' garden, although another part of me realized that his hold on me had been broken somehow, after I jumped over the wall with Carley wounded. So now I was going out like some Greek hero, after another maiden in distress. Perfectly capable maidens, by the way, and me not much of an experienced dreamer either. But isn't that how it is – heroes are made, not born. Well, at least that's how I see it.

I dreamed myself to a place full of deep, rolling fog, dark like storm clouds. I was totally disoriented. I mean, I'm used to being up in the air, and my pilot training taught me how to take care of myself upside down, falling, tipping, and not knowing which way was up. That wasn't the problem. I felt as if I had gone out of *all worlds*, like I was in some place that didn't exist at all, as if I had been snuffed out. But I also felt responsible, as if I was meant to figure something out.

The first thing I thought was "Move!" So I began swooshing my arms around (while I still knew what arms were). It was like swimming, only there was no water or air. I did move a little bit, but nothing else happened. Then I decided to do nothing. This was scary, since if I did nothing, I might forget everything, even who I was. But after a-while I did nothing a little bit harder. My mind got really quiet. I felt like some kind of a radio receiver setting up a differential. I mean, I had this clear notion—that's all I could call it, a *notion*—that if I was calm enough inside my head then something would have to come in, because my head would be quieter than the outside. Like a vacuum sucking things up."

Then into my head came the clear idea that Porphyra was nearby, and that she was lost.

So, I kept working on this mind-differential thing. It was like being an equation instead of just thinking about one, sort of made me

Anita Sullivan

dizzy, but it was better if I concentrated on that, instead of actually thinking about Porphyra. It almost became a way of navigating; I felt little cool wisps coming in, and they began to guide me. It took forever. But eventually—and it could have been days, I mean *days*—I bumped into her. It was like she was another cloud. We were both clouds. But she was a knot, a big purple knot. And I couldn't figure out where we needed to be, where we were, or how to get from one to the other. Totally impossible. So, I just kept nudging. Eventually we sort of communicated. And then I felt a kind of *snap!* It was like a book closing. A very new book. And we fell out of the sky together, to my place in Maine. We were on the grass in front of my cabin. We lay there for awhile, and then I took her inside and gave her some food.

But there was one more thing. *Porphyra had grown.* During the time she was away, she had gotten older. Not only was she taller by an inch or so, but she was, well, she had developed – I'm a guy, I couldn't help but notice – she was poking out of her tee shirt. Her eyes were different too, they had been a lovely grayish violet color, and now, well, they were the same color I guess, but you couldn't really see them. As if the cloud she was drifting in during her journey had come down, like a cataract, I don't know. Djan looks like that sometimes. She just looked older. And that's not supposed to happen here, is it?

Yike! It's enough to make me tear my hair. My sideburns, that is, since I don't have much otherwise, having what is euphemistically called a "high forehead." Not like Djan with his mat of curls, or even Mick, who has let his hair get down around his shoulders. I mean, what use is this second life – this second chance – if we're all going to be in agony all the time, or at least about the same percentage of the time that we were before? What's the point? "Agony, agony!" I can just hear

Bugs Bunny's voice saying that. I'm trying to keep my spirits up, but it's hard.

Eugenia came back from the Library today with a story about a princess in Welsh mythology called Bloduedd who was made of flowers. A couple of wizards put her together out of nine different kinds of blossoms, so she looked and acted human even though technically she wasn't. Porphyra! we all thought. She was upstairs somewhere again, not at our meeting, so we all kind of nodded at each other. This sounded like the right story. But on top of that – and this is even more uncanny – Eugenia learned that the mother of the original centaur was made out of clouds! Her name was Nephele, and she was put together by the god Zeus to look exactly like his wife Hera, to fool some guy who was trying to seduce Hera. Anyhow, the guy had sex with the cloud woman and she bore him a son named Centaurus, who was the first centaur.

Somehow we think this is all important. But we don't know how. We decided not to tell Porph, because she's busy acting like a teenager now, being unpredictable and moody all the time, and this might just upset her. But Eugenia had an idea.

"When Carley and I were in Kalypsos' garden the first time, he told us he knew we were still alive, because he could see "the silver cord." She remembered him saying those words. "So, if we went with Porphyra, back to see him, he could tell us if she had a silver cord. Then we'd know at least if she's – well, if she's like one of us."

*Oh, human you mean?* I thought, and probably the others did too.

"So, what if she's not?" said Mick. He gave a big shrug and made a face. "I would bet she's not, but so what? We stole her. We made her come here. She's fine. We love her. Why rock the boat?"

"We need to know," said Djan.

"O.K., so if she's not alive, or maybe not even human, are we going to kick her back out, back to the place we took her from?" This was Mick again.

"This does feel like something we do need to know, if it's possible," said Eugenia, echoing Djan. She winced a little. "We would have to figure out afterwards what to do about it."

"We just have to assume that *finding out* is the best thing to do," said Djan, not sounding particularly wise or decisive, which was unusual for him.

Mick made a wry face but didn't continue his argument.

"It probably all has something to do with Carley," he said.

So, it's back to Ikaria, the three of us, me, Porph and Mick. "Porph n' Mick, Porph n' Mick,' Wow! Sounds like a song. Djan and Eugenia are staying behind to look after Carley. And also because I think we're all feeling sort of weirdly fatalistic—is that the right word? Like we're in danger of being drawn over to the Dark Side if we aren't careful. As if Carley's thing with the centaur has blown our defenses, and now we're all more vulnerable. No, I've got it! We're feeling like we've gotten outside the safety zone, as if we're *not even in the original Experiment any more*, but instead we're all out there flailing around in the huge Afterlife Soup like all the other spirits and energies or whatever. So, the reason Eugenia and Djan are staying behind is more like they are acting as both a conscience and a safety committee, to make sure we stay in the bounds of what we are supposed to be doing. Yeah, that makes sense. Even if we can't put words to it, we all know there is something we're "doing," and we want to keep doing it.

So, anyhow, me and Mick, we'll fly off to Ikaria with Porphyra between us, holding each of us by the hand, and we'll save the world as we know it. I've gotta stop going off like this, but it's fun. Yes, folks, my account will probably be a little jerky for awhile, like TV news where the guy gets off in the corner and mutters into his tape recorder, "Now we're on the site, and we've marked off the coordinates. We don't know what to expect yet. There have been rumors of armed militia . . . ."

You know, a really crazy thought occurred to me. Carley goes to the Library a lot and is friendly with the Librarian. Anyhow, what if instead of writing things down one after another like I'm doing, "Today we had a meeting, and now we've decided to go to Ikaria again . . . ." What if she is *still telling the story and we don't even know it?* Maybe she's sending out unconscious messages, and then somehow it shows up in a book at the Library. I can just see it now, a shelf at the edge of one of those aisles that go off into the distance like a path into forest, only a different color. And suddenly, blam—or maybe not suddenly, maybe gradually emerging out of the mist—a Book takes shape. Another book. This is the Story of Porphyra and, and, well, the rest of us. Whatever we are in the story. That could be happening even now. And here I am blabbing away for nothing.

Anita Sullivan

# The Three

The three women sat in white plastic chairs under the olive trees and talked. They had been doing this every afternoon for 100 years. They didn't know it was 100 years, almost to the day, because they had never kept track. They only knew it was what they did, and that they never tired of it. They talked of many things: of their imaginary children, in great detail, since their real ones had grown up long ago. They did not speak of wars or quarrels with their husbands or of difficulties with neighbors, or complaints about the local government, since none of these were matters that happened any longer. Instead, the rhythms of their conversation flowed and ebbed in synchrony with random wonderings that came to their minds, "mist in the ears" as one of them put it, the weather in the huge sense of how it defined the days. Mostly, they talked about the day at hand, from beginning to end.

They were at leisure, but never bored. This was not the "boring village" of Kavafy's poem, where the country lad expresses his desire to get away to the excitement of the city. There was nowhere else for them to go, therefore they had no desire to go elsewhere. They had learned the fine art of contentment, huge contentment, the kind that makes wiggling the toes and stretching the arms and legs into a conscious ritual, and melodious, luxuriant sighing the way that one punctuates the passage of time. Dancing too. Sometimes, upon whim, they would put a tape or a CD into the battered boom box and rise, one by one, or all at once, to make a circle in the dirt. There they would kick and sway with half smiles on their faces, knowing they were not being observed. Every now and then, once a month perhaps, one of them would say, "It's a wonder we still have anything to say to each other," and after that, maybe for a few days, they would fall silent. The silence would rise and throb around them, indistinguishable from the sound of bees, flies, or the underlying tremble the wind made by strumming lightly upon columns of air. And into their three minds would come a cool breeze of fear. Would the silence take them? Had they not drunk deeply enough from the lake of Memory after all? Would they stumble together out into the field of asphodels to lie, face up and eyes wide open, beneath the white cypress tree, forever awake and forever dumb?

On this afternoon they had just begun to speak again after an especially long period of silence. The three of them, almost from the beginning, had discarded their given names and jokingly renamed themselves Clothos, Atropos and Lachesis, the three fates of early mythology. These were the formal versions. In everyday parlance, they called each other Chloe, Atraki, and Lachoula.

"I had a wonder in a dream," said Atraki.

"Tell!" said the others.

"I wondered if there are others like us loose in the world."

A long silence. Then Chloe said, "Since this is not a new wonder for us, you must have had it more strongly than before. Do you know why?"

Atraki nodded slowly. "I could hear someone's feet on the footpath to the village." She tilted her head for awhile then smiled. "Not yet. It's not happening yet, but it will."

"Not hoofs?" said Lachoula sharply, squinting a bit in alarm.

They all remembered the same thing, and looked over their shoulders with a shiver.

Anita Sullivan

"Not the centaurs again, no. They still pass by in the night sometimes."

"In the night?" said Chloe. "I haven't heard them, have you?" nodding at Lachoula. She shook her head and they both looked hard at Atraki. Into the minds of the three of them came a picture of their respective houses, the strong wooden doors behind flower-covered stone walls, doors they still closed and latched at night even though they had seen no other humans for almost 100 years.

"How many?" asked Lachoula, not referring to the centaurs.

Atraki closed her eyes to listen. Across her rosy face ran tiny tremors, her eyelashes fluttered. "Three."

Three days later their visitors came in the morning, when the three women were at home doing their work: painting, weaving, and building. Atraki was on her knees with a trowel, laying sun-dried yellow bricks into a circular pattern in her garden. She was singing. Brown and gray and yellow dust covered her clothing. She was wearing a pair of the traditional Turkish women's field pants, with wide, skirt-like legs. All three women had switched to these as their daily clothes, with much merriment about how they could never have gotten away with it in earlier days, but how comfortable and sensible the outfits were.

She heard a crunch of pebbles and looked up to see three faces regarding her with polite surprise over her waist-high garden wall. Waist high for most mortals, although because she was an unusually small person, for her the wall came to a place just below her breasts.

Atraki looked them over one by one, without smiling. Her strange green-golden eyes drew them in, marked them, and spat them out again. They seemed not to notice. But she squinted a little longer at Porphyra, noting that she did not have the *cord*. A thing that, perhaps, could be remedied.

She stood up, dusted off her hands and invited them in, as custom had decreed from the beginning of time in this part of the world. She led them down to the gate at the bottom of the garden, and they filed silently along after her, to a little terrace in a sheltered spot where the small house made a curve in back of the kitchen. Soon they were all seated on wooden stools or plastic chairs with glasses of wild cherry juice in their hands. Mick frowned through half-closed eyes at the cherries floating in the bottom of his glass. But he spoke up cheerfully: "I've been all over Ikaria, but it keeps surprising me! This is a village I've never seen. Maybe you keep yourselves hidden." Atrakis, looking again into his gray-green eyes, saw that he was keeping part of himself hidden. This surprised her, and made a small ripple on the surface of a deep cauldron of rage she was always aware of in her vicinity.

"We're here on a kind of quest," said Eden. His own senses had flashed "*witch, witch,*" to him as soon as he saw her. Something in the way she stood on the balls of her feet, as if about to fly. But out of ignorance or native wisdom, he felt no fear, only cautious optimism. He decided to tell the story in a direct way that might seem indirect, rather in an indirect way that would seem direct. The opposite of how it would have been in the "normal" world.

"We are part of a small group of human beings who came to the end of our lives, and now we are living on in a second reality. We have formed into a little company and we travel around together sometimes. Everything was going along fine for awhile, but now one of

Anita Sullivan

us is really ill, and we need to find out how to make her well again." He stopped. *Quit while you're ahead* he thought, and couldn't help making a little grimace. No matter what he said, there would be some truth and some untruth in it.

The untruth was immediately obvious. Porphyra was not really part of the company.

"I am a princess," she said. She had brought along her stuffed rabbit Lambris, and held him in front of her, sitting on her lap with his back against her stomach. Atrakis turned to look directly at the girl. Her own granddaughter had been about this age when she, Atrakis, had died.

"Is it the princess, then, who is ill?" she asked. *If they know she is not human, they might regard this as an illness.*

Mick and Eden looked over at Porphyra suddenly, a reflex reaction. They had never thought of this as a possibility.

"No!" said Mick. His own, smaller, cauldron of rage, which lived inside him, began to thrum in sympathy with that other, larger one. He and Atrakis would have been, at the beginning of time, made of the same cloth. "No, but we brought her along with us because we need to know more about her. She needs to know more about herself than just her name."

"And her color," said Atrakis flatly. "Here on Ikaria for centuries we have called ourselves the *porphyrogennita*, by which we mean 'born of royal blood.' It is all nonsense, of course, and we all know it, but it held our society together for generations and allowed us to resist Romans, pirates, Genoese, Venetians, and Turks. They saw us as the poorest set of beggars in the entire Aegean sea, but we knew they were seeing us out of one side of their heads only. From the other side, we were royal blood. And because we could see ourselves that way, we were able to refine our entire society away from the normal, into the magical, the enchanted. For us, that was our reality. And so, now, it is much easier for people to die here, because in a sense they have always been part of the Timeless Realm. I see that you, Princess Porphyra, are like us." She smiled at the little girl, who jerked slightly in her chair. But she said nothing, only held more tightly to Lambris.

"I could see immediately when you stood outside my wall that your little one had no linen cord, thus was not human in the same way that you are," she continued. *Linen? I thought it was silver.* Eden and Mick looked at each other as if they were both having this same thought.

"Well, that wraps it up," Eden was saying to himself with a little internal grimace that didn't show up on his face. "We've found out what we came for right off the bat. Time to get moving." But he didn't move.

"Yes, fine, this is all well and good," said Mick, "but – but back to the original subject, I mean – what we are really here for. We have a friend back home who is ill because of something that happened to her here on Ikaria. She, uh, – she uh – encountered a centaur!"

Atrakis stood up. Her eyes blazed and she suddenly seemed to flap around like a windmill. Out of her mouth came a hissing sound. Mick rocked forward on his chair, as if he had been pushed by a large hand, then fell back again, gasping. Then abruptly it was over. With a chuckle, Atrakis took a large swig of her cherry juice, tilting her head far back, taking her time about it. Once again she was a small, lithe, pretty young woman with masses of light brown hair tied back with a blue ribbon.

Anita Sullivan

She was shaking her head. "They move forward, and they move backward," she was saying, as if continuing a long conversation they had somehow missed. "We don't see them for decades, and then they come through the village at night like silk under the moon, with grass crowns on their heads. If you are careful, you can catch them benevolent and learn what you need to know, but it doesn't last." She turned abruptly into her house, emerging a few seconds later with what looked like a small club in her hand. She waved it around over them, and they could see it was a stubby marble rod, slightly enlarged on one end. "My pestle!" she chortled. "My magic pestle. The three of us, with these, we have given the centaurs a setback or two. Goes to show it's not only men who do all the poking and grinding, eh what!" and she broke into a peal of melodic laughter that rang through the entire garden.

Then she turned again and pointed with her pestle at Porphyra. "This one, she's got to ride on the centaur's back before he will give up his cure. After that, who knows? She might choose to come and join us here. Time for three seasons to become four, after this many centuries, is it?"

Soon they found themselves out on the village street again, plodding through the dust past crumbling stone walls, houses with no roofs, the ruins of the place. No more did they see any whole buildings; the place looked as if it hadn't been lived in for 100 years. They kept going uphill, passing a huge olive tree beside a wall that looked as if it might belong to a store rather than a house, maybe the location of the "plaka," the village central square in earlier times. But they did not see the other two women sitting in frozen curiosity on their chairs as they went by. They didn't peer into the shadows to notice the laughter and curiosity mingled in their eyes, and the mischief. Only Porphyra saw a little thickness and swirl taking place under the olive tree, and she turned as they went by to stare, wondering if she stood still even for sixty seconds, if something more solid would come into view.

## The Light Princess

They kept walking along the mountain road that wound up and down among the hills, out of sight of the sea. "What do we do now?" Mick had asked once, and Eden hadn't even bothered to shrug. They were both pretty grim, or at least silent, although the day was beautifully clear, sunny and cool. Even Porphyra did not launch into her usual lively chatter. After an hour or so they came to a small pine forest studded with ancient beehives, the place where Carley and Eugenia had met Ifigenia on their first visit to Ikaria. They remembered now her telling them about it, and because it was so lovely and quiet here they decided to rest and eat. Possibly even decide what to do next. As they lay back on the dried pine needles, Mick said, "The silence is different here, you know what I mean?"

Eden grunted and shifted from one elbow to another, lying on his stomach. "Yeah," he said, noncommittally. Then continued.

"I guess it's because the bees would normally be here making noise. And because they *aren't* here, that extra lack of noise makes for a different kind of silence than the usual one. Neat theory, anyway!" He made an attempt to laugh, but it failed to ignite.

Porphyra was busily unwrapping an egg salad sandwich.

Anita Sullivan

"When do I get to ride on the centaur's back?" she asked, after she had taken a bite. It was as if she had said, "When are we going to the grocery store?"

Eden groaned and rolled over, looking up at the sky. He didn't seem capable of speaking for the moment. Mick cleared his throat.

"Do you know what a centaur is?"

She nodded slowly. "They're horses who have human heads," she said. "I've ridden horses a lot." She giggled. "It might be easier if you could *talk* to them. Horses are a different mind set than us, you know. At least that's what my friend Lisa used to say."

They both stared at her. Mick swallowed, took a deep breath. "Your friend Lisa," he repeated slowly.

She was chewing, so she just nodded cheerfully. This was the first time she had shown any sign of remembering any kind of past life. They had come to assume she didn't even have one, that she was like some kind of paper doll, made quickly out of material at hand and set down in the middle of their story to complicate things.

"Blow me down and smother me with onions," muttered Eden. It was a thing his mother used to say. He sat up, reached into his backpack for an orange, and began to peel it while resting his elbows on his knees.

"So, you're not afraid of horses?" he said. *How ridiculous! A centaur is nowhere near being a horse. No more than a unicorn is just a horse with a horn. We shouldn't even think 'horse' when we're talking about them, it's dangerous!*

Porphyra shook her head and looked over at them with a schoolgirlish smile.

"I know how to stay on a horse bareback. I learned that when I was really small, starting off with those little horses, you know, not ponies. I never even fell off! They used to make me ride the horses pulling the chariots in the parades. Not in the races, though." She frowned, and they were silent, hardly breathing. Maybe there was something about the quietness of this grove after all that was allowing her to remember.

Porphyra looked away from them then, through the trees and over the tops of the little "village" of stone rectangles that housed the ancient bee urns, empty now for who knows how many decades. Eden had a vague feeling of redundancy, as if the three of them were a small part of a drawing someone was making of the scene, a huge sketch, and their shapes would blend nicely in with the curves and lines, the rectangular and the circular, the wild and the tame, which lay all around them and had been on this piece of earth for thousands of years. The thought was depressing and comforting at the same time, but new to him. He filed it away, thinking it might come in handy again later, both in letter and spirit.

Porphyra stopped talking for a minute and looked back at Mick and Eden, almost shyly now. Her violet eyes were, indeed, those of a woman constructed out of flowers, but a woman – for the moment – not a girl. "I know there's something about me that is making things go wrong now," she said softly. "I know that me just going away won't make it better, probably make it worse. Carley – all of you, well, not Eden, but the rest of you – you rescued me from being stuck some-where I wasn't really supposed to be. And now I have to rescue you!" She smiled, and seemed to be a little girl with yellow braids again. "I want to go find a centaur and ride it. That's what happens next, it really does. I might as well just go do it."

The fact that she stood up then, not even stopping to finish her half-eaten sandwich, told them eloquently that she was serious. And the authority of such eloquence was not to be gainsaid. They were soon moving along the road again, silent, a bit weary, taking swigs from their water bottles, and wondering where to find the nearest centaur.

"I have the feeling that we need the original one, you know what I mean?" Mick said. Eden looked perplexed a minute, then nodded. He paused. "I suppose I should recognize the original, but I might not. And you know—we might run across a lot of centaurs before we hit the jackpot." His face crumpled helplessly. "How many centaurs can stand on the head of a pin?" Mick joined in, "How many centaurs does it take to put in a new lightbulb?" And soon they were all laughing, half doubled over and reeling around in the road, howling and yipping, far beyond the actual humor of what they were saying. Porphyra screamed and threw her rabbit up into the air.

On the far western side of the island a centaur heard them, and drawn to laughter as readily as to wine, shook his head up and down, snorted, and began a slow trot in their direction. Through the rest of that day and for part of the night they moved towards one another. An aerial view would have shown their paths converging in a meandering fashion, as they sometimes doubled back or headed down a side road, while the centaur, running through the well-worn paths of goats, unicorns, satyrs, lions, and boars as well as his own kind, was never forced aside by cliffs or heavy thorn thickets. They stopped to sleep while he did not, so that by early morning they were less than half a mile apart. Because of the terrain, they actually met at the bottom of a steep cliff, on a tiny sheltered beach at the mouth of a river, where frogs were singing their strange song in the reeds. The river ended here, abruptly, at a sand bar, and made a little gully through the sand to connect itself to the sea. Mick, Porphyra and Eden were rolling up their pants legs preparing to wade across, having removed their shoes in happy anticipation of a little splash in the sea that was lapping gently onto the pebbly beach, when the centaur stepped delicately out from a grove of plane trees and trotted down to the water.

Immediately, as if they had rehearsed this scene, Mick and Eden moved backwards until they were standing next to the cliff, rigid as posts. Quashing their knightly instincts, or for that matter their brotherly or fatherly instincts, they tried to turn themselves into part of the scenery, hoping neutrality would continue to be an option. Porphyra, on the other hand, scampered across half the width of the beach, behind the creature, and climbed up a ledge onto the ruins of a small temple. Here she walked along a slab of marble floor that protruded slightly over the beach about ten feet above it, and called out softly, "Here I am, sir!" The morning breeze stirred her overalls and braids as surely as if they were gossamer, and she looked quite lovely. None of them knew the temple was very old, and dedicated to Artemis.

The beast walked over to her as sedately as a unicorn might have approached its virgin. He stood underneath her, his large curly head bowed as if he were being mildly chastised, and waited. Nimbly, Princess Porphyra leaped onto his broad back.

"It's so *huge*!" whispered Mick. "I had no idea it would be that big!"

While the two of them stood transfixed, the beast was walking away from them. By the time they were paying full attention again, girl

Anita Sullivan

and beast were disappearing down a slope back into the trees along the river bank. She was riding lightly and easily, gripping the creature's human shoulders with her hands and with her legs curled backwards, heels dug into its horse flanks. He was too broad and she too small for her to ride sitting up straight, straddling his width, but she looked oddly competent in this awkward position. Then girl and beast popped out of sight.

Eden's hands flew to his stomach unconsciously. They looked at each other.

"I feel so damned helpless. I mean we had to just let it happen, ugh! What should we do now?"

"I think we've got to follow them, don't you think?"

"Hey, you know, she could jump off! Right now! She's done her thing. PORPHYRA! JUMP OFF NOW, RIGHT NOW, IT'S O.K. JUMP OFF!" This was Eden, yelling and running into the trees. He was practically crying.

They both stumbled down the sandy bank, through tall river grasses. They were on the opposite side of the river from where Porphyra and the centaur had gone in, and the ground was swampy here. Frogs leaped out in all directions, disgruntled at the interruption. Soon they left the mouth of the river behind and were going along a sandy river valley between vines, thorn bushes, flowering shrubs, and finally in among a long grove of plane trees whose roots stuck up above the earth and this, along with a smattering of large stones, kept the going from being anything but slow and hazardous.

Although they stopped now and then to listen, they did not hear any of the few noises they might expect from a centaur moving along a river bank or even splashing into one of the many rocky pools that appeared at regular intervals along its course from the mountains. Mick and Eden crossed back and forth to find the easiest walking, and presently began to watch for hoofmarks in the soft sand, but were unsuccessful. The creature did not have much of a head start, so either it knew a secret path away from the river, up the stony hillside, or it had vanished in some more magical way.

"Maybe it went into another dimension," said Mick, almost grinding his teeth at the word "dimension." He shook his head, trying to gain control of his anger. "I used to love fairy tales when I was a kid, but now I'm really sick of them, you know what I mean?"

Without much hope they kept on going until, after an hour or so, they reached a place where the bank became so narrow and steep that it really had turned into a ravine, and they were forced to go straight up the side, leaving the river altogether.

"There must be a bunch of caves up here," Eden said hopefully, as they tramped along, pulling themselves up by branches, and almost losing their footing among loose stones.

"There are," said Mick. "I've explored around this area some. I never found any deep caves, but lots of shallow ones. It would take a pretty big cave for that guy."

Eden stopped and rubbed his sideburns thoughtfully. "I wish Carley were here," he said. "She always knows which story we are in. I can't help but wonder if Porphyra is supposed to be on her own now, for awhile. I know it sounds terrible, because centaurs, with women, well, they're basically the male principle at its worst, not much else. But she was *supposed* to ride on a centaur's back, so maybe she'll be protected somehow. Or because – " he stopped and took a deep breath, "because she's not really human."

Mick shook his head. "No, we *can't* desert her now! She's only a kid. I mean, if there's some sort of magic that makes her immune from harm, so much the better. But I don't believe it. I don't think we're in any story except our own."

"Hmm," said Eden slowly. "You know, we really should be doing better than this. Our mission here was to find out if Porph was human, and then go report back. And already, after only a couple of days, guess what? We're in trouble again. I mean, I sure as hell don't know what we're *supposed* to be doing now, but we don't seem to be pushing things forward in a positive direction."

"Hey! That's an idea!" said Mick, as if Eden had just suggested one. "We could play a quick game of paper, scissors, rock – just you and me. We don't know where to go next, so we make up three possibilities, and then we play until one of us has won three rounds, and whatever is on top at the end, well – we do that!"

"Well, if there's any magic floating around, now's its big chance," Eden agreed somewhat wearily.

So they made up three plans: *paper* would be heading back down the river to the shore, hoping to find some clue along the way, or a side path where the two had left the river bank to go up the hillside; *scissors* would be cutting their losses here and trying to find their way back to Kalypsos' garden, outside the wall, figuring that maybe the centaur spent a lot of time there; *rock* would be to stay right where they were, making daily forays outwards in a circle a short distance from the center.

At the end of the game, *rock* was on top.

"It figures, for Ikaria!" they both said, trying to disguise from each other that this was the least favorite of their choices.

# Carley Intervenes

"They've been separated!" Eugenia was saying about the same time, to Djan and Heloise. The three of them were sitting in front of a small fire in Carley's top floor bedroom, Heloise on a white sheepskin rug, the other two cupping glass mugs of hot mint tea in their hands. Carley was lying quietly on the bed, silent as usual. The fireplace was semi-circular, wedged into a curve at the smallest part of this oddly-shaped room, ("I get so tired of corners in a house!" Carley had said to the Arbiter when giving directions for the villa). It was white, resembling more the adobe of the Southwest U.S. than the traditional Mediterranean hearths, but its design did allow a small fire of aromatic twigs and branches to put out quite a large and steady heat on this cool winter afternoon.

Eugenia and Djan had been tracking their other three friends from the time they left the villa. It was a kind of crystal-gazing without the crystal; each using their own method. Eugenia simply let her eyes go unfocused and looked at whatever was in front of her as if it were a kaleidoscope, making a meaningful pattern. Inside, this pattern would take on its own motion, which she translated as Mick, Eden and Porphyra moving about on Ikaria. Djan made quick small sketches with stubs of colored chalk on dark paper and when they reached some sort of critical mass, he stared at them for a long time.

Whatever their methods, they seemed often in agreement about the results. They had noted the meeting with Atropos, (they failed to register the other two women under the olive tree). They sensed that some important information or advice may have been given during this meeting. They were aware of the centaur's path across the island before

Anita Sullivan

he arrived on the beach, and even made a mark on the island map at the point he set out from, for possible future reference. By now a large map of Ikaria hung on the wall in the cafeteria, with little colored slips of paper pinned to it as if they were closely monitoring a military campaign.

What had puzzled them both was how fast the centaur came and went, once he met up with the little group. It was as if he sank into a hole in the sand. But now, Eugenia was realizing that Porphyra had gone with him, while Djan and Mick were left behind. Hours had passed, and this was still the situation. She and Djan had completely lost track of both the girl and the beast, as if the two had wandered out of "scrying" range.

"Makes a person feel . . . positively . . . incompetent!" Djan said slowly. His eyes were closed, and his face screwed up so tightly in concentration that he looked like the preliminary blocking out of a clay image which the artist had decided to set back on a shelf for later fine modeling. Eugenia broke into a musical giggle. Djan's eyes flew open, blinked rapidly.

"I think we can help," Eugenia almost sang at him. "From here!" She crouched on the floor. Djan shrugged, then nodded and slipped out of his chair, dropping naturally into a squat. This put him right next to the dog, who was lying with her head up, paying quiet attention.

"Centaurs have better natures and worse ones," she continued. "The better ones come out like phases of the moon, only more mercurial, not on a regular basis. I think there is something we all need to learn from this creature. But we have to do it fast."

Djan nodded again. "They are creatures of the rock," he said. "but of the fire in the rock as well. Yes!" He gave a deep sigh, and his nostrils flared slightly. "We must dream, but in a different way than usual, I am thinking."

"We need Carley too, and Heloise," said Eugenia. They looked over to the bed, where Carley lay in a flannel nightgown, on her side with her back to them, looking out at the sea beyond the balcony railing. They knew her eyes would likely be open, but they didn't know what she was seeing.

"They have a strong sense of justice; in ancient times they would run in herds a moonlit night every hundred years or so; they veer violently back and forth from consciousness so high and clear that it is godlike, as if they had almost reached Theosis, the state at which a living creature merges with the divine – and a condition of animal mendacity, lewdness, greed that is something like a foundation for evil, but not evil itself. Is this clear to you as well?" Djan looked up at Eugenia, who still sat in the wicker chair. "Yes," she said. Then she added, half whispering, "I wonder if maybe the extremes have become farther apart as the centuries have gone by." She lifted her chin to fend off a doubt she didn't want anyone else in the room to have to contend with.

"Almost as if – " Djan began, then stopped himself. He stood up. "We must devise a ritual. Oh, damn it, Carley, we need you to pull us a flagon of mead, make us one of your impromptu flans, or quiches, or just a pottage of herbs to reek in our nostrils." He was allowing himself to babble, like a wizard making small preliminary whirls before the larger hummings.

"I think she can be with us in some way," said Eugenia, going over to Carley. "She has gone deep into herself, and she is poisoned, but she may be able to dream . . . to dream the way you say we must."

Anita Sullivan

She walked back towards the fire, but stood in the window, the sun stirring a wildfire in her hair. "So, what kind of dreaming are you talking about?"

Djan was sitting on the hearth making a little steeple with his fingers, bringing his thumbs and pinky fingers together under it, in and out. He stared into the small cathedral of his hands, breathing slowly.

"In some ways, oddly enough, centaurs are local," he said. "They don't exist anywhere but in the Old World. They are creatures of the Mediterranean culture. And yet, they are as old as the dinosaurs, older in fact. It puzzles me, that wisdom, which comes in some degree simply from age and experience through fire, can remain so unreliable, so occasional. It's almost as if they are receptacles for some leftover vast idea that could never come to fruition . . . or that they are in some sense Christ-like figures, taking on a punishment so that things do not become worse than they are." He looked up, his eyes almost black. "But I digress."

"You do, you do indeed!" said Eugenia, fondly and impatiently.

"I am also puzzled," he continued, folding his hands deliberately into his lap so as to change his focus, "as to how a centaur could injure a living human." He shook his head, as if puzzling once more about this. "I would think Porphyra were in more danger than Carley, yet the evidence is here." He waved at Carley's bed. "All of which goes to show that we may be setting out into dangerous territory armed with the wrong set of premises. I am perfectly willing to shift premises, but to what? *How do we reach this creature?*"

"If you can touch the clocks and never start them, then you can start the clocks and never touch them," said Eugenia softly but clearly.

Her eyes widened. Where had that come from? It was nothing she thought of herself.

Heloise made a funny little moan and heaved herself to her feet, almost stepping on her left ear as usual, which was a little longer than her right. She padded over to Carley's bed, and stood beside it sideways, as if waiting for her mistress to step down onto her back. Carley also made a funny little moan, coughed, and turned over, facing in their direction.

"I was dreaming of *The Thirteen Clocks*," she said. She began to hiccup.

"The story! Porphyra's story!" hissed Eugenia to Djan. She ran over to the bed and handed Carley the glass of water that always stood on the little table nearby. Djan stood up and came over too.

"Carley!" Eugenia said. She leaned over her friend and spoke lightly into her ear, almost as if she were blowing onto a cup of tea to make it cooler. "Porphyra needs our help again. We must send her wisdom, and the need for wisdom. We must send her sounds with no origin, the needle voice of a bird in the dusk that can go into a heart. She is the dusk now, the purple of it, and fullness and the draping down. She is the long-haired innocence of its origin. But she needs the voice of the bird, and you know that voice."

"We are dream bodies now," said Djan, taking up where Eugenia left off, or maybe both of them talking at once, chanting almost, sometimes diverging into sounds that were not words. "Much have we traveled in realms of gold. Hand in hand we go where we must go, into new realms where our individual selves have blended into a mist, a cloak of readiness. And beneath the cloak, the needle that you have in your body, in your groin, the needle of beauty and pain, that will become now the voice of a bird to penetrate the heart of the one on whose back Porphyra is riding. We go now, we will go now . . . ."

The two of them curved together over the back of the horizontal dog, towards Carley horizontal on the bed, made a certain pattern of voice and structure. An improvised pattern, but strong and unique. They stayed that way, murmuring but still, for a long time, as if posing for a painting by William Blake, while the colors in the room bled and swirled around them, and dusk, about which they spoke, came softly through the window, minus some of her usual colors. They neither left the room, nor were they in the room any longer. Only later, when they were once again aware of their surroundings and the pitch darkness and the cold, did they realize that Heloise was gone.

"Of course!" Djan said. But he neither explained what he meant nor did the others ask him.


A Most Perfect Oil


A centaur facing one direction, a basset hound standing beside him facing the opposite way, and a teenage girl holding a stuffed rabbit sitting on the creature's broad back with her legs dangling over the side. This on a stony headland, amid maquis and heather with the late afternoon sun being dumped over them as if a painter or photographer had ordered too much light and needed to use it all up quickly before the next batch arrived.

Heloise looked gravely down into the sun pooling at her feet. Her face was sad but her eyes gleamed.

"Oh, Heloise, I'm so glad you came! I couldn't get down by myself, and the centaur never would stand still beside a rock long enough. Here I come!"

And Porphyra slid carefully down the shaggy side of the beast, landing with a soft thump on top of Heloise, straddling her not-quite-so-broad back! Immediately her tennis shoes hit the ground and gave her a little jolt, but nothing like it would have been if she had jumped straight off without the intervening dog.

They sat that way for a few seconds, as if giving the photographer a chance at a second shot. Then Porphyra climbed off and knelt down beside Heloise, stroking her between her long silvery ears. She laid her head on the dog's back with a big smile on her face. Neither of them seemed in a hurry to rush off, and the large beast beside them shifted position slightly so it could see them. They could feel it looking at them, since a centaur's glance carries true weight, their eyes having been constructed at an early time in the evolution of earth's creatures.

"You can make an antidote."

The centaur spoke. Not in words, but making a sound they heard as brown and cobbled, coming to a hissing stop then resonating on afterwards as if they were inside a cave.

"You have some of my hide on your clothes, Little One," he continued. "Mix three equal sized hairs from my coat with a pound of old oil, put into it two handfuls of the flower of St. John's Wort and set it in the sun for two months. After this, gather leaves of Gentian, Tormentil, white Dittany, Zedoary, and Carline and steep in two glasses of the best white wine. Do this for three days. Combine the two, oil and wine, and boil gently in a metal vat for six hours. Strain them in a press, Add to the expression an ounce of Saffron, Myrrh, Aloes,

Spikenard, and Rhubarb, all bruised, and let them boil again for six hours. Then set the mixture in the sun for 40 days. After this, let the injured person drink three drops of it in wine. At the same time, anoint the wounded area. This will cause a healing. It has, also, the capacity to kill me, so do not return here with any of it on your body. There are so few of us remaining."

The centaur's voice slid from sand into silver dust and while they were still held still by it, and perhaps its message too, he trotted away, the sound of his hooves blending with the sound of his fading voice so that they scarcely knew he was leaving.

"Oh, no!" Wailed Porphyra, "I can't remember all that! Oh, Heloise, the centaur was telling us how to cure Carley, and I can't remember all those plant names, oh hell, oh hell!" She looked at the dog and began to cry, loudly and desperately, shuddering as she squashed her rabbit under one arm and put her hands up to her face.

Heloise bumped her head gently against the girl's leg. When Porphyra looked down, the dog was gazing up at her, her long brown eyes so full of thoughts and ideas and hope and laughing that the little girl took a step backwards, flooded with understanding. "Oh, wow! You've got it all in your head, have you, Heloise? Oh wow! Well, quick, let's go back, then, can we?"

Patiently, the dog explained: first they had to stay on the island to collect the herbs called for in the recipe.

At first Porphyra thought she would have to find a rock and scratch every name onto it that she could still remember. But then she realized Heloise knew the plants; she wasn't just remembering them, she *knew*. With the plucky spontaneity of her character, Porphyra easily shrugged off questions such as: *how many herbs were there again? And*

*what if they aren't all here? And how long will this take? And shouldn't
we get the others to help us?* She just started doing her half of the job,
which was to pick leaves or flowers from the plants that Heloise pointed out, and to find someplace to store them until they were done. Her
biggest problem was hunger, and being cold at night (or rather, half of
her being cold, the half that was facing away from Heloise).

The other problem was a way to carry the herbs. She and the
dog didn't return to the same place every night, but kept moving
through the landscape, thus it was necessary to bring the growing
collection of leaves, stems, and flowers along with them. Porphyra had
only a tee shirt on, and jeans, and she couldn't afford to go shirtless
because it was too cold at night. Finally she talked Heloise into a side
expedition into some of the deserted houses, and she found a piece of
coarse sacking material that would serve as a knapsack. Into it went
Lambris first, and with him a little pile of centaur hairs that she had
carefully scraped off the back of her jeans and placed into a plane tree
leaf, all rolled up and folded together as best she could manage. She did
two or three of these, and as a final safeguard, she slit Lambris's velvet
tummy with a sharp rock and stuffed the leaves inside him so they
wouldn't unroll and spill their precious contents.

Finding food was more difficult. First she just went without,
and drank lots of water from the many streams they crossed. On the
third afternoon they chanced upon a small village and Porphyra went in
and out of the stores along the street, most of which were open. Here,
by some odd breaches in whatever rules were guiding their actions, she
managed to find some dried olives, fresh apricots and several packages
of crackers, all of which she tore into like a small, unwinged vulture. It

was while they were pausing for this meal, in which Heloise took grateful part, that Mick and Eden discovered them.

After they exchanged excited greetings, they sat on a bench together sharing food (Mick and Eden had some wine, canned sardines, tomatoes, and cheese, since Eden turned out to be second only to Djan in scrounging skill). Discreetly, but insistently, Eden and Mick probed for information about what had happened to Porphyra after she left them, riding on the back of the centaur. But she was unable to tell them.

"I don't know," she said. She shook her head so that her braids shot out on either side. Her eyes went unfocussed. When she tried to open her mouth to say 'centaur', the word would not come. "We're gathering some herbs, me and Heloise, to cure Carley. Heloise knows what they are, I don't. I'm just along for the ride." She smiled enigmatically and bit into another apricot.

Heloise, her head resting gravely on her paws, sighed in relief. The short scene on the hillside had been a secret. Nobody in the universe except the three of them, knew what took place there. Thus must it remain, or the whole curing process would become powerless. But, being a dog, she had no way to make the girl quiet if she decided to tell too much, about the recipe, for example, or about how the centaur's deep gray eyes had bored information and a promise into their minds. How they both carried this promise inside them like an egg, or rather maybe like a small stone that would never emerge, but stay with them as an extra weight for the rest of their days. A bit of a danger, this egg/stone, should it ever begin to weigh wrongly upon their minds

Eventually Eden and Mick gave up trying to find out about the centaur, even with direct, simple questions such as a child might wish to answer, such as "Was it fun to ride on the back of a real centaur?"

"Did he talk to you?" "He didn't hurt you, did he?" "How did you get away?" To all these questions she just shook her head as if they made no sense to her. Eden and Mick looked at each other, troubled. But Porphyra was obviously unharmed, and besides, the presence of Heloise was most reassuring.

"It's a girl thing," said Eden lightly, at last, to Mick, who had an odd fleeting reaction *that's the kind of thing I would say, Eden, not you.* He made no reply, but was able to understand the remark as an anguished admission of their inability to truly penetrate the full enigma of the situation. It was also, crudely and simply, a way to help relieve the guilt and tension they had been laboring under for the past several days.

All of them were tired, dirty, and wishing to dream their way back to Carley's villa; but they felt a need to stay together, and Porphyra made it clear they had certain plants to gather, and that she had no idea how many or how long it would take.

"Carley has quite a few herbs in her garden," said Mick. He looked down at Heloise, whose head was raised off her paws, and who seemed to be gazing out over the edge of the village plaza into the trees beyond. She turned slowly to face him, and the expression on her face said, more or less, "Good heavens, Mick, don't you realize I am intimately familiar with her garden and have taken those plants into account already?"

"What if we just go over to old what's-his-name, oh, you know – Kalypsos – and get what we need?" Now it was Mick's turn to let off nervous energy. He wrinkled his face as soon as he said it, knowing it wasn't really an idea.

"So, what have you got so far?" He turned to Porphyra. She shook her head. "I don't know! Well, actually, I know we have four different plants, and we need – oh, I don't remember, at least twice that many."

Languidly, Heloise set one paw down just to the left of Porphyra's feet.

"Does that mean eleven or fifteen?" asked Mick, looking at the dog closely. In reply, the dog tipped her paw up sideways, as if to turn it into a single digit.

"Eleven herbs, then, right?" Heloise withdrew her paw and lay her head back down.

"Seven more," they said to each other. Who knew how long such a task would take? They might find six in two days and then spend a month or more looking for the seventh. They had no idea how many of them Carley had growing in her garden.

"Well, look – " Mick said, clearing his throat and taking a deep breath. "Carley's not dying, so far as I know, she's only in pain some of the time. We need to hurry, but it's not life or death this minute, if you know what I mean. I mean, we don't need to panic."

"Another thing," said Eden after they were silent awhile, and Porphyra had gone to sleep, her head resting against his shoulder. "Another thing," he said more quietly, but making sure the dog knew he was talking to her especially. "We aren't very good at finding food here. We can't really stay here much longer without reinforcements. We need to go back and do a bunch of cooking, get some clean clothes, that sort of thing, like a camping trip. We'd do a much better job. What do you think, Heloise?"

She lifted her head, gave a chortled sort of growl, then slowly unfolded her ungainly self and lumbered to her feet.

"I guess we've got our marching orders," grinned Eden, and Mick laughed.

## Essential Ingredients

It was Eugenia who noticed, fully and forcefully, that the herbs they would gather would have no names.

The morning after they arrived back at the villa, all of them were outside prowling around the terraced gardens while Heloise sniffed and pondered, slithered and tromped, and they followed behind, each carrying a handful of little cloth bags. Porphyra kept giggling when, for example, Heloise's forehead would appear like a small gray disc above a low bush, her eyebrows raised alertly, and they would all rush over to see if this was one of the seven remaining herbs for the formula. Nobody, not even Porphyra knew exactly what was going on, or what they would do with all these leaves and roots when they did finally satisfy the dog that they had gathered all that was needed. The girl remembered the centaur, but felt the information so serenely and deeply embedded into her being that it never occurred to her to speak about it. Somehow she knew they must steep herbs, set them in the sun, boil them, steep them again. But she had no idea of proportions or time, or even a clear sense of what it was all for. The connection between this gathering game (she saw it now as a game), Carley's strange illness, and her own memory of sliding off the centaur's back, did not seem to her a matter of cause and effect, but only of juxtaposition. There was real danger, in fact, that the tiny hairs she had scraped off the back of her jeans and placed inside leaves, inside the body of her rabbit, would be forgotten.

"What is it we are gathering, does anybody know the names of these plants?" Eugenia asked sometime in the middle of the morning. "I'm so ignorant of plant names. And this is a different environment. I know some of the ones in England, and even used to know some back in Oregon. But here . . . Djan, do you know?"

He came over to stand beside her, looking down on a tiny plant with thick, pointed leaves and tiny, exquisite white blossoms with yellow centers. Heloise was tapping the blossoms with one paw, and Mick was preparing to pluck some to put into one of the bags.

"How much?" He asked, after he had plucked a dozen flowers. Heloise backed away and sat down on her haunches, as if satisfied. This in itself was such an uncharacteristic action that they all turned and stared. Heloise sitting down. Normally they would have broken into laughter, since her short legs would barely bend enough to allow her behind to reach the ground, and she looked as if she would rebound at any minute, or topple over. Instead, they looked at each other, seeking an explanation.

"Shall we form a circle?" Djan asked with mock solemnity, gesturing to either side. They were on the middle terrace, with plenty of room to sit down together.

At that moment they heard a tapping on the stairs inside the house, accompanied by a muffled choking, weeping sound.

"Carley!" Eugenia said, and they all turned to look down at the French doors of the music room. Carley came limping slowly out, using her cane and blinking as if she were emerging from a cave instead of from a light-drenched house.

"What's that smell?" She said, raising her head, eyes half closed, to point her nose towards the sky. She sniffed there for awhile, then lowered her head and made the choking sound again. "Smells like a dead horse. Did somebody poison a horse here? It's awful, I'm leaving. I'm going back home, who can live in a place like this?"

They were temporarily frozen in position. Nobody knew what to do, if anything needed to be done. Carley came up the stairs to their level, leaning on her cane and still making sniffing sounds. She walked around, looking at them as if she saw them but they were not part of her present problem. Eventually she went up one more level, to the table outside the kitchen where they usually ate breakfast. On the table was the old dark green sack Porphyra and Heloise had brought back from Ikaria. Carley rushed at it and struck it with her stick, over and over.

"Phew! Oh, this is where it's coming from, oh take it away, it's killing me!"

And she picked up the sack with her cane and flung it into the bushes.

Djan and Eugenia, who had most recently been looking after Carley, moved forward first, in a unified urgency that came from realizing her condition was worse.

"The poison has gone to her brain," they both thought, or some version of this, and came up to her as she stood shakily before the round wrought-iron table staring down at it as if the offending item were still there.

"Would you like to go back inside, Carley?" Eugenia said in a normal tone of voice, trying not to sound like a nurse. "If it smells bad out here, I'm sure it will go away soon."

Anita Sullivan

"It was coming in through the window," said Carley, with some irritation. "That's why I came out here. Oh, where are the lions? Where is Heloise? I want to go back!"

"I'd be glad to help you, Carley," said Eugenia, touching her lightly on the shoulder. "I don't know exactly what you mean by going back, but I do want to help you. Maybe if we go and sit down on the soft cushions, the little sofa . . . . "

Djan, meanwhile, went over to retrieve the sack. He had noticed it earlier in the day when they all came out into the garden to look for herbs. He knew, or at least assumed that the others had brought it back from Ikaria for some reason, though nobody had discussed it the evening before when they arrived. As he went over to the flower beds to pick it up, he found himself sniffing. But he smelled nothing unusual, surely nothing like a dead animal. His head was buzzing with thoughts. Dead horse, dead centaur, same thing. That notion was going through his head, and it made a kind of sense. What was inside this bag?

The others were still down on the lower terrace looking up, ready to jump in if they were needed, but figuring the less fuss and bother the more likely was Carley to calm down again. Porphyra had jerked like a marionette when Carley flung the piece of sacking into the flowers. Her reaction had been automatic, not coming from thought, not from a rational train of thought that would go, "Oh, dear! Inside that sack is the most important ingredient of the formula we are going to put together to cure Carley. If something happens to it, we will not get another chance." But she could not visualize what was actually in the sack, nor how it got there. Still, she found herself slowly walking up the stairs and over to where Djan stood, now holding onto the old piece of flour sacking with the string holding it closed.

"This yours?" He asked her, his dark eyes boring into hers. He made no move to hand it to her. He could feel a swirl of possibilities around him like magnetic waves having a sword fight.

Porphyra nodded solemnly.

"I think we need to put it into the house somewhere, so it's safe," he said, half turning to walk in that direction. Eugenia had succeeded in shepherding Carley back through the kitchen door.

"No!" said Porphyra. She stood firmly planted, not following Djan as he had intended she would do.

"Oh, what, then, do you have in mind?" He turned courteously, squinting at her with all his native fierceness.

"Carley smells a dead horse in there," the girl said, pointing to the bag. "It's not a horse, it's a centaur, and it's not dead, it's only a small piece of it in there, not enough to smell. But Carley might destroy it and we need it for the medicine!"

She drew a great shuddering breath after having made this pronouncement, and then closed her eyes and crumpled into a heap on the warm paving stones.

Mick and Eden ran over immediately to kneel on either side of her. Heloise, meanwhile, had gone up to Djan, and reaching up, took the end of the sacking lightly in her teeth, pulling on it. She was trying to draw him away from the house.

"Yes, yes, I see." Djan gave a sigh and gently retrieving the bag from the dog's teeth, turned away from the house and came down to where Porphyra was lying.

Anita Sullivan

"She just fainted," said Eden, who was crouched down near her face to make sure she was breathing. "I don't think she hurt herself, she didn't fall splat she just kind of slid down! Should we move her inside?"

"Yeah," said Mick, "I'll help."

While they were carefully lifting the girl and carrying her into the house, Djan continued down the shallow stairs to the bottom level, outside the cafeteria. Here there was a little garden shed, painted with birds, butterflies and musical notes, yet amazingly blending well into the background next to the wall of yellowed pavement stones that surrounded the villa. He opened the door and, looking around, placed the sack onto a shelf. Behind him stood the approving dog.

"Only thee and me know it's here, Heloise," Djan told her. He shook his head and closed the door carefully. "Seems so obvious now. I know it's there, and so do you. But in this reality, memory no longer has the power it once did." He paused, directly facing the tool shed, and was quiet, making a pattern inside his head. Then he murmured something, reached into his pocket, and pulled out a piece of blue chalk. With it he drew a small figure on the paving stone in front of the shed door. It was the figure of a centaur with its head bowed, in shame.

## The Lady of Thessaly

Hello, Eugenia here. I'm going to talk for awhile. I want Carley to know everything that happened while she was ill, even if it is hard to tell this part of the story. This won't be in any normal order, because the only way I can bear to tell it is like telling a dream the way it happens, not the way it comes out afterwards. What I say might be hard to figure out, but I know Carley will understand.

They say in ancient Thessaly – I remember reading this in the library – that the sun was female, and women were birds; the moon was male, and men were horses. Thessaly is the land of centaurs. Or, at least, it's traditionally their country of origin. I don't think that matters much, but I do like the part about birds and horses.

Porphyra wasn't a bird, though, she was a girl made of flowers. Maybe flower petals are like wings. The last petals we saw of her were drifting in the breeze, white, and pale lavender, and they did look rather like the wings of butterflies, not so much birds. But I guess wings are wings.

We had gotten down to the last herb we needed, number 10 out of 11. This was about two weeks after Mick, Eden, Porphyra and Heloise had come back from Ikaria. Lots happened in between. Djan went back home to Tasmania, in a kind of mania (I couldn't help saying that) to do some research on his computer. It seems that he has Internet access there. Naturally, he can't get onto the Internet as it is now, assuming it still exists. But he can get onto how it was, frozen in time, when he died in about 2000. So, he started researching "Natural Magic" and herbal formulas from Renaissance and Medieval magicians, and even further back than that. He came up with a number of formulas that he printed out and brought back with him in his backpack.

"Heloise seems to know the right herbs we need to make Carley well. We must presume she got these from the centaur. But assuming he also told them the formula as to what to <u>do</u> with these herbs, well, it's going to be rather difficult to extract that information

Anita Sullivan

from Heloise, intelligent being though she is. Her paws and eyes are truly articulate, but – "

His idea was that the information was all transferred in a non-verbal way, animal-to-animal, and for us to "translate" it, we had to find a way to make it easy for Heloise to tell us what she knew. The rest of what she knew, I should say, since already she had helped us gather 10 out of 11 medicinal plants. So we worked and worked with her, (and she was so patient with us) until we had a formula all written down, with the names of 11 herbs, and what to do with all of them.

Porphyra was there, too, of course. But she seemed to have blocked everything out. After she fainted that day, they brought her inside and laid her on her bed, and she did wake up later and drink some water. But she wouldn't eat anything. In fact, I don't think she ate any more after that afternoon. It didn't seem to matter. It was as if she had become magic again, out of a story or a dream, the way she was when we found her, and didn't need food any more.

We took turns going back to Ikaria to find more herbs, making quick trips and managing to avoid trouble. Porphyra came with us once, she and I and Eden. We found vervain and purple loosestrife. Come to think of it, Heloise wasn't even with us, that's strange. I had forgotten about that. Porphyra seemed to remember, finally, what we needed. She also knew the last flower we were missing, which was speedwell, or *veronica officinalis*. There didn't seem to be any of it on Ikaria, nor in Carley's garden. It is a flower with delicate, light blue flowers tinged faintly with purple. Porphyra didn't know its name, but she pointed it out to us in a book in the Library, after the Librarian led us to a section filled with massive herbals from every age in history. We spent about three days in there, she and I and Heloise, until we found it. It's not particularly a rare plant, it's just that it doesn't exist on Ikaria or in the part of Italy where Carley's house is, or in Tasmania either. Besides, I think we needed the Greek version of it, the kind that grows in Thessaly, birthplace of the centaurs.

So, did we need to make a trip to Thessaly? We were all ready to go.

Carley was getting worse. She was obviously thinner, and her mind was wandering, and she seemed to have a low fever 24 hours a day, no matter what we did. Her eyes were inflamed, and red welts kept breaking out on different parts of her body, then going away, only to break out again in a different place the next day.

By this time Porphyra had eaten nothing for about 6 days, only drinking water. Eden was particularly worried, and kept offering her sandwiches until it became a kind of joke. He wasn't with us when we found her, and we hadn't really told him the whole story, how she had been caught in the wrong fairytale, and the only clue was just one sentence, so that by taking her out of the story we didn't damage it.

Eden was trying to convince himself not to panic about Porphyra, that maybe because she was not really human like us she didn't really need to eat. Maybe she had phases, back and forth. There was really no way to rationalize what was happening, we all felt the sadness gathering like a pool behind a dam, and we didn't understand where it came from. I guess Porphyra really was a flower princess, like the one in the Welsh legend, and maybe she knew it all along. Anyhow, that's how it all ended. Porphyra somehow figured out *she was made partly of speedwell.* I don't know how she knew for sure, because it wasn't a matter for guesswork. One morning she went down to the little pool at the bottom of the garden, a few steps down from the

Anita Sullivan

little garden shed with the pictures painted all over it. And she drowned in the pool. Or maybe I should say, she dissolved in the pool. Not right away. First we saw her there, sitting on a flat slab of stone in the sun, leaning against the rim of the pool with her knees tucked sideways under her and her hands resting on her knees. We could see her long blonde braids, and she looked like a little girl inside her baggy overalls, a little girl half asleep in the sun. Then Mick, who had gone down to check on her, came rushing back up to the kitchen, his face white.

"Come down quick, Porph is gone. I think she went into the pool!"

We all dashed down the hill, practically tripping on the steps, and arrived all at once. We stood in a little half circle around the pool, looking down at the water. Floating on the surface were flower blossoms, a whole bunch of them. We just started dumbly at them, hardly breathing, because we knew there was no reason to look any further for Porphyra, this was she.

We started reaching out, one by one, and gathering the blossoms into our hands. We laid them out onto the stone slab in a little pile. Eden was crying. We all had tears in our eyes. But Heloise went immediately to the speedwell, a few branches of it sticking out, and pulled them with her teeth, gently, to lay them aside in an obvious way.

"She did that," said Mick, biting his lip and shaking his head, fighting back his own sobs. "She did that." He said no more, but we understood her sacrifice. Spontaneously we all fell onto our knees and bowed our heads silently. After awhile Djan began to sing, an old chant from his boyhood in Australia. We stayed there for a long time, losing complete track of time again.

That's about it, I guess. After that we had all the herbs, and we had the recipe from an old Italian herbalist from the 16th century, so we made the potion. Some of it had to sit for 40 days in the sun, and then boil, steep in glasses of wine, and then be set out in the sun again. The whole process took about two months. Even then, we almost did it wrong, because of the most important ingredient of all. Well, I guess there isn't any such thing. The most important ingredient of all is probably love. But even though Djan and Heloise knew there was some part of the centaur's body in the old gunny sack up on the shelf in the shed, they didn't know for sure what it was, and how much of it to put in. Not even Heloise knew this. We opened the sack together and found Porphyra's stuffed rabbit slit open with a wad of mushed up leaves inside. This didn't make any sense, I mean why would they put some of the plants inside the rabbit? So we tried to sort through the mess, and Djan reminded us how Carley had smelled a dead horse, so there might be some hair or skin from the centaur inside this mush of leaves. Finally we turned Lambris inside out over the bowl, letting the leaves fall in, and any other bits of hair that might be sticking to him, trusting that the leaves would not be poison. Eden took the rabbit and we don't know what he did with it. I think Porphyra's sudden death was especially hard for him since he had died young and still missed his brother and two (I think) sisters, and was now sort of losing another sister. Or maybe Porphyra would have become more than that to him, if they lived here in this reality for a long time together. But she seems even more lost to him now than his regular brother and sisters, who might even turn up one day. It's all so strange.

The directions that Djan got from *The Eighth Book of Natural Magick* said to "anoint the affected area, and the place about the heart, and drink three drops of it in wine. It will work wonders." So, we anointed Carley (or rather, I did, since we thought it should be directly applied to her skin), and then dressed her carefully back in a soft night-gown. She was awake enough to drink some wine with the medicine in it. We did this every day until she got well, which was about a month. There was a bit of the tincture left, and we put it into a purple glass bottle and set it down in the shade behind the pool. I don't know if it's coincidence, but sometimes when I go down there to the pool, which is not often, I see white petals on the water, no matter what season.

## Part VI

### The Snake

A snake has come to live with me. It seems to have a hole beside the pool at the bottom of the garden. Maybe it is the soul of Porphyra in a new form, although I don't really believe that. Still, the idea is comforting, that she may still be alive somewhere, especially since we were never sure in what sense she was alive.

The snake is beautiful, with glittering scales of gold and orange and green. A kind of oriental potentate? An illusion? Just as Porphyra was an illusion, except she wasn't. We knew her as a violet-eyed child with very precise blonde braids and a way of holding a stuffed rabbit, and a stubborn willfulness, and on and on . . . . So what that each atom of matter is composed primarily of empty space, and therefore that the notion of solidness is false. The mountain is your beloved, nonetheless.

I am no longer concerned that one day will follow another, and another into mindless, meaningless eternity. I am no longer concerned that, as Mick would have it, some gods are snickering up their sleeves "I told you so!" As we down here in the "pre-dead" group reluctantly come to the conclusion that, well, yes maybe Death is a good idea after all, because it gives meaning to Life. If you lead your life as if you would die tomorrow, or if you lead your life as if you will live forever, what *is the difference?* All the difference in the world! And yet, no difference at all! Both at the same time. This is what I know now, after a year of being only half conscious. My internal gyro has a different proportion, I can almost see it. Maybe being wounded and healed by a centaur is such a rare, such an excruciating experience that it confers permanent enlightenment. I wish.

Using the Mayan Day-Signs has given us a new structure. Or rather, I should say, our own version of that ancient calendar system. When I was recuperating, that first month when I could walk without my cane and had no more pain, we would all sit together at a table in the shade and work out our system of days. Each day has a specific name, and a generic one. Each day has its own, fairly particular, set of characteristics. For example, on Scarlet Lunar Laughing Pig day you can do anything, but it is best not to engage in lots of physical work because you will likely do most of it wrong without even noticing it. So, on that day, you probably would plan to go to the beach, or draw, or water all your indoor plants, or go watch for hummingbirds. You wouldn't go to the Library, even though that's not work. You might dance a little. You would definitely laugh, but not too much.

Making up your day as you go along, you are constantly talking to the Name of the Day as if it were a person. And together, the two of you create a new version of each day, by reinforcing its essential nature, richly, richly. This is how we live now, all of us.

The snake appeared on Horizontal Stones Falling Water, a quiet day but one in which it is best to go out alone and explore something potentially dangerous. Most everyone else took that as a chance to do some dream traveling, but I stayed close to home. I went out walking, passed the sign that said "Via Buono" and noticed that it seemed to have grown bright, as if it had a new coat of paint. On a whim, I turned and started down that forbidden little street, but my path was blocked by a fierce thicket of thorns, and a faint hissing sound coming from inside. When I tried to pry the thorns aside, I scratched my wrist a little with a thorn, and it bled, and I had a premonition of death by poison. I looked down at my feet and saw they had become snakes, both pointing to the left. This caused me to stumble, and to limp, but I turned right and continued (my normal feet back again) down to the beach. I poked around among the stones and shells, then climbed the steps to the old villa. There I felt an urge to explore, so I started picking up paving stones to look under them, as if I were seeking a treasure.

Nothing more than that. Did I find a treasure? Yes and no. I picked up a lovely potsherd, light orange, with the pale tracing on it of what looked like a woman's face, her chin tilted back in three-quarter view. Beautiful high cheekbone. I put it into my pocket and ambled slowly home. As I came in through the gate and shut it behind me, I had the notion to go down to the pool and sit on the edge, musing in a sad and loving way about Porphyra. As I did so, a picture came into my mind of a village square in Ikaria, a village I had never visited. There was a huge plane tree off to one side, and what I was seeing was an olive tree with plastic tables and chairs under it. There were four chairs, four women sitting in the chairs, their legs stretched out comfortably in a pinwheel pattern towards one another in the center. From the corner of my eye I saw that one of them had long yellow braids. That's all. I felt hugely glad and laughed with tears running down my face, which seemed appropriate for Horizontal Stones Falling Water day. Then the snake, His Highness, crawled out from under a stone, and settled himself down for an afternoon of basking.

I sat there for a long time, basking also, and laughing at bees. The large black and yellow ones are so comical when they land on the marguerite, whose blossom is flat and tiny, a little pink plate innocently facing the sky. But as soon as the bee lands on it, Fwoom! The blossom bends down under its weight, and the bee finds itself suddenly

Anita Sullivan

gathering nectar upside down, clinging to keep from falling off. As soon as it flies off, Pop! The blossom goes back up again. Meanwhile, the bee has gone on to the next flower, Fwoom! He's upside down again. For some reason I find this endlessly amusing. So I didn't hear the bell ringing at my outside door, even though it is rather loud. Since it has only rung one other time since I have lived here, you would think I'd have noticed right away.

It took me awhile to get over to the gate, and when I finally managed to swing it open, I saw two strangers, a young man and woman. They obviously didn't recognize me either. We stared at one another wordlessly, nobody exactly sure what they wanted or dared to say, and yet I saw them without really seeing them, not registering any more than "young male and female." After awhile they both smiled shyly, and asked if they could come in. Wordless still, I held the big wooden door open for them.

They stood close together, looking around wide-eyed. I don't know what they expected. I don't know why I didn't say anything, it's not like me, but I guess I knew they were not new members of our little Experiment dropping in to join the company.

I turned and walked back to the house, figuring they would follow me, but when I stopped by the pool to look back over at them I noticed they had moved all the way across the open yard in front of this part of the wall, and up to the first terrace, the one above me. This happened much more quickly than they could have walked—even run—there, so I knew they had floated, or made some kind of jump. This gave me a little chill.

"Who are you?" I asked when I finally caught up to them, still not walking at my usual brisk pace. They were staring at me with their eyes huge, and I realized I was wearing an old white sun dress with flaring sleeves, and my hair (which is black and long) tied up on top of my head in a big knot with a gold cord, so it's possible I looked like some kind of witch or other magical creature to them. Now that I regarded them more closely, I saw how young they were, probably under twenty, and that they were identical twins.

They both opened their mouths as if trying to answer, but the only sound that came out was irregular, loud breathing. I squinted a little, and could see that something was not quite right about their substance. Like the lions, *I could see through them.* Not totally, but I could make out the shadow of the ground, the general shape of garden plants, and as they shifted position slightly, these things shifted too. I felt dizzy, and reached out for a nearby chair.

"Where are we?" The girl said finally. Her voice was high and sweet. She looked over at her brother, smiled an impish little smile, and punched his shoulder. "You there, Dan? We dreaming together again?"

Her brother's jaw shifted a little, as if it were trying to smile and be tough at the same time. But his brows came together and he looked back at me.

"Are we in a dream?" he said, almost accusingly.

*Oh, if I could answer that question for you, sir!* I was tempted to act queenly. How often does one have the chance to be on the giving end of a dream, to be the gate keeper, the guide through the mystery? I shook my head to clear it, not as if to say no, and motioned them to sit down in the shade. Something was nagging at the back of my mind, a snippet of information. Was I supposed to know who these people were?

Anita Sullivan

"Let me bring you something to drink," I said firmly, and left for the kitchen. I would call for Heloise. She would at least let me know if they were real, a thing I doubted mightily. As I was placing juice glasses onto a tray the thought struck me, "What if these are live humans having a conscious dream?" And I smiled as I remembered how the first couple of years here I had worried about waves of such people drifting into my private space at all hours of the day and night. The chances of that, I was now certain, were practically nil. These two had undertaken quite a trip to arrive at this place. Why?

They were still there when I returned, and they were able to take the drinks, and seemed to drink them. But we had no ordinary conversation.

The boy was Dan, the girl was Donna. They were looking for something, but they didn't know what. So far as they knew, they had flown here, through a sky with their arms sticking out to their sides like airplane wings. They flew over woods, quite a lot of woods, and then over water. They believed they had arrived at their destination, but were puzzled by my presence, yet they assumed that I must be a magical or sacred person blessed with important information that would help them in their quest. I liked them both and didn't want to disappoint them.

I wanted to help them find out what they needed to know, even if that meant convincing them they were in the wrong place. I began to tell them something about the situation here. But I made a huge discovery: *it was impossible to tell them the truth unless they basically knew it already.*

"My name is Carley. I used to be alive on Earth. I died when I was eighty-seven, and as I was dying, I heard a voice that told me I had a choice between dying and staying alive under certain very strict circumstances."

I opened my mouth to say these words, but they sounded ridiculous even to me. Yet anything remotely similar sounded equally ridiculous. Who is going to believe this situation except someone who has actually gone through it? I couldn't say to these kids, "You're in a dream," because maybe they weren't. I couldn't say, "This is a real place," because I don't know what kind of truth I am telling them. For all I knew they were only spirits of someone who had lived hundreds of years ago. But I didn't believe that either. *Is it possible to stumble upon this place by accident?* This thought nagged me fiercely, because I now believe the answer to that question is "No!"

Heloise was nowhere to be found, and although the lions were actually pacing quite near us, in their semi-transparent condition, they remained ornamental rather than useful, as usual.

"Are you looking for something you have lost?" I asked. Perhaps I ought to have said *someone.* They glanced at each other, shrugged, wiggled their heads back and forth as if to jog their memories. "We're brother and sister, we keep having dreams together," they managed to say. "We feel sad when we have these dreams. I guess we are looking for something we have lost, yes. But we always forget what it was!" Their eyes both filled with tears. The dream had let them down, or they weren't ready for it yet.

I leaned forward, looking at them closely, from Donna to Dan, Dan to Donna, into their beautiful, warm, hazel-green eyes. The eyes are the windows of the soul, I thought. Maybe I can plant an idea there.

"Come back again three days from now," I said softly. "Three days from now, three days from now." I felt like Glinda the Good in

Anita Sullivan

*The Wizard of Oz*. "Here, wait!" Before they might take my advice and disappear, I jumped up and ran down to the little garden shed. There on a shelf inside was a box of colored chalk. Rushing back, I reached out and took hold of their hands, one each, and made a little wriggly line with blue chalk on the top of their wrists. "This is the snake, for memory," I said, wildly. The chalk did, indeed, make a legible mark. "You will remember this dream, and you will return."

And soon afterwards they began to fade away right in front of me, with hopeful looks on their sweet innocent faces, their glowing eyes the last thing I remember before they winked out of my sight.

## The Twins

Memory, how fickle she is! The next morning I was listening to Rossini's opera *The Italian from Algiers* with Agnes Balsa singing the major female role; red-gold sun filtered through the curtains, splashing appropriately all over the music room floor, and I was dancing and feeling clearheaded and tingling with unfocussed anticipation. I decided on the spot that we needed to do some chamber music around here. The rest of the morning I spent placidly plotting ways to convince Djan to take up the viola da gamba, Mick the violin, Eugenia viola, Eden the bass. Then I switched them all around again, partly for fun, but partly to keep from being nervous about actually suggesting my idea to them. Beneath it all was a hunger to make music with other people again. Here we have before us the luxury of eternity to learn new skills . . . . I kept making new resolutions on top of new fantasies, and I totally failed to ponder the previous afternoon's visitation.

I had no idea that Eugenia had been teaching herself water colors in her wee cottage, that Mick had started a huge mosaic out of glass and colored rock behind his house, and that Djan not only played the didgeridoo but could draw animals out of his head like any old Paleolithic cave dweller. Eden, meanwhile, was venting his creative energies by fixing up his cabin in the woods, carving his own doorways and bannisters with hand tools. Part of his original agreement with the Arbiters had been to start with a house rough and small, so he could expand and shape it to his own taste as he grew accustomed to the new life. Apparently he had in mind tearing it down and rebuilding it over and over, for variety. Architecture is a passion of his. "What I really wanted was a revolving house," he grinned, "one that revolves really slowly during the day, so the light stays almost same in each of the rooms, but the view is different. But the Arbiter said that wasn't in the Plan, and of course I couldn't argue!" He stopped, an odd look on his face. "A flying house would be nice too," he added.

At any rate, in the mania of my new harebrained scheme, I forgot completely about the two visitors, even when Mick, Djan, Eden and Eugenia were there for dinner three days later, and a winter storm was coming in outside, charging the atmosphere with suspense. You'd think that would have reminded me that *three days* had passed.

Djan and Eden had started a conversation about tracking. Since our dream travels required a certain adept attention to the details of geography, we had all found ways to train our memories and powers of observation to recall specific locations that we wanted to re-visit.

"When Carley and I first went to Ikaria, it's so amazing we even ended up on the same island!" Eugenia said. "And South Dakota!"

We laughed, looking at Mick who would have landed us in North Dakota instead.

"My theory," Djan began slowly, tipping his chair back. We all smiled and sagged comfortably into our chairs. How many years would it take for us to lose the capacity for conversation? I wondered. Would we become like an old married couple whose every dialogue followed a set formula with few variations? Will our *thinking* stagnate so much that we each lose the capacity for new ideas? Sipping wine in the loving company of friends, I couldn't work up a decent attitude of anguish.

"The trajectory of a Hoopoe, for example," he was continuing. "You watch the bird fly clear across the yard, over the fence, across the road, to a tree branch down by the shore. For a bird that's the equivalent of maybe a mile or two, eh? In what way does the bird know ahead of time where it is going? They don't have a narrative, like we do, to tell them where they want to end up, to give them the map."

"The birds-eye view," I said in a small voice.

"It's just habit," said Mick with a shrug. "They get to know their territory, and they just keep doing the same thing."

Djan shook his head. "But no, think about it for a minute. Even for humans, even the act of picking up a glass of wine, or—" he smiled, "tipping your chair back just far enough that it doesn't fall over—*each time* it's just as complicated, whether you call it 'habit' or not. Humans have a verbal directive to guide us in so many of our simplest actions, even if we don't notice what we're saying to ourselves. But the bird starts flying out of a kind of urge, with a certain faith that things will show up along the way to guide him. Her." He stopped.

"Yeah, it's like radar!" Eden said, "Keeping the path true. Three flaps from the first branch the willow tree has to show up in the space just to the left of his eye, and then the wall looms up under him, a part of the wall he suddenly remembers. Yeah, it's all about suddenly remembering things as they come up, not knowing ahead of time!" He was nodding as he felt a new understanding blossoming in his mind.

But the phrase "suddenly remembering" made me suddenly remember. I felt a chill, as if the wind outside were coming through the walls. My hands started to shake. I put down my fork. "Umm . . . ." I said, getting ready to tell the story. Everyone was suddenly quiet, wondering if I had had a relapse. But at the same moment, like Macbeth seeing Banquo's ghost, Eden's eyes opened wide and he began to stand up slowly from his place. He was facing the outer windows, the ones looking out onto the garden, although it was now dark. His mouth opened wider and wider as he tried to take in more air.

We all turned. There, shimmering and hovering a foot or so above the tiles, were the twins. They looked a little less substantial this time than before, even though there was less to see behind them – or rather through them – because of the lack of light.

"Dan! Donna!" Eden said in a choked voice. Tears were running down his cheeks and I thought he was going to keel over. He slid around from his side of the table rapidly and clumsily, but then stopped. It was obvious these were apparitions of some sort, not real live people. He didn't want to scare them away.

"Dan! Donna! Are you there? It's me, Eden. I'm alive!" It was all he could say. We froze in place.

The twins seemed to bob in the air, neither making gestures nor speaking. I couldn't tell if they saw Eden or not, if he and they were

Anita Sullivan

communicating. Unconsciously we all leaned forward as if to make it happen. Let them talk! Please let them!

The twins' faces seemed to register something. Their eyes widened too, as if they saw him, and then they both broke into huge smiles. The three of them looked at one another for about a minute, without moving. Several times Eden opened his mouth, but then closed it again. Finally, the twins faded, as they had done for me. They didn't drift back through the windows, they just disappeared, not even leaving a shape in the air.

We all stayed in our chairs, sort of gasping and shaking and being quiet for a long, long time. Eden sat back down and put his face into his hands. He kept sighing, huge sobbing sighs. Eugenia finally went over and leaned on him, her head on his shoulders.

Later it was Djan who suggested gently to Eden that the twins had probably been dreaming of him. His younger brother and sister, missing him badly, probably were seeking him out in their dreams, and they had found him. This was a good thing, because now they would go home at peace, knowing he was in a good place. If they were religious, they could think of it as heaven.

Eden managed to tell us who they were, his younger siblings, high school sophomores when he had died. "I know we can't talk," he kept saying, and then breaking down into weeping. "I can't ask them any questions, how they're doing, or anything like that. They can't tell me any news. That's the rule. I know that. I just hope – I just hope – " and he broke down again.

"I do believe they saw you, Eden," said Eugenia, standing behind him and massaging his neck and shoulders. "I'm sure they were dreaming about you, and they will feel better now."

"I don't want them to come back!" Eden almost wailed. "I hope they don't keep coming! I want to ask them about Mom and Dad, and about Natalie. Is she still alive? Did she get better? But they can't tell me. It's against the rules. I don't want anything to happen to them!" And he blubbered on and on, until he finally exhausted himself and we helped him upstairs to bed.

Although we were exhausted too, we went into the library and sat sprawled around on the sofas and chairs until dawn, half talking, half dozing.

"This is weird!" said Mick. "I mean, it's like an invasion." He shivered and held his elbows. "You know what I mean? The other world again. We're supposed to be cut off from that. I just don't get it. Are things changing here, I mean really changing?"

Djan looked solemn. I thought back to our earlier conversation, when he and Eden were talking about the Hoopoe. Navigation by local memory, not by knowing the Big Picture. The way geese in their migrations work, each goose following the minute changes of the goose in front. Or people inside their houses making small daily decisions, not ever quite doing the same thing twice.

"Do you think something really is changing?" I asked, echoing Mick.

"It seems natural enough that somebody in their dream body might appear in our lives," said Eugenia after awhile. "But this was somehow so cruel. I don't mean anybody is being cruel on purpose, but it hurt Eden so much. I wouldn't want that to happen again."

"You mean other people showing up too?" Mick said. His eyes widened at the thought.

Anita Sullivan

"But it's O.K., really," I said. "It happened out of love. That's probably the only way it could happen."

New Zealand

That night I dreamed without going there. This had become unusual for any of us, so accustomed were we to traveling through our dreams. It was as if I had been deputized to do some sort of survey, and it was more efficient to come and go without dragging my full self along.

So far as I know, I dreamed of the South Island of New Zealand, along a sparsely-settled but spectacularly beautiful coastline. I was on a train, whose tracks ran along a ridge just above the end of the sand on the beach. We wound around the irregular coastline; I could see the blue water, the white foam as it broke against the shore—sometimes sand, sometimes jagged rocks—then the wet sand, the dry sand, and a silvery and ragged line of dune plants just below where the tracks were firmly set into a foundation of crushed rocks.

There were other passengers on the train, shadowy figures without faces or voices. I was looking for someone, I believe. We came, after hours of travel, to a small town, and I got off the train for awhile, maybe for several days. The town ran parallel to the beach and consisted of two rows of sturdy wooden, one-story shops for about two blocks, and then a half dozen neat little fenced cottages. The shops were separated by narrow alleys, barred at the street end by a wooden gate painted red. A whole street of red gates and small store windows painted yellow and green and blue and white. Very cheerful, but some-what bravely so, as if the population had dwindled to almost nothing, and people were keeping up a false hope with all this paint. I had the sense that in the houses on the side away from the sea, the back gardens would be filled with quiet, like my own. But I could not go there to find out.

I approached one store and a man of about sixty with mild blue eyes and a face reddened by sun and sea air came out to greet me. He didn't smile or frown, only squinted carefully and extended his hand for me to shake. We spoke briefly, I asked him a question and he answered it. I told him this was the most beautiful place I had ever seen in my life.

"In your life!" He said, and slapped his knee, laughing. "In your life, right!" Then he took me by the sleeve and led me through the red gate into a door on the side of his store. Inside was a huge space like a studio, not a single canned good or sack or box to show this was a place for selling things. Skylights in the ceiling made pools of sun on the brick walls, onto the stone floor. In the middle of the room a short man sat at an easel with his left arm upraised, painting.

"Take this man out of here," said the first man, and held his own left arm up against the side of his face as if warding off something divine or terrible. "He's been here painting the sea as long as anybody can remember. We don't know what to do with him."

"What's his name?" I whispered.

"Sam," said the first man solemnly, his voice suddenly going very deep, and he lingered over the "m" so it came out "Sam m m m m m m m" as if he were playing the cello. Outside I could hear the sea sound come up to blend with his voice. This made me dizzy through my ears, not my eyes, so I reeled a bit.

Anita Sullivan

The man called Sam rocked back and forth on his little chair. "You're in my light!" He complained, and turned around to look at me. We recognized each other right away. He had been a good friend of David's and mine, a high school art teacher from New Zealand who had retired in our town. We had many fine long evenings of conversation together.

"Are you coming back with me?" I asked.

Sam shook his head. The other man was crossing the room and leaving through the door where we had come in. Like a dragon's tail, the thought suddenly caught up with me: *he was an old man.* I hadn't seen anybody over 40 for a couple of years. What did this mean? But I turned my attention back to Sam.

"I'm a sound painter," he said proudly. "It's me job, y' know, mate!" He grinned, exaggerating his New Zealand accent, and shifted his legs slightly so he was practically straddling his chair. I looked now at his canvas for the first time, and saw that it was as large as the world. On it was a painting of the sea, but in different colors from how it looked outside, what I could see from the single window.

"All the random sounds in the world, they come snaking over here to me and I turn them into a painting. Somebody else out there is doing a weaving, somebody maybe a symphony or a story. It's not busy-work, you see." He looked up at me with his gray-blue eyes twinkling. I felt deeply comforted. Somebody had a job to do that was truly worth doing.

"How do you account for the fact – " I began, sensing the beginning of an enormous question about to leave my mouth, but I needed to start over.

"How does one keep track of oneself?" I stammered.

He lifted his chin slightly, understanding the question.

"You're always one notch behind, no matter what," he said, shifting his legs so his knees touched at one corner of the chair. How many possible positions are there for sitting? I wondered if he ever stood up. Or ate. Or slept. "You can go on and on, fast or slow, and you'll always be one notch behind yourself. You never recognize your today self because all you have to go by is yesterday, and so with the world itself, the same." He turned and looked back at his painting. "Oh, she's going crook!" He cried, and began to plunge his brush deeply into the collection of cans ranged around his feet, and to slap it with seeming wild abandon against the canvas. Soon the painting took on a pastel sheen, with the purples and greens totally engulfed by paler colors. "I like the work, the combination of hearing and seeing. The ocean gives me the day's sounds from all over the world, the groans and thuds and screeches, the angry and ugly sounds along with all the good ones. No duplicates. They make into a very, very subtle roar, the sea sound. It's up to me to interpret it. If I do say so, I'm a pretty good interpreter."

He waved his hand at the canvas, and I gazed and gazed. I was seeing the same coastline shape that I had seen from the train, all over again, but the colors were different. Therefore, was I seeing the same coastline? I rocked back and forth on my toes. I felt like an airplane must feel when it barrels down the runway, helpless to fend off the lift that its structure makes inevitable. I ran out of the room, realizing I needed to catch the train. My bare knees had damp splotches of red paint on them.

Anita Sullivan

Purity

Eden came in the next morning while I was tuning the harpsichord. He apologized for "being a hermit" for so long. Our conversation took place in fits and starts, the way the winter sun was coming through the windows. At one point, in fact, I mentioned that I would like some new glass for the windows and he brightened up. "Hey, great idea, we could make glass! I've always wanted to do some chemistry, you know, bloop! bloop!" He waved his hands around to indicate beakers bubbling. "But Mick is really the one who knows about glass. He's making a mosaic in his back yard now, I've seen it. Partly from naturally colored rocks he's picked up all over the place, but he's been getting into making his own stuff." He paused a minute, took a deep breath. "In fact, I think he's been getting into alchemy."

"Alchemy?" I felt myself stiffen. "Turning lead into gold?" I made a face as if to say, "Who would need to do that here?"

"Well, that's just what he calls it," said Eden, continuing as if I had said nothing. "He's not trying to make gold. It's more having to do with the body and the mind, and it involves plants and herbs too, which I guess alchemy never did. He's brewing up stuff and trying it on things, on himself . . . ." He stopped, and his shoulders went up a little as if he had heard himself say too much and he was trying to take it back. He looked over at me to see my reaction, and I was staring back at him with a horrified expression.

"But alchemy and herbal medicine are totally different things," I said slowly. "Good lord, Eden, this sounds serious!"

"Well, I'm not sure . . ." he said.

"But you said he was trying stuff on himself. What for? What's he trying to turn himself into? He's already perfectly healthy, we all are!" For some reason I felt an unreasonable panic rising. *The time is out of joint.* "Is it so very difficult to maintain happiness?" I went on, beginning to tilt towards anger.

"Humans are naturally curious," he began, rather lamely, and I plowed right over him.

"Damn it, if we can't learn to be happy here, where can we? Happiness is a skill. There's a difference between true happiness, joy— whatever you want to call it—and just plain relief. Most people think happiness is relief, and they spend a lot of energy trying to get that relief. From boredom, or pain, or a vague persistent sense of missing out on something better. Happiness is a skill, but it's a *passive* skill. You learn to receive it, to make yourself ready for it so it can just come and land on you, like—oh, I don't know—like bees on flowers. You bask in it, quietly!"

Eden grinned. "Oh, I don't know about quietly," he said. "You can dive around in it like a porpoise, burrow through it like a gopher, you can toss it up and let it fall on your head!"

"Good grief! You're quoting Scrooge McDuck, Eden! You're too young for the Mickey Mouse comics!" I grinned back. But quickly we both got serious again.

I told him that it sounded as if Mick were in danger of doing himself harm. "What's to keep him from poisoning himself?" I said. "Maybe, deep down, that's what he wants to do."

Eden shook his head. "I think it's more like trying for per- fection," he said.

Anita Sullivan

"It's kind of easy here," he went on slowly, "for us to go to extremes with things. I mean, well," he scrunched his forehead the way he did when he was thinking hard, "it's hard to know when you've gone off the deep end. Is there even a deep end any more?"

"I guess that's how we help each other out," I said. "One person's deep end is another person's—" I stopped.

"Egg cup!" he shot back.

"Wading pool!"

"Petrie dish!"

"What?"

We were both too worried even to go off on one of our silly word tangents. So we let the conversation drop, and agreed (without saying so) to pay special attention to Mick the next time we all got together.

But it was awhile before we were all together again. Everyone was a little out of sorts after Eden's brother and sister's visit. We seemed to be in a phase of hunkering down, or at least taking trips in twos instead of in larger groups. Thus it was that I happened to have a private conversation with Mick before our whole group finally met again for dinner in the cafeteria.

He knocked on the door of the music room one evening, after I had already gone upstairs to bed, not to sleep, but to sit with a cup of tea by the fire, just rocking. I hollered at him to come up, and he came into the room having taken his shoes off as people always did in my house, so that I thought of the poem about fog: "The fog comes / on little cat feet."

His eyes looked a little odd, as if he hadn't slept for awhile. He sat down on the hearth kitty-corner from me, hands on his knees, not looking at me.

"I've been working on some stuff," he began. Then he shook his head and started over. "I've gotta figure out – I'm right on the verge of something really important, and I need some help." He stopped again. I just sat quietly. Quickly running through my mind was a thought I had tried to avoid ever since that first day when he came to my gate: *he's not quite up to this new life.* It wasn't an attitude of superiority on my part that allowed this thought, but rather a vague sense that Mick was just not doing well. He was not "ripening" or "maturing" or whatever it is that we are supposed to be doing here above and beyond the usual childhood-to-adult sequence we manage in our regular lifespan. Instead, I had the nagging fear that his peculiar intelligence was driving him down an enticing side path.

"Tell me about it."

"I need you to talk Eugenia into having sex with me," he said. Whatever I was expecting, it wasn't this.

"I'm serious."

I closed my eyes and took a deep breath. When I opened them again, he was still talking, oblivious to me, the way people will do when they're in pain and don't realize theirs might be less than yours. He was going on about purity, getting rid of toxins, moving to a higher level of awareness through clarity of mind and spirit, transformation. I had heard this kind of thing before. I interrupted him.

"Why are people so damned seduced by the idea of purity?" I half snarled. "Why don't we concentrate on what it is to be fully human! Isn't that, ultimately what we're *here* for, to be fully human? What does purity have to do with it? Pure what?"

"Fully human doesn't mean the same thing here that it did before," he said quietly. Obviously he had thought about this. "Now we are leading the way, we're doing something different, something ordinary humans haven't ever done before, not ever. I thought at first it was just going to happen, no matter what we did. All we had to do was stay alive here. But lately I've come to realize it won't ever happen if we don't take an active part."

"But the very fact that you are here indicates some sort of active part, you nitwit!" I thought this, but said nothing

He went on, not looking at me directly, which for him always meant he was keeping something back. "You know, I just recently figured out – " he laughed a little, "Isn't it crazy, that we are still figuring things out here? I mean, really *obvious* things that we should have known before!" He paused, and I found myself looking at him as if he were getting ready to go away for years, and I was trying to impress his image on my memory – I was cataloguing things: the firelight on his skin, the shape of his upper arms coming out from the dark red tee shirt. This was an action from an earlier time, and it surprised me to find myself doing it now. We don't have to do that anymore, we are able to see each other every day from now on. Does this make us indifferent to one another? Impulsively I reached out and touched his leg. He jumped.

"What are you doing, Mick?" I half whispered.

He swallowed, and looked away. I felt my throat tighten. What did I need to say? Why had he come to me, and not to Djan? Because I am a woman and he wanted me to use my influence with Eugenia to help him carry out an experiment. This strikes me as incredibly calculated behavior, which I don't like or understand.

". . . people have always just survived. Nature doesn't require that people *thrive* in order to stay on the planet and keep going as a species. It's the *survival* of the fittest, remember?" He was talking again, and I had missed some of it. "But there isn't any overall drive towards the finest possible. I've never understood that, but it's just how it is. Now we really have the chance to *thrive*. We can have the best nutrition, the best health, the optimum stimulus – we can refine ourselves into whatever is possible for human beings to become. A kind of purifying process." His eyes were glowing with almost religious fervor. I tilted my head and squinted at him, deliberately showing my skepticism.

"Is that where alchemy comes in?" I said flatly. I was annoyed, even a little hurt that he seemed to be using me.

"Who told you that?" He said, then realized it must be Eden, and laughed. "Oh, well, then you already know a little about what I'm doing. I've got a kind of chemistry lab, complete with retorts and beakers and pipettes and siphons. I've been refining things. Plant essences mostly, and working with crystals too, so 'alchemy' is really quite a loose term. But I don't see why it shouldn't include organic material. We need to get away from the stupid distinction between 'living' and 'dead' matter anyhow. It's all alive in some sense, on a huge spectrum."

He took a deep breath, and went on as if finally noticing my presence and answering the question I might have asked. "I get my instructions from dreams, and some of these old herbals we were using in the library, and from—" he stopped himself, and shrugged. "It

Anita Sullivan

doesn't matter really. The point is, finally, after so many years of being cloudy inside my head, I'm finally starting to see clearly. I've slowed down enough, and every now and then I really *see*. I can actually feel my body changing, a kind of purifying process . . . ." He laughed and looked directly at me for the first time, no longer manipulating, just plain embarrassed.

But I said nothing. Not so much because I wanted to smoke him out, but because I really wanted to see what he did with the purity argument. It's a very powerful one, tied inextricably with the religious impulse, and I've always wanted to be convinced. Is not purity the highest state of all? Don't we want to rise, gradually, through levels of clarity and beauty to become one with the eternal Mind, or the Divine, that is the Universe? In some sense or another, most religions aspire to that. And here we are, a group of humans who can bypass many of the usual human handicaps and go directly to this blazing path if we so choose, because we are playing by a totally different set of rules. Isn't he right, shouldn't we actively be trying to become divine, or some such?

He talked on, making idealistic noises, but I found myself less and less listening to his words, and instead giving way to a swelling emotional image, the impression his spirit was making upon my own. "He is dying," I thought, in surprise, and then remembered that none of us has any guarantee of immortality, even here. I felt miserable, and frightened.

"I've always hung with uncertainty," I said, rather lamely. As he continued to talk I looked into the fire and remembered the hummingbird I had been seeing during that strange, lonely, first year in this villa. I remember that I had been certain it was a sign of Mick and

Eugenia, two good friends. I had seen many hummingbirds since, and other birds as well, but not really seen them the same way. What had happened to that first bird? Had it died by now? How long did hummingbirds live?

I tried to work up a longing for purity, and failed. If I hold a glass of wine up to the light and think "how beautiful!" then put it down and forget, how does that differ from never having done it at all? It does differ, I know that. What I need is not purity, but the answer to this question, "what is the difference?" And I think the answer has already come many times, it is simply a matter of increasing its frequency.

Only towards dawn, when he returned to the original purpose of his visit, did it even occur to him that talking about sex might cause me pain.

"Why sex with Eugenia, why not with me?" I had said rather harshly at this point, an attempt at humor, but also out of curiosity, and even a jibe at myself.

His eyes widened and I could see his jaw tighten. Mick, a normally glib talker, was suddenly struck into silence. I tilted my head a little, smiling; yet unaccountably my eyes filled with tears. He was looking down, and in a little while I saw his own tears falling, and his shoulders shaking. I went to sit beside him, even though there was not much room on the hearth, and we stayed in that awkward position for awhile. Although that brought our conversation effectively to a stop, I thought at the time that he didn't want to continue because he was being sensitive to the fact that I had been mortally sickened by an encounter with what amounted to the "male principle," a centaur, and

Anita Sullivan

he was probably feeling guilty for dumping his purity and sex and alchemy ideas on me. What I didn't consider was that he might be so far gone in his notions of purity that he would regard me as having been irreparably sullied by this experience; for the injury had registered in his mind as if it had been an actual rape, rather than something more like a ritual version of one. And he had completely overlooked the possibility that this attitude might not sit too well with me.

Gently I steered him into agreeing that we needed to call a group meeting. We could even put sex on the agenda if that would make him happy, set up some ground rules, check out what people were feeling on the subject. For the time being he seemed fixed on this as the next and most necessary step in whatever ritual he was devising for the advancement of the human species: duality as acted out between the male and female principles, leading to unity. Or some such.

"I still have to be convinced that 'purity' is necessary," I said, my final position for the night. "I think it's an innately seductive and dangerous idea, Mick, is what I think."

"We need to be *doing* something!" He said, standing up and stretching elaborately, ready to leave. "We shouldn't be just sitting a-round like people in a nursing home for crying out loud! We're ob-viously part of a larger process going on, but if we pay no attention, we get used. I'm not a control freak or anything," he said, again not look-ing directly at me. His expression was opaque, veiled. "I'm willing to go with the flow, but I do think there is a flow, you know what I mean? We're getting stagnant here, I can't stand it!"

I shrugged. "Yes, Mick, I certainly can agree this is an import-ant enough issue that we need to see what the others think, don't you agree?" He nodded, and I went on in a rush. "My view is that what we're all *doing* here may be experimental, but it's not a matter that can be thought out in advance, nor analyzed in an intellectual way; it's more like following the story."

The story is still ahead of us, moving shadow-like along. Doesn't matter if we run to keep up with it, or if we stop, it's always moving at the same distance before us, making it seem as if we are following it when we are not.

"Oh, what the hell, maybe we're just talking about love!" Mick said, as we parted our ways, both totally exhausted, just as the sky was growing light. "Forget frigging purity, let's call it love!" He opened his arms to give me a hug. But it was one of those light, careful hugs that people give when they're trying to be physical without being sexual with one another. This is the way Mick always hugged, I remembered. Right then I wanted to wrap my arms around him in a huge bear embrace, burning through to some kind of core. Now that would be alchemy!

But I only sighed, returned his wimpy hug in equal measure. No, I thought, we're talking about two human beings who see the world totally differently. "It's turtles all the way down, kid!" I assured him, and reeled off to my couch. I could hear him cackling all the way down to the gate.


Ninety-Nine Times as High as the Moon
"Grant us, in the absence of sleep, serenity."
George Seferis.


"Evolving is not something one can do on purpose." Djan was tilted back in a chair so far it would have gone over it if hadn't been

Anita Sullivan

propped against the back wall of the cafeteria. His booted feet were stretched out under the table and he was drinking his second beer.

*Why do men always wear their shoes when they don't have to?* I was idly wondering, a wonder I have wondered oft before. I was simultaneously savoring a glass of sauvignon blanc and wiggling my free toes in their straw sandals.

"I'm not even sure we can do *purity* on purpose . . . but maybe that's just me rationalizing my laziness," Djan went on before Mick could open his mouth, though I'm not sure he wanted to any more by this time. After an hour listening to him explain, the rest of us had all put pretty much of a kebosh onto his alchemical aspirations. We just plain couldn't work up an interest; it sounded too much like work. Like dogma too, in disguise (my opinion).

Mick was shaking his head in frustration and disappointment. He strode back and forth in front of us like a saint mistakenly hauled before the Inquisition. Or rather, more like a member of the Inquisition hauled before a panel of saints. We forgave him right off and went back to our wine and the essential things. Our inclinations at that moment at least, were away from clarity, higher consciousness, the possibility of evolving into a higher species, blah blah blah, and more towards a semi-conscious awareness of something resembling serenity. It wasn't even the usual apathy that accompanies a state of physical comfort. More than that. We were talking so far at cross-purposes as to be almost unintelligible to one another.

"Loosen up, Mick," said Eugenia, sipping a glass of retsina and nibbling on focaccia with artichokes and olive paste. She was looking at him fondly but with a puzzled expression. "You sound like a religious fanatic," she said. Then she sat up straight and took a deep breath. "I'm sorry, I know you're serious about this. But you sound like one of those tent preachers, telling us we'll all go to hell if we don't do this or that. Pretty soon you'll be telling us we have to start renouncing worldly pleasures." She paused and stared at her wine glass for a moment. "We're not all sitting here getting drunk and then going home to sleep it off, same old routine. Don't you understand, Mick, we're actually *happy*. It doesn't get any better than this!"

"And the reason – !" This was Eden, who was over at his own table with its candle in the middle, working his way through a salad, a pizza and an Italian soda. "The reason we can call this – " he waved his hand around the room, "happiness, instead of some big-deal higher ecstasy – is because it doesn't go away the next morning! This is sustainable happiness, a deep contentment. You don't have to flagellate yourself, or shoot something into your veins for it, it's just natural!"

I nodded vigorously. Couldn't have said it better myself. Djan grunted, squinted, and swigged his beer, tilting his chair back again and relapsing into his own version of happiness.

Mick had outlined briefly but clearly his "alchemical" plans, not knowing it would be such an uphill battle. He had brought along a small set of vials for each of us, hoping to persuade us to start a new regimen. When pressed, he had to admit the vials contained a concoction that would act as a physical purge (required fasting included according to a rigorous schedule), followed by an escalating series of hallucinogenic drugs. These, combined with a very complex set of ritual body positions and exercises, would start us on the way to becoming pure enough in body and mind to begin focusing in earnest on the spirit. He had worked it out carefully. It was all new, he assured us, not just a tired re-run of New-Age ideas, or even a resurrection of

Anita Sullivan

shamanistic practices from "native" cultures. "This stuff comes from people who are way more advanced than us, who have lived through a slew of reincarnations. They know what they're talking about. They are way beyond being human any more. It's just a place we need to be going, and we have the capacity, we can go there! I mean, we are in a different starting place now, like being up above the atmosphere! We have got to do this, it's like – like bringing all the parallel realities together in one big bang!"

He was practically inarticulate in his excitement. We understood the rational force of his arguments. We all felt our own doubts gathering and drifting, but breaking apart again like wispy clouds in the face of a robust full moon. As for me, I was too recently a recipient of concoctions from herbal recipes myself to want any further experimenting along that line right at present. And what did he mean by *people who are way more advanced than us*? This wanted looking into.

"The downfall of the rational mind," murmured Djan, taking a deep breath and puffing out his cheeks, then releasing his breath in a long quiet hiss.

"Reason is not the highest human faculty," I murmured myself. I had figured that much out even when I was still alive the first time.

"I don't think I'm talking about reason," said Mick, shaking his head. "This is way higher than that."

"Well there's a relief!" said Eugenia. It was an odd remark for her, since she is rarely cynical.

"We already know what we need, it's a matter of finding out," said Djan. But he didn't seem to care if we heard him, he wasn't making a pronouncement.

I nodded again. "I think the fact that we just plain *don't want* to do what Mick is suggesting, I think that is worth paying attention to. Body wisdom is what I call it."

"You're all so damned complacent!" Mick shouted. He shook his head again, and then slumped down into a chair at the end of the room, over where the huge windows swooped down into a kind of sash in the corner.

Djan's chair came down again. He rested his elbows on his knees (after carefully placing his beer bottle onto the table), bowed his head for a little, and then lifted it. Try as he would not to seem like a tribal leader, he nevertheless was one. It didn't pose a problem of hierarchy for us, though, since we tend to be such poor followers.

"We shouldn't dismiss Mick's ideas so casually this way. I believe we need to be clear and totally honest with one another and with ourselves. To harbor a difference of philosophy this profound might be impossible in such a small group as this. If we can't talk it out, we may have to resort to the oldest solution of all, which is simply dividing ourselves up again."

There was a collective intake of breath as it finally hit us. This was the core issue, our community. I saw Mick suddenly go very still.

Djan sat looking around at all of us, gently nodding his large grizzled head.

"I've got something to say, then," said Eugenia very matter-of-factly. "I think it's been an incredible blessing that we have found a way to be together, all of us. I love our times together, and I truly think this is the heart of the Experiment, our community. People simply can't live alone. If you think of this in a scientific way, I believe we've already done the most important thing, by figuring out how to be together. We couldn't stay sane otherwise. I like very much the *way* we have gone about our lives together. Speaking for myself, I like the spontaneous nature of our life here, that we just feel our way along, day to day. I trust that completely. So, I guess I feel that things are basically fine. It makes me uncomfortable to think about doing what you suggest, Mick. I don't see the need for it." She shrugged, "I feel that taking a deliberate action to <u>improve</u> ourselves is a contradiction in terms. That's just how I feel. End of sermon." She tried to smile, but her smile died away and she lapsed into a kind of worried silence.

Eden was rustling around and it was obvious he wanted to speak next.

"I don't have anything profound to say," he began. "But Djan is right, this is important, and I have a feeling we really need to thrash it out. I know we've already talked, and I think we all get the idea of what Mick has in mind." He looked over at Mick with a little apologetic grin. "I guess you think we're all pretty dense, Mick, and that we really don't get what you're saying. But seriously, I believe this represents a huge gap here. I mean, it's really – there's really a big difference in philosophy between your attitude and what seems to be the attitude of the rest of us. I don't mean we're all united against you, no, I don't mean that at all. It's kind of like, what is that term in physics? Inertia! Yeah, we are putting up this big wall of inertia, but it comes from a deep place, it doesn't come from being lazy, or – I don't know – corrupted? You've got to trust us, Mick. We aren't all a bunch of, what is it? Hedonists, you know, featherhead pleasure seekers wallowing in our comforts – " he waved his hand around the cafeteria, "our welfare state here. And here's Mick like the old Puritan work ethic, issuing a warning to keep us from going downhill. But I really think something else entirely is going on here, and that's what you're not seeing, Mick. I think we're building something, each of us separately, and also together. We seem to have developed an integrity that keeps us from just wallowing in surface pleasure. I don't mean we're invincible, and that we can't be corrupted, but I don't think the best way to proceed is to keep—I don't know, flagellating ourselves to make sure we keep our noses clean. Sorry, that wasn't too eloquent." He stopped with a rueful expression and sighed.

My mind was whirling. Words and phrases were going through, like "intellect" and "gut feeling," and "purpose" I kept waving them off. Will this boil down to a senseless confrontation, where both sides are convinced they are right and nobody really understands what is going on?

"What is really going on here? That's what we need to know," I said. "I mean, Mick could be right, we're all sinking into a kind of primitive state, and *we don't even know it*. I don't believe that, but what do I know? On the other hand, Mick could be wandering off into some crazy side path himself, seduced by this notion of purity, a kind of Darwinist desire to evolve to a higher level of being human. I think the immediate question is simply this: do we change the way we are conducting our lives, or don't we? And if so, why? And if not, why not?"

I stopped, and everybody looked at me as if they expected me to go on. I grinned.

"I'm done for the time being, believe it or not. Although I think if somebody could just recite the right poem, that would make a lot of things much more clear all at once. I'm serious."

"Is poetry rational?" Djan couldn't help asking.

"It has its own logic," I said. "And I believe maybe that's the kind of logic we need right now. A normal rational discussion of these issues probably won't get us anywhere." I shrugged and looked over at Mick. It was an invitation for him to say something.

"I'm just as irrational as the rest of you," he said, with an attempt at a laugh. "In fact, I thought I had practically a Ph.D. in it, because I was a dream therapist for so long. I learned the language of dreams, the symbolic language. And I believed all reality was just one huge dream. I still believe that, but in some sense it doesn't matter so much here. I wish we could break the thing away from rational versus irrational. I mean, don't you *feel* anything about this? I'm going on my gut with this stuff, I promise you. It's an energy thing, you know what I mean? Aren't you bored just sitting around day after day, taking little trips. I mean, we don't really have any purpose here. It seems to be paradise, but really it's only the ground floor. We still lack the *capacity* for enjoying it the way we should, for seeing it. Don't you feel any kind of a drive to get more clear? It's like a chance for permanent ecstasy. Like permanent orgasm!" He chuckled.

Djan broke in here, "Aristotle said, 'humans all naturally desire happiness.' But he didn't really define what that was. Is it a plateau or a mountain path? Is it the end or the way? Philosophically I like to think of humans as permanently active, permanently becoming, always ill defined. It's more exciting that way. And yet – here – " he waved his hand around, "there seems to be the chance for rest. A chance to *stop*. I for one am not particularly concerned whether I'm pausing on a wide rock on the mountainside, or on the mountain top itself. I believe not caring about the difference is, in itself, a kind of wisdom, and not easily come by nor maintained. As if there is truly a heaven and we have arrived in it. I for one would like the chance to relish that state for as long as I am capable. Am I alone in this?"

Eden, Eugenia and I were nodding. We were also growing a bit weary with talk. Our need for comfort was surging to the surface again. I smiled.

"But it's not natural for people to sit and do nothing, no matter how good it feels!" Mick said, but his voice sounded less convinced than before. "They stagnate. I feel that. People always have to make themselves do stuff that's good for them."

"So we're splitting hairs like the ancient theologians," said Djan wryly. "Are we stagnant or are we happy?"

"Do we need a kick in the butt or an eye pillow?" Eden said quietly, and I snickered.

"Are you bothered by not feeling useful in this life here?" Eden continued, turning to Mick. "Does it have to be this purification routine—which seems so rigid—or could you achieve the same goal some other way? We did it once, remember, at the House of Bees." He stopped, as if surprised at his own recollection of this. "There may be other similar opportunities. Perhaps we should be actively pursuing them." He looked around at all of us, but we were losing steam.

Mick was sitting by this time, on a chair at a table next to Eden. He was just sitting straight up in a chair, hands on his thighs, staring in front of him. For the first time that evening a thought crossed my mind: *he has taken something.*

He said nothing in response to Eden. None of us wanted to speak any more until Mick had a chance again. Especially me, I felt like a stupid blabbermouth. Where have the rest of us gone that Mick hasn't been able to go?

"I sometimes see wolves at the edge of my garden," I said, unable to keep my mouth shut. "Or at least I used to, before you all came." Everyone was quiet, suddenly listening in that cautious way that people do when they are afraid they might hear something really looney and uncomfortable. This worried me, because they all know I've fully recovered from my illness. But I blundered on. "I really think it's more like the Old Woman Who Swept the Cobwebs out of the Sky. Ninety-nine times as high as the moon. It was a quiet little job, behind the scenes. Yet without it, the universe would come to a stop. It would get all gummed up!" I smiled. "I think we're doing basically the same thing." I shrugged. "Brooms and buckets, behind the scenes. Maintenance. It's hard work."

Then I remembered one of the wolves was boredom, but the other one was madness.

"Be nice if we knew more about it," said Eugenia, almost crossly, and I wanted to hug her.

Mick started shaking his head, swinging it from side to side like a kid experimenting with how to make himself totally dizzy. He stopped just before I was ready to run over and start slapping him, as if he were hysterical.

"I'm not talking about *work*!" He said, almost spitting the word out. "I'm not talking about doing good work for the world, saving the world. I'm talking about frinking human potential! Our potential! I haven't stopped to figure what kind of big picture we all fit into, I just know that we, here, the five of us, have this incredible possibility – I mean, it's like we've been chosen for a big test. We could take advantage of this amazing situation to do stuff no humans have ever had a hope of doing before. And we're failing!" His voice rose to a kind of wail, and he stopped, and went suddenly all rigid again, like a puppet whose master had hung him up on a peg behind the stage and gone off to lunch.

We were all quiet, mulling this over. The room seemed large, dark and hollow, and seemed to be ticking, loudly, like an enormous clock.

Eden stood up and went over to Mick. He put his hand on Mick's shoulder.

"Mick, you're a grown-up human being for crying out loud. Go on out and evolve like hell and leave us behind in the mud if you want to. Don't let us hold you back. After all, you know there are others out there. We're probably a hopeless lot, and maybe you're right, and you should give up on us – for now at least. But don't go away and forget about us, please keep in touch. We're friends."

This moved Mick suddenly to tears, and he sat there with his head down for awhile, his shoulders shaking, Eden's hand still on his shoulder. I caught myself feeling once again irritated with Mick for disrupting our routine (our sweeping work)! But almost immediately I felt irritated at myself too, as reason quickly reminded me that I had done the same not long ago, by running afoul of a centaur. We have to stick together, to see one another through each phase of this life.

"In sickness and in health," said Djan clearly, not muttering to himself for once, and I caught my breath.

"Poetic logic!" I said, pointing in comic exaggeration to Djan, and smiling through tears of my own.

Anita Sullivan

Yuriko

*"If you cannot trust the dog, the faithful one? And is this anyway a dog?"*

Brigit Pegeen Kelly


The night crickets were starting to sing in the high grass as she came around the corner of the barn, although some light remained in the upper sky. Gray. *The color of Wednesday.* She rolled this phrase around in the back of her mind where it could resonate quietly like distant thunder and lend a slight drama to a scene she was approaching with great care. It was all here: the light, the sound, the prickle of late summer grass on her bare ankles, and beneath, a slight odor of the rotten, the crushed, the sere. She could sense all of this drifting through the atmosphere like substantial but invisible people in satiny easy chairs, all filthy rich and yet austere. Yuriko chuckled at the image, and began to run.

She thought of the small silvery flash that used to appear at random intervals just in front of her face – a week, a month or half a year apart like a baby meteor surfacing briefly in the wrong dimension. She had never told anyone; and only registered it in her own mind as a quick joy, totally inexplicable. But how it made her feel each time was how she felt now: a secret signal from a place she did not know. Now it was larger and more evident, but with all the benefits remaining of secrecy. *To know without being able to name.*

"Am I dead?" She wondered, glancing over at the side of the barn, and behind it to the house that would be starting to glow now if anybody were in it. But she had searched the house from top to bottom, and all the rooms were clean, empty. Gently clean, not squeaky and damp as if someone had been through them recently with mops and sponges to erase all memory of who had lived there.

"I live here, with Masako and Andy, my husband and son," she told herself. "But now they are gone. Or I am gone. Or are we living here at different times?"

This had happened recently. Had she been ill? She could dimly visualize Masako, her husband, stocky and comforting with his warm brown eyes and the endearing streaks of gray in the thick lock of dark hair over his forehead. He had been bending over her, putting cool towels onto her forehead, murmuring words of comfort that she couldn't understand. Andy, a taller version of his father, had been bouncing up and down behind him, wanting to help, frightened, waiting for orders to jump into the car and drive thirty miles to the nearest town for help. They were both wearing white shirts, thick brown belts, gray khaki pants, their usual outfits when they were working at home in the shop, building recumbent bicycles. The barn had been remodeled for the business years before, after Masako came home from Vietnam unable to hold down a job any more, and he had started compulsively repairing bicycles. So many bicycles in Saigon, so many patient, bicycle mechanics scarred from war wounds standing beside their tools, one on each block, hoping someone would break down on their street. He was trying to make up for something. His father had been a computer engineer in Nagasaki, his mother taught Japanese to foreigners in a government language institute. He was expected to follow them into a profession. This was always a source of tension in the family.

Now they were all gone. And she was suddenly awake again, alive, after being unconscious for – how long? She woke up in the late afternoon feeling relaxed and clear. As if somebody had come in while

Anita Sullivan

she was asleep and carefully taken away certain memories, allowing others to emerge, to flex themselves lazily and slowly swell into a warm dominance. Warm and clear, that's how she felt in body and mind.

That her life had totally changed, she had no doubt. She knew Masako and Andy would not come back, that she had the option of staying on at this house without them, and that nobody else would ever appear again in this place as long as she chose to stay here. A blissful feeling of solitude overwhelmed her.

"Why am I not sad?" She thought. "I don't miss them. I'm not afraid. I'm not even curious."

She was running out into the field beside the barn because the grass was beautiful there, and she knew if she went out there and died, or died again, she would be all right. If she didn't die, it would be a place to stand for awhile, maybe all night, until she knew what to do next. Always before, she looked out into this empty abandoned field from the windows of the shop, whenever she was in there helping with the bicycles. Or she walked past it on the path around the house on her way to drive to her job at the hospital. Or she saw the corner of it from the bedroom window. This field, its color and configuration, the irregular and comical hump of Mount Atherton on the far side beyond the woods, the old pear tree splayed right in the middle of her line of sight from the barn window – all of this floated beside her every day of her life since she had married Masako eighteen years before and come from Chicago to this place. It was as if she had taken on, right from the start, a double existence: her house and family on one side, and this field on the other. Although she had walked in the field any number of times, she seemed never to have actually been there at all; as if she couldn't go there truly until after she died.

And now she ran out into the middle of it and stood, panting slightly, facing the mountain. Squinting through her lashes, she looked directly and fully at one blade of grass bending in front of her, along the length of its body to the sturdy seed-head that was drawing it back down towards the earth. She ran her eyes back and forth along its curve as if she were assessing one of her patients in the hospital. She breathed slowly as if adjusting her rhythm to the geometry of the grass blade's ascension from the earth, the equation of its over and its up. She wondered if she would ever speak again, and while she was wondering this, and no other wonder had entered her mind, she was aware of a dim thickening taking place on the other side of the grass blade. The thickening soon replaced the darker background that had been there before, and effectively obliterated the silhouette of the grass from her vision. Her eyes snapped into a different focus, and she found herself looking over at the form of a silvery-gray basset hound with extremely long ears. As if the entire field had revealed itself to be something not quite what she had assumed. Yuriko's mouth opened and she heard herself laughing.

In her wolfish wisdom, Heloise took Yuri to Mick's house rather than to mine. Thus, we didn't know about her for months, nor did we see Mick during that time either. But we had assumed he might be absent for awhile, even though we didn't want that to happen.

"It's like the split between Heraclitus and Parmenides, if you'll cast your minds back," said Djan. "Heraclitus said the primary force in the world is Becoming, and Parmenides said it was Being. For Heraclitus, everything was always in motion, nothing really existed but was always on its way to something else; for Parmenides there could be no true motion in the world, because that would imply a place where Something was Not, and this was, of course impossible." He paused and puffed on his imaginary pipe. He actually did have a sort of bamboo pipe-like device he kept in his pocket, more like a thick piece of grass. I have no idea whether it had a taste, but it was a new habit for him.

"I think we have a similar split here. Inevitable, I suppose, when you get enough people together, some kind of major disagreement will turn up eventually."

"I suppose we represent Parmenides?" I said, wrinkling my forehead in disbelief. "But that makes us sound so stodgy. I was always more of a fan of Heraclitus myself."

Djan coughed, his pipe almost fell onto the ground, but he caught it with a deft flick of the wrist, laughing.

"My assumption," he said, and his shoulders were shaking. I had never seen Djan so completely overcome by sheer mirth. "Was that Mick represented Parmenides, simply because his idea of purity seems so fixed. The One instead of the Many. But there I go again. You're quite right, from his point of view we are the ones who are fixed." He shook his head, and I knew he would go back home and puzzle it all out, and that we would likely hear the results of his puzzling.

Mick's absence had made us all uneasy and restless. We continued to seek one another's company with the usual sporadic regularity, yet we sometimes sat around in an almost surly silence, like a group of passengers waiting for a late train. Eden and Djan took to playing tavli, the ancient board game, off in a corner of the cafeteria; Eugenia spent time with a drawing pad, obsessively prowling the inside and outside of my villa, sketching patterns. I found excuses to wander to the limits of my estate, especially exploring the old road that led away from the seashore and up into the hillside. I started composing music late at night. I went to the Library almost every day. We hardly knew what we were hoping for at best, or fearing.

On top of that, we simply missed Mick's company.

"I feel as if I'm distracting myself rather than living," Eden muttered one afternoon, as he came in from a run on the beach. "But I don't know what else to do."

We had just about decided to go looking for him, figuring he wouldn't be at home (where we would not have access), but was probably out taking instruction from some of those higher beings he hinted at.

"Maybe he's ended up in a good place, like the House of Bees," we kept telling ourselves. Besides, he doesn't like the idea of being rescued, even if he needs it.

"But it's really rude of him, not to let us know where he is. He knows perfectly well how much we care about each other!" This could have been any one of us speaking.

Finally we decided to go back to Ikaria again, not so much because we really expected him to be there, but on the principle of the joke about looking for your lost glasses – not where you actually lost them in the dark – but under the streetlight, where "you can see so much better." Besides, I had a hunch the "people who are way more advanced than us" he referred to, might just as well be Kalypsos and Georgia as anyone else. For some reason I had lost my earlier fears about returning to this strange garden, which for me might seem to be a center of bad karma, and thus a place to avoid. I felt in some way immune, as if my presence might even deter danger from everyone else.

And then Mick showed up one afternoon with Yuri. Only Eugenia was there with me, in the kitchen at the table drinking mint tea and working on a picture puzzle. Suddenly there they were in the doorway to the terrace, side by side, holding hands like lovers. Mick, looking a little smug, but brown and fit, and beside him a small, slender woman with a heart-shaped face framed with straight, black hair, dark brown eyes. There was a silence around her like a cloud, and in fact one of my first reactions suggested *she is mute*, but she was not. At the same time, now that I think back on it, Heloise showed up behind them, like a shadow, and I realized how little she had been with us lately. What was this dog up to? Impulsively I called out, "Heloise!"

Mick and Yuri jumped. They also turned to look, but the dog had disappeared. Still, this broke the ice a little and allowed some sort of normal introductions to take place. This is Yuriko, she's someone I met a few months ago. She's staying with me. She's a physician. *There are others out there* Eden had reminded Mick, that long night when we had rejected his plans for active evolution, or group purification, or whatever he had concocted for us all. Was Mick now introducing us to the first member of his renegade group? I felt wary. No, rather, I felt foolishly paranoid. *So what if he operates by different rules, we still owe him kindness.*

We made a place at the table for them and offered them tea. I tried to relax and treat this like a normal social visit. Yuri, at least, had been living with Mick for a few months, long enough to learn the skill of dream travel. Mick explained that they had, indeed, been traveling together.

"So, we don't know you," Eugenia said gently, turning to Yuri. Mick had been explaining things about her, but so far she had only smiled and nodded. Did she speak only Japanese? For all we knew, Mick might be fluent in that language. We could probably live with one another for a thousand years and some of the most obvious facts about each of us would never come to light.

"I'm new at all this," she replied in totally unaccented English, her voice husky, as if she had been a smoker all her life. "Mick has told me—that I must have died, or rather almost died. But I have no memory of it, that's the strange part. My last memory is of my husband and son taking care of me after I fainted. But I don't think I was seriously ill. Then I woke up and they were gone. But it all felt like it happened a very long time ago, as if I had recovered already from my grief. As if there was a whole life in-between that now I don't remember. So when I woke up and found myself in the field beside my house, I felt totally at peace being alone. And then the basset hound came and brought me to Mick's house." She smiled, a mischievous, mirthful little smile.

"You all have houses you live in, with yards and gardens," she was continuing. She shook her head and with one hand flipped a sheaf of her hair back behind her right shoulder. "I don't have a house, it seems."

"Yes you do, you have my house!" Mick said, a trifle boorishly I thought.

"I might have stayed in my own house," Yuri continued softly, paying no attention to Mick. "But the dog brought me here, to Mick's."

Anita Sullivan

She shrugged. Her right hand made a quick little motion forward, and it occurred to me that she had once smoked but given it up. Or maybe not?

Eugenia had an odd expression on her face, a kind of comic frown. "Heloise," she said, to nobody in particular. "That's the dog. She brought you to Mick's."

Suddenly I caught my lower lip in my teeth. Whose side is this dog on, anyway? Was she actively recruiting new acolytes for Mick? But there is no way on God's green earth that Heloise could do harm to us, or to anybody, of this I was as certain as—well, as Parmenides! I broke into a silly grin and gave a huge sigh of relief.

"So you don't have a house." I said.

"I can't go back there," she said, shrugging her shoulders slightly. I was aware then of how slender and small she was, yet well shaped. A child woman. I remembered that, being a physician, she might know something about drugs. She and Mick seemed comfortable and familiar with one another, yet she seemed fully mature, not likely to come easily under the influence of his peculiar zealotry.

"It's not because she can't dream," said Mick, looking fondly at Yuri. "We've been other places. A few. And we came here today, quite easily." He smiled and looked quite like a man at ease, just showing off his girlfriend to friends, not one who is slyly trying to advance his plans to gain power.

"Are you wanting advice?" I asked blandly. I wanted to rush on, to say, "Why don't you go ask those way more advanced folks you've been consorting with? Surely we aren't pure enough for you!"

"I don't think so," said Mick, disarmingly. I had been looking at Yuri. He can be so honest that you forget how subtle he is. But inside, my defenses were crumbling before the onslaught of simple affection, and I was glad of that. Live and let live. I caught Mick's eye, which had gone all leafy, forest shadow-and-sunlight. When he's like that, he might as well be the centaur's cousin for all I can figure him out. I gave a huge sigh and fell back in my chair.

"You know, we could call up Eden and see if he can design you a house," said Eugenia. "He's quite fantastic with wood." She was half laughing. The situation was strange for all of us; we were like billiard balls wandering around looking for comfortable slots to roll down into.

Yuri folded her arms and tilted her head in a lively thoughtful manner, as if she were only now pondering this question for the first time. She looked sideways at Mick in a deeply affectionate way that translated to both me and Eugenia that they were, indeed, lovers.

"I don't really know what I can have, so it's hard to know what I want," she said finally. It was a truly honest answer, and I felt relieved. Then she added, suddenly, as if she had been thinking about it for a long time but only now was voicing her conclusion. "But I would really like to live on Ikaria."

Anita Sullivan

## Part VII
### The Lodge Dock Florist

Eventually plans were drawn up for Yuriko's house. She seemed open to suggestion, though she had in mind a steep, rocky hillside high above the sea, with only a single pine tree for vegetation. It was a spot she had already visited with Mick, we figured out later.

"The goats have eaten the rest," she said. "All I have to do is keep them out, and things will grow back." Then she added, "But I do want one goat for my own. She or he won't eat much!"

"You going to milk it?" Eden asked, looking at her with respect.

Yuri shook her head. "No, I just want a pet goat. It's one of those things I've always wanted. A black and white one . . . ." She looked off into the distance.

The time came for us to go have a look at the site. And that was when we discovered we couldn't find Ikaria any more. Like Parzival's castle, it was behaving like one of those magical places that has no real location, but only shows up when it wants to be found.

"But we were just there!" wailed Mick, after our first attempt landed us back in the central domed area of the Library, and feeling lucky to be there. When you dream travel intending to land in a familiar place, and that place has disappeared, the resulting confusion can be dangerous. "Yuri and I went there without any trouble!" Since we already knew they had been to Ikaria together, this fresh admission on his part didn't seem to bother him. And indeed, it only added to our general bewilderment.

280

"What happened?" we all asked at once, each of us fully confident that we carried a vivid image of the island.

Although we did not manage to arrive in Ikaria, we had followed the usual protocol: staying in physical contact by holding hands during the journey. All of us reported a strong wind accompanying our travel, the sound of the wind grew louder and louder until it stopped abruptly in front of an enormous, dark hedge-like wall. Each of us felt immediately that this was a barrier we could neither penetrate nor fly over. It was totally unfamiliar—and carried with it no sense of geographical position—so we didn't know the protocol for making it dissolve, or getting around it.

"It was like 'Boing!'" Eden said, demonstrating by reeling backwards. "There was no way past that thing. It didn't seem to be hard, like a stone wall, more like, oh I don't know, a thicket of brambles. What's that fairy tale where the princess goes to sleep and the rose thorns grow for 100 years around her?"

"Sleeping Beauty," I said.

The experience was so final, so strong, that we decided not to try again immediately. Shaken, we returned to the cafeteria for a conference.

"This is something new," said Djan, confirming what we were all thinking.

"You think the Arbiters, the folks in charge, have finally caught on to our shenanigans and decided to clamp down on us?" I said, trying to put a light side to things.

"We're having way too much fun," said Eden, nodding.

Mick nodded too. "It feels almost like evil," he said, "You know what I mean? Ikaria is like that, you know. Out of bounds. Not evil, I mean, but definitely not what you'd call a safe zone!"

"But why stop us now?" Eugenia said slowly. "We've been there so often, and—" she smiled around at all of us, including Yuri, "we've gotten into so much trouble. It's like closing the barn door after the horses have left. I think this comes from Ikaria itself."

"Like a joke!" said Eden, but he was serious. "A puckish little prank the island is playing, just to show us what it can do."

"But Ikaria is a serious place!" Mick said. He was sitting forwards on a chair with his hands clasped loosely between his knees, looking between us rather than at us. But his attitude was different than it had been last time, when he sat in much the same place as a suppliant, an apostate even. Now he seemed like a teacher. "A whole lot of important experimental work is going on there. I mean a whole lot. The island is like a huge portal. All kinds of stuff, people and other creatures, come and go freely there. Stuff like 'alive' and 'dead' or 'real' and 'unreal' don't even count. There's a lot of sheer power kicking around, though, and probably quite a bit of *danger* if you come with the wrong attitude. I mean, there are folks there who really know stuff, and you better pay attention!" He shrugged and smiled. My eyes were open so wide they almost hurt. This was Mick with a changed attitude. Or at least, somewhat changed.

"Well, it sure seems like this huge portal is closed for repairs," Eden said. "If you guys have been there recently and you can't even go back, what do you think is going on?" He looked from Mick to Yuri. But Mick, as if he had said too much, only shrugged.

"Do you think it's because I'm intending to build a house there?" Yuri said. We all looked at her in surprise. We had grown so accustomed to our own rhythm of talking together, and here came a new voice, low, musically resonant but almost hoarse. What does she mean? I wondered, as if she had said something totally strange.

Djan looked up with something like a hopeful expression. "Hah!" He said, but then lapsed into silence again.

"But who?" said Eugenia, after nobody else responded to Yuri's question. "I really can't believe this has to do with an intention on anybody's part. I don't think somebody is in charge of Ikaria, and they have now decided that the island is forbidden territory for us. I mean, what's so unusual about us—are we not pure enough?" She stuck her tongue between her teeth at this, for her, bold remark, and looked over at Mick.

"I wonder," I said, following up on what Eugenia had said, "if maybe we need to find a way *through* this hedge, or forest or whatever it is. Like the prince in 'Sleeping Beauty' Only I can't remember exactly what he did."

"The right words," said Djan, but again did not elaborate.

"I think I should try to go back by myself," said Yuri. "I mean, you have all been there together before, and now your way is blocked, so it *could* have something to do with me. Maybe I need to clear the way." She looked at Mick, as if there was more to what she was saying than the rest of us could know.

"Did you meet Kalypsos?" I blurted out before I could stop myself, directing my question to Yuri. "I feel his hand in all of this." I cringed slightly, as if expecting a roll of thunder from asking the wrong question at the right place, or vice versa.

Anita Sullivan

She ducked her head and examined her hands. Then she shook her hair back with a lift of her chin and looked directly at me. "Yes, I did," she said. "I want to work with him."

The silence that followed this statement was palpable in its variety: you could almost hear the individual reaction of each of us as we slid emotionally and intellectually through shock, suspicion, amusement, curiosity, fear, disbelief, concern, and annoyance. I glanced at Mick to see if he was behaving like a proud teacher whose pupil had passed her test. But his expression was inscrutable.

Eugenia took a deep breath and said, "You are a physician, Yuri. Does that have something to do with why you want to work with Kalypsos? His plants . . . ."

She nodded, looking suddenly a little frightened and even on the verge of tears. "He offers apprenticeship," she said softly. Then she gathered courage and looked directly at Eugenia. "I want to go through his initiation process. Mick has already begun it."

"Good god!" said Djan. We all looked at him, not because his reaction was eloquent, but because something in the tone of it suggested more.

"Do you realize what this means?" He continued, turning his palms up and looking at the ceiling. For a few minutes he breathed heavily, as if he were a shaman working himself up to the next level of his trance. "It means we have arrived at a point in this life where change is truly possible. Not only possible, but likely. Not only likely, but now, it seems, inevitable. In short, a wall has been breached, and god help us what will come in or out, and how."

You could have heard a pin drop. But Djan wasn't done.

"You rascal!" He said to Mick, and his voice was almost devoid of expression. "You have brought us into your camp after all. That's why we can't get into Ikaria, not because of punishment or testing, but simply because it has *moved*, and something else is where it used to be. But I don't think we can ignore this matter, because it's on our path. *And we are on a path!*" His last sentence was almost a roar. I closed my eyes for fear of seeing him grow large and fill the room like a smoke monster, or a temporary lion.

## Diversion to Australia

"I am not ready for this," Djan said, later that evening. Nothing had been decided, but a kind of understanding prevailed, we were all on our own again. Nobody had urged another trip to Ikaria right away, and nobody knew what else to suggest, so eventually everyone went quietly off into the night. Skulked, I might better say. For the first time since I was a child, I felt the palpability of something called 'sin,' and it annoyed me. Was Mick right after all? Were the rest of us blindsided by willful apathy? I remembered David's old joke. "If there really is a hell, and I've been sinning all these years, I want my money back. I'm in the wrong universe!"

Unusual for him, Djan stayed behind. We went up to the room above the kitchen where the little sofa was perched before another of my curved fireplaces. He sat hunched in a small rocking chair; I pulled my knees up and made myself comfortable on the sofa.

"I'm going back to Australia for awhile," said Djan. "Would you consider coming along?" He looked at me intently for a few seconds, then away again. I felt his gloom, but he wasn't asking me because he wanted someone to cheer him up. I was honored and intrigued.

"The Dream Time," he murmured, as if to give me a hint. But it was partly his usual extraordinary way of catching onto my thoughts before they became words. Then he continued. "I feel a need to go and touch base with something invariant, before setting out again into – into whatever is about to start happening. We seem to have blown our chances for stability, for paradise even . . . ." He stopped, and his face scrunched a little as if he were trying to keep from weeping. "Likely that was inevitable as soon as we all found a way to be together. Yet paradise in solitude is, in my view, totally impossible. So, pick your poison. And we have." He swallowed, took a deep breath and looked at me again, reaching out one hand, palm up, in entreaty.

"Is paradise a kind of purity, then, after all?" I said, hearing my voice splash like a pebble into a puddle.

His chin went up and his eyes gleamed. "Overarching," he said. "That is, I would suppose there must be perfection in the aggregate, while the details would necessarily remain flexible. And we, being human, are ever awash in details. I suppose, come to think of it, this is how Mick's view differs from, er, at least my own. He may believe there is such thing as a perfect human life that can actually be *lived*, rather than merely contemplated." I said nothing, and he continued.

"The Dreamtime is changeless. It is a Story that only happened once, and has been happening all along, but is the same story. Only one story, as if such a thing is truly possible. Like the hedgehog instead of the fox. Like a parade example of Parmenides' philosophy, or his world you might rather say. Yet, it worked for so many thousands of years . . .

I feel the need to go back and touch it one last, last—time. Because I think, at last, it may be truly . . . done."

I reached out and placed my palm under the back of his hand, lifting it slightly, then put my other hand over the top.

"It seems like we're actually making something" I said. "I feel like we're becoming a new set of Elders, of brand new mythological beings. Maybe like new Dream Time beings even. Is this true? I mean, can what we do over here actually have any bearing on the world—down there? The one we left behind?"

"Well, there's no success or failure in the large sense," he said, and then made a wry little face. "And I'm coming to believe—or at least to hope—that we cannot do as much damage as we might imagine." He stood up and came over to sit beside me. We sat there, touching shoulders for a long time, not saying anything because we both felt our thoughts turning into large, inchoate masses. Or at least I did. After a long time, it might have been hours, Djan reached over and put his arms around me and I leaned towards him. Before we could fall over together onto the sofa, which was much to small for two people to lie on, we rose together and stumbled dreamily upstairs to my bed. It was probably the best way we could have chosen to go to Australia.

## The Lady Bicyclist

"Silence is like wine," I was saying to Djan as we sat on a flat gray rock under a sky so blue that surely fire must have been that color at the origin of the world. "There are so many different varieties. The silence of my garden, for example, is very different from this, I don't

Anita Sullivan

know how . . . . I'm suddenly *rabid* to make a list of all the kinds I can think of!" I bounced on the rock in excitement.

Djan scrunched his eyes to indicate he had heard me, but said nothing. For a moment I wished Eden were here, because he would have turned the question into a listing game, which is what I wanted to happen. 1. The silence between certain phrases in a piece of music; 2. The silence at the bottom of my sock drawer; 3. The silence inside of a dog . . . I giggled.

We were in Arnhem Land, a stretch of the North Australian coast, and we were sitting in front of a series of shallow, cave-like overhangs painted by a long-extinct tribe of Aborigines. We had been camping out here for days, lying on our backs in thin sleeping bags feeling the contour of the ground beneath us at night, especially the endless variety of small, lumpy (and sometimes thorny) desert plants and their attendant small stones. *A little kingdom in middle earth*, I thought once at maybe two a.m. as I wiggled in a vain attempt to find a comfortable position. Why do I have so many bones? Humans are not meant to lie upon the earth, and why ever not? Surely, surely we were designed for a different planet than this!

Patiently, Djan had explained the myth of Nargorkun and his wives, how he had been bitten by mukul, the green ants, and as a result became ill, and swelled up into the shape and size of a monster. His two wives helped him create the world. In his swollen capacity as a god, Nagorkun made laws for the world, and these laws were taken out into the world by two creatures called Narkundeeundee who went like missionaries to the clans, teaching people. They had green eyes made of bees wax. And on, and on, and on. . . . My own eyes glazed over at the details.

"Why do you call this invariant?" I wondered to him. "I mean, these kinds of stories are obviously made up by someone. There's such incredible detail. How does a person dare to get up in the morning, they might violate a law by just the way they get out of bed!"

He shrugged. "I can't explain that part," he said. "It's a way of life that you must begin early, and be deeply immersed in to under-stand." He raised his eyes again to the vivid, elongated figures on the wall in front of us. Nargorkun's two wives, who were sisters, were flying sideways across the rock; they had perfectly round white heads like medieval madonnas with haloes; inside their heads two black dots for eyes, but no mouths. Their skinny white arms made a "W" shape on either side of their heads, above the stick-like bodies. But these were not the drawings of children. I shivered.

"Where did Nargorkun go?" I asked in a whisper.

"I don't know," he said. "But for sure he's gone now, for his people are no longer here to keep him alive."

I mashed my lips together for a minute, thinking, and trying to keep myself from blurting out questions too soon. Mythology is full of disasters that happen because of questions.

"Don't you think maybe it's O.K. for Nargorkun to be gone now?" I asked gently.

"That's precisely what I would like to know," he said, and sighed hugely. "My father brought me here once," he continued slowly, "and told me the stories. I don't know in what way he believed them anymore but he was carrying out the Law of Telling. He couldn't help himself."

During the day, in the early morning when it was cool and in late evening, we wandered between the stones, huge boulders scattered randomly around the gently rolling earth as far as we could see, although downhill in the purple-gray distance we could see the possibility of more level, unpocked land. We found a waterfall going down into a narrow creek whose water looked almost black, but tasted divine. I washed my hair in it, and bathed like a princess in a pool that only came up to the top of my legs when I stood up, but if I knelt in it, my breasts would float comically on the water. Sometimes, but not often, Djan would come into the pool with me, and we would make love in the way of water creatures. But generally he was in a frame of mind of an ascetic, practicing abstinence. Maybe it was the influence of Nargorkun and all his laws about sex. Maybe if we stayed here long enough, we would start thinking like Mick, and devising rituals for achieving greater purity. Under this sky, atop this earth with its vast array of sounds and silences, each gesture seemed vast, and it became incumbent upon the human form to accommodate its gestures to the larger pattern. No, not "purity" any more, but harmony. And harmony with a teensy bit of variety, so as to allow something to build. I sighed and once again lapsed into a sensation of my own vastness. I could feel all my molecules seeping away from me into the stone. This was a place of Earth first, then Fire, then Water – Air last. And Stone, primarily of Stone.

Since we had all the time in the world, it became clear to me that Djan wished to remain here indefinitely, even possibly for years, until he came to an understanding about the nature of this ancient culture, and the suppleness of its relationship with the land. Myself, I didn't want to stay that long. I wanted to go back to my garden.

I also, irrationally, wanted to ride a bicycle. At home, the road was too short; too soon I came to the limits of my territory. Here there was a long, deserted dirt road, reasonably packed down, disappearing over the horizon in both directions, and it made me long for *wheels*. No motors, just the silence of whirring circularity propelling me over the ground with more rapidity than my legs could do. As Djan paced the cave walls and mulled the implications of the past upon the future, I found myself drifting more often up the rise to the narrow dirt road and sitting on it, visualizing bicycles. I remembered a book I had read years ago called *Need for the Bike*, by a Frenchman who had bicycled all over France but never chose to bring himself up to the level of athletic prowess necessary for competing in the Tour de France. In French, it was *Besoin de Vélo*, which always made me smile.

But the usual method of asking for supplies, (and 'bicycle' might very well have slipped through the system), simply didn't work anywhere else except at home. The Arbiter and crew did not acknowledge us out of context. Djan and I had brought enough food and bush-survival equipment to last a couple of months, so we wouldn't have to keep shuttling back and forth, with the ever-present possibility (especially now, since our recent experience with Ikaria) of not being able to get back to the same place. I didn't dare dream myself back home, send out for a bike, and try to come back here with it.

So, I sat in the sun and obsessed about riding with the wind in my hair, the full-body effort of pedaling down this seemingly limitless packed-dirt road beneath an unblemished, rich, bright, outrageously domineering blue sky. And the image gave me simple pleasure. My head became silly with the simplicity of it; my head grew round and white and mouthless, like the wives of Nargorkun. I remembered a

Greek song called "The Lady Bicyclist," and began to sing it as I strolled along the dirt road, farther and farther away from the caves of Nargorkun. Maybe I could become an Aborigine Ancestor, singing the world into existence, and at least there would be a bicycle-shaped boulder to my credit.

But soon I turned back, unwilling to risk getting lost, still humming the song sporadically. And by the time I got back to the section of road just above the little basin where the shallow caves began, I realized I was flying. That is, my feet were not on the ground but a few inches above it, still moving back and forth as if I were walking, but sawing through pure air. It was so simple.

It was as if I were riding a bicycle without the bicycle.

I willed myself to land, and ran down the slope calling "Djan! Djan!" making a small avalanche on the way. I found him just turning slowly away from a rock surface, his hand up with the index finger pointing towards the wall, as if he had been directing a play. He had an odd look on his face, like fierce wonder. When he saw me he bowed slightly and gestured more sweepingly towards the wall.

There was a petroglyph of a woman on a bicycle. No question about it, very clear. A modern bicycle, with gears neatly pecked in; and her hair was blowing in the wind.

I went a little crazy then and started riding around in the air in front of him, whooping like an Indian on a horse and saying "Gee Haw!" Which was of course totally inappropriate. He laughed a little and tried to reach up and take me by the elbows, but it was no use, my mania had to run its course. When I was a little calmer we sat down firmly on the ground and stared at the rock drawing. It was in a spot that had been blank before, unlike much rock art, where new drawings were etched or painted right on top of old ones.

"The drawing. It's brand new. It just appeared," he said. As if I needed to be told. He said nothing about the fact that I had been flying around in front of him.

"It's me, on my bicycle!" I said, barely able to speak with excitement. I told him how I had been wishing for a bike, then found myself airborne.

We kept staring at the wall. I went over to it to examine it closely, and sure enough the petroglyph was bright white, the way they all are before the patina of age forms on them.

"Do you think this is how it was always done?" I said, wrinkling my nose a little to indicate I didn't believe that.

He positively pouted at me. "What do you mean, exactly? Utilizing two minds instead of one?"

"Oh, lordy!" I whispered. I wasn't thinking about that, only that the petroglyph had appeared spontaneously, without hammer or chisel. I guess I was imagining a "little magic creature" behind the rock, a Mimi perhaps, and I was playing around with the notion that all Australian rock art had been part of the original "Dreaming," meaning that humans had nothing to do with it. But he was suggesting that we had done it ourselves, together, with only our minds.

"Does this mean we have some kind of power?"

He shook his head very slightly, as if fending off such an idea, and closed his eyes. He was sitting cross-legged, barefoot, and suddenly he looked gray and old. I thought of the Irish legend of the youth who is taken off to the land of the Immortals, and returns home for a quick visit, only to crumble into dust when he gets off his horse. "Don't leave me, Djan!" I felt like crying out, and I put my hand on his right shoulder and kept it there.

"It's as if old passageways are being opened," he murmured. "Not as if new rooms are being added to the house."

"Do you think it's something we can do on purpose?"

"No," he said. "Yes and no. Some kind of delicate relationship between need and circumstance. Rather quirky, I imagine." He smiled.

"Hmfff!" I snorted. "We really are making up the rules as we go along. How do you tell the rules from the results any more? I mean, Djan, if *we* are in charge of making up a whole new mythology for the world . . . !" I couldn't help it, my mouth fell open and I just let it hang there.

"You know," he said, shaking his head. "In the end I believe it's all local. It always has been. We've just brought the bicycle into the North Australian Stone Age, one tire, one gear, one rider at a time." He reached over and ruffled my hair across my face.

"Well, we're not going to take over the world, any road!" he said, rising and stretching. "Let's go cook something, eh?"

During the next few days we were prowling around secretly hoping we could make another petroglyph. It was like being a volcano and not knowing when you were going to erupt next. This bicycle petroglyph could have been just a one-off event, but we both felt it wasn't, because we both felt different. Something had fallen off, allowing a clearer way of seeing.

"I see things shorter," I said one minute. "I see things with rounded corners," I said another minute. "The colors are the same but the shapes aren't. The nature of *solid* is different for me. Also past and present. I keep seeing rocks tumbling down hillsides and people being stabbed and screaming, and rolling down the hill with the rocks, and armies advancing across landscapes, and horses rearing, and a million other actions, and it all seems suddenly natural and normal, but still *dreadful*. And so intense. I suddenly understand violence and evil in a new way, but I still don't like it, but I understand it more as color and shape. It's like how things were *before the Story*."

I was babbling all of this to Djan, not at once, but in spurts. The rest of the time we didn't talk much, because nothing much needed to be said. We knew a time would come for me to go back to my villa, and that he might or might not come along.

We didn't make any more petroglyphs, but this one stayed. Meanwhile I kept practicing my flying, so that now I could fly with my feet straight down, or stuck out behind me. I wasn't able to go any higher than about ten feet, but I'm not sure I wanted to anyway, since I get dizzy easily. I enjoyed cruising around the landscape, exploring places I couldn't have reached before, perching now and then in the top of a small tree when I could find one. But when the time came for me to leave, Djan wasn't ready yet. He had already made two trips back to his house in Tasmania for food, books and blankets. But on a beautiful blue afternoon in what seemed to be autumn, I said goodbye and told him I must leave.

"Maybe Ikaria has finished moving around, and when you come back, it will be in a place where we can all go find it again," I said.

He looked at me with a smile in his eyes that made his whole countenance glow. I felt it as love, and I glowed back. Quietly I took his hand and kissed it. Then I threw my arms around his neck and gave

Anita Sullivan

him a total body hug, a long one. "See you, Djan," I said, and flew off to a quiet rock where I could dream myself home.

## Yuriko's House

I came home to springtime in Italy, since the seasons are the opposite here from in Australia. Spring! How could I ever have missed it before? I jumped out of bed and ran into the garden. (I always wake up from my dream voyages in bed. I find this sort of quaint and endearing, the Administrative mind at work, ever attentive to detail.)

Everything seemed to be in flower, even the vegetables. I sat on the warm flagstones with my knees up and my arms wrapped around them, closed my eyes, intending to sink into a reverie. But the airs were loud with chattering voices. The plants were talking among themselves in little spits and surges, wavelets breaking onto the bridge of my nose, squiggles of scent shimmying across the bottoms of my eyelids, shafts of pressure lightly twanging across my forehead as if I were being anointed again and again.

"Where have you been?" was the general message. *WHERE HAVE YOU BEEN?*

Where, indeed? How could I have not noticed them before in this clear and poignant way, my plant creatures? There were persons in my garden, many persons. Companions galore. I could have lived alone all these years after all, and not been without company. "Could you loosen the soil just a teensy bit around my roots?" Hibiscus asked, in a slightly husky tone, very orange in its flavor. The green blither of Fennel wished me to douse it all over lightly with warmish water; sturdily ethereal Sage needed a bit of calcium worked delicately into the soil around its base; Clematis was simply broiling and needed some shade . . . . How could I have been so oblivious to all these sweet souls before?

I spent a week totally in their service from morning to night. I didn't fly or play the harpsichord the entire time, hardly ate, slept badly. It was an excessive way to be initiated into a new phase in my life. I piled my hair up on top of my head again, tied my loose trousers around my ankles with old strips of cloth, and gave myself up to this new obsession. Near the end of that period I found myself on a spring evening of outrageous limpidness, half reclining on the steps leading from the top terrace to the middle one, my right shoulder resting on Heloise's warm and furry side.

I sat up and looked at her through narrowed eyes.

"Heloise!" I practically growled. WHERE HAVE YOU BEEN?

But she is totally lacking in the ability to feel responsible. She turned her head gently in my direction and I was looking again into her light brown eyes. They took me down a swift path between silvery beech trees, an outdoor cathedral with no altar, only the endless dappled path. I gasped. If she had spoken—and she didn't emit even a groan or a sigh—she might have said, "How long does it take you, each time, to notice when I am somewhere else, and why is it always MY responsibility when you come to your senses?" We hugged.

"Look at this!" I said, and flew around the garden in the dusk like a huge moth. I realized then that if all my friends were suddenly lost to me, I could stay here alone and be content. The richness of the world was now more available to me than before, and time had split open like a squash, its stringy sinews exposed for further exploration.

Anita Sullivan

Eventually, though, I noticed that nobody had come to visit me for a long time. So one morning I called Heloise and went upstairs to the sofa with her. She lay down at one end, and I bunched myself comfortably up at the other. "Hello, fellow crittur!" I grinned over at her. And then I gave a huge sigh. "You know as well as I do, Heloise, that we need to go back to Ikaria. And this time I'm just going to let you be the guide."

The inscrutable basset hound placed her long chin onto her silken gray paws and regarded me blandly. This time the trip was different than ever before. I didn't fall into a hypnogogic state, and then slip into a dream space. Instead, I flew us over. Somewhat like a pilot, I extended my new-found flying skill to include Heloise and the sofa— except that it wasn't a matter of "power" coming from me, rather a useful stillness that *allowed* the process to happen. At any rate, we landed with a mild clatter on stones, and when we climbed off the sofa I saw that we were on a steep, barren hillside overlooking a road, after which the hill continued for a long ways, more gradually down to the sea.

When I turned to look up the hill I saw the familiar shape of Eden bent double in working position. He was busy troweling around some rocks on a terrace for a small stone house with a slate roof. "Yuriko's house!" I cried, and started running. Heloise at a more leisurely pace padded after me, her large paws not finding much purchase on the stony, steep surface.

Eden looked up and a big grin broke out on his face. "Hey, glad to see you! It's about time!" he said.

Panting, I reached level ground and flopped down onto the dirt. Beside me and above me was the house, three stories going up the hillside in tiers, each with its outer stones nicely smoothed and the space between them caulked with white lime. The windows were odd-shaped, but fitted with hand-blown glass framed for opening, and with the traditional shutters on either side, now held at half-open position. They were painted a lovely forest green.

"Where's Yuri?" I asked.

"She's over working at Kalypos's" said Eden, pronouncing it so it sounded like 'kalip-SO-sis'. "He's mainly teaching her what plants to grow here on this hillside. Right now, I mean. But she's bringing some of his ideas over here, with his permission. The magus thing, you know." He waved his hand as if I would know what he was talking about, and so he wouldn't have to go any more into explanations. I nodded, sorting through the questions crowding up in my mind, and finding that none of them was really taking urgent and pointed shape, but that they were all bumping around softly like rubber toys in a bathtub. I giggled.

"Eugenia's here quite a bit, too," he said. "She finally brought the drawing she's been working on for years and years. Said she wanted it to be here, on the wall, when the house was done. She's in there now, painting. The walls, I mean, not her drawing!" He grinned and came over to sit down beside me. "Would you like a drink?"

My eyes widened and I bit my upper lip. Should I be jealous? Was I now a stranger? Had my friends gone over to the 'other side' while I and Djan were in Australia? Maybe I should show off how well I could fly . . . .

"Tell me, Eden, what's going on," I said, after he had gone inside and brought me a mug of cool water.

He nodded. "We figured out a back way to come over here, to Ikaria I mean," he started. I knew I could count on him to completely confuse me, and then straighten it all out if I just waited long enough. I looked around for something to lean against, and saw a gnarled old pine tree at the edge of the unpaved section of the terrace. Underneath it, tethered to a rope, was a little goat with black shiny fur and a white forehead. The rope that tethered him was soft and fat, and looked about half as big as he. I laughed and stood up.

"Yuriko has her goat!"

"Yeah, his name is Rubato."

"Oh!" I laughed again. Only a musician would come up with such a name.

"He has nothing to graze on right now, but Kalypsos says we can grow some really good grass up here, and various other ground covers. And we're working on a cistern behind the house, and there's a little river down there too . . . . "

Rubato shied away from me and tried to bite my hand. His strange yellowish eyes reminded me a bit of the centaur, and I felt my stomach tighten.

"Typical goat," said Eden, shaking his head. "But she likes him. I think he's a royal pain to tell you the truth."

I came back to his part of the terrace. All around were scattered large stones of all shapes, none of them very flat. I saw mallets and wedges and a great deal of rock dust. Eden looked hot, tired, fit and happy.

"Did you build this house?"

He shrugged. "Some," he said. "I mostly designed it as we went along. Yuri and Mick and Eugenia did a lot of the work, though the stone cracking is the slowest. We got Petros in to help us, and a group of – well, I guess you'd call them spirit helpers!" He took a deep breath, looking at me cautiously. "Some slave labor, folks working out their time in a sort of purgatory here. Some transvestites, old warriors, pimps, people who've been on the wheel a long, long time. I didn't think it was such a good idea, but what else could we do? Petros apparently runs a kind of sweat shop, very informal, very ad hoc. Ifigenia was a big help in totting up the bills, and we got it all squared away so they won't be coming back later to demand back wages. I could never have done the rock crushing myself in a million years."

I swallowed. "Can I help?"

"Oh, sure, now that you're finally here." He looked at me a little more closely. "We missed you. You and Djan. But you know how it is, we all do our thing." He squinted a little and looked down the hill to the sea. "I'm just so thankful to get back to Ikaria. It's now sort of the hub of things. We didn't really have one before, I mean your place was a fine gathering spot, but it was still your place, you know. Like being guests. But here . . ." he waved his hand around the entire hillside. "It's like we can bring our work here, and be doing something together instead of being by ourselves and just visiting each other like we were before. You'll see what I mean."

*But what about Mick and his purity thing?* I wanted to ask, but wasn't sure if it was even relevant any more.

"What about Mick?" I said.

He must have known I would get around to that question sooner or later. His guileless blue eyes widened in his effort to figure out which kind of honest answer might be best. We smiled at each other.

"He's still working with Kalypsos too," he said slowly. "I don't truly know what all he does over there. I think he gets into tubs of plant elixir and tries to turn himself into a half plant person; he picks herbs from morning to night and plants them from night to morning; he douses and scrubs and dribbles fluids onto his wrists. He's evolving into a higher species." His voice was warm, but there was a slight edge to his tone that warned me not to persist with my questions. Something had happened I didn't know about. Maybe I couldn't know about. I felt rather sharply forlorn, but oddly enough, not frightened or jealous.

"Do you all live here, on Ikaria, now?" I asked after we had sat awhile and looked out through half-closed eyelids at the sea, far below and filling the horizon as well.

"Nah!" he grinned, and at last he caught on to how weird I was feeling. I could feel him adjusting to it, wheeling in almost like a hawk coming back to its nest at the top of a cliff. "It's like going to work, Carley. Remember that? Only not in the bad old way it used to be. Here, we go home to sleep most nights, or for a week at a time. And then we come back here to this house for our together work. It's Yuriko's house, but since she came to choosing it kind of late, and since we all had a hand in it, this house belongs to all of us. It's not something we decided, it just came about naturally." He shrugged slightly and looked briefly over at me. "This new arrangement allows us to have a better distinction between private and social, actually less of a distinction than before, more unified. It's hard to explain, but I like it a lot. And here in Ikaria—" his voice took on a more complex timbre, an enthusiasm I had never heard in it before, "Here in Ikaria life is much more interesting. There's an actual society, some people like us, you know—growth potential," he smiled at the phrase. "But it's way more complicated, like a whole bunch of stories all coming back to their home base and mixing it up." He shook his head with a funny delighted expression on his face. "I think you'll get the hang of it right off. Djan will too. I hope he comes back soon."

I sighed, loudly. "I guess we really were away a long time."

"Yeah, where have you been anyway?" he said, and shot a keen look at me. "Not taking any unauthorized trips on your own, I hope?"

"Isn't it neat how we are still polite with one another?" I grinned, looking right back at him. "It's really a good thing.

"Oh, was I being polite?" He said lightly. And when I didn't reply, his forehead scrunched a little as he tried to figure out why I had said that. Meanwhile, I decided to put him out of his misery, and I told him about our visit to Australia, the rock art, and how I had learned to fly. He was especially interested in the flying and asked for a demonstration. We stood up.

"I don't know if I can do it on demand," I said doubtfully, and then I rose about six inches off the ground and proceeded to float right into the front wall of the house with a little "splat," dislodging some whitewash dust.

"Looks like you could use a wee bit of practice," he said with his front teeth clamped together and a huge silly grin on his face.

I looked at him standing there in his tee shirt and white floppy hat, and I looked at the healthy chaos of stones and small tree, goat and dust and plant pots waiting for new tenants, and the unframed doorway leading into the house that would be filled with light, and our laughter and talk, and the talk and laughter of who knows how many new voices in the weeks and years to come. I felt tears stinging my eyes.

"Did you really do that, or was it just smoke and mirrors?" Eden was saying, his face serious now, a little puzzled.

I hobbled back across the terrace and sat down, a little dazed, rubbing my temples, while at the same time wrinkling my forehead to think.

"It's like that story—I think it was Hans Christian Anderson—*The Emperor Has No Clothes*, where the emperor was really going around naked but everybody pretended he still had clothes on."

"I always hated that story," said Eden.

I nodded. "Me too. And besides, this is the opposite. I really am flying, but it's so hard to believe, that I feel as if I'm just pretending!"

"Maybe that's the problem, you gotta believe it's happening, or else it doesn't," said Eden, almost immediately shaking his head at what he had just heard himself say.

"No, this is definitely a physical thing, like walking or riding a bicycle," I said. "It's not like the flying we do in dreams, or at least the flying around we've all been doing together to get from one place to another. You know, where we imagine ourselves somewhere." I looked down at my feet, now firmly touching the ground, and I began to have doubts. How firmly? How far off the ground? I was remembering also that my most recent trip to Ikaria on the sofa with Heloise was more like "a physical thing," and less like "imagining."

"This kind of flying I'm doing is as much putting the earth down as it is you going up—if that makes any sense," I continued, by way of clarification.

"Is that why you only rose up about four inches from the ground?" Eden asked, not a trace of humor in his question.

"Well, I thought it was more like six inches," I said in a dignified manner. "But I guess maybe flying is an enormous phenomenon with many aspects, and I am only doing the baby steps so far. You might call it 'the initial fooling,' where I am still close enough to the ground that people might hardly even notice. I used to have flying dreams that way, where I was flying down the sidewalk in a city standing up, and it seemed quite normal. But at some point, I wonder, maybe we start crossing over from the dream territory into the physical realm. I mean, I've learned a brand new human action here. I'm flying around while I'm wide awake!" I swallowed, feeling a chill along my arms and under my ribs.

"But it's so silly!" Eden said in bewildered exasperation. "I mean, here we are all of us, dead for years, and still alive, and flying around from one place to another through our dreams . . . and here you come along and actually *fly* . . . . Well, maybe we should say *float*—but anyway. What's the big deal, it's just all part of the way things operate here!"

"It's another shift," I said slowly, nodding my head because I was imagining myself as Djan speaking. "It's another shift, is all I can say. A sign that something really is *changing*. Flying like this isn't just a psychological trick, it's an actual skill that you can learn, as if you were re-activating some kind of an obsolete knob inside you like your appendix or something, or as if you were growing a new knob. I can feel it. And I just bet that in a few months or years we'll all be flying. Maybe not across the seas, and maybe not through time, but at least short distances."

Anita Sullivan

He was quiet a long time, looking off across the sea. Then he turned with a cheerful grin. "So, Mick is purifying himself for no reason after all," he said, with some relief.

"Oh no, no, no!" I shook my head. "I don't know what Mick is doing, but he's on a different track. We can, after all, do harm to ourselves, we can still die. But, Eden, I really believe that no matter what we do out of *sheer curiosity*—as long as there's not greed or malice, cruelty, any of that—we can't do anything wrong, can we?" My voice croaked a little. "It's just not possible for us to harm each other, is it? Just ourselves?"

He closed his eyes. Then opened them and came to sit down beside me. "Yeah, I think you're right. There's no real incentive for good old-fashioned evil—you know, sloth, envy, anger, lust—the seven deadly sins. Maybe the incentive for that stuff really is blocked." He shrugged. "I for one don't want to experiment with inciting myself to acts of harm . . . ."

I shivered slightly. "I don't really think we're *blocked*," I said in a small voice. "So, maybe what Mick is doing is useful, his version of learning to fly, I don't know." I stopped for a breath.

"He's been reading Plotinus," said Eden cautiously. "I think it's made an impression for the good."

"How do you mean?"

He squared his shoulders and wrinkled his forehead, ready to say more. "All that Medieval duality talk has complicated his big purity idea, or at least confused the issue enough for him that he's postponed his dire predictions. At least he's lightened up some, and he's stopped being so single-minded, the way he was before. And Yuri's been a good influence, since she really knows something about plants. So, anyhow, go on with what you were saying."

"I don't know how much power we actually have to change things, but it's certainly different than it was before, I mean even different from how it was right after we died and took up this new life." I was figuring things out as I went along, as I always do. Acting out the very philosophy I was preaching, come to think of it. "But I think reality is a thing always in the making. The Universe is being made up as it goes along, even though it's very, very old. I believe that the universe—meaning everything there is—might be vulnerable in some large sense. Yes, this is what I mean! I think we have an obligation to be acting in a way that sharpens our instincts always in the direction of beauty, so that *in case the universe is vulnerable* we don't begin to shift things in a bad direction."

"So, you do think it's possible to do something wrong, then?" he said. I'll hand it to Eden, he does pay attention when you talk.

"Yeah, I guess I do."

"Whoah!" He said softly. Then we both just sat for awhile, comfortably in the sun. Heloise was snoozing in the shade of the little pine tree, almost touching Rubato, and I wished I could just jump up and start doing my share of the ongoing work. But I was suddenly over-come with a need to leave, a sense of obligation I had almost allowed myself to forget. I needed to go now, before Eugenia came out of the house to welcome me back (why hadn't she done that already?) Or before Djan suddenly landed in our midst fresh from Australia, or Mick and Yuriko came back from their work with Kalypsos, or before Ifigenia might drop in for a visit, or one of Petros' strange "spirit helpers." I wasn't ready to face any of them just now, I had some other reason for this particular trip to Ikaria and I had best go find out what it was.

Then Eden stood up, picked up a shovel, and leaned on it briefly, looking down at me with an odd expression of affection. "Well, Carley, then I don't think I'll ask for flying lessons right away. You're obviously the flier in the group. Our chief story teller too. Besides, I used to fly for a living . . . ." He added that last sentence with a puzzled look, as if it had just occurred to him.

"I gotta get back to work," he continued. "You want to help?" He added, "I could use someone to mix plaster. Or maybe Eugenia needs something too."

"Not yet," I said, and got heavily to my feet, like a bird that doesn't do very well on land. "I've got something I need to do, but I'll be back soon. Much sooner this time, I promise!"

And in less than a minute I rose above the ground and began to float a bit unsteadily towards the top of the hill.


Abelard


Into the mountain fastness I flew, but slowly, as my lack of ability to rise above treetop level did hamper my speed. As I topped the first hill, the one above Yuriko's house, and banked to the northwest and thus into the island's central mountain range, Eden's question "Is it all smoke and mirrors?" Came back to mind. In fact, it pierced my consciousness like a shout, or as if it had been an icicle—maybe some-one *removing* an icicle from my heart or eye, as in the story of the *Snow Queen*.

"Yes!" I cried out, tilting my head back to the row of cumulous clouds that were bumping along on the tops of the pointed cedars ahead of me. "I'm not really flying! I'm not really flying! Ta da, ta da, ta DAH!"

The *not really* swung around to take the place of the *really* so quickly and easily I know that balance had been ready to tip in my mind for quite some time. I had no trouble substituting one for the other. "Yes!" I thought again. "This is how it is!" Not just with flying, but with growing old, with dying, with living, and especially with that dreadful business of there always being another moment coming along to supersede the marvelous, final, perfect one you have just experienced. What *seems* can rise like a mist to act as a reality in itself, and we can live there as long as anywhere, in content. A certain delicate care is required – more in the nature of an art, I would say – to maintain this state of affairs. "Our little company then, we may not really be alive at all. We're one reality removed. We're somebody's lucid dream. Or maybe we're dreaming ourselves, and we're just getting better and better at it, until one day there won't be any difference at all any more between seems and is. That's what the Arbiter and his minions were hoping to accomplish!" I thought, and was hugely delighted by this new possibility. There is a truth to this life that never was possible before. I need not be concerned about living each moment as if it were my last, or of squandering this enormous generosity of beauty and time by my mortal inability to live intensely enough; for even if I die, or rather *when I choose* to die, my last moment will already have been sounded long before, but the smoke and mirrors will make it not so. That is all the comfort I truly ever sought in the first part of my life, but never found. Now I have found it.

Anita Sullivan

While I was sorting through this brand new inchoate mass of notions (they occurred in a clump, as thoughts often do, and I am spreading them out as if they arrived in a neat sequence), at the same time I was being careful to navigate around oaks, cypresses, pines, and to adjust to sudden updrafts and breathtaking views down long dry canyons in the direction of the sea. But soon the sea was no longer in view; I was rapidly moving into the treeless, boulder-ridden central shoulder of the island where only goats and falcons roamed. The clouds were closer too, and I surely didn't want to try flying through them, so I kept them firmly in the corner of my eye as I scanned the ground below. What was I looking for? Surely it would be obvious, and I wouldn't have to spend days camping out, lying on the lumpy earth again. My goodness! Is that the voice of a cranky old woman starting to emerge?

I soon learned that my flying skill is not yet fully constant; it seems to occur in spells, and when a spell runs out, I am grounded for awhile wherever I happen to be. In this case, I landed on a boulder just above a little church, at a place so high that I could see water on both sides of the island, very dimly in the distance, closer on the East side than the West. "Set in the silver sea," I muttered, and stepped down off the boulder. To my right was a level place with several concrete picnic tables, and below that, the church with its familiar Byzantine proportions. I can never pass up a chance to explore a country church, no matter how plain it might look. I started picking my way carefully over the loose stones.

As I was moving along, making a bit of a clatter, I heard a noise coming from behind me. Far below, since this was rather a cone-shaped hill, I could see the beginning of the tree line again, the "lodge dock florist" of the Red Riding Hood tale, except that on Ikaria only the cypress trees were "lodge" and everything else held down by wind, sun and lack of water. But the noise was too close to be coming from the forest. It sounded like heavy breathing, not a human breath. I froze, facing away from the sound.

From the corner of my eye I saw a dark shape come up on my right side and stop beside me. In the split second before I turned to look, I knew it was a wolf.

"So much for Seems!" I thought, looking down at this solid, glorious creature. "Wake up!" I sang softly in a voice that could have been my mother's, shortly after I was born. "Wake up, Carley, wake up! This is all a dream."

The wolf looked at me, its tawny eyes taking me in from top to toe in a completely non-judgmental gaze of full intelligence. I felt terrified and honored at the same time. Also, I felt clear, as if I were made of glass that had been recently cleaned so you could see all the way through, with everything in-between on full display. A kind of purity, come to think of it.

Meanwhile I gazed and gazed at the whole length of this animal of dark gray, thick fur and arrested power, feeling as if my eyes were sending out rays, as if I were shining down on him (I never questioned that this was a "he" wolf). He stood quietly, looked away from me again. *Let's go!* He said, inside my mind.

*Where?*

*To the one who is waiting.*

*Who?*

*She, the one who is waiting for me.*

*Heloise!*

Anita Sullivan

*The very one.*

I didn't question the wolf any further, such as, "Why do you need me to take you to Heloise?" Of course the wolf needed me; I was designated to make the proper introductions. More than that, it's how the story is working here. We have already changed the original version where the wolf eats grandmother and maybe eats Little Red Riding Hood too. But no! This wolf is Abelard. He has arrived so that we can change that story too. My skin prickled at the thought of a litter of wolf-basset puppies in our future. What will Djan think about that?

I knew another reason that Abelard had come at last: so that we now could die. Not that we couldn't have before, of course, but now it could be a positive act. For we have the means, at last, to do it right. It won't come from wearing out, cruel chance, or simply to make room for new life, as it always has done before. Now it will come as the culmination of an understanding. The understanding has already started to show itself—as a melting of the edges of things, a dispersal of the animate into energy, a shift in seeming as a quality, an apprehension of the visible as rhythm, of music as lace. This is as it should be. We will leave Abelard behind with Heloise to hold the fort, in case.

The wolf and I stepped down the hill together, and instead of exploring the church, we turned into the dirt road that wound down the hillside through the boulders in the direction of Yuriko's house.

The End.